Irish author **Abby Green** [...] career in film and TV—[...] [...] of a lot of standing in the rain outside actors' trailers—to pursue her love of romance. After she'd bombarded Mills & Boon with manuscripts they kindly accepted one, and an author was born. She lives in Dublin, Ireland, and loves any excuse for distraction. Visit abby-green.com or email abbygreenauthor@gmail.com.

Jackie Ashenden writes dark, emotional stories, with alpha heroes who've just got the world to their liking only to have it blown wide apart by their kick-ass heroines. She lives in Auckland, New Zealand, with her husband, the inimitable Dr Jax, two kids and two rats. When she's not torturing alpha males and their gutsy heroines she can be found drinking chocolate martinis, reading anything she can lay her hands on, wasting time on social media or being forced to go mountain biking with her husband. To keep up to date with Jackie's new releases and other news sign up to her newsletter at jackieashenden.com.

FROM ROME
WITH SCANDAL

ABBY GREEN

JACKIE ASHENDEN

MILLS & BOON

First published in Great Britain 2024
by Mills & Boon, an imprint of HarperCollins*Publishers* Ltd,
1 London Bridge Street, London, SE1 9GF

www.harpercollins.co.uk

HarperCollins*Publishers*, Macken House, 39/40 Mayor Street Upper, Dublin 1, D01 C9W8, Ireland

ISBN: 978-0-263-32022-0

09/24

This book contains FSC™ certified paper and other controlled sources to ensure responsible forest management.

For more information visit www.harpercollins.co.uk/green.

Printed and Bound in the UK using 100% Renewable Electricity at CPI Group (UK) Ltd, Croydon, CR0 4YY

'I DO' FOR REVENGE

ABBY GREEN

MILLS & BOON

This is for Susan Drennan McGrath, AKA Susie Q.
She was right by my side during my quest for
publication, encouraging and supporting me every
step of the way, opening a bottle of bubbles to celebrate
a rejection letter because it came with 'notes'!

She never doubted I could succeed and, 60+ books
later, I still can't quite believe that I have.
But she was right. Friends like this are rare
and I'm incredibly lucky. Thank you, Susie Q <3

CHAPTER ONE

VITTORIO VITALE POURED himself a generous measure of whiskey. Irish. The best. He raised the glass to the view of Rome, bathed in early-afternoon golden sunlight. His domain. Finally. He took a sip of the golden drink and the liquid burnt a trail down his throat before settling in his belly, sending out a glow.

A glow of intense satisfaction. Today was the culmination of all of his—

He frowned when the buzzer on his desk sounded. He'd asked not to be disturbed under any circumstances.

Irritation needled over his skin. He pressed a button. 'Tommaso, I specifically requested—'

'Sorry, sir, I know. But…um…your— Wait a second! You can't just—'

The door to Vito's office swung open and a woman appeared on the threshold. His eyes widened. A woman in full wedding regalia. The white dress looked complicated and fussy, with a high neckline and long sleeves. Lace over lace. Stiff. Formal. The voluminous skirt filled the doorway.

Her face was bright pink. Hair sleek and pulled back. A veil was trailing from the top of her head. She clutched an extravagant bouquet in one hand; the flowers looked stiff. Even from here, Vito could see the whites of her knuckles.

His assistant appeared behind the woman. Vito sent him a look and said, 'It's fine, Tommaso.'

Vito put down his glass. He'd have to delay his celebration for a moment. He thought of the woman he'd arranged to meet later, one of Italy's most beautiful models. Tall, willowy, long dark hair like silk. Stunning body. He really didn't want this interruption to affect his plans.

But evidently he would have to deal with the woman he'd been due to marry, about two hours ago.

He flicked a glance at his watch and put out a hand. 'Miss Gavia. Please, come in.'

Flora Gavia was so angry she could barely see straight. Had Vittorio Vitale just looked at his watch? As if she was inconveniencing him? The man who she'd waited for in the vestibule of the church for an hour? Before realising with sickening inevitability that he wasn't coming?

The anger of her uncle was still palpable, his face mottled with rage—even more so after an aide had whispered something in his ear. He'd turned to Flora and screamed at her that it was all her fault, that everything was ruined. And just before he'd stormed off with his wife, her aunt, in tow, he'd said, 'What little use you were to me is now gone. You've been nothing but a burden and a drain for fourteen years. You're dead to me.'

In that moment, Flora had gone numb, putting her emotions on ice. It had been too huge to absorb that the people who had taken her in at just eight years old were effectively walking away from her, leaving her on her own.

But then something had broken through as the guests had filed out of the church whispering and staring at her—*anger*, at the man who'd done this to her. Vittorio Vitale.

And now she was here facing him and she was momentarily blinded by his sheer masculine beauty. Tall and broad. Powerfully muscular. He more resembled a prize athlete than a titan of industry. A billionaire.

Short, thick dark hair. Swept back from a high forehead. Bone structure that would make anyone weep with envy. Sharp blade of a nose. A hard jaw. And that mouth. When she'd first seen him she hadn't been able to take her eyes off his mouth. Lush and tauntingly sexual.

Much to her shock—because she was extremely sexually inexperienced—she'd imagined him doing things to her with that mouth. And that had been *so* unsettling because no other man had ever made her think of such things, and the marriage between them wasn't remotely based on romance. It was to be strictly business. Except there *was* no marriage. Because he'd stood her up.

Flora blinked. The anger surged back and it was disconcerting. She didn't get angry. She was generally well disposed to most people and situations, believing in good outcomes. And that people had good intentions. But in the case of Vittorio Vitale, it was blindingly obvious his intentions had been nefarious all along.

He didn't even look guilty or remotely contrite. He looked almost…bored. Dressed in plain dark trousers and a white shirt. Top button open, sleeves rolled up.

Flora shook her bouquet at him, scattering petals on the floor. 'You're not even dressed for a wedding. You never intended on marrying me, did you?' That fact was becoming painfully obvious.

He came around his desk and perched on the edge, crossing his feet at the ankles and putting his hands in his pockets. He couldn't have looked more louche.

He said, 'Truthfully? No. It wasn't cold feet.'

She looked around the office, taking it in for the first

time. It was at the top of a sleek modern building right in the historical centre of Rome, which was saying something about the influence of the person who'd built something like this here.

Floor-to-ceiling windows on two sides framed amazing views of the ancient city. The iconic shape of the Colosseum was just visible in the distance.

Flora dragged in a ragged breath. Her head was spinning. She looked at him again and this time tried not to notice how gorgeous he was. Feeling bewildered now, more than anything, she asked, 'Why?'

Vittorio's jaw clenched. He looked as if he wasn't going to say a word. She bit out, 'I think I have a right to know.'

Vittorio took his hands out of his pockets and folded his arms. 'That's fair enough. What did your uncle tell you?'

Flora swallowed and remembered the tirade he'd subjected her to. 'Not much.' He'd never told her anything really.

Vittorio frowned. 'Are you aware that your uncle's business is disintegrating as we speak?'

Flora's gut clenched. Her uncle *had* seemed more preoccupied than usual lately. Her aunt even less civil. They'd stop talking as soon as she walked into a room and rudely ask her if she wanted anything. The fact that she'd agreed to a marriage of convenience at her uncle's behest seemed to have been forgotten pretty quickly.

'No, I wasn't aware. I'm not privy to his business dealings.'

'You were privy to this marriage arrangement, weren't you? You were under no illusions. You knew you had a way out in six months if you wanted it. You had nothing to lose.'

She'd agreed to the marriage for lots of reason but also because there'd been the get-out clause after six months. She'd always felt indebted to her uncle for taking over her guardianship after her parents and younger brother had died, tragically. He'd put a roof over her head.

It hadn't been perfect by any means, but she'd been able to stay with family, and in one of the most beautiful cities in the world.

Her uncle could have left her to an institution, or boarding schools.

But then he wouldn't have had access to your trust fund, pointed out a little voice.

Flora reminded herself that he'd needed that money for her education and maintenance. To pay for the house staff to stay behind on holidays to watch her while they'd travelled around the world.

The fact that there was nothing left of her inheritance, according to her uncle, just showed how expensive it had been to take care of her. As he'd pointed out to her, this marriage was to be as much about protecting her future as for his benefit. He'd told her that he couldn't live with himself if anything happened and he couldn't provide for her or give her an inheritance. This marriage would protect them both.

She'd owed her uncle, for everything he'd done for her. But today that debt had ended in spectacular fashion.

'You asked for the six-month get-out clause,' Flora pointed out.

'My insurance in case things didn't go as planned, so I wouldn't be caught out. Your uncle didn't like it, but he didn't have much choice.'

In case things didn't go as planned.

Flora wasn't sure what that meant. The acute embarrassment hit her again. The anger resurfaced.

'How could you?' she demanded emotionally. 'How could you do something so heartless and cruel? Do you have any idea how it felt to stand there and wait? How humiliating?'

* * *

Vito looked at the woman before him. Something twisted a little in his gut. His conscience. So he did have one after all.

But then he felt something more disturbing. An awareness. Up to this point, because he'd known what he had planned, he hadn't engaged much with Flora Gavia, seeing no point in acting out a charade of courtship. And she'd seemed happy that he'd kept his distance. The engagement had been short in any case, only a month from announcement to today.

So, he hadn't really noticed her much, aided by the fact that she'd always seemed to hover on the edge of the room, or on the edge of a group, never planting herself in front of him, as most women did.

They'd had dinner together with her uncle and aunt, but her uncle had dominated the conversation. All Vito had had was an impression of Flora that she was quiet and a little mousy. Brownish hair. Brownish eyes. Pretty…but unremarkable.

But suddenly, here in his office, she was transformed. Maybe it was the dress, fussy as it was. Maybe it was makeup. Her hair was pulled back and sleek, showing off her face. She had high cheekbones. And her eyes were much bigger than he remembered and not a dull brownish at all, but a startling shade of gold and brown. Long lashes.

Her mouth was far more lush than he recalled. Lush enough to make him stare. To wonder how on earth he'd missed this before. An electric charge sizzled in his blood.

His gaze drifted down over the dress, where her breasts moved up and down with her agitated breath. They were high and full. Small waist. Shapely hips. A classic feminine figure and one she'd kept hidden under shapeless clothes before now.

Basically she'd never made an impression. He'd never wanted to look twice. But now he was looking. Twice.

She shook the bouquet at him again. 'Well? Don't you have anything to say?'

Vito dragged his gaze back up. Petals were strewn all over his floor. Her veil was askew, and then, as if realising that, she made a face and pulled it from her head, throwing it down. Her sleek chignon was coming loose and Vito had the absurd urge to go over and loosen it completely so that her hair fell down over her shoulders.

He'd never seen it down and the fact that he noticed, and, worse, had a desire to see it down, was very irritating.

She said, 'Answer me. Please.'

Vito looked at her. There was a catch in her voice this time. His insides curdled. Was she going to cry? He went clammy at the thought, his head filled with unwelcome memories of his mother's grief-ravaged face. Unwelcome memories of not being able to fix her pain.

But Flora didn't look as if she was going to cry. She looked...confused.

Vito said, 'You really didn't know?' He didn't trust her as far as he could throw her. Clearly she was up to something, perhaps trying to salvage what she could out of the debacle unfolding for her uncle. He would play along for now.

She held up her hands, the bouquet beginning to look very frayed. 'Know what?'

The sense of triumph Vito had been feeling only a short time before was still palpable. 'As of today, coinciding with the wedding—'

'You mean *non*-wedding,' Flora pointed out.

Vito inclined his head. 'However you'd like to describe it. As of today, your uncle's business is in free fall and I now

own most of his shares, enough to take control. He thought
we were doing a deal. We weren't. I was. To crush him.'

Flora looked even more confused. She started to pace,
trampling the veil under her feet, the bouquet an extension
of one hand as she gesticulated. 'So what…? You're saying
it was just a corporate takeover? Then why would you need
a convenient marriage and why the theatrics?' She stopped
and looked at him.

Years of anger and grief had calcified into a hard stone
in Vito's gut. 'Because this wasn't just about a corporate
takeover, there was more to it. A lot more.'

Flora looked at him. She stabbed the air with the bouquet. 'Like what?'

Tension filled Vito. 'Like the fact that your uncle was
responsible for ruining my father's business and ultimately
for my father's suicide and my mother's subsequent death.'

Flora's hand with the bouquet dropped and the flowers
slipped out of her hand to the floor, joining the veil. She
swallowed visibly. 'I'm so sorry, that's awful. I had no idea.'

She looked stricken. Her acting ability irritated Vito. He
straightened up and looked at her. Right now she embodied
the Gavia family, and he despised them.

'Your uncle didn't even remember me when we met. My
name didn't register. I was able to come in and decimate
his business and social standing and not once did it occur
to him that the name "Vitale" should mean something to
him. That it should remind him of the man whose business
he ruined from the inside out, causing my father to be accused of corruption, to lose his good name and standing.
He almost went to jail, but at the last moment your uncle
begged for mercy from the authorities, playing the saviour,
when he'd been behind it all.'

He didn't mention the way he and his parents had been

ostracised overnight, by friends and neighbours. How they'd lost their home. How his very first proper girlfriend had stopped taking his calls, and had soon reappeared hand in hand with one of Vito's best friends. The double betrayal had been immense. He'd learnt there and then that there was only one person you could rely on. Yourself.

Vito said grimly, 'Your family name and business go back generations, my father was the first in his family to make a real success of the business and your uncle saw him as a threat, which was ridiculous. Your uncle could have bought him off a hundred times over, but he went after him, for sport, and to let him know that his ambition was to be punished. My father died of shame, by his own hand.'

Flora's eyes were huge. 'And your mother...'

Vito was angry he'd exposed himself to this woman. That her eyes and the manufactured emotion were affecting him. He'd never sought sympathy in his life and certainly not now from a member of the family who had destroyed his.

He said in a clipped voice, 'She got sick and we didn't have the money to pay for private health care. She died while waiting for treatment. Treatment that could have saved her. That's all you need to know.'

Flora's anger drained away. She was shocked. And yet, at the same time, she wasn't shocked. Not any more. Not after her uncle had just cut her loose so brutally. Not after he'd so obviously used her in a business deal. 'I had no idea.'

Vittorio made a dismissive sound. 'Don't make a fool out of me. You might not have known my story, but you were as invested in this marriage as your uncle. That six-month get-out clause would have ensured your wealth for life. There was no downside for you.'

Flora looked at him. His beauty mocked her now, because it was cold and cynical.

Her uncle had already told her that if she exited at the six-months mark, that money would be his. She hadn't even cared. She'd seen it as a means to escape from a marriage in name only, if she'd needed it. The truth was that she'd agreed to the marriage primarily out of loyalty to her uncle but also for more complicated reasons. The fact that she'd found Vittorio Vitale totally fascinating. If unbelievably intimidating.

Somewhere, in a deep and shameful place, she'd known that a man like him would never choose a woman like her, and so she'd indulged in a little fantasy. Believing for a brief moment that when they married, perhaps a man who'd barely looked at her might look at her properly...see her as a woman.

The thought of anything more had felt far too audacious to even contemplate.

When he'd stood her up today, she'd been reminded in a very comprehensive and cruel way that nothing could incite a man like him to marry her. Not even a business deal. She'd even wondered if she'd been the one to ruin it all, just by not being alluring enough. Certainly her uncle had made her feel as though it had been her fault.

But it hadn't been because this man had never intended on following through with his part of the arrangement.

She said dully, 'I was just a pawn to try and maximise my uncle's downfall. The marriage plan was a particularly creative and cynical touch.'

It wasn't much comfort to know that she hadn't necessarily been instrumental in this process. It was almost more insulting. She really was that inconsequential.

Now Vittorio was sneering. 'Oh, please, spare me the

self-pity. Your uncle was the one who suggested the marriage. He obviously saw an added bonus to going into business with me. Insurance for life. I won't deny I saw the benefits of embarrassing him socially when he handed me the opportunity. You were in it together, why on earth else would you have agreed to a marriage of convenience with a total stranger if it wasn't for your own benefit too?'

Flora clamped her mouth shut. She wasn't about to articulate to this cold, judgemental and vengeful man her complicated feelings of loyalty and gratitude to her uncle, a man who patently hadn't deserved any of it. If anyone was the fool here, it was her, the full extent of which was becoming horrifyingly clear.

No wonder her uncle had kept her inside like a hothouse flower for years, while all along planning on selling her off to the highest bidder. He'd been keeping her out of sight and away from any kind of influence. He'd even had her home-schooled!

She'd presumed he was just being overprotective and it had made her feel cared for. She felt nauseous now when everything began to make awful sense. Had she really been that starved for love and attention? Her twisting gut told her the answer. *Pathetic.*

Vittorio's excoriating look just flayed Flora further. She felt as if she'd lost three layers of skin. She muttered, 'I need to go.'

He put out a hand. 'By all means, you know where the door is.'

Flora turned and went towards the door, the dress moving stiffly around her. His cruel callousness stopped her though. She turned around again. 'I'm very sorry for what happened to you and I can understand your need to see justice done.'

She pointed to herself. 'This was not the way to do it

though, far from it. What you did today reduced you to my uncle's level. You're just as mean and ruthless. You humiliated me for sport.'

For a moment he didn't react, then he said, 'Nothing happened to you today that you won't have forgotten about in a week. Believe me, I could have been far more ruthless with your uncle. He still has assets. He has a way back if he wants to work for it. And you have your own funds from your parents.'

Flora's mouth opened. 'How do you know about that?'

The fact that he obviously didn't know that her inheritance was already totally depleted was something she wasn't going to divulge. Sickeningly, a memory came back, of her uncle persuading her to sign a form allowing him access to her inheritance before she came of age—he'd told her it was for her benefit but after these revelations, she knew that that action had not been for her benefit. Her naivety made a hot flush of mortification rise up.

Vittorio shrugged. 'It came up when I was investigating your uncle. If anything you should be thanking me. You're free now to live your life, out from under your uncle's shadow. You're twenty-two, you have your inheritance. Today isn't the cash-in day you'd hoped for, but I've no doubt you can manufacture a strategic marriage all of your own, once everyone has moved on to the next salacious news story.'

Flora, somehow, found it within herself to push down the rising nausea and lift her chin. She said, 'You know what? I should have suspected something when you never pushed for us to meet alone or have a conversation. This is the most we've talked since we met. I thought you were just being a gentleman.'

Vittorio shook his head, eyes glittering like obsidian. Hard. Cold. 'I'm far from a gentleman.'

Flora hitched her chin higher. 'I know that now. And you're right about something else. I am free to live my life. I hope I never see you again.

'You—' she pointed at Vittorio with a trembling finger '—are not a nice person.'

Something caught her eye and impulsively she pulled the engagement ring he'd given her off her finger. It was a large, ostentatious diamond, in a gold setting with more diamonds either side. It weighed a ton. She resisted the urge to fling it at him, and put it down on a nearby table. 'You can have that knuckle-duster back. And by the way, I didn't mention it at the time because I didn't want you to feel bad, but you have no taste.'

It was probably the meanest thing Flora had ever said to anyone and she immediately felt awful, but before she could forget what this man—and her uncle—had put her through she turned and walked out.

Her dress took up most of the elevator as she descended and as she walked through the ground-floor lobby she willed the nausea to stay down and finally made it outside, sucking in lungfuls of air.

People stared as they walked past but she was oblivious. Panic now replaced the sense of nausea. She had nothing. No one. Nowhere to go. She was completely alone and she was only realising now that she'd been alone all along because her uncle and aunt had never really cared for her.

They'd taken her inheritance!

And that man back there? Flora couldn't imagine him caring for *anyone*. He was cruel, cold, heartless, ruthless, cynical, mean— She stopped. Took a breath. And realised that amidst the panic, there was also something far more fledgling rising up. A sense of...liberation.

Vittorio was right about one thing. She was free now. Totally free. Free of that sense of loyalty and obligation she'd had since her uncle had taken her in.

She looked around her as if seeing the world for the first time. She was on the precipice of something both terrifying and a little exhilarating. What would she do? Where did she go from here? The panic crept back, but she forced herself not to let it overwhelm her.

As she stood there on the pavement outside Vittorio's offices, in her wedding dress, with her hair coming loose, Flora said to herself, *Think. Think.* The first thing to do— find a bed for the night and get rid of this dress. And then... she would tackle tomorrow.

Flora turned left and set off, head held high, ignoring the looks and jeers from a group of young guys on mopeds. She would find a way. She would. She had to. She had no choice. There was no one she could ask for help. She was on her own now. And that was okay. She believed in the goodness of people—*most people*—and that good things would happen. With this blind faith guiding her, she disappeared into the streets of Rome, the train of her wedding dress trailing behind her.

Vito stood at his window for a long time, drink forgotten. He was unsettled by what had just happened.

You think? jeered a voice.

He ignored it. The truth was that his focus had been solely on Umberto Gavia for so long that when Gavia had proposed the marriage of convenience, Vito had gone along with it, seeing it purely as a bonus addition to his overall takedown of the man.

And, as Flora had never really made much of an impression, he'd found it easy not to think of her as a person, standing in a church waiting for him, because of course he'd always known he wouldn't be there.

But she hadn't known that. And he hadn't really thought of those consequences beyond the inevitable social embarrassment they'd cause Umberto Gavia. But now he did think of her. Because she'd stood right in front of him reminding him she was a consequence. A person who, if she was to be believed, hadn't had much of a clue as to what was going on.

And yet she'd agreed to the marriage. So he'd just assumed that she and her uncle were in cahoots. Therefore she'd deserved—

What? demanded a voice. *To be humiliated in front of Roman society? To be judged and punished like her uncle?*

Yes. A Gavia was a Gavia. It hadn't just been Vito's family that Umberto had decimated, it had been countless others. When Vito had looked into his practices to build his case against him, he'd found even more heinous acts committed against people.

But Flora hadn't just behaved like a cold-hearted Gavia. She hadn't come to him cajoling or begging or crying or looking for sympathy. She'd been angry. Confused. Bewildered. And she'd looked genuinely upset when he'd told her about his family.

Vito told himself he'd be an idiot not to suspect it had been an act. An attempt to salvage what she could for herself.

You are not a nice person.

Vito had never claimed to be *nice.* He'd stopped being nice right around the time when his mother had slipped away, her body ravaged by illness. That had been the moment when he'd set his sights on making sure that Umberto Gavia would one day pay for his actions.

And that day had come. He hardened his heart. Flora Gavia would be fine. She had a huge inheritance from her own parents—her father had been Umberto's brother.

But he hadn't been involved in the family business, so why punish her?

Vito pushed that aside. Her father might not have been directly involved, but she'd been brought up by Umberto since she was a child. She was practically his daughter.

No doubt he'd see her at a social function soon, looking for a replacement husband. Or, she'd have returned to join her uncle wherever he'd sloped off to.

She would be fine.

The Gavia family hadn't survived for generations without brass necks, and, as Vito had told Flora, he hadn't decimated Umberto Gavia as much as he could have. The man was badly wounded financially and socially, but he could return if he worked for it.

Vito knew that Umberto was essentially lazy though, so he didn't expect to see him around any time soon.

As for Flora... Vito had to admit reluctantly that he would be intrigued to see her again. The Flora who'd just accosted him here in his office had shown a far more intriguing side of herself. If Vito had met that woman before today...he might have felt very differently about leaving her standing at the altar.

But he had. And now it was done. He could move on. He picked up his drink and threw what remained of the whiskey down his throat. But somehow, this time, the glow of satisfaction felt a little dulled and a distinctly acidic aftertaste lingered in his mouth and stomach for a long time.

CHAPTER TWO

Six months later, Rome

'VITALE! WHERE THE hell have you been?'

Vito forced a smile at the man who'd called at him. He made his way through the crowd of Rome's most monied and exclusive people in one of its oldest and most venerated hotels.

There had just been a charity auction at an annual fundraising event and people had paid eye-watering sums for things like yachts and Caribbean islands, all without batting an eyelid.

He used to take this scene for granted, but lately...he'd been finding such displays of wealth tedious.

A woman's hand landed on his arm. He looked down. Long perfect nails. Blood red. Perfectly tanned skin. The ubiquitous diamond bracelet. His nose wrinkled at the perfume. Too heavy. He looked up and registered a model whom he vaguely knew. Beautiful. Stunning. He waited for a beat. *Nothing.*

He took her hand and lifted it from his arm. Her eyes widened. Immediately incensed. Vito moved on towards the man he knew. 'Roberto, *ciao*—'

At that moment, there was a loud crash, what sounded like a hundred glasses breaking and shattering. Vito looked around and saw the back of a waitress. She was bending down and trying to deal with the tray that had just fallen, spilling its contents of glasses.

He didn't take in much detail apart from her black skirt and white shirt. Brown/golden hair pulled up into a bun. A space had formed around her as if people were repelled by the scene. Something about that irritated Vito. He went over and bent down, picking up the larger pieces of glass.

She immediately said, 'Oh, please don't, I'll get into even more trouble.'

Something about her voice made him go still. He looked at her and even though her face was turned away, there was something about the curve of her cheek and jaw that made him stare.

As if aware of him staring, she looked at him. He saw her eyes widen and the colour leach from her face.

Flora Gavia.

Vito frowned, trying to take in what this was. Flora Gavia, an heiress, member of the hated family, dressed as a waitress at an event. *Not* dressed as a socialite.

'You…what…?'

Flora looked at something over his head and hissed, 'Please leave me alone.'

She muttered to herself as she continued picking up shattered glass. 'I'm in so much trouble. There's no way they'll take me on after this—'

Vito put his hand around her wrist. It felt unbelievably slender and delicate. Her scent hit him then too, floral with a hint of musk. Instantly pleasing.

She looked at him. 'What are you doing?'

He looked down. 'You're bleeding.'

She looked down to see blood seeping from a finger. She groaned. 'Now I'm really in for it. They *hate* blood.'

Before Vito could make sense of that, someone was arriving and apologising profusely. 'So sorry, sir, please, let us deal with this.'

Vito was all but pulled to standing by a veritable team of event staff who huddled around Flora and within seconds, like magic, she and the tray and all the broken glass were gone. The place was pristine again. For a second Vito wasn't even sure if he hadn't hallucinated it.

But then he noticed the slightly pink stain on the floor. Her blood. And that made him feel a surge of such a mix of emotions that he couldn't even name them. What he did feel was an urgency to go after her, to see if it really was her.

'Hey, Vitale, didn't that waitress look very like the Gavia woman you stood up at the altar?'

Vito looked at the man who'd come to stand beside him. He forced a smile again. 'I have to go, if you'll excuse me?'

Vito didn't wait for a response. He strode off the ballroom floor and out to the lobby. He stood there for a moment, not even sure where to start looking, but then he saw a figure with hair pulled up into a bun. Black skirt. A denim jacket over her shirt. A crossbody bag. Black sheer tights. Flat brogues.

She was walking quickly towards the entrance and Vito didn't think. He moved, and caught her just before she was about to disappear out of a side door. She looked up at him and went pale again. 'You.'

'Yes, me,' Vittorio Vitale said grimly, with his hand wrapped around her arm. Flora's finger was still throbbing under the makeshift tissue bandage but she was hardly aware. Of all the luck, and all the people she could have bumped into, it had to be him, in her moment of total and utter humiliation. She couldn't think of anyone who would get more out of this.

'Well?' she said pugnaciously. 'When you've stopped looking at me and getting pleasure out of seeing me scrabbling around the floor picking up broken glass in front of the most important people in Rome, I'd like to get on.'

If anything, the man looked even more gorgeous than Flora remembered. He was dressed in a classic black tuxedo and the material did little to disguise his powerful body. She could see the bunched muscle of his biceps and felt a little woozy.

Lack of blood.

That was it.

He was shaking his head. 'What are you doing here?'

She looked at him and then gestured at herself with her free hand. 'Do I really need to spell it out?'

He didn't answer, he just looked over her head and then tugged her with him, across the lobby to the reception desk, where a manager jumped to attention, barely glancing at her. 'Signore Vitale, how can I help you?'

'I'd like a room, please.'

Flora's mouth dropped open as she watched the manager issue Vittorio with a room key without so much as an eye-flicker. Now he was leading her across the lobby to the elevator. They were inside the small but luxurious space before Flora pulled her arm free and found her voice. 'What on earth do you think you're doing?'

Vittorio stabbed at a button. He said, 'That's what I'd like to ask you.'

Flora said, 'As it happens, before you accosted me I was going home because I've just lost my job. Tonight was part of a month's trial, and I failed.'

Vittorio looked at her as the elevator ascended. 'Since when are you working as a waitress?'

Flora pretended to look at her watch and said tartly, 'As

of about ten minutes ago I'm no longer a waitress. It was a short-lived career.'

The elevator doors opened onto a quiet corridor with plush cream carpets, soft lighting and walls painted in hues of cream and gold.

Vittorio stepped out but kept a hand on the door, stopping it from closing again. He sounded impatient. 'Please, Flora, I think we need to talk.'

'About what? I think we said all that needed to be said on the day you stood me up at our wedding.'

A muscle in his jaw pulsed. The muted sound of voices came from nearby. He glanced away and Flora had an urge to smack his hand aside and quickly press the button to escape but at that moment an elegant older couple appeared.

The woman smiled at Flora and even though Flora was being offered an opportunity to use this couple as an excuse to stay in the elevator and travel back down, something else inside her compelled her to step into the corridor, out of their way, signalling that she was with Vittorio, even though she couldn't have looked more mismatched with her white shirt, black skirt and serviceable shoes.

The doors closed again and Vittorio was heading for a doorway at the end of the corridor. Flora followed him, her feet sinking into the carpet. It had been months since she'd inhabited surroundings as salubrious—not that her uncle's palazzo had even been that luxurious. It hadn't been comfortable. It had been more like a museum, stuffed with antiques and forbidding portraits of ancestors who looked nothing like her.

Flora had taken after her English mother's side of the family, perhaps something else that had never endeared her to her uncle.

Vittorio was standing in the open doorway now and look-

ing at her as he undid his bow tie with his other hand. He
cut a rakish figure with stubble lining his jaw.

Before taking a step over the threshold Flora commented,
'You obviously do this a lot.'

'What?'

'That manager didn't even blink when you asked for a
room.'

Vittorio's mouth quirked ever so slightly on one side.
'That's probably because, as of about a month ago, I own
this hotel.'

'Oh.' Flora felt exposed. She'd been imagining that it was
a regular occurrence for Vittorio Vitale to appear with a
woman demanding a room at short notice. As if he would
do that with a woman like her!

He stood back. 'Please, come in.'

Flora took a breath and walked past him. His scent tick-
led her nostrils, sharp and musky with woodier undertones.
All at once sophisticated but also with an edge of something
indefinable. Very masculine.

She was very conscious of her own scent—eau-de-kitchen.

The room was palatial. Then she saw more rooms leading off this main one. It was a suite. With windows looking
out over Rome. Flora could see a terrace outside.

She saw Vittorio reflected in the window, behind her.
Tall and indistinct. She forced herself to turn around. 'Why
do you want to talk to me?'

His bow tie was undone now. Top button open. He spread
his hands out. 'What are you doing here like this? Why
aren't you with your uncle? I heard he was last seen in
South America trying to make a name for himself where
he's less known.'

That stung. Vittorio knew more than she did. Her uncle
hadn't been in touch since that morning at the church.

Feeling hurt and hating that weakness, she said, 'What my uncle does now, or where he is, is none of my concern. I haven't seen him since that morning six months ago.'

Vittorio's brows snapped together. 'What?'

Flora shrugged. 'It's like you said, I was free. I did my own thing.'

'What was that exactly...that has led you to this?'

The humiliation of his very public abandonment and the way he'd cast her out of his office as if she was nothing but an irritation made her say, 'You know what? I don't owe you any explanations. If you don't mind, I have somewhere to be and I need to go.' Because it was going to take her at least an hour to get back to where she lived on the outskirts of the city.

She moved back towards the door and Vittorio asked incredulously, 'You really burnt through your inheritance that quickly?'

Flora stopped. Didn't turn around. She felt like laughing and crying all at once. The inheritance she'd never seen! Because her uncle had taken it. The truly pathetic part was that she'd never really known how much was there. She'd been too young to know at first and whenever she'd brought it up, her uncle had been vague and assured her he was taking care of it for her. No doubt this man, Vittorio Vitale, who had rebuilt his family's name and fortune, would laugh himself silly if he knew the full extent of her sad story.

As frigidly as she could, she said, 'Yes, that's exactly it. I squandered it and now I'm working in menial jobs. Goodbye, Vittorio, have a nice life.'

She was almost at the door when Vito broke out of his trance and said, 'Wait.' He was reeling. Nothing made sense. He knew something was very off but he wasn't sure what it was.

Flora stopped. There was something fragile about her from the back. Her hair pulled up into a high bun. He realised that she'd lost weight. He had a strong aversion to letting her out of his sight. He put it down to needing to know what she was up to, because it was something. Even if it didn't involve her uncle.

'Look, can I offer you something to eat? Drink?'

For a long moment she didn't move and then she turned around. She'd definitely lost weight. He could see it now. Even as he also noticed the same curves he'd noticed before, when she'd been in that wedding dress. Breasts high and full.

His body tightened in response.

Not appropriate.

It hadn't been then, and it wasn't now.

She said, 'Actually, maybe a sandwich, please.' Then almost as an afterthought, she said, 'And some sausages, if that's okay.'

Vito picked up the phone and made a call, then put it down again. She was hovering by the door, still in her jacket. 'Sit down, Flora. Make yourself comfortable. Can I get you something to drink?'

With almost palpable reluctance she came back in and perched on the edge of one of the sofas. *Not* the reaction Vito was used to from women.

'A glass of water, thank you.'

Vito went to the lavishly stocked mini-bar and took out some water for her and a small bottle of whiskey for himself. He put the drinks in glasses and came back over, handing her the water. He said, 'If you want something stronger, let me know.'

She shook her head. 'No, this is fine, thank you.' She took a gulp of water.

Vito noticed something and cursed softly. 'You're still bleeding.'

She lifted her hand and blood was trickling down her finger. 'I'm sorry, I didn't realise—'

Vito was already on the phone issuing an order. He put the phone back down and said, 'Come into the bathroom, let me see it.'

Flora was rummaging through her bag clearly looking for something. 'It's fine, I have another tissue here somewhere—'

'Flora—'

Her head came up and she looked at him.

He said, 'Let me see it, please.'

Flora lifted off her bag and stood up. Vito went into the bathroom and turned on the light. She followed him in.

He said, 'Give me your jacket.'

She slipped it off and he draped it over the back of the door. Then he took her hand in his and peeled off the make-shift tissue bandage. He muttered, 'Didn't they have any plasters?'

'I didn't hang around to find out. The boss was *so* angry.'

Vito looked at Flora. This close, he could see freckles across her nose. It felt curiously intimate. Her cheeks went a little pink. *She wanted him.* Vito was used to women wanting him but this was different. He sensed she'd never admit it, never mind use it.

She said, 'What is it? Have I got something on my face?'

Once again he was struck by how...pretty she was. With no make-up or adornment. Huge eyes. Long lashes. Those cheekbones. A mouth that was pure provocation, lips full and soft.

How had he not noticed before?

He knew how—because he'd been so fixated on her uncle.

He shook his head. 'No, there's just something…different about you.'

With visible self-consciousness, she touched her head with her free hand. 'It's probably my hair. I don't straighten it any more. Can't afford to. And I never could do it myself.'

Vito could see that it looked a little wild, with curly tendrils close to her hairline. He curbed the urge to free it and see it spill over her shoulders. He turned on the cold tap and put her finger under the water, hearing her intake of breath.

There was a knock on the door outside. Vito said, 'Hold it there until I get back.'

He could have sworn he heard a muttered *'yes, sir'*, but he went out and opened the door and admitted the room-service attendant who had arrived with a trolley containing the food and a first-aid kit.

Vito thanked him and tipped him and brought the first-aid kit into the bathroom, where Flora was still dutifully holding her injured finger under the water. He turned off the tap and dried her hand with a small towel, careful to be gentle.

He noticed her nails were short. Unvarnished. He took a plaster from the kit and placed it over the cut, saying, 'It was deep.'

Flora said, 'Thank you. You didn't have to do that.'

Vittorio threw away the wrapping and closed up the box. 'It was nothing.'

Impressed by his practicality, she asked, 'Where did you learn to do that?'

He looked at her, amused. 'Put on a plaster?'

She flushed. 'Some people are squeamish.' She remembered cutting her leg badly on barbed wire when she'd been smaller and going to her aunt. Her aunt had almost fainted on the spot, causing such a commotion that her uncle had had the house staff attend to her aunt before they'd even noticed that Flora was the one who required urgent attention. She'd ended up in hospital needing stitches.

She took her hand back, cradling it to her chest. It suddenly felt as if there were no air in the room. But before Flora could move or say something, Vittorio said, 'My mother was ill, as I mentioned before. I nursed her for a time. Medical stuff doesn't make me squeamish.'

Flora recalled what he'd told her about his parents. The reason for his revenge mission on her uncle. She could empathise.

Vittorio said, 'The food is here. You should eat.'

Food.

Flora's stomach rumbled faintly. It was the reason she'd stayed. Because she'd learned in the last few months not to look a gift horse in the mouth. She wasn't too proud to accept food, especially when it wasn't just her she had to think about.

She followed Vittorio back out to the suite. He'd taken off his jacket and his back was broad under the shirt, tapering down to slim hips. The trousers did little to hide the definition of his muscular buttocks.

He was standing at a trolley and lifting a silver domed lid from a plate. Flora's eyes went wide. A toasted sandwich with fries. Sausages on the side. She'd never seen anything that looked so delicious.

Vittorio put the plate of food on the table and pulled out a chair. 'Please, sit.'

Flora did. She picked up a chip and popped it into her mouth, almost closing her eyes at the salty tastiness. She noticed that there was no other food. 'Aren't you hungry too?'

Vittorio shook his head. 'I'm fine.'

Flora picked up the sandwich and was about to take a big bite out of it when she stopped. 'Can you not look at me? You're making me feel like an animal in the zoo.' In fairness, she conceded, he probably wasn't used to the spectacle of women actually eating in front of him. Her aunt had eaten like a bird and only Flora and the staff had known of the midnight trips to the palazzo kitchen where she would binge periodically, out of sight.

Vittorio looked at his watch. 'Actually, I need to speak to someone downstairs. I'll let you eat in peace.'

Flora felt a surge of relief not to be pinned under that obsidian gaze for a minute. He started walking to the door and then stopped and turned back. 'You'll be here when I get back.' It wasn't really a question.

She said, 'I do have to leave soon.'

'I won't be long, a few minutes. And then I can take you wherever you need to go.'

Flora immediately balked at the thought of him seeing where she was staying. 'Oh, no, that's fine, but I'll wait until you come back.'

He left and Flora took advantage of the privacy to polish off the sandwich and fries. She drank the water. And carefully wrapped up the sausages in a napkin.

When she was finished she put her jacket back on so she'd be ready to go when Vittorio got back. She would thank him for his hospitality and leave and go back to a world where he didn't exist. And hopefully she wouldn't have any more unnerving encounters with him. He stirred up way too much inside her.

When Vito returned to the suite it was empty. He felt an instant sense of panic mixed with regret mixed with irritation.

Disappointment.

He hadn't met many people he could trust and there was no reason why Flora Gavia would be any different.

But then he noticed that the French doors were open, leading out onto the balcony where a figure stood at the wall, and he felt exposed for his initial reaction. Why should he even care if Flora Gavia disappeared into the ether again?

Because he wanted to know what was going on.

He had the same slightly unsettling sense that he'd had the day she'd walked out of his office in the wedding dress—that he'd missed something huge and vital. Then, he'd reassured himself that it was nothing. He was just used to having all the information and leaving nothing to chance. He hadn't expected her to confront him on the day of the wedding.

She'd walked out of his office leaving more questions than answers. And now there were even more questions. Vito didn't like loose ends or things that didn't make sense. That was how you got caught out.

The fact that Flora Gavia was working as a waitress for an event company and that at least one person had recognised her was a potential problem. Perhaps it was part of a plan with her uncle. Perhaps she *was* now working solo, but until Vito knew for sure he'd have to keep her close.

CHAPTER THREE

FLORA WAS MESMERISED by the view of Rome from this vantage point. She was so engrossed she didn't hear Vittorio return and nearly jumped out of her skin when he said from behind her, 'Your hair is down.'

She whirled around to see a look of shock on his face. She put her hands to her head. *This* was why her aunt had insisted on her keeping it straight when out in public. Its natural state was curly and wayward and untameable. Untidy.

'I took it down because my head was sore.' She started bundling it up again but Vittorio put out a hand.

'No, stop.'

She did. Dropped her hands. She realised now that he didn't look shocked, disgusted. He looked shocked, transfixed. She felt a swooping sensation in her belly.

He said, 'It's...beautiful.'

Flora felt heat come into her face. She was glad of the darkness. 'Thank you. It was my mother's... I mean, I inherited it from her.'

'Your mother was English.'

'Yes. My father was... Italian.' Obviously. Her father had been her uncle's brother. She felt seriously woolly-headed around this man.

She said, 'I should go. I really need to get back.'

'You have a boyfriend?'

Flora's eyes nearly bugged out of her head. The thought of having had the luxury of time to have a boyfriend was almost comical. She shook her head. 'No, no boyfriend but I do have responsibilities and where I live…it's a little bit different. I have to be back—' She stopped. Vittorio Vitale didn't need to know the minutiae of her living arrangements.

She said, 'Look, I just need to go now, okay? Thanks for the food…and for—'

'Losing you your job?'

She looked at him, surprised. 'It wasn't your fault. I dropped the tray.' Well, it had been a little his fault, she'd heard someone call his name and had seen him and she'd been in such shock that she hadn't looked where she was going and had bumped into something. But she wasn't about to reveal that.

'If I hadn't tried to help you it might not have been so bad.'

Flora made a face. 'Perhaps. Although, my track record for holding trays wasn't great to begin with. That was the third one I've dropped.'

'Ah,' Vittorio said.

'Funnily enough my uncle didn't consider learning how to hold trays full of glasses to be of importance in my schooling.'

'And yet that's what you're doing.'

Vittorio sounded curious. Flora went back into the suite. 'I just need to get my bag and then I'll be gone.'

'I'll give you a lift.'

Flora was putting her cross-body bag over her head of unruly hair. She tensed. 'That's really not necessary, I'm out on the edges of the city.'

'I insist. I want to make sure you get home safely.'

Flora thought quickly. Maybe she could get him to drop her off somewhere nearby so he wouldn't see where she actually lived.

'Okay, then, if you insist.'

'My car is downstairs, let's go.' He picked up his jacket on the way and led her back out of the suite, to the elevator and down to the lobby. In the lobby though, Flora froze. Her event manager boss was also in the lobby and had seen her.

Vittorio saw her reaction and said sharply, 'Who is that?'

Flora said miserably, 'My now ex-boss.'

Vittorio said, 'Wait here.' And he walked over to the man, who Flora could see was going pale in the face. There were a few words exchanged, mostly on Vittorio's side, and the man was now going red and nodding frantically.

Vittorio came back and took her arm in his hand, guiding her out of the hotel through the main entrance. She looked back at her ex-boss, who appeared to be in some kind of shock.

They were outside the hotel now, going down steps to where a low-slung silver bullet of a car was waiting. A young valet was holding open the passenger door and Flora got in gingerly, feeling awkward, having to contort herself a little. The door closed.

Vittorio got in on the other side, deftly starting the car and manoeuvring them out into the Rome traffic. Flora gave him a general address of where she was staying. She didn't want to distract him further but curiosity overcame her and when there was a lull in traffic she asked, 'What did you say to him?'

Vittorio was looking ahead, and Flora took in his strong profile. The man didn't have a bad angle.

He said, 'I told him that I didn't appreciate the way he treated his staff and unless he demonstrated a less punitive work environment in future, I wouldn't have him manage an event at my hotel again.'

'Oh.' Flora absorbed this. Not what she might have expected of the man who had been ruthless enough to ruin her uncle and stand her up on their wedding day. She also hadn't expected his hospitality. Or how gentle he'd been tending to her finger. The plaster was wrapped around it snugly. It was no longer throbbing, or bleeding.

He drove with easy confidence. Fast, but not too fast. He didn't need to show off. Her uncle had always terrified Flora with the way he drove.

Before she realised it they were in the quieter residential areas of Rome. Exactly where Flora had directed Vittorio. He said, 'Where now?'

'You can just let me out anywhere here.'

Vittorio was driving slowly and looking at the very sleepy/closed apartment blocks. 'Tell me which one. I'm dropping you to the door, Flora.'

Flora.

The way he said her name gave her flutters. She could sense he wasn't going to take no for an answer. She sighed and gave him the address. It was around the corner.

He pulled up outside and got out before she could move, opening her door. The entrance to where she stayed was a nondescript gate. Flora stood in front of it, feeling awkward. Vittorio loomed large under the street lights. It made her even more conscious of what was behind her.

She said, 'Okay, look, thank you for the lift. I can take it from here.'

He was frowning though and looking over her shoulder. 'What is this place? Some sort of...hostel?'

She seized on that. 'Yes, it's a hostel and guests aren't welcome inside.'

At that moment the gate opened behind Flora. An older woman stepped out. 'Flora? Are you okay?'

Flora nodded. 'Fine, Maria, this…er…gentleman was just dropping me home.'

'Okay. Because we need to talk, Flora. I'm afraid that it's not going to be possible for you to stay if you want to keep Benji here too.'

'Who's Benji?'

Vittorio's question couldn't distract Flora from the stomach-dropping panic she felt. She'd known this was coming but still…

Maria's voice was dry. 'Benji is Flora's baby.'

Vittorio stared at her. 'You have a baby? How on earth…? You were pregnant when we were due to get married?'

Maria barked out a laugh. 'Not a real baby.'

Flora put up her hands. 'Stop. Both of you.' She looked at Maria and turned her back on Vittorio. 'When do I need to move out?'

Maria's expression was soft, kind, but regretful. 'Probably as soon as you can. The inspectors could turn up any day now and if they find Benji…'

'I know. And the last thing I want to do is get any of you into trouble, when you're doing such amazing work.'

'Work…what work?' Vittorio asked.

Before Flora could answer, Maria said, 'Who is this man? Can you trust him?'

'With this information? Yes, I believe so…'

'Okay, well, I'll leave you to talk and then we can figure out where you're going to go.'

Flora felt weary. 'Okay, thanks, Maria.'

The other woman went back inside, shutting the gate securely again. Flora looked at Vittorio. His arms were folded. He wasn't moving until he got answers.

First question. 'What is this place? It's not just a hostel, is it?'

Flora shook her head. 'It's a women's aid centre, so I'm sure you can appreciate the need for sensitivity and discretion.'

'What on earth are you doing in a women's aid centre…?' His brows snapped together. 'Did someone do something? Did something happen?'

'No, nothing like that. I ended up here…through somewhere else and they let me stay for a miminal fee. I worked for them to help out.'

'You ended up here…?'

Flora swallowed. 'Look, it's really none of your concern. You should go.'

One thing Vito was very sure of was that he was going nowhere until he'd got to the bottom of why Flora was living in a women's aid centre.

He said, 'Who, or what, is Benji?'

Flora looked as if she was going to argue but then she said, 'Okay, fine, wait here. I'll be back.'

Vittorio leaned back against his car. It was quiet here. Residential. Nondescript. The perfect place for a women's aid centre. He could appreciate that. Flora was gone for about ten minutes and Vito was just appreciating the fact that no one ever kept him waiting when she reappeared with a bundle of what looked like scraggy fur in her arms.

'This is Benji. I found him in a skip a few weeks ago. He's blind in one eye.'

It was a dog. A puppy. Of indeterminate breed. Beagle-ish. With white and grey and a bit of brown. One brown eye and the other one was cloudy. The dog was curled trustingly against Flora's chest. Vittorio put out a hand to stroke him and the dog's hair went up and he growled, which sounded a little comical coming from something so small.

Flora said unapologetically, 'Sorry, he doesn't like men much.'

Vito pulled back his hand. 'Fair enough.'

He thought of what the woman had said. 'You have to move out because of the dog?'

Flora nodded. 'No animals allowed. They just don't have the facilities but it's heartbreaking because a lot of the kids who come here have had to leave pets at home. There isn't space for a garden. They really need to move to a better facility but they can't afford it.'

'What are you going to do?' Even as he asked the question, a plan started to formulate in Vito's head.

Flora bit her lip and Vito wanted to go over and tug it loose, press his own mouth against hers. Slip his hand under all that hair and tug it so that her head fell back, giving him deeper access to her—

'I'm not sure. Maybe Maria will know someone.'

'You're coming home with me.'

Flora looked at him. The colour drained from her face. 'That's preposterous.'

'If we'd got married, you'd be living with me now.'

'Well, that never happened because you stood me up, remember? And even if we had married, we'd be getting divorced now. Six months have passed.'

'You never know, you might have found me easy to live with and decided not to get divorced.'

Flora smiled sweetly. 'The same goes for you—you might have found me too irresistible to let go.'

Neither said anything for a moment and then Vito saw some colour come back into Flora's cheeks. He took advantage of what he knew. 'What if the inspectors turn up tomorrow? You don't want to be the cause of getting the centre shut down.'

Now she looked stricken. 'Of course not.'

'Then if you leave with me tonight, you'll be ensuring their safety.'

She looked tortured. It was almost insulting. But then from the moment she'd stormed into his office in the wedding dress, *no*, from the moment they'd met, she'd never shown much of an inclination to spend time with him. He couldn't remember a time when a woman had been so uninterested. From the age of puberty, Vito had known that he possessed a rare power. He'd never taken it for granted but he'd used it to his advantage when he'd had to.

She looked at him and Vito was struck again by her huge eyes. Her hair curled wildly, falling over her shoulders.

'Okay, but just for one night, and then I'll sort something out. Okay?'

Vito shrugged. 'Sure.'

'I'll go in and get my things. I won't be long. I have a carrier for Benji.'

'Do you need help?' Vito stood up straight.

She shook her head. 'No, it's better if you don't come in. Strangers, especially male strangers, aren't exactly... welcome.'

Vito put his hands in his pockets. He was rarely in a situation where he was ineffectual. It was eye-opening.

Approximately ten minutes later, Flora reappeared with a wheelie case in one hand and a pet carrier in the other. She handed Vito the wheelie case and said, 'I'll sit in the back with Benji so he doesn't get scared.'

Vito stowed the case. 'I've put in a call to my housekeeper to ensure there are provisions for a dog, and some food.'

'Thank you.'

Driving back into the city, Vito glanced in the rear-view mirror and caught Flora's eye. For the first time since seeing her again he noticed shadows under her eyes like delicate bruises. He felt a clutch of something unfamiliar in his gut. Unfamiliar but not unknown.

Concern.

For a Gavia of all people.

Conflicting emotions tangled together, and the suspicion that he was being monumentally naive not to suspect that this woman was up to something. He needed to find out what was going on. 'So how did you end up in the women's aid centre?'

He glanced at her in the rear-view mirror again and she was avoiding his eye, biting her lip. Then their eyes met again and he felt it like an electric shock. His hands gripped the wheel tighter.

With almost palpable reluctance she said, 'I, er…was in a hostel in the city and someone mentioned the aid centre, that they were looking for a volunteer to help out and that there was a place to stay, if you did.'

Vito frowned. 'Hostel…what kind of hostel?'

'A homeless hostel.'

It took a second for that to sink in and when it did, Vito almost crashed the car. He swerved and a driver shouted expletives at him. He pulled into a layby and turned to face Flora.

He said one word. 'Explain.'

'Do we have to do this here? It might be better when you're not driving.'

'I'm not driving,' he pointed out. And then, 'Are you saying you were homeless?'

'Only for a couple of days.'

Vito couldn't sit there. He got out of the car, pulling his jacket off and throwing it aside. He felt constricted. He opened the passenger door and pulled the seat forward and said, 'We need to talk.'

They were on a quiet leafy street on the way back into the city, the moon shining bright. She got out. The dog made a little pitiful sound and she said something reassuring. For a bizarre moment Vito almost…envied the dog. Ridiculous.

Flora stood and faced him.

Vito folded his arms. 'Tell me everything that happened after you walked out of my office.'

Flora gulped. She might have imagined this scene in her weaker moments when she would have enjoyed seeing Vittorio Vitale grovelling a little, but now that he was in front of her looking positively…nuclear, it didn't feel as good as she might have imagined. She almost felt as though she should be apologising.

'When I left your office I had nothing. Nowhere to go. Not a cent of money.'

Vittorio shook his head. 'How?'

'I told you I hadn't seen my uncle since that day. He told me in no uncertain terms that any use I'd had was no longer valid. I did try to go to the palazzo but it was already closed up.'

'But what about your inheritance?'

Flora shook her head. 'My uncle plundered it over the years. I stupidly signed a form granting him access until I was of age.'

'In all the investigations we did, no one noticed that it was gone.'

'Well, it was.'

Vittorio sounded grim. 'He must have doctored the accounts. I had no idea you were destitute. I assumed you had that money, or that you'd just leave with your uncle.'

Flora repressed a shiver. 'No way.'

Vittorio cursed softly. 'You're cold. Let's go.'

She wasn't cold but he was already ushering her back into the car and closing the door and within seconds they were driving again, until they entered the historic centre of Rome. Not far from Vittorio's offices and where her uncle's palazzo had been.

Vittorio came to a stop outside a discreet building. A doorman jumped out and took Vittorio's keys. Another attendant took Flora's battered case and Vittorio said, 'Does the dog need to be taken around the block? Damiano can do it.'

Flora took Benji out of the carrier and attached his lead, handing it to the young man. She said, 'Thank you.'

The little dog trotted off happily. Vittorio said, 'He obviously doesn't dislike all men.'

Now Flora felt irrationally guilty. 'Um…no…mainly just the tall ones.' Who looked intimidating. She kept that to herself.

Inside, the apartment building was sleek and modern, belying the older exterior, which she figured must be protected as a lot of structures were in Rome. Vittorio obviously favoured a less traditional aesthetic, and, having grown up in the stuffy Gavia palazzo, Flora found she appreciated the clean lines.

They ascended in the elevator, Flora very conscious of still being in her waitress uniform. The doors opened directly into the apartment, a reception hall with marbled floors and a massive round table upon which sat a vase full of colourful blooms.

The apartment seemed to take up the entire top floor

with massive rooms, tall ceilings and an outdoor terrace. A housekeeper met them, an older woman, Sofia. She showed Flora a dog bed and bowls for food and water and assured her they'd have more things tomorrow.

Flora was about to protest that they probably wouldn't still be here but Vittorio was saying, 'Come into the living room. It's more comfortable.'

The room was filled with couches and chairs. Coffee tables stacked with books. Modern art on the walls. Muted colours. It was soothing. Flora had an urge to curl up on a couch and sleep for a week. She tried to hold back a yawn.

Vittorio was looking at her. He said, 'You should go to bed. You're exhausted.'

She didn't protest. As much because she *was* exhausted but also because she needed to try and absorb everything that had happened this evening since she'd heard someone say his name at that function, causing a chain of events leading to here.

Vittorio instructed Sofia to show Flora to her room and she dutifully followed the older woman down a series of corridors, to a door. Inside was a massive bedroom suite with dressing room and en suite. Even a living room with TV.

Sofia showed her where her case had been stowed and where there was a robe and toiletries. The woman's kindness made Flora feel emotional. After growing up in the sterile environment of her uncle and aunt's guardianship, she'd experienced more compassion and kindness in the last six months than ever before in her life. And from people who had the least amount of resources.

And yet... Vittorio had shown her kindness this evening. Disconcerting. The last person she would have expected to help her. She would have assumed if he'd seen her waitressing like that he'd either laugh or completely ignore her. Step over her as she'd picked up the broken glass. But he hadn't done anything of the sort. He'd stood up for her.

And now he was taking her in.

Flora's head was starting to throb. When Sofia had left, she explored the suite, and the lure of the luxurious marble bathroom was too much. She stripped off and stepped into a shower the size of a room and almost groaned with pleasure as steaming hot water sluiced down over her body.

She hadn't experienced this level of a shower in months, or actually ever, because the plumbing in the Gavia palazzo had been about the same age as the palazzo. So this was... heaven. She even succumbed to the lure to wash her hair, an epic feat at the best of times.

When her aunt had first seen her hair in all its natural glory when she'd been a child, she'd been so horrified that she'd made sure that it was always straight, ensuring Flora was subjected to rigorous hair-drying and straightening by a member of staff at least once a week.

When Flora emerged from the bathroom, swathed in a robe and with a towel wrapped around her head, she lay on the bed, promising herself she'd just have a quick rest before she finished drying off. But then her eyes closed and the throbbing in her head finally stopped and everything went blissfully dark and quiet.

Vito was pacing back and forth on his terrace. The dog had been returned to the apartment and was now sniffing on the terrace, stopping to wee on a plant every now and then. It had started howling when it had realised Flora was nowhere to be seen and so Vito had risked a bite, scooping the animal up into his arms, to try and keep him quiet. The dog had looked at him suspiciously for a long moment, nose twitching, and had then promptly curled into a ball in his arms. Until he'd squirmed to be put down again.

Vito's head was reeling.

Was Flora telling the truth?

His gut told him the answer. Why on earth would she have gone to such elaborate lengths on the off chance she'd run into him again to play on his sympathies?

He hadn't even been due to attend that function earlier. It had been a last-minute decision, purely because he'd wanted to check on how the hotel was doing.

Everything he'd learned this evening made a kind of sick sense based on how Flora had behaved in his office that day.

The day you stood her up in public.

His conscience pricked.

She'd been shocked. Bewildered. And then, stoic when leaving. Not hinting for a second that she was walking out into…nothing.

So, was she really a victim of her uncle too? If so, then Vito had done her a serious injustice.

He left the puppy momentarily to go to Flora's room. The door was ajar and he pushed it open. For a second he couldn't see her but then he made out a shape on the bed and went in further.

She was on top of the covers, in a robe. A towel half on, half off her head. Dark brown and golden curly strands escaping. Her chest was softly rising and falling. One bare leg was exposed. Pale. Long and shapely.

Vito's pulse tripped. He felt like a voyeur. A little flash of something white and grey and brown streaked past his feet.

The dog.

It had obviously followed her smell and was now trying to jump up onto the bed. It was too high.

The dog looked at Vito with huge pleading eyes. Vito

cursed and scooped it up and put it on the bed, where it went and curled straight into Flora's side, into a little ball of fluff.

Vito walked back out of the room before she could wake and witness him staring at her as if he'd never seen a woman before.

Flora Gavia was already exposing him in ways he'd never anticipated and, as much as he trusted that this wasn't some elaborate ruse, he definitely wasn't letting her out of his sight until he knew for sure.

CHAPTER FOUR

WHEN FLORA WOKE she felt as if she was emerging from the deepest and most peaceful sleep she'd ever had. When she opened her eyes she had to squint. It was bright daylight. Her phone was on a nightstand beside the bed and she looked at it and jackknifed up to sitting, the damp towel falling off her head. She groaned. She could only imagine what state her hair was in.

It was lunchtime. Later than she'd ever slept in her life. And she was in Vittorio Vitale's apartment. In his guest room. And where was Benji?

She got up and washed herself and pulled on a pair of faded jeans and a T-shirt. She couldn't do much with her hair so she just pulled it back into a bun.

She left the room and made her way down corridors, eventually emerging into the living room. She saw French doors open and heard an excited yapping. She followed the sound to see a young man in a suit throwing a ball for Benji. The man looked up and went red. She recognised him as the man who'd admitted her to Vittorio's office on the wedding day. 'Miss Gavia, I'm Tommaso, Signore Vitale's assistant. I'll let him know you're up. He's in his home office.'

He'd fled before Flora could say anything and Benji was running around her feet excitedly. She picked him up and snuggled him close. She frowned then as a half-memory, half-dream returned. Had Benji been on the bed with her last night? And had someone come to take him that morning?

Flora thought of Vittorio coming into the room and seeing her sprawled on the bed in complete disarray and a flush of heat climbed through her body. And of course he chose that moment to appear in front of her, when her face was glowing like a beacon.

He was dressed in black trousers and a light blue shirt, top button open. He said, 'You must be hungry. Let's have lunch. Tommaso will take Benji out for a walk.'

Tommaso appeared again and whisked Benji away. Flora said redundantly, 'Thank you, but I can take him out myself. I don't expect your staff to dog-sit. Anyway, we'll be leaving soon.'

Flora had been following Vittorio into a room off the living room. It was a dining room, through which she could see a kitchen and hear someone whistling. The domestic sound was comforting.

Vittorio pulled out a chair where there was a setting laid out. Flora sat down. Vittorio sat opposite her. He said, 'It's no problem. Tommaso is happy to help. So, where exactly are you planning on going?'

Flora was distracted by Sofia appearing with a light pasta starter that smelled delicious. She looked at Vittorio. 'I'm sorry, what?'

'You said you'll be leaving soon. Where are you planning on going?'

Flora's insides cramped a little. She didn't have anywhere to go. And with a dog in tow that would be even more challenging. She affected an airy tone. 'Oh, we'll find somewhere. I have some contacts.'

'Not many places will take a dog.'

Flora wanted to glare at him. She didn't need to hear her fears articulated back to her. 'I'm sure we'll be fine.' She speared a piece of pasta and put it in her mouth.

'So far you've been on the streets, then in a hostel and then a women's aid centre—your track record hasn't exactly been...stellar.'

Now Flora felt defensive. 'I did the best I could with what little I had. The wedding dress didn't fetch as much as I'd hoped.'

'You sold the dress?'

'It was all I had to sell.'

She saw Vittorio go pale under his tan at the thought of her being driven to drastic measures, and said hurriedly, 'It never came to that. It wouldn't have.'

'It could have,' he said darkly.

'Well, it didn't. I sold the dress for a few hundred euros and that kept me going.'

'It was worth thousands.'

Vittorio had bought the dress. Flora said, 'The second-hand designer wedding-dress market isn't as robust as you might think.'

'You could have made a lot more for the engagement ring, but you left it behind.'

Flora recalled what she'd said to him. 'I'm sorry for saying you had no taste. That wasn't very nice.'

Vittorio pushed his half-finished plate away. He emitted a sound halfway between a bark of laughter and incredulity. '*You're* sorry? I'm the one who sent you out into the streets to fend for yourself.'

Flora squirmed a little. 'You thought I had money.'

'Why didn't you tell me?' Then he made a face and said, 'I wasn't exactly receptive to hearing your side of things.'

'You could say that, yes.'

Sofia came and took the starters away and returned with mains of chicken in a white wine sauce with baby potatoes and salad. Flora tried not to behave like someone who hadn't had a square meal in months, but it was hard.

She forced herself to leave some food on the plate and had to stop herself asking Sofia if she could bag up the leftovers for Benji. As if reading her mind, though, Sofia winked at Flora and said, 'Don't worry, Benji will get some choice pieces of chicken.'

Flora grinned at Sofia. Who would have known she'd find such a sanctuary in Vittorio Vitale's home? She looked at him and he had an arrested expression on his face. She stopped smiling. 'What is it? You keep looking at me as if I've got something on my face.'

He shook his head and cleared his throat. 'The fact is that we both know that you've got nowhere to go.'

Flora sat up straight. 'That's not true, I have lots of...' She trailed off and sagged back a little. She never had been much good at lying.

Sofia brought coffees and biscotti. Flora took a fortifying sip. As the tart strong drink went down her throat she said, 'I'll find something. It's not your concern.'

'Well, I think it is. I feel responsible for letting you go the last time without ensuring your well-being and security. I was distracted and blinded by besting your uncle. I don't like to admit it, but you were peripheral to my agenda with him and this time I'm going to take responsibility for my actions.'

Now Flora was suspicious. 'What's that supposed to mean—take responsibility?'

Vittorio stood up and walked over to the window, hands in his pockets. The action drew the material of his trousers taut over his muscular buttocks. Then he turned around and Flora had to avert her gaze up, guiltily.

'What that means is that I have a proposition.'

Now Flora felt nervous. 'Vittorio—'

'Call me Vito. The only person who called me Vittorio was my mother when she was angry with me.'

Flora's heart squeezed at the mention of his mother. 'Very well... Vito...' she faltered. It felt incredibly intimate calling him Vito. Now she knew why he hadn't invited her to address him as such before, because in his eyes she'd barely existed.

He'd just apologised for that.

'What kind of proposition?' And when she said that, why did she feel an illicit flutter of awareness across her skin? This man had no interest in her. Not like that.

'The reason your uncle proposed a marriage arrangement was for his own benefit, of course, but also because he knew the media was speculating about my...social life. My bachelorhood. The fact that it was potentially affecting my business. He saw an opportunity and grabbed it.'

'And then you grabbed it right back,' pointed out Flora. Using her as the unfortunate pawn.

Vito conceded that with a nod of his head. 'But the fact remains that there was some logic in your uncle's plan outside his own nefarious aims. And the situation hasn't changed.'

Flora frowned. 'Meaning...'

'Speculation is still rife as to my...love life. Standing you up at the altar didn't exactly enhance my reputation.'

Flora's heart quickened. 'So you don't...have a girlfriend at the moment?' She winced inwardly. A man like Vito didn't do girlfriends. She recalled seeing a picture of him in the papers shortly after that fateful day—he'd been at an event with one of Italy's most beautiful models. The gossip had been intense. She'd actually been grateful that she wasn't recognisable or else the paparazzi would have had a field day documenting her fall from grace.

Vito was shaking his head. 'No, there's no one in particular.'

A spark of something dark made Flora say, 'Just casual lovers, then.'

Vito's jaw clenched and then he said tightly, 'Actually, not even casual lovers for a while. I haven't had much interest.'

Flora's silly heart skipped again. 'It's none of my business.'

'It will be.'

'How's that?'

'What I propose is that we get back together.'

'But we never were together, not really.'

'True. But that doesn't really matter. If we're seen to be together again, it'll restore your reputation and it'll stop the speculation about my private life.'

'It wasn't much of a secret that our marriage was a business deal,' she pointed out, still stung by some of the whispers she'd heard from people leaving the church.

'Of course, he was never going to marry a mouse like her. A man like Vittorio Vitale needs a real woman.'

It was that comment in particular that had galvanised her to come to his offices to find him. The thought of more humiliation wasn't particularly appealing.

He said, 'So who's to say that it's not something else now? Something more.'

That audacious thought sent an electric charge across her skin. But of course he didn't actually mean it. It was a hypothetical question. Flora shook her head, struggling to understand. 'But why…would you want to do this with me of all people? You hate me.'

Vito shook his head. 'Not you. Your uncle.'

She frowned. 'But won't he benefit from you being seen with me?'

Vito's mouth thinned. 'If anything it'll highlight his exile even more. He wouldn't dare come near me.'

Flora shivered a little. She'd seen what it was like to be on the wrong side of this man.

'I... I'd have to think about it. I've made a bit of a life for myself. I know you might not think it's much, but I have hope for the future, that I can survive. Me and Benji. We just need help getting on our feet.'

'Which is what I'm offering you.'

'What *are* you offering exactly?'

A look came into his eyes that Flora didn't like. It was something between knowing, cynical and weary.

'What do you want?'

Her mind went blank. What she wanted she'd already got in a way—freedom from her uncle. A life of her own. She was happy to work for her own security.

'What's your price, Flora?'

She looked at him, eyes narrowed. There it was, the world-weary cynicism. She rebelled against it. Even after everything she'd been through, loss, pain, grief, the sterile care of her uncle and aunt, she still retained some sense of hope and a belief in good.

A little rogue inside her urged her to play him at his own game. She lifted her chin. 'I want money, Vito. Isn't that what everyone wants?'

Vito didn't know why he felt so...disappointed. Underneath it all, Flora Gavia was like everyone else, every other woman. She wanted to feather her nest. And he was offering her exactly what she wanted.

Whether or not she'd manipulated him to this exact point, he still wasn't sure and that irritated him. Even now when she was brazenly saying she wanted money.

But then...something about the expression on her face caught him. Her eyes. As if she was mocking him, or...felt sorry for him. Instantly he felt exposed.

'What is it? What are you up to, Flora?'

She stood up. She was slight in her jeans and T-shirt, but he was acutely conscious of her curves under the thin material of her top. The tiny waist he'd noticed on the wedding day. Hips flaring out. The swell of her breasts.

This was a mistake. The woman was a serious irritation and maybe he should just let her and the damn dog—

'You're unbelievable,' she said, cutting through his thoughts. 'You're the most cynical person I ever met. Even worse than my uncle, and that's saying something.'

Vito's face was like stone. 'Everyone has a price, Flora, whether they like to admit it or not.'

Flora was about to deny that but she clamped her mouth shut. Maybe she was being hasty here. Vittorio Vitale was one of the most powerfully wealthy men in the world. There was a lot he could do. Maybe she did have a price.

She looked at him. 'If I did want something...it wouldn't have to be for me, would it?'

He frowned. 'Like what?'

'I don't know...yet.'

Vito shrugged. 'You get to decide what you want to do with it. No strings attached.'

It being whatever price she deemed she was worth for Vito to pretend that they were back together? The notion was so ridiculous that she almost felt like laughing. But then she remembered her uncle and aunt, and how every conversation had revolved around money and who had it or didn't.

She remembered that they had plundered her inheritance. All she'd had left of her beloved parents.

Vittorio Vitale was a man from that world. Where everything revolved around money and power and ambition. No wonder it was the only language he knew. He'd been bereaved as a young man and had set out to avenge his parents, accruing great wealth and power along the way.

Motivated by revenge. And yet, since she'd seen him again he'd shown aspects of himself that she never would have expected of the cold and ruthless man who had stood her up on their wedding day. Flora's head was whirling.

'I have to think about all of this… I'm going to go for a walk. I'll find Tommaso and send him back. I'm sure he has more to be doing for you than walking my dog.'

Flora had slipped out of the room before Vito could say anything else. He couldn't really believe that she wasn't negotiating terms. That she wasn't immediately naming a price.

It had been so long since he'd dealt with anyone who didn't look at him as if calculating how much they could get out of him—business colleagues and women—that it was more than a novelty. It was disconcerting. He had nothing to bargain with. And that made him feel a little…redundant.

If he had nothing he could offer Flora then would she even stay? And why did that suddenly matter?

Because she intrigues you and you want her. You want the woman who you stood up at the altar. You haven't forgotten her in six months.

This situation was unprecedented. Vito had never had to think much about pursuing a woman he wanted, never intending on a liaison lasting long. Because his main focus had always been on building up his business and taking Umberto Gavia down.

But now, he wanted a woman who came with strings attached. More than strings. A dog. And yet it wasn't making him reconsider. He was too hungry for her.

He'd taken that model out—on the evening of the day he'd been due to marry Flora Gavia. It had been intended as a very clear message to Umberto Gavia and the world that Vito was triumphant.

But that evening and date had been a disaster. He'd been distracted. The model—he couldn't even remember her name—had been uninteresting and not remotely appealing to Vito.

And now, in light of what Flora had been facing when she'd left his office, the memory left a distinctly sour taste in his mouth.

Since that day, Vito had found that the life that he'd been living—high-octane working and socialising—had suddenly felt…a little empty. He'd put it down to the anticlimax of taking over Gavia's business. And so he'd put his head down and used the time to consolidate his position, to make sure that he was invulnerable to any kind of attacks in the future.

But as soon as he'd laid eyes on Flora Gavia again something had pulsed back into life inside him. A desire to engage again. Desire for a woman. Hunger.

The fact that it was *her* of all people was not entirely welcome, but he assured himself that even if she was up to something, he would be prepared. It wasn't as if he wasn't expecting it.

A little voice reminded him that he'd felt something for her on the wedding day, when she'd appeared in that dress. He'd noticed her then. She'd made a mark, a mark that hadn't been made before. Because he hadn't noticed her previously. Or had deliberately chosen not to. Not wanting the distraction.

But now he was distracted. And he was going to do whatever it took to persuade her that he at least owed her sanctuary. As for anything more than that…he'd seen the way she blushed whenever he looked at her. He knew when a woman wanted him. They were both adults. If she was prepared to admit that she felt the same chemistry as him, then perhaps this offer of sanctuary could become something much more mutually satisfying.

He went back into his home office and made some calls. When he heard a light knock on the door, he looked up to see Flora framed in the doorway, the dog in her arms looking pretty content.

Vito could empathise. He stood up. 'Please, come in. Can I get you anything?'

Flora came in and stood on the other side of the desk. She shook her head. Some of her hair had come loose from her bun and was framing her face in curly tendrils.

Once again Vito wondered how on earth he hadn't appreciated her allure until the wedding day, and now.

She put the dog down and he ambled around the room, sniffing. She said, 'I've had a think about your…proposition.'

Vito waited, feeling unexpectedly tense. He really wasn't sure which way this woman would go and usually he read people with ease.

She looked at him. 'I've decided that I'll stay. I'll agree to this plan…to appear as if we are together. It can only help me regain some sort of dignity and respect and give me an opportunity to give something back.'

'Give something back…what do you mean?'

'I'd like you to give a generous donation to the women's aid centre. They need every euro they can get and they need new facilities. I know that's a lot to ask but—'

'Consider it done.'

Flora's eyes widened. 'You mean…you mean that you'll donate, *and* help them get new facilities?'

Vito shrugged. 'I invest in charities all the time, and they're a great cause. They should have been on my radar before now.'

'But it could mean…millions.'

'They need it. You said so yourself.'

'Yes, but I wasn't thinking you'd just agree and offer so much in one fell swoop.'

'Maybe I'm trying to impress you.'

Flora blushed. Vito's body tightened all over.

She said, 'You know you're an impressive guy, but I'm not here to be impressed.'

Vito was struck once again by the way she seemed to be so determined not to take advantage of his interest. To flirt with him.

Curious, he asked, 'What do you want for yourself?'

She shook her head. 'Nothing, really. Oh, no, wait, I'll need help with vet bills for Benji…but I'll pay you back for that when I can.'

'The dog. And the women's aid centre. Nothing for you.'

She looked at him as if he were talking in tongues. 'I've never had anything…so I'm not sure what you mean. My uncle put a roof over my head and hired tutors. I believed that he used my inheritance for that. Now I know he used it for a lot more. But I can't be bitter about it because what's the point? The money is gone. He got his due in the end. I can't say I'm sorry that he is where he is.'

'But what about *your* future?'

Now Flora looked shy. 'I'd like to do some kind of a course. I've always been interested in design and graphics. I helped the women's aid centre come up with a new logo.'

'I could pay for a course.'

Flora shook her head again. 'I know you could, without even blinking, but my independence is important to me. My whole life was spent feeling obligated to my uncle. He never let me forget that he was taking me in, caring for me—'

'While embezzling you,' Vito pointed out.

'Yes. That too. But if I do a course, I want to pay for it myself. I'll get a job and make my own way. Maybe you could just help with some references or something like that…'

Vito couldn't quite compute this. If Flora was playing a game, it was a very long one. He should know—that was what he'd done with her uncle. But, in his gut, he felt he knew the answer. There was no game here.

For a disconcerting second, Vito felt as if the ground beneath him were shifting. Moving. As if he might have to put out a hand to steady himself. But the only thing within reach was her. And he hadn't had to use anyone to steady himself in a long time. Hadn't needed it.

He pushed a piece of paper and a pen across the desk. 'Write down your contact at the women's aid centre and I'll put my team in touch. They'll set up a meeting and we can ascertain the best way to go about helping them.'

Flora sat down on the chair behind her, almost as if the stuffing were knocked out of her. 'That's really amazing. Thank you.' She wrote down a name and pushed the paper back.

Vito felt something unfamiliar in his chest. A glow. Warmth. Then a little line furrowed between her brows and she said hesitantly, 'So how would this work exactly? How would we show people that we're…together?'

* * *

Flora still felt a little as if the wind had been knocked out of her. She couldn't believe that Vito was agreeing to her request with such speed and generosity. Okay, so he was rich enough to do something like this, but she wasn't used to rich people being generous. Her uncle had been one of the meanest people she'd ever known.

He perched on the edge of the table now and his thigh was in her peripheral vision. She had to fight not to let her gaze drop.

He said, 'We'll go to social events together. Which will mean being photographed together. Which will inevitably draw interest once they realise who you are…but we can spin it that after the wedding was called off, we met again and reconnected and a real relationship grew out of the ashes of the business deal.'

He was *so* cynical. 'You sound like you have it figured out.'

He shrugged lightly. 'We need to be prepared because the press interest will be intense. But I'll make it clear that it has nothing to do with your uncle or mending any bridges.'

Flora felt a small pang for her uncle but then quashed it. He didn't deserve her concern or sympathy. Her own father had moved away from Italy to get away from his brother, not liking his business methods, and the only reason Flora had ended up with him was because her parents obviously hadn't expected that something so tragic as a fatal accident would befall them, and there had been no guardian mentioned in their will. Her uncle had been her only next of kin.

It was only in the last six months that his act of benevolence in taking her in had taken on much darker hues.

She forced her mind back to what Vito was saying. 'So

we'd just have to appear together...but won't people know we're not together when they see us? We're not a couple.'

A gleam came into Vito's eye. It made Flora's skin feel suddenly tight and prickly. He said, 'We'll have to make it look like we're a couple.'

'How, exactly?'

Vito stood up and came around the desk. He held out a hand. Flora's heart thumped. She looked at it suspiciously. Vito said, 'It's just a hand, Flora, it won't bite you.'

No, maybe not. But the thought of putting her hand in his suddenly felt like a ridiculously audacious thing to do. She lifted her hand and slipped it into his palm. His fingers closed around hers and he pulled her up to standing.

Since when had he moved so close that their bodies were practically touching? All Flora could smell was him. Musky and woodsy and spicy. Masculine. She wanted to close her eyes and breathe deep. It was an effort not to do that.

She had to look up. He was so much taller than her. He made her feel incredibly petite. Delicate. He was looking at her. His gaze moving over her face, resting on her mouth. It tingled. She had to swallow. Her throat was dry.

'What are you doing?' she asked, trying to break the languor that was spreading through her body.

'I'm showing you how we might have to...touch. Interact. To make people think we're together.'

'Oh.' Flora's brain didn't seem to want to function.

'You see,' Vito was saying, 'I don't think we'll have to pretend all that much.'

'We won't?'

He shook his head. He lifted his other hand and before Flora knew what he was doing, her hair was loosening from its confinement and falling around her shoulders. Vito was looking at her, running the long strands through his fingers. Flora felt as though she wanted to purr.

Then he said, 'The truth is that I don't think either of us will have to pretend.'

She lifted her gaze to his and her heart stopped at the look in his eyes. It was smouldering. This close she could see flecks of gold, like little fires.

He wanted her.

It hit her right in her solar plexus, and deep in her core. Between her legs a pulse throbbed, making her press her thighs together as if that could stem the damp, hot reaction.

She knew it was important to try and hang onto some dignity here. It must be so obvious that she fancied him and he was just a very good actor making her believe that he wanted her too because there was no way it could be real.

Vito tipped Flora's chin up and his head lowered. Every part of her quivered with anticipation. And when that firm, sexy mouth touched hers, she knew in that instant she'd never be the same again. He was scorching her alive, from the inside out. She'd never felt anything like it.

His hands moved, cupping her face, holding her so that he could entice her to open up to him, which she did on a helpless sigh. And then the scorching became an inferno when his tongue touched hers.

Flora was lost in a swooning dizzy dance. Time had stopped and all that existed was how it felt to be kissed by this man, her whole body being set alight from between her legs to her breasts.

She didn't even realise she was clutching his arms to remain standing until he pulled back for a moment. Oxygen got to her brain. She opened her eyes. She loosened her death grip on his biceps. Tried to make sense of what had just happened. Vito was watching her, eyes glittering.

There was a sound from the ground. A growling. Flora looked down to see Benji glaring up at Vito. She bent down and scooped him up, as much to do something with her trembling hands as anything else.

She took a step back and eventually said, 'Wow. I mean, yes, okay, I see what you mean. That was…very convincing. If I didn't know better I'd think that you did really want to kiss me. But then I've never been kissed before so I guess I wouldn't really know the difference.'

He frowned. 'I wasn't trying to convince you of anything. I *was* kissing you for real. I do want you, Flora. The electricity between us is off the charts.'

Her belly swooped alarmingly and her legs felt weak. 'I… Okay, that's good, then, isn't it?'

She sneaked a look at Vito. He was frowning. 'Wait a second…you just said you'd never been kissed before… Are you innocent?'

Flora's face burned. Benji was squirming in her arms so she put him down again—the traitor—and stood up. Of course Vito must have noticed her gauche inexperience, even if she hadn't just admitted it.

There really was nothing to say except to admit the bald truth. 'Yes, I'm a virgin, if that's what you mean.'

CHAPTER FIVE

VITO LOOKED INCREDULOUS. No doubt virgins were as mythical as unicorns in his very cynical world. He said, 'But… how?'

Now Flora felt self-conscious. She wrapped her arms around herself. A minute ago she'd been melting and now she felt cold. 'I didn't have much of a social life. I was home-schooled. When I graduated, my uncle preferred to keep me at the palazzo, helping him and my aunt to host their parties.'

'You could have left,' Vito pointed out.

Now Flora felt even more vulnerable. 'I could have, yes. But somehow, whenever I contemplated it, my uncle always said something that made me feel like I hadn't paid my dues yet. And when I asked about my inheritance he told me he had it tied up with stocks and shares, trying to make sure I got the most out of it. Then…the marriage deal with you was struck…and for the first time I felt like maybe I finally had a way out. My dues would be paid.'

Vito took a step back. He was shaking his head. 'This changes everything.'

Flora immediately feared for the women's aid home. 'Are you going back on what you promised?'

'No, of course not. But we don't need to appear in public. I won't put you through unnecessary scrutiny.'

Flora struggled to understand. 'But…you just said you wanted me?' She'd never felt as exposed as she did in that moment.

'I do want you, more than I've wanted a woman in a long time.' He sounded grim.

The relief that flooded her was nothing short of humiliating. But she couldn't help asking, 'So…what's the problem?'

Vito's jaw clenched. He said tautly, 'I don't sleep with innocents. I won't be your first lover, Flora. And I wouldn't be able to stand next to you and not touch you. After a kiss like that there's only one way it would end. In my bed.'

A wave of heat pulsed through Flora's body as she thought of where they might be right now, naked limbs entwined, Vito's hands exploring every inch of her flesh—she shook her head, desperately trying to dislodge the images.

She tried to claw back any sense of dignity she could. 'Well, it's very presumptuous of you to imagine that I would have allowed that to happen.'

She wanted to cringe. Who was she kidding? He'd just kissed her and she'd been ready to climb into his skin. She wouldn't have put up a word of protest.

Vito said, 'If you could have resisted, then you would have had more control than me.'

The thought of driving this man so crazy with desire that he wouldn't be able to control himself was heady.

Flora forced herself to parse the information. She asked, 'What is it about my virginity that is so off-putting?'

Vito was pacing again. He stopped and faced her. 'I'm not the man you want as your first lover, Flora. I can't promise anything more than having fun while we both get what we need and want out of this…relationship. You deserve someone who really cares for you. Who'll be gentle.'

Flora felt like growling. There was a fire burning inside

her. A fire this man had set alight. The last thing she wanted was gentle, or someone who cared for her. She wanted this man. Only this man. He'd already ruined her and he'd only kissed her!

'I didn't know you held me in such high esteem.' She couldn't help sound mocking.

Vito scowled.

She uncrossed her arms from around herself. 'What if I wasn't a virgin?'

'We wouldn't be having this conversation.'

Flora shivered. They'd be doing something else. 'So what happens now?'

'I'll do what I promised and help the women's aid centre and you're free to stay here until you get a job.'

'What about your precious reputation?'

A muscle in Vito's jaw popped. He said, 'I'll live with it.'

'I'm sure there are any number of women who'd be willing to act the part. Women who aren't virgins. The question is why haven't you just chosen a suitable woman before now? Why me?'

The truth? Because no other woman had appealed to him enough to even play out a fake relationship for the sake of it. Until Flora. She had inspired the notion. No other woman had made him want to seduce her in a long time. Until Flora.

Except what had happened just now hadn't even been a seduction, it had been blunt and seriously lacking in finesse. But he'd had to kiss her. He'd had to *know*. And now he did and now he couldn't see anything else but her.

But he couldn't have her. He had a rule. He would not sleep with innocents. There was too much of a risk of emotional attachment. And he was not in the market for emotional attachment.

That way lay loss, grief and pain. After losing his parents, Vito had vowed that he would never let anyone close again. And he hadn't. And that wasn't going to change.

He had no desire for a wife, or family. He had no desire to lose everything again. He'd built himself up from the ashes of grief once, he wouldn't be able to do it again.

And while he knew rationally that there was no reason to believe he would suffer such loss again, there was also no guarantee that he wouldn't. And he wasn't prepared to take the risk.

Coward.

He had his business and that was all he needed, along with taking his pleasures when and where he could. Restoring the Vitale name and turning it from a byword for shoddy work practices and whispers of corruption into something respected and revered was his life's work. If he could ensure his name became an enduring brand, eclipsing the name Gavia for ever, and if his success benefited others less fortunate, then that was all the legacy he needed.

He said, 'This conversation is over. You're welcome to stay until you're on your feet. But that'll be the extent of our relationship.'

'Flatmates.'

'Essentially.'

Her eyes narrowed on him and, for the first time since he'd met her, Vito saw something that looked suspiciously calculating in those golden-brown depths. But then it was gone.

She bent down and scooped up Benji and said, 'Okay, fine. I'll stay out of your way as much as I can. You'll hardly know I'm here.'

Vito watched Flora leave the room, her wild hair spilling down her back. He wanted to reach out and wrap a lock of that hair around his hand and tug her back and finish what they'd started.

He cursed. What a time to discover that he really did have a conscience.

Later that evening, Vito was back in the apartment after spending the rest of the day in the office. A day where he'd been distracted and irritable. A day where he couldn't stop replaying that kiss in his head. Probably one of the most chaste kisses he'd ever experienced but one that had left him on fire.

And then he'd had to endure an interminably boring business dinner.

He hadn't seen Flora or the dog on his arrival back at the apartment. Sofia was gone for the day. He presumed Flora was in bed. It was late. He imagined her in bed, alone, her hair spread around her head like a halo… He took a healthy swig of his whiskey, hoping the burn would eclipse the other burn.

He was standing at the window, looking out over the view of Rome. It never failed to buoy him up. To remind him of how far he'd come. Restoring his father's legacy and pride in the family name.

What's it all for, though, if you've no one to leave it to? Is a brand really going to last without someone to protect it?

He scowled at his reflection and at the insidious doubts infiltrating his head. He was quite happy with his life of no entanglements. And today he'd had the sense to walk away from a potentially explosive one. *Flora.* An innocent.

Just at that moment, he caught a moving flash of silver out of the corner of his eye. He tensed and turned around. 'Flora? Is that you?'

Nothing for a beat and then, from outside in the hall, 'Um, yes, it's me.'

'What are you doing?'

'Going out.'

Vito frowned and put the glass down on a table. He walked to the door and looked into the corridor that led to the reception hall and almost choked at what he saw. Flora, but not Flora. A different woman. His brain was melting and his entire body was going up in flames.

Somehow he managed to croak out, 'What are you wearing?'

Flora was trembling all over but refused to let Vito's re-action put her off. She knew the dress was audacious. It was why she was wearing it. It had been a hand-me-down from one of the women at the shelter, along with the match-ing four-inch stilettos that she could barely walk in. The woman had said, 'Take it—with your figure it'll look amaz-ing.' Flora had taken it, as much out of politeness as any-thing else.

But this evening she'd realised it was perfect for what she needed.

To get rid of her virginity.

If she couldn't do it in this dress, then she might as well take a vow of chastity. Vito had laid down a gauntlet earlier. Even if he didn't know it. Flora had realised that she didn't want her innocence to hold her back. She had no great ro-mantic illusions after growing up in a loveless environment. This was a very practical decision. She wanted Vito, there-fore she needed to remove the impediment: her virginity.

She said, 'I'm wearing a dress.' But even as she said that she winced. It was just a scrap of material really. Thin straps and a low V-neck, with hundreds of little silver me-dallions stitched into the fabric that moved and shimmered with every breath she took. She couldn't wear a bra with the dress so she felt very conscious of her breasts under the thin material.

It fell to her upper thigh, just about scraping the edges of decency.

Vito's eyes were almost bugging out of his head. He said, 'That's not a dress, that's an invitation to sin.'

His reaction galvanised Flora. 'Good, I was hoping for that effect.'

His gaze moved up to meet hers. 'Why?'

'Because if my virginity is such an impediment I intend to get rid of it. If you won't be my first lover, then I'll find someone who will. You made me realise today that I don't want my innocence holding me back.'

She turned around to leave and prayed that she wouldn't humiliate herself by falling flat on her face in these ridiculous shoes.

Vito said from behind her, 'Where are you going?'

Without turning around, she said, 'I'm going to Diablo. I hear it's the best nightclub in town.'

'Do you know how much it costs to get in?'

Aiming for more confidence than she felt and going off what she'd heard about the club—that if they deemed you alluring enough they would let you in for free—Flora said, 'I don't think it'll be an issue, do you?' She really hoped it wouldn't be. She was counting on this dress being enough of a distraction to get her in.

'That place is full of sharks.'

Flora was in the entrance hall now and she turned around. 'You'd know, I guess.' She didn't mean it as an insult, merely as a fact.

Vito's face was stony. But he said, 'Something like that.'

Then he shook his head and came towards her. Flora

stood her ground. He said, 'You won't find the kind of man you want in a place like that, Flora.'

'You don't know what kind of man I want.'

I want you.

She turned around again and was almost at the private elevator doors when Vito said from behind her, 'This is crazy.'

She pressed the button and the doors opened. He said, 'You wouldn't dare.'

She just said, 'Watch me,' and stepped into the elevator.

CHAPTER SIX

VITO ENTERED THE dark decadent space, lit up by strobing lights. The thumping bass of the music reached all the way down to his bones, but he noticed none of it. He was looking for a wild-haired temptress in a glittering excuse for a dress.

'Vito, man! Where the hell have you been?'

Vito ignored the greeting.

He got to the other side of the bar where he stood at a railing. The dance floor was below and thick with people, their sinuous bodies moving in time with the music. Heads thrown back, arms around necks, bodies pressed together. It was temptation and sin and decadence and he wondered what he'd ever seen in it. It all seemed a little desperate and tacky to him now.

Full of predators.

Like you.

Vito made a face, scaring off one woman who had been approaching him.

And then, a flash of silver caught his eye and he saw her. She was on the edge of the dance floor, surrounded by a group of men. Of course she'd got in. He couldn't imagine a bouncer in the world denying her entry. She was holding a delicate flute of sparkling wine. She laughed at something one of the men said but Vito could see that she didn't look entirely comfortable. They were hemming her in.

Then she looked up and over their heads, straight at him. She lifted her glass in a salute and then downed the drink in one, handing her empty glass to one man while taking another by the hand and leading him onto the dance floor.

The man looked as if all his Christmases had just come at once. Vito was going to kill him. He refrained from vaulting over the rail onto the dance floor and took the stairs.

His blood was pounding along with the music, but with one refrain, *Mine, mine, mine.* He had forgotten all about his conscience. The minute he'd seen Flora in that dress his conscience had turned to dust.

She was his and he was going to have her, over and over, until he could breathe again.

Flora was feeling a little dizzy after downing that drink in one go. A little reckless, but when she'd seen Vito standing at the railing scouring the crowd for her, she'd wanted to taunt him.

She was done with men trying to keep her in a box. First her uncle's palazzo and now Vito's plush apartment. She wanted to live. She wanted to be devoured. The only problem was that the only man she wanted to devour her was more likely to drag her out of here and scold her than devour her.

The man she had pulled onto the dance floor was now dancing energetically opposite her, his avid gaze firmly fixed on her breasts. She smiled weakly. This wasn't panning out exactly as she'd hoped. It felt a bit tawdry.

But suddenly he was gone and in his place was a man about a foot taller, and broader and altogether more dynamic. *Vito.*

She stopped moving and looked up. And gulped. His gaze was on fire. His face was stark. Jaw clenched. Flora put her hands on her hips. 'I'm not leaving.'

'Yes, you are.'

'No, I'm not. I'm having sex tonight and if you don't want it to be with you then please get out of my way.'

'You will not be having sex tonight with anyone *but* me,' Vito breathed.

The music was almost deafening but Flora heard that as clear as a bell. Her heart thumped. 'What did you say?'

He reached for her and put his hands on her waist. He tugged her closer until their bodies were touching. She could feel the ridge of his arousal. Her heart rate went up to a million beats a minute. He was still wearing his work clothes, white shirt and dark trousers. He should have looked ridiculous. He was the sexiest man there.

He said succinctly, 'You heard me.'

She had heard him but she didn't quite believe him. Maybe he was just trying to get her out of this den of iniquity.

'What are you saying exactly, Vito?'

Vito moved his hands around to her back, hauling her closer. His hands were on her bare skin. She was throbbing. And down between her legs, she was damp.

He said, 'I want you, Flora.'

'But you didn't want to be my first lover.'

'Let's just say I've reconsidered.'

Flora could see the day-old stubble on his jaw darkening it, making it look even harder. She reached up and touched him there, feeling the short bristles, imagining how it would feel on her skin.

He took her hand and pressed his mouth to her inner palm, darting out his tongue. Flora's legs nearly gave way. Vito held her up. He took her hand and said, 'Come on, we're leaving.'

He started to pull her off the dance floor and Flora's insides were somersaulting. At the last second, though, she stalled and he looked back at her, impatience stamped all over his face.

For her.

She said, 'Can we just…stay for one more song? I've never been to a nightclub before.'

Vito looked at her and something flickered over his face—surprise. But then he nodded. 'One song.'

Flora tugged him back onto the dance floor, the beat of the music in time with the pounding of her pulse. For the first time in her life, as she danced—inelegantly, she was sure—in front of a man who was looking at her as if she were the only thing on the planet, she felt young and free. Vibrant. Alive. *Seen.* That revelation made her stumble a little. Vito caught her. She didn't want to think about that too closely, how it felt to be seen for herself and not as someone who was just tolerated. It made her feel emotional, and she didn't want to delve into emotions. She wanted the physicality that Vito was offering.

She looked up at him and said, 'Okay, I'm ready to go.'

The journey back to Vito's apartment was made in silence. Once again he drove with a quiet confidence that impressed Flora. Even more so when she thought of those hands and what they would shortly be doing to *her.*

Her whole body felt as if it were vibrating. Maybe the after-effects of the club and the music but more likely the effects of Vito's hands on her. His eyes.

She sneaked a look at his profile as he pulled to a stop outside the building and the concierge came out to park the car. His face was still set in those stark lines. She felt a prickle of unease. 'Vito, if you've changed your mind—'

He looked at her and she stopped talking. He said, 'I've never been more sure of anything in my life.'

Flora licked dry lips. 'What's that exactly?' Because if he was about to say that he wasn't going to do this then she was jumping straight into a cab and going back to the club.

'You and me. I am the only first lover you will know, Flora. You're mine.'

A thrill so electric went through her at his possessive declaration that she quivered with it. 'I… Okay.'

He got out of the car and tossed the keys to the concierge, and came around to help her out. He kept hold of her hand, leading her into the building, to the elevator. The doors closed. Flora took the opportunity to slip out of the shoes, picking them up with her free hand. She muttered, 'I don't know how women wear these all the time.'

The elevator doors opened and before Flora could take another breath, Vito had taken her shoes, thrown them aside and she had her back against the wall beside the elevator doors and his hands were either side of her head.

The air sizzled. Or maybe she was just sizzling.

He said, 'If this evening's stunt was designed to make me change my mind, it worked.'

Flora frowned. It was hard to concentrate when he was so close. *Had* she set out to drive him to pursue her? All she could remember thinking was that if she wasn't a virgin then they could make love.

'I…hadn't really thought it through in such detail. I just wanted to get rid of it so that I could…maybe we could… you know…'

'Make love?'

Flora nodded, relieved that he understood. She looked at his mouth. 'Can we stop talking now?'

He answered that by putting his mouth on hers and she

melted into him, hands fisting his shirt to stay standing. His hands were on her face, in her hair and then on her back, fingers spread over her skin.

She ached between her legs. A physical pain to have him touch her there, but he drew back and said harshly, 'Not here, like this.'

He scooped her up into his arms and carried her down the corridor into his bedroom. Flora lifted her head and said, 'Wait! Benji.'

Vito didn't break his stride. 'Taken care of. I asked Damiano to keep him in the security room tonight. We'll get him in the morning.'

We. Flora's heart turned over. He hadn't just forgotten about the dog. And now they were truly alone. No interruptions. Vito was going to be her first lover. And she already knew that his mark on her would be indelible. Perhaps fatal. But she didn't care about that now. She was hungry. Starving. For something she'd never known could exist. Desire. No, lust.

She'd always imagined wanting to have sex with someone would feel a little tepid. But this was like a storm, building and building deep inside, threatening to blow her apart.

Vito put her on her feet. She suddenly felt self-conscious. Very aware that she would be joining a legion of women before her and that inevitably she wouldn't stack up next to them.

But Vito was looking at her as if he'd never seen a woman before and Flora clung onto that illusion. He said, 'I want to see you.'

Flora quivered inwardly. No way was she baring herself while suddenly feeling so vulnerable. 'You first.'

Vito didn't hesitate. His shirt came off and Flora barely had time to ogle at the hard-muscled perfection of his chest before he was undoing his trousers and pulling them down, kicking them off.

Now he wore just briefs that did little to hide the bulge. Flora watched wide-eyed, fascinated, as he tugged them down and off too, freeing his impressive erection.

Flora's insides squeezed tight. Then she realised she was squeezing her thighs together as if that could stem the flow of damp heat. Of sheer lust.

Without even making the conscious decision, she reached out and touched Vito's chest. His skin was warm and firm. Dark hairs dusting his pectoral muscles. A line of hair dissected his abdomen and went all the way down to the thicket of hair between his legs.

Hard, powerful thighs. Slim waist. He was intimidatingly perfect. She dragged her gaze back up. She was filled with a sense of their disparities in everything—but mostly experience. 'Vito… I don't know if this is such a good idea. I'm not…experienced, as you know…you're bound to be disappointed…'

He put a finger over her lips. Then he took it away and said, 'Do you want to do this?'

Flora couldn't help but nod. 'More than anything.'

'Then let me see you.'

Flora's heart thumped. She brought a hand to one strap of the dress and pushed it down over her shoulder. Then the other. The dress lowered and clung for a second to her chest.

Vito reached out and, with a flick of his hand, the dress fell under its own weight, all the way to the floor, leaving Flora standing before him wearing nothing but her underwear.

She heard Vito's sharp intake of breath. She was too scared to look at him, see his reaction. There was a stillness in the air. Eventually, he breathed, 'You are…more beautiful than anything I imagined.'

She looked up. He'd imagined this? His eyes were so dark she couldn't read them. He closed the distance between them and cupped her breasts, testing their weight and shape, thumbs moving back and forth over hard nipples.

Flora bit her lip. And then Vito was dipping, capturing her mouth with his again, angling her face up to him so that he could plunder deep. She wrapped her arms around him, opening up her body to his. There was no point where they didn't touch, breast to chest and hips to belly and thighs. It was intoxicating.

Flora felt weightless for a moment and then she realised that Vito was putting her down on the bed. She was dizzy, with desire. He drew back. A lock of hair fell onto his forehead and she reached up and touched it. It made him seem younger, carefree.

He took her hand and captured it, pressing his mouth to her palm again. Tasting her. Need was like a taut wire inside Flora. She said, 'Vito, please… I need you.'

He looked at her. 'I want to make sure you're ready. Your first time might hurt a little.'

She shimmied out of her underwear, throwing the slip of material aside. 'I'll be fine. I'm not made of glass.'

'No,' he breathed, his eyes moving down over her body. 'You're not, are you?'

Still, he didn't move fast. He put his hand on her, between her legs. Flora opened for him, trusting him implicitly. He explored her with a finger, then two, seeking where she ached, finding where she was so hot and wet. Moving in and out, making her hips circle and her head go back.

Then he was thrusting deep, massaging her inner mucles, and Flora was helpless to stop a wave of pleasure breaking her apart. She couldn't breathe for a long moment, absorbing the magnitude of what had just happened.

When she lifted her head, she saw Vito rolling a sheath onto his erection, and then he positioned himself between her legs, holding the full weight of his body off hers.

Even as the last flutters of orgasm were still pulsing through her body, Flora was hungry for more. She tilted her hips towards Vito. He smiled and said, 'Patience, little one.'

She wanted to scowl but then he was nudging the head of his erection against her body and she sucked in a breath when he breached her entrance. He kept going, watching her reaction, inch by inch, until she felt so full that she couldn't breathe, but then she did take a breath, and another, and Vito pulled back out, before moving in again and starting up a rhythm as old as humanity.

Flora was no longer human as she was swept up into a vortex of building pleasure—so intense it almost bordered on being painful. She wrapped her legs around Vito's waist and he sank even deeper, emitting a curse that would have made her smile if she hadn't been so focused on reaching the pinnacle shimmering just out of reach.

But then Vito lowered his head to her breast and took a nipple into his mouth, sucking deep, biting gently and the peak broke over Flora with no warning, making her cry out, her back arch, and every muscle in her body clench tight. She was barely aware of Vito's own guttural cry as his big body jerked against hers, both of them falling over the edge and down into an ocean of endless pleasure.

Dawn was lightening the Rome sky outside but Vito was hardly aware. He was standing, with a towel slung around his hips, a few feet from the bed. He'd just taken a shower and was already lamenting washing Flora's scent from his skin. That made him nervous. This whole situation made him nervous.

He didn't do this. He didn't take women in off the street. He didn't sleep with virgins. He didn't watch lovers as they slept.

But…she was a vision. On her front, one arm raised. The plump flesh of her breast visible. Enticing. Wild hair spread out around her head, reminding him of how he'd wrapped it in his hand as he'd thrust into her over and over again and had chased a pinnacle of pleasure he'd never reached before.

That's because she was innocent.

No. It had been more than that. Vito already knew that what had happened last night would only get better. He felt it deep inside. There was something unprecedented about their chemistry.

Making love for him had always been pleasurable but not…transcendent.

A sense of panic clutched at his gut. A sense of claustrophobia. But then he forced it back down. Reminding himself of all that he'd been through. All that he'd mastered. A woman couldn't undo that, no matter how amazing the sex. And that was all it was. Amazing sex. He wanted to bark out a laugh at himself, for almost losing it. Over a woman. Over sex.

Vito was a loner. He had no intentions of that changing. He would never suffer the awful excoriating pain of loss and grief again.

But first, he had to set some boundaries and make sure Flora knew that, outside sex, there would be no intimacies. He would take her back to her own room. He didn't indulge women in his bed after sex.

He bent down over the bed, intending to scoop Flora up, but she opened her eyes and saw him. Vito was instantly distracted when that gold-and-brown gaze widened on him.

She moved, and came up on one arm, her breasts swaying with the movement, causing his body to tighten as desire surged.

She looked deliciously sleepy, and well loved. *Sexy.*

He would move her in a minute, but first, 'How are you feeling?'

She frowned, as if gauging, and then with a slow, shy smile, she said, 'I feel good…amazing.' She looked at him. 'I wasn't sure for a second…if it wasn't a dream. But you're not a dream, are you?'

She reached out and touched his clean-shaven jaw with a light touch, but it seared Vito all the way to his gut.

She said, 'You're real. What happened…was real.'

Vito, quite against his intention to scoop her up and take her back to her own bed, found himself flicking off his towel and climbing back onto the bed beside Flora, breathing in her scent and revelling in the way her body curved against his.

His blood was already pounding, hunger clawing. Why on earth would he take her back to her own bed when she was here now, *his*, for the taking? He asked, 'Are you sore?'

She went a little pink. 'Just a bit tender…but I want you again, Vito… Is that too much? Too forward?' She buried her head against him as if she was embarrassed and Vito felt something disturbingly close to an emotion fill his chest. He pushed it back down.

It was just amazing sex.

He tipped her chin back up and looked at her. 'No, it's not too much at all. I want you too. But this time…we're going to take it slow…'

He heard the hitch in her breath as his hand moved over her belly and down, exploring her tender flesh and bringing them both back to an urgency that didn't remain slow for very long.

CHAPTER SEVEN

WHEN FLORA WOKE it was bright daylight outside. She looked at her watch and jackknifed up to sitting. Lunchtime. Again. She'd never been so slovenly in her life.

And then she went still as several things registered. She wasn't in her own room. She was in a very rumpled bed. *Vito's bed.* She was naked. And she had a delicious feeling of languor running through her veins. As if she wanted to just lie back down and luxuriate in the feeling of having been so thoroughly...loved.

A little shiver went through her. It wasn't love. It was just sex. Amazing sex. She'd never known it could be like that. So...all-encompassing. So transformative. She did feel transformed. As if her cells had been realigned and now she was a different verison of herself. *A woman.* Who had awoken to her sensuality.

But the thing that loomed largest in her head now was how considerate and gentle Vito had been. *And not gentle.* But that had been because she'd been urging him on, to stop taking such care.

Heat filled her face now as she remembered how at one point she'd bitten his shoulder. She'd bitten him. Like a mad thing. She buried her face in her hands and cringed.

'What's wrong? Are you hurt? Sore?'

A small bundle of fur landed beside Flora on the bed at

the same time as she heard the voice. Benji. Her dog, who she was neglecting terribly, expecting everyone to take on her responsibility.

And Vito, standing in the doorway, dressed in dark trousers and a short-sleeved polo shirt, looking as if he'd just stepped out of *Vogue Italia* for men. She pulled the sheet up over her chest and drew her knees up, while scooping Benji up against her chest, like a shield. He licked her face.

She felt vulnerable and prickly. 'You should have woken me. I should've been up, walking Benji and—' She stopped.

Vito raised a brow. 'And what? You don't have anything to do. Relax.'

Before her life had imploded on that fateful wedding day she'd been busy running the palazzo for her uncle and aunt. And in the last six months she'd been in survival mode. She felt redundant. 'I need to get a job.'

'And I'm sure you will...but after last night I think we're back to Plan A.'

'Which is?'

'Pretending we're back together. I don't think the PDA will be an issue now, do you?'

Flora wanted to scowl at his arrogant self-assurance even though she'd been the one who had all but seduced him!

'I...yes, I guess so.' She couldn't very well say no, now, could she?

Vito glanced at his watch. 'Sofia has prepared some brunch for you and then the glam team will be arriving.'

'The glam team?'

Vito looked at her. 'A stylist and her team of hair and make-up staff. We'll be attending our first function this evening.'

'This evening!' Flora squeaked.

Vito looked at her. 'You've been to social events before.'

ABBY GREEN   89

Flora shook her head. 'Not really, not outside my uncle's palazzo. He didn't really approve of me attending events that weren't hosted by him.'

Vito was silent for a long moment. 'Did he ever let you out of that palazzo?'

Flora said, 'Of course, I was free to come and go. I'd go to the market with the housekeeper. Or when they were away that's when I'd go out to museums and art galleries.'

'You didn't meet with friends? Go to parties?'

Flora felt self-conscious. 'Not really.' *Never.* She confided reluctantly, 'I had no friends. Like I told you, I was home-schooled.'

Vito came into the bedroom. 'Have you ever left Italy?'

Flora shook her head. 'No. Not since I came here from London after my parents and younger brother, Charlie, died.'

Vito's eyes widened. A look of pure disgust came over his face. 'That man kept you locked up like Cinderella. All you were missing was two evil stepsisters.'

Flora found it hard to breathe for a moment. She'd never had anyone else evaluate the life she'd taken for granted before. And the loyalty and obligation she'd felt to her uncle was still there, like a scar.

'I can't really complain. I had a roof over my head—I lived in a beautiful palazzo. I got my education.'

Vito made a rude sound. 'That palazzo was like something out of a nineteen-fifties film set, straight out of the Cinecittà movie studios.'

A surprised laugh at Vito's accurate assessment came out of Flora before she could stop it. She put her hand over her mouth.

But still, the impulse to be loyal made her say, 'I think my uncle just appreciated another era.'

Vito snorted. 'He appreciated not spending money on anything but creating misery, more to the point.'

Flora sobered. Vito was right. She'd always known her uncle kept her all but locked up, but she'd convinced herself it had been for her protection and security. Now she could understand that he'd done it so that she wouldn't leave before he could get his hands on her inheritance.

The sense of years spent locked out of the world suddenly made her appreciate what was happening here now with Vito. She was being awoken in more ways than one. She felt a sense of urgency. 'What time is the glam team coming?'

'Three o'clock.'

'And what time do you have to go to the office?'

'About half an hour ago.'

Flora summoned up all of her courage and threw back the cover and stood up from the bed. Naked.

'Well, then,' she said, 'as you're already late, what does another half-hour matter?'

Vito's face flushed and his eyes narrowed on her body. For a moment she imagined Vito leaving her standing there, walking away, but then he scooped up Benji, who had trotted over to smell his feet, efficiently put the dog out of the room, closed the door and stalked towards Flora, shedding clothes as he did.

By the time he reached her he was naked. His body gleamed in the sunlight flooding into the room and Flora took her opportunity to really look at him, marvelling at his sheer perfection.

'Keep looking at me like that and we'll be here until tomorrow.' Vito growled, reaching for her, and placing his hands on her waist. She was pressed up against him and she quivered all over at the contact. His erection pressing against her lower belly.

Breathless, she looked up and said, 'And that'd be a bad thing because…?'

Vito took a skein of her hair and wrapped it around his hand. He said, 'Because I have every intention of showing you off this evening and making sure everyone can see the jewel that has been locked away for too long.'

Emotion caught at Flora before she could stop it. Making her chest tight. In a bid to defuse it and distract Vito from just how seismic his words were to her, Flora reached up and wrapped her arms around his neck and then they were falling back onto the bed in a tangle of limbs and sighs and murmurs that grew more frantic and desperate as they lost themselves in each other again.

Flora was looking at herself suspiciously in the mirror. Even Benji was looking at her suspiciously. With his one good eye. Flora said reproachfully to his reflection in the mirror, where he was sitting on the bed behind her, 'It *is* still me, Ben.'

She sniffed her wrist where the stylist had instructed her to spray some perfume. It was heady—musky rose and something lighter. She liked it even if it didn't feel remotely like her. Maybe it was the scent putting him off.

Because visually, she was almost unrecognisable. Flora had never had a fantasy of being transformed like Cinderella, but if she had…she was living it right now.

The stylist and her team had just left and finally Flora was able to take in the magnitude of what they'd been working on all afternoon. She blushed, thinking of how when she and Vito had emerged from the bedroom after a couple of hours indulging in exploring each other with a thoroughness that had left Flora limp with an overload of pleasure—the glam team had been waiting for her.

Flora had felt like a naughty child caught playing truant. Vito had left her in the hands of the team, but not before she'd heard him instructing the stylist, 'Under no circumstances is her hair to be straightened.' That had caused another rush of emotion to Flora's chest, making her feel as if a layer of skin had been removed, exposing vulnerabilities she'd pushed down for a long time.

But then Vito had left and she'd been sucked into a whirlwind of having her hair trimmed and styled, nails manicured, a facial, her entire body measured to within an inch of its life, all leading to this…vision in the mirror.

The dress was a very pale pink blush colour, strapless and cut across her chest to reveal more cleavage than Flora was comfortable with, but the stylist had assured her it was not too revealing. The bodice was tight and then from her waist the dress fell to the floor in whimsical layers of silk and chiffon.

It was deceptively simple and Flora could barely feel it when she moved. As if it were made of air.

She wore a simple diamond choker and a diamond cocktail ring on her index finger. Diamond stud earrings.

Her hair had been styled in such a way that it was still natural but a little more tamed. The hairdresser had left her some products, telling her they would work miracles. It had been pulled back on one side and held in place with a diamond clip and then teased to flow over the other bare shoulder.

Her make-up was minimal, much to Flora's relief. Or, to be more accurate, she'd been made up to look as if she were wearing very little. Some dusky shimmery blush colour on her eyes, lashes long and black. Eyebrows plucked and shaped. Blush on her cheeks. Her mouth looked plumper— as if she'd just been kissed. She was tempted to find a tissue to make it look less…provocative but then she heard a sound coming from the doorway and turned around.

Vito.

Flora instantly forgot her preoccupation with herself. Vito was wearing a tuxedo. She'd seen him in a tuxedo just a couple of nights ago but that had been unexpected and she'd been too distracted to really appreciate the full effect.

But now he was in front of her and she was going to be going out with him and pretending that they were together as a couple…suddenly it was all a bit overwhelming.

Vito frowned. 'What is it? You've gone white.' He was beside her and guiding her to a stool nearby, making her sit down before she could protest. In truth her legs had turned to jelly. The impact of him in the tuxedo, what had happened between them in the last twenty-four hours, added to the sense of overwhelm.

Flora struggled to get air to her brain. Her heart. Vito smelled delicious, which only scrambled her brain cells even more.

Vito handed her a glass of water. Flora took a gulp. She handed it back. Looked up. 'I don't know if I can do this.'

Vito was putting the glass down. 'Do what?'

'Go out with you.' She shook her head. 'I know people think that I come from this very privileged background, but *you* know that's not the case. I've never really been to a society event. That's one of the reasons why there were so many people at the wedding that day, because most of them just wanted to gawk at me.'

Vito's jaw clenched. 'Flora, if I'd thought for a second about how that day was really going to impact you—'

She waved a hand. 'It's not your fault. How could you have known?'

Vito took a step back and held out a hand. 'Come here.'

Reluctantly Flora put her hand in his and let him pull her up. He put his hands on her shoulders and she felt the zing of electricity all the way to between her legs. Her body was like a finely tuned instrument around this man. She could only hope that he felt a smidgeon of what she was feeling but it was unlikely, he was so much more experienced.

He turned her to face the mirror. 'Look at yourself.'

Flora resisted telling him that was exactly what she'd just been doing and what had led to this minor attack of nerves. She looked at him. The first thing she noticed was how tall he was behind her. And his hands, on her shoulders. His skin so much darker than hers.

'Not at me,' he scolded. 'At you.'

Flora rolled her eyes but then did as he asked. He pulled her back against him and she could feel his chest rumble against her back when he spoke. 'You are beautiful, Flora. And I'm ashamed to admit that I was so blinded by your uncle that I didn't notice it properly until you arrived in my office the day of the wedding.'

Flora's gaze met his. Her heart flipped. She felt shy now. 'I noticed you…as soon as I saw you.'

'When you were hiding in the shadows.'

That impacted Flora in a very deep place where she harboured her worst fears and insecurities. 'You were very intimidating.'

'If I had not been so consumed with revenge, I would have noticed you more and maybe things would have been… different.'

Flora gave a little snort. 'You still wouldn't have married me.'

'No, of course not. I'm never getting married. But maybe… we would have realised this mutual desire a lot earlier.'

Flora shook her head and stepped out from under his hands, facing him. 'No, you hated him too much to be associated with anyone close to him.'

Vito looked at her broodingly. 'Perhaps.'

'Anyway,' Flora said, 'I'm glad things worked out the way they did. All ties were finally cut with my uncle and I found my freedom and independence, and I'm never giving it up for anyone again.'

But you'd consider it for this man.

That revelation gave her a jolt. On no planet was it likely that she and this man would be anything more than a fleeting interlude. For whatever reason he fancied her right now, but she was sure it wouldn't last long and he wouldn't keep indulging her like this. His guilt would be assuaged and he'd be moving on to the next woman.

And that was okay. Flora wasn't even sure where she really saw herself, or what she wanted long-term. Her uncle had kept her so confined that she was just enjoying her independence and feeling young and free.

And enjoying Vito, a little devil prompted.

Vito looked at her and saw the heat coming into her face before she could stop it. He said approvingly, 'That's good, you've got a little colour again.'

Terrified he'd see just how much that was down to him, Flora said, 'We should probably go?'

Thankfully Vito didn't argue or say anything else. He led her out of the room and Flora made sure to install Benji in the kitchen area with his bed and treats, before they went down to the ground level where his driver was waiting.

In the car, as it moved through the traffic, Flora thought of the way Vito had so summarily declared he wasn't going to have a family. She turned to him. 'If you really have no intention of marrying or having a family, then what's all this for, if not to leave a legacy to pass down?' She put out a hand to encompass the city beyond the car.

Vito shook his head, supremely unconcerned. 'I don't need a family to leave a legacy. I lost the only family I ever had and I have no intention of living my life in fear that it'll disappear again. My father's name will endure, I've made sure of that.'

Flora's heart squeezed. She could understand that sentiment, after losing her own family. But she got distracted from pursuing that line of conversation when she saw where they were going. One of Rome's most iconic buildings that housed a venerated museum. It was hosting an event that evening to celebrate a new exhibition with all proceeds from the VIP guest tickets going to charities.

She saw the glittering crowd entering the building, and the sense of panic and overwhelm came back with a vengeance. She couldn't see one woman with her hair down. They were all wearing complicated up-dos and their hair was sleek and shiny.

Flora gripped Vito's hand. 'My hair, Vito, it's too untidy. We should have put it up.'

He looked at her and his mouth quirked. 'Nonsense, you'll be a sensation.'

Flora felt queasy. She didn't want to be a sensation, she wanted to just slip into the crowd and not be noticed and then leave again. But now the car was stopping and Vito was getting out, straightening his jacket and coming around to open her door and putting out a hand. Too late to turn back. She'd set this chain of events in motion when she'd tried to sneak out of his apartment last night looking to find someone to relieve her of her innocence.

And she hadn't failed. Her skin got hot at the memory

of what had happened. She'd had a driving force to be with this man in spite of any obstacles like her virginity, and so now she had to fulfil her part in this arrangement.

Flora let Vito pull her out of the car. Her dress fell around her legs in soft folds. She took a deep breath.

'Ready?'

She nodded, mentally steeling herself for the experience.

What she was unprepared for were the photographers lined up along the red-carpeted steps, calling out, *'Vito! Over here! Who is your date, please?'*

They didn't recognise her. The same photographers who had been outside the church waiting for her to emerge after the humiliation of being stood up didn't recognise her. On that wedding day the priest had been kind enough to let her out of a back entrance where he'd had one of the church staff in a car waiting for her.

Her uncle and aunt had just cast her off. She'd had nowhere to go…and in that moment she'd been so angry and humiliated that she'd directed the driver to take her to the only place she could think of. Vito's office. She hadn't even known if he'd be there, but he had been. As if it were a normal working day. Adding insult to injury.

'Vito, who's your date?'

Vito squeezed Flora's hand before saying, 'Don't you recognise Flora Gavia?'

There was a moment of almost comically hushed silence and then it was pandemonium with shouting and flashing lights, but Vito managed to get them to the top of the steps and into the foyer of the museum before Flora could absorb the enormity of what had just happened. Vittorio Vitale declaring publicly that he was back with his jilted bride-to-be.

She looked around. Guests were being funnelled up a wide central marble staircase. She'd been to this museum when it was open during the day. Not at night, like this, when it had been transformed. A massive crystal chandelier was overhead, emitting a golden light. Flowers adorned every space, and all along either side of the staircase, sending out heady scents.

The medieval frescoes on the ceiling almost paled in comparison. Flora was so busy looking up that she collided into Vito's back when he stopped. He looked at her and she mumbled, 'Sorry.'

They were on the first level now and being directed into a massive ballroom, or, as Flora knew it, one of the museum's vast rooms, usually stuffed with artefacts from ancient Roman times. That had all been cleared out and now this room was full of Rome's high society being served by waiters wearing black and white. Much as Flora had been doing, not so long ago.

Vito took two glasses of champagne from a tray and handed her one. She took a sip, wrinkling her nose at the bubbles. Golden lighting imbued everyone and everything with a kind of celestial glow. French doors were open onto a wide terrace, which she knew overlooked beautiful landscaped gardens.

'You've been here before?' Vito asked her.

'Of course…with my tutor for schoolwork. Not like this. Although,' she amended then, 'when I was older, finished with schoolwork, I loved coming to the gardens. There's a cafe and you can sit for hours watching people come and go.'

'I'm surprised your uncle gave you the freedom to do that.' Vito's tone was dry.

'Well, he didn't. I did it when they were away on business or travelling.' Flora felt self-conscious now. 'You must think I was very weak to let him have such a hold over me.'

Flora sneaked a look at Vito but he was shaking his head.

'Not at all. I think it must have taken immense courage and fortitude to withstand that hostile environment and emerge with such a forgiving nature.'

Flora felt a glow inside her. But before she could respond to Vito's comment, they were being interrupted by what turned into a long line of people vying for Vito's attention, and all sending Flora more than curious glances.

She heard someone say nearby in a loud whisper, *'Is it really her? I don't think so...she wasn't that pretty.'*

Vito must have heard it too because he wrapped an arm around Flora's waist and turned to face the person behind the whisper. Two women, whose faces went pink. Vito said cordially to one of them, 'Ah, Contessa, I do believe you must know Flora Gavia?'

The woman smiled but it wasn't friendly. She didn't like being caught out. She put out a hand. 'Of course, Miss Gavia, how nice. I dined at your uncle's palazzo many times. How is he?'

Flora took her hand and shook it firmly and said with a bright smile, 'I have no idea. I'm sure that, wherever he is, he's up to no good.'

She heard a stifled snort next to her but didn't look at Vito. When he'd recovered himself he said, 'If you'll excuse us, Contessa?' and he smoothly guided Flora away and they went out onto the terrace.

When they were outside he let out a proper laugh and Flora smiled ruefully. He put his hand on the terrace wall. Fairy lights strung between trees in the garden made the space look like a magical wonderland.

He said, 'I don't think I'll have to worry about you handling yourself with the vultures.'

Flora shrugged. 'They never scared me. They're just snobs.'

Vito turned to face her, with his back to the wall. 'What does scare you?'

Flora knew exactly what scared her. But she was reluctant to divulge it to Vito. But then she thought, he now knew her more intimately than anyone else… She looked at him. 'I'm scared of being invisible.'

He didn't say anything for a long moment and then he glanced over her head behind them and said, 'I don't think that's something you'll have to worry about any more.'

She looked behind her to see most of the crowd gawking at them. She blushed. She wanted to bury her head in Vito's chest and that surprised her. Since when had he become a safe harbour?

'They're just bored and looking for a scandal.'

Vito reached for her and pulled her close. She fell into him with a muted swish of layers of fabric. He was tall and solid. *Hard.* Flora's blush got hotter.

He said, 'Then let's give them what they want, hm?'

And then he kissed her, blocking everything out, including the fact that she'd just revealed to him her worst fear, cultivated after growing up in a house with people who hadn't seen her. Who'd all but stepped over her.

It had been a long time since she'd felt noticed or seen and the fact that it was happening here with the sworn enemy of her family was too much to get her head around right now. So she pushed it aside and revelled in Vito's desire, because she was aware of another fear developing— the moment when he would look at her and not see her or want her any more.

Hours later, in Vito's bed, Vito was somewhere between waking and sleeping. Flora was a soft and delicious weight against him, one leg thrown over his thighs. He waited for a feeling of claustrophobia. It didn't come. Only the hunger.

They certainly had caused a stir earlier that evening. Flora had captivated the crowd in a way that had taken even him by surprise. Not because he'd underestimated her beauty but because he could see how her innate goodness shone out and took people unawares.

She'd defused the cynicism in the room without even opening her mouth. It had evoked something in him that he hadn't ever felt with a woman before. A need to protect. Against the women who would chew her up and spit her out so fast her head would be spinning and the men who wanted her.

So, actually, Vito had felt two things. Protective and possessive.

His mind cast around desperately for reasons why she evoked these things in him.

It was the guilt.

He felt a sense of relief. That was it. The guilt he carried for having sent her out to the streets. Even though she didn't hold him accountable. He'd almost prefer it if she did.

Earlier, on their way back to his apartment, in the car, she'd asked him, 'So what is it that scares you? Not much, I'd imagine.'

Vito had instinctively felt the need to close up, shut down the conversation, but then he'd recalled her fear of being invisible and how that had struck him deep. He'd felt something similar when his parents had died and he'd suddenly been on his own in the world, without a family. With nothing but his name and the clothes on his back. And revenge in his heart. Having to somehow resurrect himself from the pit of grief and loss.

He'd felt her looking at him with those big gold-flecked

eyes. So he'd admitted it, that his fear was of losing everything. Again.

She'd said, 'That's why you don't want a family?'

Vito had countered, 'That's why I choose to focus on my business because no matter what happens, even if I lost it all tomorrow... I won't be destroyed. Things and businesses can be rebuilt, people can't.'

He'd looked at her then, her face in shadow. He'd asked, 'Do you remember your family at all?'

She'd shaken her head. 'No, not that much. I was very young.'

Vito wasn't sure he entirely believed her but he wasn't about to delve into any more personal territory. He was only interested in the physical. Not the emotional or psychological. When they had arrived back at the apartment Vito had taken Benji from Flora and said, 'I'll take him out, you get ready for bed. *My* bed.'

When he'd arrived back and gone into his bedroom he'd seen the evening gown carefully draped over a chair and the jewellery neatly lined up on the dresser. Something about that had caught at him, which had annoyed him.

He hadn't been able to see Flora. But then the curtain by the French doors had moved and he'd gone over to see her standing with her arms on the wall, in a robe, bare feet. Not waiting for him seductively in the bed, like another lover. But here, enjoying the view. That little clutch at his chest again...

Flora moved now beside him in the bed, bringing him back from the ledge of his thoughts. She slid a hand across his chest, nails snagging on a nipple. Vito sucked in a breath. Even now, he felt the impulse to put some distance between them, to send her back to her own bed, to set boundaries... but now her mouth was on his skin and he felt the wet heat of her tongue and the impulse died a fiery death.

She knew where he stood, he'd told her in no uncertain terms there was no possibility of a long-term relationship with him, so why not let the boundaries blur and enjoy the moment?

He drew her up and over him, so her entire body lay over his, breasts against his chest. He could feel the scrape of her nipples. Her hair fell around them in a wild curtain of waves and curls. She looked sleepy but delicious.

He said, 'Open your legs.'

She did, her thighs going either side of his hips. With his hands and mouth and then his whole body, he brought them to the edge and back countless times, until their skin was slick and Flora was begging incoherently for release, and only then did he thrust so deep that they both fell together in a cataclysm of pleasure so intense that any sense of control Vito had wielded for those brief moments while staving off this pleasure felt like a very hollow victory.

CHAPTER EIGHT

'WOULD YOU LIKE to go to New York?'

Flora looked at Vito from the other side of the dining table where they were having breakfast. A spoon upon which was heaped granola, fruit and yoghurt was stopped halfway to her mouth.

'Seriously?'

He nodded and wiped his mouth with a napkin. 'I'm opening a new office there and I've been invited to some social events.'

Flora put the spoon back down. There was a fizzing excitement in her belly. 'I've always wanted to go to New York.'

'Well, then, you'll just need your passport. We'll be leaving tomorrow.'

The fizzing excitement leached away. Flora sagged back. 'I don't have a passport.'

Vito looked incredulous but then his expression darkened. 'Let me guess, your beloved uncle didn't deem it necessary because he didn't allow you to go anywhere.'

'Something like that. It's been on my list of things to do but I hadn't got around to it yet.' Flora felt pathetic. Who didn't have a passport? 'I won't be able to go.'

Vito shook his head. 'Yes, you will. You'll come with me right now to my office and we'll do whatever it takes to arrange a passport.'

'But that can't be done in a day.'

Vito arched a brow. 'There's not much I can't achieve in a day.'

Now Flora felt stupid. As if a bit of bureaucratic red tape would stand in Vittorio Vitale's way.

'Are you sure? I don't want to cause work for you and your employees.'

Vito held out a hand. 'Come here.'

Flora's heart palpitated at the look in his eyes. She still couldn't really believe that she was here, with this man, and that last night she'd been dressed like a princess from a fairy tale—a fairy tale that had turned into something much more X-rated when they'd arrived back at the apartment.

She got up from her chair and let Vito take her hand, pulling her onto his lap. He said, 'I know I asked you if you wanted to come to New York but it wasn't really a question. I need you there.'

Flora's heart fluttered, but before she could lose herself in a little daydream Vito was saying, 'After all, we have a plan to execute—show everyone that we're a couple.'

She went a little cold inside, even though Vito's arms were around her waist. 'Of course,' she said as lightly as she could. She extricated herself from his embrace and went back to the other side of the table again. 'How could I forget?'

She didn't look at him but she could feel his gaze on her as she studiously ate some of her breakfast.

'Flora…'

Reluctantly she looked up. He said, 'You need to understand that this is just a temporary thing…for as long as we want each other. That hasn't changed. The sex between us is…intense, but it's just sex. I won't want more and when the time comes we will be moving on with our lives. I will make sure you're set up. That's the least I can do for you after—'

Flora put up her hand. Vito stopped talking. She hid the dangerous pang near her heart because she *did* need to hear him spell this out. Because she knew deep down that his effect on her had already impacted her emotionally in a way that she feared was more comprehensive than she liked to admit.

She said, 'I've just gained my independence and freedom. I won't be giving that up for anyone for a long time. If ever. The man who will persuade me to one day consider entering into a relationship will have to be very special, someone I can trust. You don't have to worry, Vito. I know exactly the type of man you are, and I might have been sheltered all my life but I'm not so naive or self-destructive to think for a second that you'll ever want more than this affair.'

Vito didn't say anything for a long moment and then, 'You don't trust me.'

Flora's eyes widened, he sounded almost…*hurt*. Ridiculous. The man was impervious to anything she could ever inflict on him. 'I do trust you. I trusted you with my innocence, didn't I? But don't worry, I would have to be the biggest idiot on the planet to trust you with my heart.'

Vito stared broodingly across the plane to where Flora was curled up on a seat, asleep. Benji was a fluffy ball beside her. She'd looked so crestfallen when he'd said the dog couldn't come to New York that he'd suddenly found himself moving mountains to make it work, ensuring Benji had all the right documentation, vaccinations and health checks.

Flora was wearing new clothes supplied by the stylist,

soft black leather skinny trousers and a cream silk shirt. Her hair was loose. Feet bare.

But all Vito could think about was what she'd said the day before: *'I would have to be the biggest idiot on the planet to trust you with my heart.'*

Her words should have made him feel assured that the little telltale dreamy look he'd seen in her eyes didn't mean that she was confusing amazing sex with emotion.

But instead of feeling assured, or relieved, he'd felt… unsatisfied. Unsettled.

She'd spoken of meeting a man some day who she could trust enough to be in a relationship with. Ridiculously, Vito had felt insulted that she evidently didn't consider him trustworthy. And worse, he'd felt an almost violent sense of rejection at the image of her with another man.

He wasn't used to feeling possessive of a lover. To the point of almost…jealousy.

He shook his head at himself now. No, it wasn't jealousy, because as soon as this desire burnt out he would be ready to let her go, to find this man she could trust with her heart.

This relationship with Flora was different from anything he'd ever experienced before because of what had happened six months ago. They had a history. And Vito had been instrumental in Flora being put in a perilous situation for the last six months.

He was ensuring that she would not be in that position again—he owed her that much. The fact that they shared this crazy chemistry was something neither of them could have foreseen. It would burn out soon, it always did, and then they would both have got what they wanted from this brief interlude and they could get on with their lives.

The dog lifted its head at that moment and looked balefully at Vito, as if he'd heard his thoughts and was warning him to tread very carefully.

Vito rolled his eyes at himself. He was losing it. He opened up his laptop again and resolved to focus his attention on work but then Flora's husky-sounding voice said, 'Where are we? Was I asleep for long?'

Vito looked over. She was deliciously tousled and sleepy. She stretched, which made the silk shirt ride up, exposing her belly.

Desire surged and Vito mentally cursed her for messing with his head. He closed his laptop and said, 'We're about halfway, which is perfect timing.'

She looked at him. 'Timing for what?'

He stood up and held out a hand. 'To show you where the bedroom is.'

She frowned. 'But I just had a nap—' She stopped and blushed. 'Oh.'

'Oh,' Vito echoed, his blood pumping at the thought of introducing Flora to the decadent side of private air travel.

Flora put Benji down into his dog bed on the floor and slipped her hand into his. Vito pulled her up and led her down to the back of the plane, telling himself that the more he indulged this desire, the sooner it would burn out.

'Wow, just…wow.' Flora's eyes didn't feel big enough to take in the entire view spread out before her. Central Park, surrounded by the iconic sky-scraping tall, elegant buildings. One of which she was at the top of, on a terrace. The streets were far below, the sounds of the traffic barely piercing through to the atmosphere up here.

She tore her eyes off the view for a moment to look up at Vito, who was staring at her. She flushed. 'I must seem like such a hick to you.'

He shook his head and turned to look out at the view too. 'No, everyone should have this reaction when seeing one of the world's most famous views for the first time.'

'Did you?'

Vito's mouth quirked. 'I hate to say it but probably not. I was so consumed with restoring my father's good name and making sure I was on your uncle's tail that I'm sure I barely glanced at this view.'

Flora felt a pang near her heart at the thought of Vito being so driven in his quest to mete out justice that he hadn't even looked around him to see the beauty of the world he was conquering.

Her body still felt heavy and also sensitised after what had happened on the flight. They'd been asleep in the bed after making love and the attendant had had to wake them as they were due to land shortly. Flora had been so mortified at their decadence that she hadn't been able to look any of the staff in the eye.

Vito had looked at her with a smile around his mouth, and the thought of him being amused because he'd done this a hundred times before with other women had had Flora picking up a magazine to throw at him. He'd merely laughed then.

Benji was zipping around on the terrace full of beans after the flight. Flora welcomed the diversion from thinking too much about how Vito made her feel. 'Can I take him to the park for a walk?' She had a sudden vision of Vito accompanying them. Like some sort of real happy couple.

Vito said, 'Of course. You can do whatever you want, Flora. The city is yours.' He put out a hand.

Flora gulped. The thought of being able to move around in a city like this as if she had some sort of right to be there and take up space was daunting.

'I think I'll just take him to the park...' Feeling shy—

which was ridiculous when she could still feel his hands on her body—Flora said, 'Are you busy now? You could come with us…'

Vito shook his head, suddenly turning brisk. 'I have to go straight to the offices to meet with the managers.'

It was early afternoon in New York and Flora's stomach rumbled. She hadn't eaten much on the plane. Vito said, 'The chef here will prepare you some lunch.'

Embarrassed at her very normal bodily functions, Flora said, 'It's fine, I'll find a hot-dog stand or get a pizza slice.'

'You have your mobile phone?'

Flora patted her back jeans pocket. 'Yes, sir, all programmed in with all your numbers and your assistant's number.'

'Call me if you get lost or if anything happens. Straight away.'

Flora looked at Vito and rolled her eyes. 'I might not have been here before but I'm not completely clueless in a city. Rome is pretty big and cosmopolitan, you know.'

To her surprise he took her chin in his forefinger and thumb and planted a swift kiss on her mouth. It burned. He drew back, eyes dark, unfathomable. 'I'll see you later. We have a cocktail party to attend on the other side of the park. My house manager will unpack the bags and I've arranged for a glam team to come at five to help get you ready.'

Flora felt simultaneously hurt at the thought that she evidently needed so much help but also desperately relieved that she didn't have to try and tame her wayward hair or do her own make-up.

'Okay, see you later.'

And then he was gone, taking his force field of energy and charisma with him. Flora breathed out. The thought of a walk in the park and some respite from Vito wasn't altogether a bad thing.

* * *

'Stop fidgeting.'

Flora sighed at Vito's admonishment and dropped her hand from the hem of the dress.

She whispered at Vito in the back of the car, mindful of the driver in the front. 'It's too short.'

Vito put his hand over Flora's on her thigh and said, 'It's the perfect length. And you weren't worried about the length of your dress when you went to that club looking for your first lover.'

Flora's face burned. No, she'd been completely wanton. 'This is different,' she pointed out. 'We're not going to a nightclub.'

'And you're not looking for a lover any more.'

Heat filled Flora's body. No, she wasn't looking for a lover. She had *a lover*. The thought was still thrilling.

Vito curled his hand around Flora's bare thigh. He said, 'Want me to show you how perfect your dress is?' His hand moved up her thigh, pushing the hem of the dusky pink cocktail dress up even higher.

Flora put her hand on his. She whispered, 'We can't, the driver.' But an illicit electric charge was already making her ready for Vito's touch.

He issued a command that Flora barely heard and within seconds a privacy window had gone up between them and the driver. He turned to face her and pulled her closer. Flora was only aware of him and this space cocooning them from the outside world.

Vito's mouth covered hers and she allowed him full access, her whole body vibrating with desire as his tongue touched hers. His hand crept higher up her thigh and tacitly Flora opened her legs wider.

She could hear Vito's hum of approval in the back of

his throat and she felt a jolt of pure adrenalin when his fingers pushed aside the flimsy gusset of her underwear and stroked into her with expert precision.

Flora gasped into Vito's mouth as his fingers worked to bring her to a rapid and shuddering climax, her whole body trembling in the aftermath.

As much as it excited her that he could do this to her, it also scared her a little. It was as if once he touched her she wasn't remotely in control of her own autonomy. She opened her eyes and was mildly comforted to see the stark look of hunger on Vito's face. On an impulse she put her hand on him, where his body was hard under his trousers. She suddenly felt audacious. His eyes glittered. He said, 'If we weren't just minutes away from our destination I wouldn't stop you.'

Flora took her hand away and straightened herself as much as she could. She stored up the fact that there were things she could do to push this man off his axis as much as he did to her. Maybe on the way home…

'What are you thinking?'

Flora looked at Vito, affecting an innocence that this man had stripped her of with her full consent. 'Nothing at all.'

Flora heard him mutter something that sounded like *temptress* and resolved there and then to definitely turn the tables on him on the way home. But first she had to navigate an upmarket social event and she just prayed that the stylist who'd told her to wear this strapless thigh-skimming cocktail dress wasn't sending her out to make a fool of herself.

The cocktail party was taking place on the rooftop of one of the tall buildings almost directly opposite Vito's apartment on the other side of the park. The crowd here was different from in Rome, a little more relaxed. Flora was relieved to see that she was far from the only woman baring so much skin.

People here were curious about her but they didn't have the same intense interest as the people in Rome, understandably.

The entire terrace had been set up for the party and was being hosted by one of New York's grand dames.

'It's basically a very exclusive networking opportunity,' Vito had told Flora when she'd asked the purpose of the party.

There were delicious-looking canapés, but each time a waiter appeared Flora resisted the urge to taste one, knowing that she'd end up with caviar down her chest or some other catastrophe.

Vito was locked in conversation with a couple of other men and Flora was staring wistfully at another tray of canapés leaving her sight.

'I get it, too nervous to eat in case it goes everywhere?'

Flora turned to the woman behind the voice. A beautiful blonde woman with her hair swept up in an elegant chignon, exactly the kind of up-do Flora could never achieve.

She smiled ruefully. 'It's that obvious?'

The woman—who sounded English—chuckled and gestured to her own classic sheath of a sleeveless dress in a light cream colour. 'Let's just say I can empathise. Tell you what, I'm starving because I didn't have lunch, we only arrived in from London today, so why don't we go and eat together and then we can make sure we're still presentable?'

Flora grinned. She hadn't expected to meet someone so friendly in a place like this. 'Deal,' she said and let the woman lead her away from Vito to where caterers had a table set up groaning under a veritable feast of food.

'Who was the woman you were talking to during the party?'

Flora turned to Vito in the back of the car. 'I'm sorry,

was I meant to stay by your side? I was just hungry and so was she and I was too scared to eat any of the canapés in case I spilled something and so was she and so—'

Vito put a finger to Flora's lips. He shook his head. 'I don't expect you to stay by my side. You're a free agent.'

He could feel Flora's breath against his finger and he got hard. He pulled his hand back, cursing her effect on him. Cursing her for distracting him all evening—either when she'd been beside him, with her scent and presence and her body, poured into a dress that emphasised her tiny waist and shapely hips and generous breasts, or even worse when she hadn't been beside him. When she'd been talking to someone else.

'That's good,' she said. 'If I ever went to a social event with my uncle, say if my aunt was ill, or away, he'd expect me to stay right beside him and remember everyone we talked to. He'd quiz me on the way home.'

Vito's conscience pricked. 'Like I am now?'

Flora shook her head, making tendrils of her hair move around her face. Her hair hadn't been straightened, but it had been pulled back into a low bun. Acting on instinct, Vito said now, 'Turn around.'

She did, giving him her back. Of course he was immediately tempted to pull the zip of her dress down, but he resisted. He wasn't a teenager. *Maledizione.*

He pulled the pins out of her hair and it slowly loosened and fell down her back and around her shoulders.

'Oh, that feels so good,' she murmured.

Vito speared his fingers in her hair and massaged her skull. She groaned softly and that only made him harder. He gritted his jaw.

'So, the woman? I'm just curious because she looked familiar.'

'Her name is Carrie Black—'

Vito's hands stopped moving. Flora turned her head. 'Do you know her?'

'She's the wife of the man I'm hoping to do some business with, Lord Massimo Black. He's primarily a philanthropist but he does invest in choice businesses. What were you talking about?'

He could see Flora bite her lip. She turned to face him more fully now. 'Just chit-chat really. She was lovely.'

Flora suddenly looked nervous. 'Actually...she recognised me.'

'How?'

'They'd been in Rome when the wedding...didn't happen. The paparazzi didn't get any shots of me afterwards but the tabloids had some old pictures of me from something with my uncle. When she realised I was here with you she said she hoped I'd made you grovel for what you'd done.'

Vito couldn't exactly fault her sentiment. The guilt he felt at all but throwing Flora out onto the streets was still like a burr under his skin. 'What did you say?'

'Something about you having your reasons.' Flora's mouth quirked. 'She said she hoped you were going to bring me to Tiffany's or Cartier for a suitably expensive grovel gift.'

Flora's mouth stopped quirking and she said quickly, 'I told her of course I wasn't into anything like that. And how you'd let me bring my dog to New York. She gave me her number and told me to call her if I wanted to meet up. She has her children here but she said a walk in the park might be nice some day.'

Vito thought of how he'd had a conversation with Massimo Black and the man had expressed interest in meeting

Vito again to discuss things further. Meanwhile Flora had been exchanging numbers with his wife.

Normally when Vito brought a date to a social function, it was purely as an enhancement with the prospect of sating his libido. He'd certainly never experienced *this* kind of scenario: a woman actually helping him to foster other connections. It was disconcerting, because it made him realise that perhaps insisting on being a lone wolf was a weakness. And that having someone by his side in a more meaningful way could actually be an advantage, beyond just presenting a superficially more respectable image.

Flora said, 'I hope I didn't do or say anything to damage your relationship with Carrie's husband.'

Vito realised that she looked anxious. He shook his head. 'Not at all. And it's not your responsibility to be concerned for my image or business concerns.'

Now she looked embarrassed. 'Oh, of course, I know I have no influence.'

'Oh, you have influence, Flora, don't worry about that.' Vito reached for her and pulled her closer, leaving her in no doubt as to exactly how her influence affected him. 'You couldn't but be an asset to the people around you. You're a nice person, Flora Gavia, and that's a miracle considering who you had to grow up with.'

To Vito's surprise, Flora's eyes looked suspiciously bright. 'That's a really sweet thing to say.'

Vito felt a little winded for a moment. No one had ever accused him of being *sweet* before, certainly not a woman. He was acutely aware of Flora's relative naivety and innocence, not just physical, and once again he felt a sense of protectiveness that he couldn't stem, even though it unnerved him.

He assured himself again that, for all of that naivety

though, she knew what was happening here and she had no false illusions. In fact, out of all the women he'd been with, she was the least likely to believe in fairy tales. They both had their respective past traumas to thank for that.

She looked shy now and her cheeks were pink. 'Actually, there was something I wanted to do earlier but we didn't have time...'

Vito recalled her hand on him, shaping his body, and he issued a command to put up the privacy window, but also to drive around until he told the driver differently.

He said, 'We have all the time in the world now.'

He watched as Flora, with her tongue between her teeth, set about freeing him from his trousers. He had to call on every ounce of control he possessed not to spill right there, watching as she took him in her hand and moved it up and down as if fascinated by the way he looked in her hand.

He was about to tell her to stop, he wouldn't be able to hold on and he would make a fool of himself, but now she was lowering her head and her breath was feathering over his sensitised flesh, and he had to put his head back and grit his teeth so hard it hurt as she wrapped her mouth around him and his universe was reduced to that hot sucking heat.

When Vito had fallen over the edge of pleasure and control and Flora came back up again, a very feminine smile on her face, Vito cursed himself for ever thinking she was naive or innocent. She was no such thing. She was a temptress through and through and he was an idiot to think otherwise.

When Flora woke the following morning she found she was getting used to the sensation of her body feeling heavy with a sensual lassitude. The night came back in fragments, the car on the way to the party, the way Vito had made her come apart, and then afterwards how she'd made *him* come apart. It had been intensely satisfying to see his face flushed, eyes glittering, looking at her as if she'd just stunned him.

But then, when they'd returned to the apartment, he'd shown her in no uncertain terms who was the master here. Undoubtedly him, in spite of her little victories.

She heard a sound and cracked open one eye to wince at the bright daylight flooding into the bedroom.

She opened both eyes and felt a small furry weight launch onto the bed, landing beside her. She snuggled Benji close.

'He's been fed and walked already, by Matthew, the housekeeper. You can go back to sleep.'

Flora looked up to see Vito standing in the doorway in a three-piece suit, hair still damp from a shower, jaw clean-shaven. He looked so gorgeous it almost hurt.

Feeling a little exposed and defensive, she said, 'I'm not usually so tardy. I'm blaming you for keeping me up late.' And yet he managed to get up, no problem. She came up on one elbow, holding the sheet to her chest.

Vito leaned against the doorframe with folded arms. 'There's a credit card in your name on the table in the hall. Go shopping or make an appointment with a spa and treat yourself. My assistant can book you in. You deserve a break, Flora. It's nothing to feel guilty about.'

For someone who'd lived her life feeling indebted to the people around her and being as useful as she could be to mitigate that feeling, it was totally counter-intuitive to her to put herself first.

Flora said dryly, 'I don't think there's much left to wax or buff.' She looked at him, wondering if she was missing some vital piece of 'mistress' behaviour. 'Unless you would like me to do…something else?'

She thought of the fact that she wasn't shaved *down there*, and blushed. He hadn't seemed to mind, but maybe—

But Vito was shaking his head and coming back over to the bed, sitting on the edge and reaching for the sheet, twitching it away to look at her. Her blood instantly got hot. He said, 'You are perfect. You don't need to do a thing. And, as tempting as you are, I'll have to resist for now. I have a meeting in half an hour.'

He got up again and Flora pulled the sheet back up, lamenting his control. Pushing him out of that control was fast becoming her favourite thing.

'See you later?' She hoped she didn't sound as eager as she felt.

He grimaced slightly. 'I have a business dinner later. You don't have to wait up.'

So Flora had a whole day stretching ahead of her to see this fascinating city and get her head around what this was with Vito. Not a bad prospect.

'Later, then.'

'Later.'

He looked at her so intensely for a moment that Flora almost imagined that he couldn't help himself and would— but no, he was gone. She slumped back onto the bed. Benji crawled up and licked her face. She wrinkled her nose. 'Just us now, Ben, a whole day to explore and amuse ourselves.'

For the first time, because she was used to her own company, Flora felt a little hollow pang of loneliness. But before it could even register she pushed herself up and out of the bed, resolved to make the most of this amazing opportunity in one of the most iconic cities in the world.

After all, this affair with Vito was finite and she would have to get used to being on her own again, sooner rather than later, she had no doubt.

CHAPTER NINE

WHEN VITO RETURNED that evening he felt wrung out, but also couldn't deny the frisson of anticipation that had been growing ever since he'd made his excuses from the most boring dinner on the planet to come back to the apartment. And now that frisson was getting stronger.

He entered the apartment, pulling open his tie and the top button of his shirt. Clothes had never made him feel as restricted as they had since he'd been with Flora Gavia. A unique experience, as if he just wanted to be naked all the time. He smiled a little grimly at that notion.

He made his way through the softly lit apartment looking for her. He noticed things. Some dog toys on the ground. A pair of her trainers. A top on the back of a chair. More flowers than he would usually have in the apartment. He stopped and looked around. It looked...lived in. A novel concept for Vito when he was used to moving through spaces he inhabited without leaving much of a ripple.

Disconcertingly, it appealed to him. It made him feel somehow— He heard a sound and he looked to the doorway leading to the bedrooms and every coherent thought went out of his head.

Flora was standing there, lit with a golden glow, in a simple but devastatingly provocative silk negligée with thin straps. With one flick of his finger it would fall away from her body.

He was hard in an instant.

She looked a little dishevelled. She'd been sleeping. She said, 'I thought I heard something.'

Vito regretted not bringing her to dinner. She would have made it so much more interesting. But she would have distracted everyone. *Him.* He walked towards her. 'What if I'd been an intruder?'

'I'm sure Benji would have barked the block down and alerted me.'

The dog in question looked up sleepily from his bed and put his head back down. The most ineffectual guard dog ever.

Vito was just a foot away from Flora now. Her hair was spilling over her shoulders, wild and making his fingers itch. But then he remembered something and put his hand in his inside jacket pocket. He pulled out a long slim box and handed it to Flora. 'For you. Carrie Black was right. You do deserve a grovelling gift.'

Flora looked shocked. And reluctant. 'You don't have to give me anything.'

'Will you take it if I tell you I went in and chose it myself?'

Now she looked curious. She saw the name on the box and sucked in a breath at the iconic jewellers. 'Vito, this is too much.'

'You haven't even looked at it yet.'

She eventually took it and opened it and sucked in another breath. Vito had actually gone into the shop on a whim earlier, when they'd been stuck in traffic and he'd spotted it.

He'd noticed this necklace almost immediately and he'd known she would love it. It was a simple gold flower, with delicate petals and a lustrous pearl in the centre, on a gold chain.

For a second he regretted choosing something so...personal. Why hadn't he just chosen a diamond bracelet or something more bland? Too late now.

Flora stroked it with a finger. 'Vito, it's lovely.' She looked up at him. 'How did you know?'

Now he felt a little exposed. He shrugged. 'I saw it and thought of you, your name. Flora, flower.'

He took the box from her and took out the necklace, holding it up. 'May I?'

Flora nodded and turned around, lifting her hair up and off her neck. Vito reached around in front of her and placed the necklace around her neck, closing the clasp.

When it was closed he brought her hands down and her hair fell back down. She turned around. The necklace sat just below the hollow of her throat on her pale golden skin. She touched it. 'Thank you, you really didn't have to do that, but I love it.'

Without even asking her, Vito already knew that her uncle and aunt had most likely been very negligent in giving her anything or marking occasions like birthdays. They'd been too busy fleecing her of her inheritance.

Vito put the empty box down and took Flora's hand, leading her back towards the bedroom. He'd given up trying to put a boundary between them by using two bedrooms. Easier just to give into the inevitable.

In the bedroom, he stripped off with efficient speed and then he looked at Flora. The gold glinted against her skin. Vito found that, in spite of the sense of exposure, he liked seeing it there.

His gaze travelled down. The top of the slip rested just over her breasts. He could see the hard nubs of her nipples pressing against the fabric. He controlled himself though. It was important. To make him feel as though he weren't fraying at the edges and losing sight of what was important to him. Making an indelible success of the Vitale name so no one would ever question his father's integrity again. He couldn't think of that now. He'd worry about that later.

He looked down and could see the darker shadow of where the honey-golden curls covered her sex. He imagined her already hot there. Damp. *Ready.*

'Vito…' she said a little breathlessly. 'You're killing me here.'

He looked at her and moved closer. 'Good, because you're killing me too.'

He cupped one breast covered in that slippy silk and bent his head to target and suck the hard flesh of her nipple into his mouth. She gasped and speared her hands in his hair.

He caught her against him and she wrapped a hand around his straining flesh. Vito almost lost it there and then but somehow he managed to get them onto the bed, roll protection onto his length and finally sink into her slick tight embrace. It was fast and he couldn't control it. Vito felt Flora's body contract around his and he gave in, letting the pleasure take him where it wanted—to oblivion. Their bodies were so entwined that he couldn't have said where he ended and she began and, right then, he didn't care.

The following afternoon Vito was aware of the meeting continuing behind him. But he was brooding as he looked out of a window that commanded breathtaking views of downtown Manhattan. This *should* be a moment for him to really appreciate just how far he'd come and how successful he'd been in restoring the Vitale name.

But instead of feeling a sense of triumph he was distracted. Thinking of Flora's expression earlier at breakfast when he'd shot down her request to do something for him, to make herself useful.

She'd said, 'I had a nice time yesterday, it's not that I don't mind my own company, I'm used to it. But I just feel a bit…redundant. Maybe I could help? I'm good at office stuff, photocopying… I wouldn't mind getting teas and coffees. I'm not too proud.'

Vito had leaned over to her and pressed a swift kiss on her mouth before saying, 'You might not be, but I am. I'm not having my lover fetching tea and coffee for my staff.'

He'd stood up to leave. 'I'll be back in time for dinner this evening.'

Flora had perked up. 'I could cook.'

He'd reminded her that they had a chef to cook. She'd tried to hide it but Vito had been aware of her disappointment.

Didn't she get it? That it was enough for him that she be with him when he needed and in his bed when he wanted? That was all he asked of any woman he chose.

But she's not like the other women.

Ha! As if he needed that reminder. He'd bought her that necklace. He still felt exposed just thinking about it.

She'd said to him that morning before he'd left, 'I'm sure someone will have a use for me.'

Vito had been sorely tempted to remind her of exactly how useful she was, in his bed, but he'd resisted the urge. Partly because it had unnerved him, how strong it was to just…give into their mind-blowing desire.

He looked out over the city skyline. She was somewhere out there, in this vast city, on her own, doing…*something.* Making herself useful! And he was curious. Because he was sure that whatever she was doing would surprise him. Curious, and also a little envious if he was completely honest. For the first time since he could remember, work and his relentless ambition felt a little…hollow. The lure of being with Flora as she discovered the city was appealing. More than appealing.

He was so tempted to text her and check what she *was* doing that he deliberately didn't. Had he forgotten that she was a Gavia? And even though he was fairly certain now that she hadn't been involved in any of her uncle's nefarious activities, by allowing her to distract him like this, it was almost as if he were still allowing them to sabotage his business.

He turned away from the view and back to the meeting and said, 'Where were we?' and put all thoughts of Flora out of his head.

Three days later.

Vito was ready to admit defeat. He'd spent the last few days throwing himself into his work schedule in a bid to pretend that Flora wasn't taking up as much of his mental energy as she was.

But he was losing it. Not even slaking his lust with her in bed at night made up for the fact that, during the days, he'd more or less left her to her own devices and had then painted himself into such a corner with work that when they'd returned to the apartment last night after an event, he'd had to take an important work call.

When he'd finally managed to terminate it, blood humming with anticipation, he'd come to the bedroom to find Flora on the bed, in that silky negligée, but fast asleep. She'd looked like Sleeping Beauty, and as innocent.

Something had made him hold back from waking her. A sense of exposure that was becoming all too familiar. And the desperation that had clawed at him to have her. It was growing stronger. Not weaker.

But now he found that his need to know where she was and what she was doing was superseding everything else. Even work.

He rang his housekeeper and was informed that Flora was out. 'Doing what?' Vito asked as civilly as he could.

'Um… I believe she's walking dogs.'

'You mean *the* dog. Benji.'

'No,' his housekeeper responded, 'I mean *dogs*. She got talking to one of the neighbours the other day who was telling her she couldn't get out because she had a sprained ankle, so Flora offered to take her two dogs on her walk. By the time she came back from that walk, a couple more neighbours were asking her if she could walk their dogs too.'

Vito absorbed this. He terminated the call, feeling more distracted than ever. He turned to his manager. 'You have everything in hand for the rest of the day?'

'Of course, I'll call if anything comes up.'

Vito left, not even sure where he was going or what he was doing. He instructed his driver to take him back to his apartment. It was late afternoon anyway, so not entirely inconceivable that he'd be stopping for the day, but for him, a man whose single-minded focus had been on work since he was a teenager, it was a novel sensation.

The car pulled up outside the apartment building and Vito saw her. She was waiting to cross the road. His blood and pulse leapt. She looked…like a wild-haired nymph. She was wearing rolled-up jeans, a worn T-shirt—none of the sleek clothes the stylist had packed for her. Trainers.

And she was holding leads attached to at least six dogs. She crossed the road in front of the car and disappeared into the building. Vito got out and went up to the apartment.

When she returned with just Benji, presumably after dropping off the other dogs to their respective owners, Vito was waiting in the reception room. She saw him and stopped. She smiled. 'Hi. I didn't expect to see you back so early.'

Vito ignored the prick of his conscience at her obvious happiness to see him. 'Clearly. Were you going to tell me about your little entrepreneurial side hustle?'

Flora frowned. 'You mean the dogs? You saw me?'

Vito nodded. Her face flushed. He forced himself to focus and not think of making the rest of her body flush with desire.

Now Flora looked wary. 'What's wrong? Am I not allowed to help people?'

Of course she is.

'You're not charging them to walk their dogs?'

Now she looked disgusted. 'Of course not. They're your neighbours. And they're very nice. Mrs Weinberg sprained her ankle—'

Vito held up a hand. She stopped talking. He said, 'I'm sure they're lovely people. But you're not a dog-walker.'

Flora pushed some hair over her shoulder, agitated. 'I can be whatever I want to be.'

'I thought you wanted to be a graphic designer.'

Flora folded her arms across her chest. 'You don't want your...*lover* to be seen doing menial work. Is that it?'

Vito forced himself to sound unconcerned when the need to know everything she did suddenly seemed more compelling than anything else. 'I'm not a snob. I'm just curious. Indulge me.'

She threw her hands up. 'Because I was bored and I'm not used to sitting around doing nothing and I don't want to go shopping or to a spa. I want to be of use.'

Vito's hands itched to show her exactly how she could be of use.

She said, 'I did try to tell you, yesterday evening, but all those people wanted to talk to you at the event, and then you were on the phone when we got back and then… I fell asleep…and you didn't wake me.' Now she avoided his eye.

Vito didn't like the reminder of how he'd been overcome with duelling desires, to wake her and to walk away. She was fast becoming an obsession, if she wasn't already.

'I didn't want to disturb you,' he said now. A little voice mocked him. *Liar.*

Suddenly Flora looked shy and she said, 'I got something for you. Wait here.'

Vito watched her leave the room. Benji came over and sniffed around his feet but before he could cock his leg and mark his territory on Vito, he lifted him up and went to put him outside. The dog licked his face and Vito felt a little glow in his chest. He put him down on the terrace and pretended that the dog wasn't getting to him.

Vito went back inside and Flora was there, holding out a small black box. For some reason Vito had an almost superstitious reluctance to take it. No woman had ever bought him anything. Not since his mother had died.

But he couldn't ignore it. He took it and opened it to see silver cufflinks in the shape of eagles' heads, beautifully engraved.

Flora was saying, 'I saw them in the window of an antiques shop. They made me think of you, like an eagle, soaring above everything and biding your time until you could swoop down and take your vengeance for your father, and mother.'

It was uncanny but Vito had always had a fascination with birds of prey since he was a small child. He'd watched endless nature documentaries, much to his parents' bemusement because they lived in a city. But Vito had known that birds of prey stalked cities as much as out in the wild. He'd seen birds of prey high in the sky over Manhattan. The line between civilisation and nature was very thin.

The fact that Flora had picked these out made him feel acutely exposed, a sensation that was becoming far too familiar. He snapped the box shut. 'Thank you, but you really shouldn't have gone to the trouble.'

'It was no trouble.' Flora looked a little dejected but Vito was too full of conflicting emotions. Then she said quickly, 'I paid for them out of my own money,' and the emotions in Vito's chest and gut intensified.

He shook his head. 'You don't need to pay me back for anything, Flora.'

He was realising the full extent of just how far over and beyond the boundaries this situation had gone. Flora was like no other woman he'd ever been with. She was breaking all the rules and making up new ones. And through it all his blood was hotter for her than ever. The thought of this ending made him feel desperate. She wasn't out of his system yet. Surely it wasn't too late to restore some of those boundaries…

He handed back the box, even as bile rose from his gullet at what he was doing. 'You should return them and get your money back. I don't need anything.'

Flora's face became expressionless. Vito felt a cold finger trace down his spine. He had an urge to say, *No, wait, stop, I'm overreacting,* but Flora was already taking the box and putting it in her pocket. 'They were meant as a gift, not payment, but I should have realised that you'd be used to something a little more…sophisticated.'

She was turning away and Vito reached out and caught

her arm. She turned back but avoided his eye. He tipped up
her chin with his finger. Her eyes were guarded. He said,
'I don't mean to be ungrateful. It was a really thoughtful
thing to do. Thank you.'

That sense of desperation was back but now it was because he wanted her to stop looking like a stranger. Unreadable. He took his hand down and said, 'How would you
like to go to a show this evening? I don't have any engagements lined up.'

Flora shrugged minutely. 'Sure, that sounds nice.'

'Any show in particular?'

She smiled but Vito could see it was forced. The bile was
almost choking him now. Flora said, 'Surprise me.'

So Vito did what he would normally do in a situation
with a woman he was sleeping with—he went for the show
that was the most in demand and the hardest to get tickets
for. And even though that put him on ground that felt a little
firmer, he knew that Flora was the one woman he couldn't
impress so easily.

Flora was finding it hard to get swept away by the exuber-
ant show on the stage, just feet from where they were sitting in a VIP box. She was still incredibly hurt after Vito
handed back the present she'd got for him. She'd seen him
look at the cufflinks with an arrested expression. But then
his face had shuttered and he'd handed them back, and she'd
felt like the biggest fool.

He'd proven that you really couldn't buy anything for
the man who had everything. And he'd handed them back
because he had obviously wanted to send her a message—
don't cross the line. He'd managed to put her back in her
place *and* remind her that her finances were paltry.

She should have taken the hint from the fact that she'd

barely seen him for the last few days, clearly demonstrating his focus was on work and not on her.

And she shouldn't be hurt because if he had the ability to hurt her, it meant that he'd got a lot closer than she'd realised.

Who are you fooling? jeered a voice.

She knew it was already too late. He'd sneaked in under her skin and she was falling for him. And it was so humiliating because he'd stood her up at the altar in front of all of society, and the only reason he was still indulging her was because for some crazy reason he fancied her, but underneath that was the very obvious guilt he felt that he'd punished her along with her uncle. And she was still a Gavia. Vito would never commit to anything permanent with someone from his sworn enemy's family.

The minute he stopped fancying her, she'd be an unwelcome guest. There couldn't be less holding them together. Lust and guilt. And yet, as hurt as she was by his very obvious wish for her not to push the boundaries, he was the first person who had come into her life and seen her for herself, uniquely. Fatally, she knew she couldn't walk away. Not yet. His desire for her was calling to the deepest part of her where she'd locked herself away to avoid being hurt for so many years.

She was blooming to life under his gaze and even as she knew it was futile, all she could do was pray that he wasn't the only person who would ever make her feel like this. Desired. *Seen.* Because of one thing she was certain—Vittorio Vitale did not share the same depth of feelings.

That night when they returned to the apartment after the show, there was a silent intensity to their lovemaking, as if today had been a marker on the ground signifying that the end was nigh.

Flora shuddered against Vito as the powerful waves of her orgasm ripped through her body with Vito not far behind, his powerful body jerking in the throes of his own climax.

He lay over her, in her, for a long moment. Flora's legs and arms were wrapped around him and she knew she should move but she couldn't seem to. She knew that she was selfishly storing up these little moments so that she could take them out at a later date when this was all a distant memory.

Eventually, though, Vito pulled free of Flora's embrace but, to her surprise, he lifted her up and out of the bed with him, bringing her into the bathroom. He put her down gently and turned on the shower, the space filling with steam as the hot water ran.

He pulled her in with him and she protested weakly, 'My hair!'

Vito said, 'It's fine.'

Flora turned her face up to the spray, giving into Vito's ministrations as he washed her and her hair. His big hands running over every inch of her body, breasts, belly, hips, between her legs, until she was hot and slippery all over again.

When he was done, she lathered up her hands and explored his body, revelling in the freedom she had to trace her hands and fingers over hard muscles and powerful buttocks. And the muscle between his legs, standing stiff and proud. She wrapped a hand around him as his mouth found hers, and he put a hand between her legs, fingers seeking and finding where she ached, and together, with their breathing getting faster and faster, they came to climax again under the hot spray.

Afterwards, Vito's head was resting on the wall, over Flora's. He said with a half-chuckle, 'I didn't actually intend for anything but washing ourselves.' He moved back and tipped up her chin. Water was running in rivulets down his face and neck, onto his chest. Even though she was sated beyond anything imaginable, Flora already wanted to put her tongue there and follow them down his body.

'But,' he said, 'you're impossible not to touch, to want. What are you doing to me, woman?'

'I could say the same of you.' Flora felt prickly and vulnerable and still a little hurt after what had happened earlier.

Vito looked at her for a long moment but then broke the contact, turning off the water and moving out of the shower, taking a towel and wrapping it around Flora's body then taking another towel and rubbing her hair, before wrapping it up turban style.

Then Vito roughly dried himself, and, naked, led her back to the bed. She stopped in her tracks. 'I should probably go to my own room. My hair is damp.'

Vito looked at her. Flora's heart thumped. Since she'd been with him she'd shared his bed, his room. But now, maybe it was time to start putting some distance between them.

Vito's hand tightened on hers. She had a sense that he was going to agree with her, but then he said, 'You're not going anywhere, unless you want to.'

Putting it up to her. Flora knew she should break the contact, put some space between them, but fatally she heard herself saying, 'No, it's okay. I'll stay.'

They got back into the bed. A taut silence stretched between them. Flora was simultaneously deliciously tired but also energised. She also felt, after what had happened, and the way Vito had so brutally rejected her gift, a certain recklessness.

She turned on her side and put her head on her hand, studying him. But as she did, something inside her melted.

His eyes were closed and his lashes were long on his cheeks. Face softened but no less stunningly handsome in rest. A hint of stubble lined his jaw. His nose was aquiline, and she wanted to trace its noble shape.

She thought of a small, dark-haired version of Vito, with his impenetrable eyes and intense nature, and to her surprise a yearning rose up inside her and it terrified her, because she'd never gone so far as to imagine having a family of her own. And what that would be like. The thought of it now felt akin to standing on the edge of a large canyon and taking a step out into thin air. Free-falling into space. With nothing to hold onto.

Vito made a small move and Flora tensed, imagining him waking and finding her like this—daydreaming of a future that could never be. But then he snored gently, indicating that he was already asleep, and Flora made a decision. She got out of the bed again, and silently made her way to the bedroom she'd never slept in. It was time to face up to the inevitable.

CHAPTER TEN

'YOU WEREN'T IN the bed this morning.'

Flora avoided Vito's eye at the breakfast table. 'No, I, ah, felt bad about my hair getting the sheets damp so I moved into the other bedroom.'

'Is this going to be a regular occurrence?'

Flora forced herself to look at him and her heart flipped over. He was clean-shaven. She said, 'I think it's probably a good idea.'

After a long moment Vito said, 'You're probably right.'

Then Flora said mischievously, 'Actually, it's because you snore.'

Vito raised a brow. 'That's funny because so do you but I'd never be so rude as to mention it.'

Flora's mouth dropped open. 'No, I do not.'

'How would you know?' Vito pointed out.

Flora closed her mouth. She picked up a small pastry and threw it at him. He caught it deftly. He grinned and the flip-flopping of her heart got worse. Then Vito took another gulp of coffee, wiped his mouth and stood up, saying, 'By the way, we're leaving for London this afternoon. I have to stop off en route back to Rome. Is that okay?'

Flora looked at Vito. She felt as if she were on a roller coaster, living at the speed of Vito. She nodded her head to indicate she didn't mind, even as the thought of London filled her with a sense of disquiet. She hadn't been back there since the accident that had killed her parents and brother, after they'd left her at a friend's house for a sleepover. She pushed it down deep where all the other painful memories were stored.

'How long will we be there?'

'Just a couple of days. There's an event to attend, and I'd like to meet with Massimo Black.'

Flora was slightly cheered at the prospect of seeing Carrie Black again. Then she thought of something. 'Oh, I promised Mrs Weinberg I'd take the dogs out again this morning and do a little shopping for her.'

Vito looked amused. 'You do realise that anyone living in this building can afford to have their dogs walked and their shopping bought whenever they want?'

Flora just smiled sweetly. 'Maybe they do, but maybe they're also just lonely and want a bit of human contact. Is that so bad?'

Vito shook his head and came around to her chair and bent down, putting his hands on the arms, caging her in. Flora's pulse leapt.

Vito said, 'You're too good to be true…or are you?'

'What's that supposed to mean?'

Vito shook his head and stood up again. The implication that she was somehow faking being nice cut Flora deeper than it should. Damn him.

She said, 'Don't you get tired of being so cynical all the time? Maybe things…and people are just as they seem.'

Vito's expression hardened. 'Maybe, in some small corner of the world, but not in my world.'

Now Flora felt sad. 'Then your world must be a very lonely place.'

A glint came into Vito's eye. 'Not so lonely…for now.'

And on that, he turned and left the room. Those two words rang in Flora's head for the rest of the morning: *For now... for now.* As if Vito hadn't already made it clear as a bell that this was very finite, the message had just been well and truly drummed home.

London sweltered in the humid heat and under moody grey skies. A storm was imminent. To Flora, the weather felt as if it were an outward manifestation of the storm brewing inside her. The storm that told her all of this—between her and Vito—would explode sooner or later and she'd be left in the debris, shattered and hoping that she could pick herself up and start again.

Feeling maudlin, and not liking it because she strove hard to maintain a sunny attitude, Flora looked around the suite at the top of one of London's most iconic and exclusive hotels. She *should* feel as if she was fitting in. After all, she'd chosen her travelling clothes with care—cream pencil trousers and a matching silk blouse—pulled her hair back into a tidy braid because Vito had warned her about the British paparazzi because apparently they kept an eye on private planes arriving at the airport, hoping to catch celebrities.

Flora had almost forgotten about all of that thanks to the relative anonymity in America.

The suite was luxurious. Sumptuous. Thick plush carpets. Muted grey-and gold-trimmed decor that allowed the art and antiques to shine. Exquisite furniture.

But somehow all of this opulence only made her feel unkempt and volatile. As if this world were mocking her, saying, *You never really belonged, not even with your uncle...*

Just then, Benji came into the room, and started sniffing around the leg of a chair that looked as if it had been in

Louis XVI's court and, before he could cock his leg, Flora scooped him up and brought him out to the terrace.

When she'd put the dog down, Flora realised what it was that was bugging her, apart from being back in London after all these years, and the fact that she was falling for a man who saw her only as a lover and a vehicle to restore his reputation.

While Vito did make her feel seen in a way that was dangerously seductive, she also felt a bit like a piece of flotsam and jetsam being carried along in his current and at any moment, much like the way he'd announced they were coming to London, he might simply announce—

At that moment, as if conjured out of her tumultuous emotions, Vito appeared in the doorway. He was wearing a shirt and trousers. Casual. He looked up at the sky. 'It's starting to rain. You should come in.'

But Flora stayed rooted to the ground, emotions bubbling up before she could stop them. 'I don't have to do anything.'

Vito looked at her. 'There's a downpour starting.'

'So? It's only rain.'

Vito's gaze narrowed on her. He stepped out onto the terrace. 'Flora…what's going on?'

She struggled to articulate what she was feeling and finally she blurted out, 'I'm not just some sort of doll that you can pick up and put down and move around.'

Rain was falling now and it was heavy. Vito was shaking his head, hair beginning to flatten against his skull. He said, 'That's the last thing I think of you.'

They were getting drenched already, in just seconds, but Vito didn't seem inclined to move. Flora had to raise her voice over the rain. 'You just…need to give me notice, okay?'

'Notice of what?'

She bit her lip. 'Notice of when you don't want me any more. When it's over. You can't just announce it one morning, that you're done with me. Over breakfast.'

'Maybe you'll be done with me before I'm done with you,' Vito said. Flora absorbed that notion, as unlikely as she knew it was.

She said, 'Maybe I will, maybe you'll wake up one morning and I'll be gone.' Moving on with her life, going after her dreams and goals, even if they were still a little hazy. Flora had a sense of appreciation in that moment of how she'd survived in those first days after the wedding debacle. She could do it again, and she would. Perversely, the man who she knew would inevitably cause her untold emotional pain was also the person helping to remind her of her own agency and strength. A contradiction she didn't want to untangle right now.

Vito moved closer then, putting his hands on her waist, hauling her into him. She could feel every hard sinew of his powerful form. Their clothes were plastered to their bodies by now. The sky flashed with lightning and thunder rolled.

Vito said, 'No way, you're mine.'

Flora reached her arms up and wound them around his neck, arching herself against him. 'For now,' she said, echoing his words back to him but, even as she was reminded of her own strength, she hated to admit that she didn't feel as if she'd won any kind of victory.

She pressed her mouth to his and his hands speared in her hair, holding her in place so he could plunder her and stamp his very essence onto her. He lifted her then and brought her out of the rain and through the suite to the bedroom, and their sodden clothes were peeled off. He stood before her, every muscle sleek and taut, and she lay back on the bed. 'Make love to me, Vito.'

He came over her on two hands, and she opened her legs to him. He said as he joined their bodies in one single cataclysmic thrust, 'You're mine, Flora. *Mine.*'

She was his, for now, and he was hers, and she revelled in his possession, knowing that it wouldn't last.

The following day, Vito was distracted in his meeting. He'd given up trying to fool himself that he could avoid thinking about Flora. He texted her to see where she was—she'd mentioned going for a walk with Benji that morning. They had a function to attend that evening and he'd arranged for a glam team to meet Flora at the hotel. Even though he usually preferred how she looked before they teased her hair into some sort of up-do and put make-up over her freckles.

The after-effects of making love to Flora after that rainstorm lingered in his blood and body. He hadn't been able to get her words out of his head or the intensity of the way she'd said them.

'I'm not just some sort of doll...' and *'Maybe you'll wake up one morning and I'll be gone.'*

When Vito had woken that morning, to find Flora curled against his back, one arm draped over his waist, a hand splayed on his belly, he'd put his hand over hers and he hated to admit it, but he'd felt a sense of relief and he'd thought to himself, *Not today.*

But he wasn't fooling himself. It might not be today but it would be one day. Either he would end it because he would look at her and not want her, or maybe she *would* be the one to leave. And shouldn't Vito welcome that? After all, it wasn't as if he wanted anything more with this woman.

'Vito?'

Vito looked around. He hadn't even realised that his thoughts had propelled him up out of his seat and to a window. His phone pinged and he looked at it. A message from Flora with a location pin to a residential street in Mayfair. He frowned. What was she doing at a house in Mayfair?

He turned to the people around the board table. 'Can we wrap this up? I have somewhere I need to be.'

The fact that Vito was speeding through a meeting that would normally have absorbed one hundred per cent of his attention barely impinged now. He needed to go to Flora.

Flora was standing in the back garden when she felt the little hairs rise up on her arms. *Vito.* He'd come. She hadn't expressly asked him to but on some level she'd wanted him to come.

He came and stood beside her and asked, 'Are you interested in buying this house?'

Flora shook her head. 'No, of course not. They were having an open viewing. I had no idea it was up for sale.'

'So...why are you here?'

Flora swallowed. 'It was my home, with my parents and brother. I grew up here for eight years. After they died...my uncle sold it and the proceeds went into my inheritance.' She made a face. 'Well, what *would* have been my inheritance.'

Vito came and stood in front of her, obstructing her view of the large verdant garden. Benji ambled around nearby, sniffing the border hedging.

Flora forced herself to look at Vito, but her chest was tight and she was afraid of the emotion swelling up inside her. It had affected her more than she'd thought, when she'd first seen the number on the house and realised that the one for sale was her family home. She'd gravitated there without even knowing what she was doing.

Vito said quite seriously, 'Do you want it, Flora? I can buy it for you.'

A half-strangled laugh came out and she put her hand to her mouth before lowering it. She shook her head. 'No, I don't want the house. To be honest, I don't even remember all that much. A lot of my life here... I think I blanked it out afterwards. It was too painful to remember. We were so happy here. Me, and my parents and my little brother. But sometimes I think it can't possibly have been that perfect.'

She saw something beyond Vito and she grabbed his hand. 'I need to check something.'

She brought him down the garden to a tree at the end. Old and gnarly. She let his hand go and crouched down and pushed some leaves aside. When she saw what she was looking for on the trunk she felt a moment of pure happiness. She said, 'Look, it's still here.'

Vito bent down beside her. 'What am I looking at?'

Flora traced her finger over the etched words and spoke them out loud. '*"Flora and Charlie and Truffles."* I carved this not long before the accident.'

'Who was Truffles?' he asked.

'Our dog, a big shaggy golden retriever. I had to leave him in London. My uncle wouldn't let me take him to Rome.'

Vito stood up from his crouched position. Flora sensed his bristling energy. When she stood up his face was thunderous. She said, 'What's wrong?'

His eyes were obsidian. Flora shivered a little. It reminded her of how he'd looked in his office when she'd confronted him after the wedding debacle. He said, 'What your uncle did to you—it makes me want to go after him all over again and pound him to dust, make sure that he will never—'

Flora put her hand on Vito's arm. 'He doesn't deserve your anger or any more of your energy.'

Vito shook his head. 'Why are you *not* angry?'

'Because I didn't have that luxury for a long time. I depended on him solely. And it wasn't his fault that my parents and brother died, that was a freak accident on a rainy night after they'd left me at a friend's house. If anything, it was more my fault than his.' Flora admitted the thing she'd tortured herself with for years—if she hadn't wanted to go to her friend's house that night then maybe…

Vito was shaking his head. 'Not your fault. And it certainly wasn't your fault that your uncle then stole your inheritance.'

Flora shrugged. 'Money hasn't ever been that important to me.'

'Maybe because you felt you didn't deserve it? For living when they didn't?'

Vito's words stabbed Flora right in the heart. How could this man, who so coldly and cruelly handed her a public humiliation of the worst kind—standing her up on their wedding day—also be able to intuit one of her deepest and most shameful fears?

'Maybe,' she had to concede sadly. 'Why should I have benefited from an inheritance that my brother would never see because he was dead?'

'Why shouldn't you? I didn't know them but I'm fairly certain they wouldn't have wanted you deprived of it.'

Flora wanted to get Vito's suddenly far too perceptive focus off her. She walked away from the tree, leaving it behind. She asked, 'If your parents hadn't died…would you be different, do you think? Would you have achieved so much?'

'Who knows? Circumstances shape us into what we are, what we want. Maybe if my father hadn't been ruined I wouldn't have had the same hunger to succeed.'

Flora wrinkled her nose. 'You're ambitious… I think you would have still ended up where you are.'

'Maybe you're right, but I think I would have come up against your uncle sooner or later. He couldn't handle any competition. He would have come after me.'

She sneaked a look at Vito. He still looked ridiculously sexy even against this very domestic backdrop. Curious, she asked, 'Are you happy now that you've got your revenge?'

He stopped walking, as if her question had surprised him. 'I can't say it feels all that different apart from the fact that I'm not so consumed with one thing. If anything…it's been a bit of an anticlimax.'

'That's probably delayed grief. I can't imagine you took much time after your parents' deaths to grieve?'

He started walking again. 'Did you?'

'I was eight. I didn't know which way the world was up. I know that I didn't cry. Not for a long time.'

'But you did cry?'

Flora's chest squeezed. She nodded. 'Eventually, in quiet moments.' Wanting to move away from the painful subject of grief, Flora asked, 'Would you have had a family by now if you hadn't lost everything? If you hadn't been so intent on seeking justice?'

Vito shook his head. 'It never really interested me. I never felt it as a lack, as something that would fill a gap. My father, even before things got bad, was a workaholic. We spent a lot of time together primarily because he would take me to work with him. My mother hid it, but she was sad. I think they couldn't have more children and she never really got over it. So we were very tight. A unit. They loved me and I loved them. I didn't miss siblings so I've never particularly wanted children. I don't think I'd be a very good father.'

He'd more or less told her this already. She felt as if she

was pushing for something, not even sure what. For him to admit that maybe he wanted more out of life than being a lone wolf? And that he wanted her to be a part of that?

He turned to face her, blocking out the few other people who were still in the garden. He asked, 'What about you?'

It hit her then, like a ton of bricks, standing here in the back garden of her family home, surrounded by bittersweet memories. She said, almost to herself, 'Yes... I want a family. Some day. I'd like to try and recreate that happiness, in spite of the grief and fear of loss.'

'I'm sure you'll get it too, Flora. You'd deserve it. But I'm a selfish man, I want what I want and it's not that.'

Flora tried to ignore the way her insides clenched as if in rejection of his assertion. Her future wasn't bound with this man. She tipped up her chin. 'And what do you want?'

He reached for her. 'Haven't I been making myself very clear? I want you, Flora.'

She went into his arms willingly, and let his mouth transport her out of this place and the memories and, *worse*, hopeless dreams. Dreams Flora had never acknowledged before.

That evening the event was taking place in London's most exclusive art gallery. It was a huge art auction to raise funds for a collection of different charities. Flora turned to Vito when they were in the vast open space. She wanted to say something to him before he got swallowed up by a steady stream of worshippers.

She caught his hand and he looked down at her. Her face got hot and she momentarily forgot her train of thought. Her blood was still pulsing after what had happened not long ago. When Vito had come into the dressing room after the glam team had left, he'd taken one look at her in the slinky black silk evening gown, and the air had crackled with electricity.

What had happened in the space of the next half-hour had been fast and furious and Flora's nice, neat up-do had sadly come apart and now her hair was wild and untameable and flowing over her shoulders.

She wanted to scowl at him because, while she felt as if what they'd been doing was written in scarlet letters across her forehead, he looked pristine and serene.

He arched a brow. 'What?'

Flora forced herself to focus. He was too distracting. 'I just wanted to say thank you. I got an email from Maria at the women's aid centre earlier and she told me about their new premises thanks to your donation. They will have an acre of land, which will allow kids to bring their pets. You have no idea how much that means...' Flora had to stop, she was feeling emotional.

Vito squeezed her hand. 'After today, I can imagine exactly how special that is.'

Flora looked up at him. She felt as if she were drowning. The connection between them was so tangible, was it really just on her side? Could he not feel it too? Or was she just grasping at straws because underneath the taciturn vengeful billionaire he was actually a person who could be empathetic and that was all?

Before she could wonder too much about it, there was a tap on her back and she turned around to see Carrie Black. Flora was so full of excess emotion and relieved to see a familiar, kind face that she impulsively hugged the other woman. Her husband was greeting Vito. Flora pulled back, mortified. 'I'm sorry, this probably isn't the place for spontaneous bursts of tactility.'

Carrie Black laughed and hooked her arm into Flora's.

'Oh, believe me, I'm just as glad to see you. Let's leave the men to talk while we do some celebrity spotting. I'm sure I saw Harry Styles just now.'

Flora let herself be whisked away by Carrie, relieved to be moving out of Vito's orbit for a little while. She was far too raw after seeing her family home earlier and the explosive lovemaking.

Vito had lost sight of Flora and Carrie a while ago, and he knew his attention should be on Massimo Black, but it wasn't.

Massimo Black said wryly, 'I understand what it's like.'

Vito looked at him. 'What?'

'To be consumed.'

Vito felt exposed. 'By...?'

'A woman. I'd never experienced anything like it until I met Carrie.'

Vito was already shaking his head as if to deny that his relationship with Flora was anything like what this man had with his wife but Black didn't notice and was saying, 'You know, based on your reputation before, I wasn't inclined to invest in your company, but now that we've met and I've seen you with Flora, it's given me a new perspective. To be brutally honest, you can thank her that I'm willing to invest.'

Black held out his hand and Vito realised that this was it. The man was doing a deal, or committing to doing a deal, here and now. Vito took his hand, shook it firmly, feeling a little stunned. 'Thank you, I didn't expect that.'

Black said, 'I don't play games, Vitale. I've no time for it.'

Vito pulled his hand back. His conscience pricked. 'What if... I wasn't with Flora?'

Massimo Black said, 'Then I don't think we'd be having this conversation.'

'So if I wasn't with her, or in a relationship, then you wouldn't want to invest in my company?'

'It might seem old-fashioned but you're a much more solid bet for me if you have cares and responsibilities outside yourself. I don't think you're letting that woman go any time soon, are you?'

Vito thought of letting Flora go, of not having her near him, in his bed, and he felt dizzy. It receded quickly. He just wasn't done with her, that was all. So he could honestly respond by saying, 'No.'

At that moment Carrie appeared by her husband's side and Vito caught an inkling of what Black was saying when husband and wife looked at each other with such intimacy that he felt as if he was intruding.

He cleared his throat. 'Wasn't Flora with you?'

Carrie looked around. 'She was. She just— Ah, there she is.'

Flora approached from behind Vito and he took in her face. There was something about her expression that made him look twice. She was pale. Her smile was forced. He reached for her hand but she was holding her clutch bag. He frowned but had to respond to Massimo Black, who was saying to Vito, 'I'll have my assistant set up a meeting before you leave London?'

Vito smiled. 'Yes, that'd be good.'

Carrie smiled at them both. 'Goodnight, hope to see you again soon.'

The warmth between the women was genuine and Vito had a sense again of how it could be to have someone by his side who could enhance his life in ways he'd never considered before. As Massimo Black had said, if he weren't with Flora, Massimo wouldn't have considered working with him.

And wasn't this what he'd set out to achieve by having her by his side? He'd just never expected that she would be so effective. The other couple had walked away. Vito glanced at Flora and now she looked a little green. He took her arm. 'Are you okay?'

'I have a bit of a headache.'

'Do you want to go?'

She nodded. 'Maybe, if that's okay. You don't have to go. I can get a taxi.'

A sense of disquiet filling Vito now, he said, 'No, it's okay. Massimo Black was the person I wanted to speak to and I have. We can go.'

They walked outside and Vito's driver met them. The journey back to the hotel was in silence. Not like Flora not to be chattering. Vito didn't like it. When they got to the suite, Flora didn't meet his eye. She said, 'I think I'll go to bed in the guest room, so I don't disturb you.'

Vito was pulling off his bow tie. 'Flora, are you sure it's just a headache? Do you need a doctor?'

She shook her head quickly, her hair moving around her shoulders. 'No, it's not that bad, I'll take some painkillers and go to sleep. I'm sure I'll be fine in the morning.'

Vito told himself he was overreacting. He said, 'Okay, goodnight,' and watched Flora slip off her shoes before walking out of the room, Benji trotting loyally at her heels. He felt the urge to trot after her.

He realised that he and the dog weren't all that different. He scowled at the notion and turned away, going to the drinks cabinet to help himself to a shot of whiskey, ruminating on the potential deal with Massimo Black and the fact that having Flora in his life was central to that development.

CHAPTER ELEVEN

FLORA HATED TELLING white lies. She didn't have a headache. She had heartache, and there was no painkiller for that. She lay in bed for a long time staring up at the ceiling.

She'd overheard the exchange between Massimo Black and Vito, a fluke of hearing her name mentioned and being screened behind a plant. She'd practically heard the cogs turning in Vito's head as he'd all but assured Massimo Black that he was in a committed relationship with Flora.

But then, Flora could hardly blame Vito. At the start of this…unorthodox arrangement, he'd admitted that being seen to be in a relationship would be good for his profile, and also for hers, to restore some of the dignity he'd stripped her of when leaving her standing in that vestibule at the church.

And she knew how important Massimo Black was. If he invested in Vito, it would send him onto another level. The kind of level where his name and business would be immortalised.

Flora wouldn't deny him that. She loved him. She wanted him to succeed. But she also knew that she couldn't continue to harm herself by pretending things hadn't changed, for her. Because she'd fallen for him. She knew Vito wouldn't welcome that, no matter what kind of deal hung in the balance.

Or maybe she was being supremely naive, maybe the ruthlessness she'd seen on that day of the wedding would reappear and he'd have no problem continuing an affair while knowing she was in love with him.

But was she really contemplating telling him? Potentially having him end things, or, worse, being prepared to have him ask her to stay for the sake of his career? Either scenario made her feel nauseous.

Flora couldn't sleep. One thought dominated over everything. It was the more probable likelihood that Vito would end things if he knew how she felt. The thought that tomorrow could be the last day she would see him. Because if she told him, once he knew, that would be it. Galvanised by a cold dread settling her body, Flora got out of the bed and padded through the suite, lit only by moonlight.

She pushed open Vito's bedroom door. He was sprawled on the bed, bare-chested, sheets tangled around his waist, as if he'd been thrashing in his sleep. Something squeezed in Flora's chest.

She walked over to the bed and, as if he sensed her, Vito's eyes opened. He came up on one arm, hair sexily dishevelled. 'Flora? Is that you?' His voice was husky with sleep. Rough.

She stopped by the edge of the bed. She nodded. 'It's me. My headache is gone.'

Liar.

She ignored the voice. She needed Vito, even if it was just one more time.

He put out a hand and she took it, like a drowning woman reaching for help. He pulled her onto the bed and she landed on her back, looking up at him. His gaze roved over her face. She realised he looked pale. He said, 'I was dreaming, that you were gone and I was looking for you and I couldn't find you and—'

Flora put her hand up on his face, his jaw rough with stubble. 'Shh, I'm here. I'm not going anywhere.' As she said that she knew she was putting a nail in her own coffin, because she knew she wasn't going to tell Vito anything for the moment. She was too weak. She wanted him. And she wanted to cling onto this while he wanted her just for a little longer.

Two days later.

Rome glittered under the evening sun, everything bathed in gold. They were in the back of Vito's car being driven to his apartment from the airport. Flora's hand was in Vito's while he took a call on his phone. When he was finished he slid the sleek device into his pocket. He looked at her. 'I'm sorry about that.'

Flora lifted her shoulder in a little shrug. 'Don't be, you're working.' Then she asked, 'The meeting with Massimo Black went well?'

Vito and Black had had a long meeting in London the day before. Vito nodded. He smiled. It made Flora's heart ache—because she was happy for him and she knew she'd never get to see the long-term results of their partnership and friendship.

'We're signing contracts next week. He and Carrie want to take us out to dinner to celebrate. You'll come with me?'

Vito lifted Flora's hand and kissed the inside of her palm. Her heart rate doubled. Could she hold out for another week? To ensure that Vito's future was secured? When every day she was falling deeper and deeper in love? She forced a smile. 'Of course.'

Vito's gaze narrowed on her. 'Are you sure you're okay? You haven't seemed yourself since the other night.'

Damn him for noticing. Why did he have to demonstrate an ability to read her when her own family, who had taken her in to care for her, had barely noticed her at all? And she was the niece of this man's sworn enemy!

She smiled again, this time not forcing it. 'I'm fine… just a little tired.'

'I don't have any engagements this evening. We could… get a takeout?'

Flora sat up straight. 'I could cook!' Then she remembered that she'd suggested it before and Vito had nixed the idea. She prepared herself to have him scoff at her suggestion.

But he looked at her with an indulgent expression and his mouth quirked. 'That would really make you happy?'

Flora nodded. She'd always loved cooking, ever since one of her uncle's housekeepers had taken her under her wing when she'd been much younger.

Vito arched a brow. 'I'll expect more than pasta arrabiata.'

Flora narrowed her eyes on him. For the first time in days she was out of her head and not thinking about the future hurtling towards her. 'Challenge accepted.'

Vito watched Flora from the doorway of the kitchen, a place he didn't frequent all that much. He usually ate out, or had a chef cook. So it was a total novelty to see the woman he was currently sleeping with moving around the space with such dextrous ease.

She was wearing cut-off denim shorts. They must be her own. And a plain white shirt. Her hair was tied up into a messy knot on her head. Bare feet. No make-up. Shirt sleeves rolled up. The buttons on her shirt made his fingers itch to slip them free of their holes, exposing her voluptuous breasts to his hungry gaze.

He diverted his gaze up. She was doing something with rice and breadcrumbs. He asked, 'Where did you learn to cook?'

She glanced at him and back down. 'One of my uncle's housekeepers. A woman called Gianna. She was from Sicily. My uncle used to pay her extra to take care of me if they went away.'

'He didn't even hire a nanny?'

Flora shook her head. Vito felt the all-too-familiar burn of anger towards that man, but then he recalled Flora's hand on his arm in the garden of her old family home, her telling him not to waste his energy. It was slightly unsettling to realise that she seemed to have a way of diluting his anger.

Flora popped a cherry tomato into her mouth. Vito felt envious. Even Benji was lying on the ground just looking up at her.

'You really would be happier here than at a gala function in an evening gown, wouldn't you?'

She looked at him then and a sense of exposure prickled over his skin. She had been off the last few days but here, now, she seemed like herself again. It was mildly disturbing—for a man who had never been around a lover long enough to notice her moods—to realise that he'd become so attuned to Flora.

She looked a little sheepish. 'I used to hate it when my uncle asked me to host parties with him if my aunt was away. I never knew what to do or say. I felt awkward. But going to events with you…dressing up, that was more fun. I didn't feel that awkward.'

Vito shook his head. 'You're not awkward, Flora, far

from it.' She wasn't. She was genuine and warm and probably the nicest person Vito had ever met.

She pointed her knife at him and said, 'I hope you're not coming to dinner like that.'

He looked down at the sweatpants he'd put on to work out in the gym. And the faded T-shirt. He looked back up. 'What is the dress code?'

She cocked her head to one side and then said, 'I don't think we need to go full black tie but a suit will suffice. You don't have to wear a tie.'

Vito felt something flip over in his chest. This whole scene...was so seductive. When his parents had died, any such memories of domestic harmony and happiness had died too. He'd clamped down on ever wanting to experience it again. But here, now, he felt a very dangerous sense of... yearning. A sliver of a window was opening up the dark spaces inside him— He shut it down ruthlessly because that way led to loss and pain and grief. He didn't want this. He wasn't in the market for it.

He wondered if he needed to say something to Flora... Was she in danger of forgetting the basis of this relationship?

He opened his mouth but she said, 'Go on, shoo, dinner will be ready in an hour. I don't want to see you until then.'

Vito closed his mouth. Flora wasn't looking at him. She was engrossed in the task. He assured himself he was being ridiculous. Soon enough, she would be getting on with her life, going in a direction that would take her far away from Vito, because he knew their worlds were unlikely to collide again. He waited for a sense of relief that didn't come. Irritation prickled.

Maybe *he* was the one who needed reminding of what this was—a brief mutually beneficial interlude before they both got on with their lives.

* * *

Flora adjusted herself in the mirror. She'd showered and left her hair down. Minimal make-up. On a whim she'd picked out a daring bronze silk dress, figure-hugging and with a cut-out over one hip, the ruched silk leaving one shoulder totally bare. It fell to the knee and when Flora put it on she felt sexy and young.

She left her feet bare—what was the point of wearing shoes? But then, she recalled telling Vito he had to wear a suit and at the last moment she paired the dress with gold strappy sandals.

Her heart was skipping beats as she went back to the kitchen to prepare the meal for serving. Ridiculous that this should feel like a date even though they weren't going anywhere. And when Flora knew that even if Vito had lost interest in her, he probably wouldn't admit it until after he'd done the deal with Massimo Black.

But, if how he touched her and looked at her still were any indication, their chemistry was as potent as ever. She couldn't imagine ever wanting a man as much as—

'Well? Will I do?'

Flora looked up from where she was arranging arancini balls onto two plates. Her heart stopped beating. Vito stood in the doorway, practically taking up the entire space. He wore a white shirt and dark trousers that moulded so faithfully to his body that she could practically see his musculature.

His hair was still damp, swept back. Jaw clean-shaven. She caught a whiff of his scent—earth and leather and so sexy that she wanted to close her eyes and navigate her way to him by smell alone.

It was almost as if she'd never seen him before, his impact on her was so acute. Somehow she found her breath and got some oxygen to her brain. 'You'll do.'

He came into the kitchen and that dark gaze swept her up and down. Her skin tingled all over when she saw the appreciative flare in his eyes, turning them molten. *For her.*

He said, 'You look…edible.'

Now her legs wobbled at the thought of him actually— Quickly, before her thoughts could turn into an X-rated movie in her head, she thrust the plates at him. 'Take these through. I'll follow.'

'Yes, ma'am.'

Flora gathered herself and ran some cold water over the hectic pulse at her wrists before joining Vito in the dining room. He saluted her with his glass of white wine. 'To you, Flora. This looks amazing.' He gestured to the table she'd set. She'd picked flowers from the terrace and created a little posy in the centre of the table. She felt embarrassed now for going to such lengths. She blushed. 'It's nothing. Please eat while the arancini is still warm.'

The traditional Sicilian dish of risotto balls mixed with cheese and then covered in breadcrumbs and deep-fried was one of the first things Flora had learned how to cook.

Vito took a bite of one and closed his eyes. He said, 'The best arancini I've ever tasted.'

Flora beamed and blushed even more. 'You're just saying that, but thank you.'

'I'm not. I won't lie and say I have the most sophisticated palate on the planet, but I know good food when I taste it.'

Flora took a bite and when she could speak, she said, 'Your mother wasn't a good cook?'

Vito made a face. 'Not the best, no. And my father had no interest. We lived on a lot of processed food, which I know is sacrilege to most Italians.'

'Sounds like your mother had more interesting things to be doing. Did she work?'

'She did admin for my father a few days a week while I was in school. I think, when they didn't have more children, she resigned herself to her time not being dominated by a larger family, but I knew she was sad.'

'That must have been very tough, because it's only recently that women are opening up more about things like that, and men.'

Vito inclined his head. 'Exactly. Who knows what support she might have received today?'

Flora took a sip of wine. 'You said before that you didn't miss siblings?'

Vito shook his head and sat back, wine-glass stem between his fingers. 'Not really. I can't explain why... I had lots of friends on our street.' He gave a rueful smile. 'I probably liked being the sole focus of their attention, if I'm honest.'

Flora's heart flip-flopped. He constantly surprised her with moments of self-deprecation like this. Originally she'd thought he was a man of her uncle's ilk, ruthless and cold and obsessed with power, but he wasn't like that at all. He'd come by the way of power in his pursuit of revenge, yes, but he was obviously innately talented and intelligent. And, underneath it all, he was kind. He'd taken her in when she was sure he still hadn't trusted her. Maybe he still didn't fully trust her. That sobering thought burst a little of her rose-hued bubble.

She forced a bright smile. 'Ready for the main course?'

Vito nodded. 'That was delicious, thank you.'

Flora cleared the plates and came back moments later with the main, tender fillets of steak with a sauce made from olive oil, lemon, garlic and oregano. Fragrant and tasty. This was accompanied by roasted rosemary baby potatoes and crisp steamed vegetables.

Vito made appreciative sounds as he tasted the steak. He wiped his mouth. 'This is amazing. Did you ever think about being a chef?'

Flora was flattered. She'd only ever cooked for her uncle and aunt and they'd never made a fuss like this. 'I do like cooking, but I don't think I have enough of an interest to pursue it.'

'You still want to do graphic design?'

Flora nodded, swallowing her own mouthful. 'Yes, I was always doodling, even as a child. My mother's father was a pretty well-known artist so it's in the family. The English side, at least.'

'There were no relatives on that side who could have taken you in?' Vito asked.

Flora shook her head, pushing down the old grief and pain. She'd successfully blocked it out for years but it felt so much closer to the surface now, since she'd been with Vito. As if their intimacy was dismantling her defences.

'No, my mother was an only child and her parents died relatively young, too. So my uncle on my father's side was all I had.'

Vito wiped his mouth and said, 'I have something for you.'

Flora was about to ask, *What?* but he was gone, out of the room. He came back a minute later and handed Flora a business card. She read the name of a solicitor she'd never heard of—a specialist in inheritance law. She looked at Vito. 'Should I know this person?'

'You will,' he said enigmatically. 'I've retained him to liaise with you about receiving the inheritance you're due.'

Flora couldn't compute what Vito was saying. She frowned. 'But my inheritance is gone. Spent.'

Vito shook his head. 'I told you that I didn't wipe out your uncle completely. He still has a healthy stash of money. Not enough to start again but enough to live on. I contacted him and threatened him with legal proceedings if he didn't pay you your inheritance plus interest. It's at least—'

When Vito mentioned the amount, in the millions, Flora's head spun. 'I knew it was a lot but I had no idea...' She focused her gaze back on Vito. 'But how...?'

'It'll probably wipe out most of his disposable income, but he knows he can't afford the legal bills, and more importantly he knows that he's in the wrong. He would face the courts for embezzling his own family. The last thing he wants is to face extradition proceedings back to Italy. This solicitor just needs to meet with you to initiate the proceedings that will transfer the funds into your account.'

Flora thought of her uncle and aunt, and her conscience pricked, even now. Vito read her expression and said, 'Flora, I could very easily give you this money, but I know you wouldn't take it. It has to come from your uncle. He owes you this. He should never have taken what your parents left to you—do you think they would want what happened to you?'

Flora recalled that last image of her parents' loving smiles in the car as they'd left her at her friend's house. They'd adored her and she them. Of course they'd want her to be looked after.

The fact that Vito had done this for her... Emotion squeezed her chest and all the way up to her throat, making her eyes sting. No one had ever shown her an ounce of consideration since she was eight years old. Except for this man.

He reached for her hand, visibly concerned. 'I thought this would be a good thing?'

She nodded and tried furiously to blink back the tears and swallow the emotion. 'It is…it is…it's just that no one has ever advocated for me before and I should've been able to do it for myself, but I always felt so guilty when I imagined standing up to my uncle because he took me in—'

Vito reached for her and pulled her out of her chair and over onto his lap, thighs like steel under her bottom. Her blood heated even in the midst of this emotional storm.

He held her and said, 'That man took you in because he saw an opportunity. He didn't do it out of genuine love or concern. You owe him nothing. He owes *you*.'

Flora said quietly, 'I think when something has been drummed into you from when you're so young…it's hard to let it go.'

'He didn't see you, Flora. He never appreciated who you really were. You deserved so much more, and you have a lot to offer in whatever field you choose to go into.'

Flora looked at Vito, feeling emotional. That was one of the nicest things anyone had ever said to her.

He saw her.

The knowledge of that was so seismic and so overwhelming that she had to focus on his physicality to stop her mind from spiralling out of control.

This close she could see the deep fiery gold depths in his eyes. The long lashes. High cheekbones. A fierce swelling of love and emotion swept up inside her. Terrified she might say something before she could stop herself, she pressed her mouth against his, trying to transmit all the emotion she was feeling without revealing herself.

He accepted her kiss and opened to her, letting her explore him as he'd done her a thousand times by now. All at once familiar and wholly new. One of his hands moved to the bare skin of her hip and waist, revealed by the cut-out of the dress. He caressed her there, sending her pulse sky-rocketing. Flora welcomed this physical distraction from the emotion. He wouldn't thank her for that. She drew back after a long drugging moment to pull air into her lungs and brain. She looked down. She still felt dangerously emotional and seized on something to defuse it. 'Let's go dancing.'

Vito arched a brow and he moved minutely, leaving her in no doubt about how he was feeling right now.

Hard.

'I'd be quite happy to stay in.'

Flora was tempted but she was also afraid she'd reveal herself. She stood up from Vito's lap. She gestured to her dress. 'I think this deserves an outing, don't you?'

Vito scowled. 'I'm not sure if I want anyone else to see you in that dress.'

Excitement sizzled along Flora's veins. She loved his possessiveness. 'I've only ever been clubbing that one night…' She trailed off, remembering what had happened, when Vito had brought her back here and made love to her for the first time. It felt as if years had passed and it felt like yesterday.

Vito stood up and took her hand and said, 'Very well, then, let's go out, but I can't promise that I'll last long.'

Flora thrilled at that. Within minutes they were in the back of Vito's chauffeur-driven car and heading into the city. Flora took in people strolling along pavements, enjoying the balmy evening. Lovers hand in hand. Families with small children, eating gelato.

For the first time in her life, she felt really, truly free. And hopeful for the future, in spite of the inevitable heartbreak she faced. She'd weathered storms before. She would weather this.

Would you? Really?

For a second, a sense of utter desolation washed through her at the thought of never seeing Vito again, except in magazines or on TV. The kind of desolation she'd only felt once before, after losing her family.

'What is it? You look like you've seen a ghost. Have you changed your mind?'

Flora shook her head. She needed distraction now more than ever. She looked at Vito. 'I'm fine.' Impulsively she added, 'Thank you.'

'For what?'

'For looking out for my interests when you had no incentive to do so.'

He shook his head. 'I had every incentive, after what I did to you. You deserve it, Flora. You deserve to live the life you inherited.'

'Still… I'm your enemy's blood and you've forgiven me, that's a lot.'

'I'm your enemy's blood and you've forgiven me…'

Flora's words resounded in Vito's head as he led her by the hand to a roped-off VIP booth in the nightclub. They'd unsettled him. Made him doubt himself for a moment, and his instincts to trust Flora. Made him wonder if he was being a monumental fool to have believed she was as pure and kind as she seemed.

After all, her social reputation was now restored and she would receive her full inheritance, making her a very wealthy woman in her own right. Would she have achieved this without Vito? Not likely—he was the only one with the ability to turn the screws on her uncle.

Had she orchestrated this whole affair? Vito had to force himself to remember that it was him who had spotted her at that hotel. The hotel owned by him. What were the chances that she would be serving at an event there?

Irritated with himself for allowing seeds of doubt to take root, he ordered a bottle of champagne. He watched Flora looking around, taking in the club and the glamorous clientele. Strobing lights painted everything a rainbow hue of glittering colours. She was smiling, and in this light Vito could almost convince himself there was a satisfaction to it, as if she'd done what she'd set out to do.

He shook his head. Paranoia didn't suit him. It made him feel out of control. He reminded himself that, even if Flora had set out to regain her inheritance through Vito, it was no less than she was due. He wasn't wrong about her cutting ties with her uncle—there had been no contact between them and her uncle's reaction to having to hand over Flora's inheritance had been vitriolic to say the least.

The champagne arrived. Vito handed Flora a glass. She smiled and took a healthy gulp, wrinkling her nose. Then the beat of the music changed and Flora put down the glass and said over the heavy bass, 'Come on, let's dance.'

Vito would have protested that he didn't *dance*, he usually came here to choose a lover and leave. He'd never actually come to a place like this to enjoy the music. But Flora was leading him down onto the dance floor and turning to face him, lifting her arms in the air, swaying to the music. He noticed men around them look at her, and then at him, and then hurriedly away, once they saw his expression. He felt fierce. Possessive. In spite of the doubts he was suddenly entertaining.

He reached for Flora, telling himself that it really didn't matter if she was out to get all she could from this liaison because he would have done exactly the same.

The fact that she might not be all she seemed shouldn't

disappoint Vito because he'd stopped believing in myths and fairy tales a long time ago and that hadn't changed.

Flora still felt as if she were floating when they returned to Vito's apartment a couple of hours later. The champagne had gone straight to her head, in spite of the food, and she felt deliciously tipsy. She swayed slightly when she bent down to remove her sandals in the hall and stood up again giggling, one sandal still on. Vito looked at her and then she hiccuped, which made her giggle again. She whispered loudly, even though there was no one to hear them, 'I think I might have had a little too much champagne.'

Vito smiled, but there was something about it that registered with Flora as being *off*, but she was too tipsy to figure out what. She slipped off the other sandal and tossed it aside.

She threw her arms wide and declared, 'Take me to bed and make love to me, Vito.'

He came towards her and said, 'I think we might just get you tucked up for now, hm?'

He swung her up into his arms, and her head swirled for a second. She muttered, 'Spoilsport.' She spied the opening of his shirt and explored underneath with her fingers, caressing his skin.

'Flora…' Vito said warningly.

'Hush,' she said, suddenly feeling quite sober as another type of inebriation took over. Desire. She pulled his shirt aside, undoing a couple of the top buttons to give her access to more skin, and pressed her mouth there, drinking in his scent, tasting his skin with her tongue.

She felt his arms tighten around her. He was walking them into his bedroom now and he placed her down on the bed. Flora looked up at him. He stood for a long moment and said, 'You should sleep.'

But Flora felt no more like sleeping than she did not breathing. He turned and went towards the door. Flora stood from the bed and said, 'Wait, Vito…'

He stopped and turned around. Flora found the catch at the top of her shoulder and undid it, making the top of the dress fall to her waist, baring her breasts. It clung perilously to her hips. She made a minute move and the dress fell all the way off to the floor. 'Oops,' she said.

She could see Vito's body stiffen. Her blood rushed in response. He came back towards her, shedding his jacket as he did. He stood before her, tall and intense. She shivered at the look in his eyes, shivered with anticipation.

'Flora, are you trying to tempt me?' he asked.

'Is it working?'

A muscle in his jaw pulsed. 'Yes, damn you. Are you sure—?'

Flora closed the distance between them and lifted her hands to undo the rest of his shirt buttons. 'Yes, Vito, I'm sure. I'm a little tipsy, that's all. I know what I'm doing and what I want.' She looked up at him as she spread his shirt wide, revealing his chest. 'And what I want is you. *Now.*'

Vito was naked in seconds and tumbling back onto the bed with Flora. She revelled under his delicious weight, his hard planes and surfaces and the very hard evidence of his desire for her. She wrapped a hand around him, widening her legs, inviting him in… The head of his erection touched her sensitive skin, Flora's entire body waited on a bated breath and then Vito huffed a curse. 'You're a witch. I need to get protection.'

Flora hadn't even noticed. She'd wanted Vito that badly. Or had she known on some deep level and been prepared to take the risk? Flora's conscience pricked.

Before she could overthink it, Vito was back and sliding between her legs again, and with one smooth thrust he drove deep into her body, stealing her breath and sanity.

All of the emotions Flora had been feeling earlier and suppressing rose up inside her now. She was too raw to hold them back. As the storm broke over them, too strong to resist, Flora cried out with the pleasure and beauty of it. Her body spasming around Vito's for long seconds, loath to let him go. Legs wrapped around his hips. Arms around his neck. Breasts crushed to his chest.

It hadn't been like that before. She pressed her mouth to his shoulder, tasting the salty tang of his sweat, revelling in it. He went to move, to extricate himself, but Flora said, 'Wait, don't move.'

She had some instinct that she wanted to imprint this memory onto her brain for ever. How it felt to have Vito in her, over her. So entwined that she didn't know where he ended and she began.

And at that moment it bubbled up inside her, the need to tell him, to let him know, and as he said, 'Flora—' she blurted it out.

'I love you.'

CHAPTER TWELVE

FOR A LONG moment there was silence. Then Vito detached himself from Flora's embrace. She winced as sensitive muscles released their grip on his body. He got up from the bed in one fluid athletic movement and went to the bathroom, presumably to deal with the protection.

It gave Flora a second to pull a cover over herself and pray that she hadn't actually uttered those words out loud, that she'd just thought them in her head. But she could already feel the chill in the air, chasing across her skin. Trickling down her spine. There was no hint of inebriation left. She was stone-cold sober.

Vito reappeared, tying a towel around his waist. His face looked blank.

She'd said the words out loud.

Flora sat up, holding the sheet to her. 'Vito—' But he held up a hand, stopping her. She closed her mouth.

'What did you just say?'

Flora bit her lip. She could say *nothing* and try to blame it on the sparkling wine and the moment, but everything in her resisted against it. She couldn't hold it in.

'I said I love you.'

He shook his head. 'Why?'

Flora looked at him. 'You want me to tell you why I love you?' The thought of trying to articulate everything in her head and heart terrified her.

He looked frustrated. He ran a hand through already messed-up hair. 'No, I mean… I don't know. I mean, *how*?'

'I fell in love with you. I didn't plan on it, Vito… I didn't expect it.'

Now he sounded accusing. 'I told you from the start what this was. I never promised anything more than just…this.'

'I know,' Flora said miserably, any faint hope that he might have greeted her declaration differently turning to dust.

'What is this?' he said. 'Are you playing some sort of game? Now you've got your inheritance and you want to see if you can get more? A serious commitment?'

Flora went cold. She felt more exposed than she'd ever felt in her life. And she'd asked for this. She'd revelled in Vito actually *seeing* her, except he hadn't seen her at all. The pain was immense.

She said, 'Can you hand me a robe, please?' She couldn't conduct this conversation naked under a sheet with the touch of Vito's hands still warm on her skin.

He disappeared into the bathroom and returned with a robe, handing it to her. Flora pulled it on while trying not to expose her body. Ha! That horse and the entire herd had bolted a long time ago. She stood up from the bed, tightly belting the robe around her. The fact that Vito's gaze dropped over her body and back up, sending frissons of awareness all over her skin, was like a betrayal now.

She folded her arms over her chest. 'I guess I shouldn't be surprised that you're still as cynical as you always were. And who's to say that I'll even collect my inheritance? That's tainted money.'

'Flora, that's your money. You can't *not* take it.' And then he muttered, 'You'll probably hand it all over to a charity anyway.'

Flora pounced on that. 'One minute ago you're accusing me of being an opportunist and now you're saying I'll give it away. Which is it, Vito? Who am I really?'

He looked at her. 'That's just it. I don't know.'

Flora looked at him as her insides knotted. She'd believed that he'd seen her. The worst thing was that Vito had an air of defeat about him. Resignation.

You do know me, she wanted to shout at him. Grab him by the shoulders and shake him.

But evidently she was the fool here because he was literally telling her that, even now, after all this time spent together, he still didn't trust her.

And could she even blame him? She was a Gavia. And it was always going to come down to this.

Still, she seemed to have some instinct for self-flagellation because she heard herself saying, 'It means nothing to you that I love you?'

His expression had turned to granite. He shook his head. 'I'm sorry.'

Flora needed to escape then, to go somewhere to lick her wounds and take a moment to assess how she could still be breathing. She backed away. 'I should check Benji…we didn't…when we came in. I'll go back to my own room and tomorrow…'

'We can talk in the morning.'

Mere minutes ago, Flora and this man had been so entwined they'd been one person. Now it couldn't be more glaringly obvious that that had been just an illusion.

She turned, and somehow left the bedroom. Like an automaton, she went to check Benji, taking him out to the terrace for a few minutes and then back inside. She carried him to her bedroom and lay down on the bed, with him tucked against her body.

* * *

Vito stood for long moments at his window, as the faintest trails of dawn started to light the sky outside. He waited for a sense of relief to start spreading through him—the relief that always came when things ended with a lover. Whether it was after a night, or two nights, or a week. Because a week had always been his limit before. But not with Flora. It had been several weeks. How many? He wasn't even sure. For some reason his brain wouldn't function. It was stuck on a loop like a broken record, a loop of Flora's declaration: *'I love you.'*

She didn't love him. She couldn't.

She'd told him: *'Don't worry, I would have to be the biggest idiot on the planet to trust you with my heart.'*

The fact that he remembered those exact words wasn't something Vito cared to think about now.

The notion that she could have somehow come to trust him enough to give him her heart was unthinkable to Vito. The thought that perhaps she'd seen something in him—something worth loving—made no sense to him. His life had been consumed with revenge and mining his hurt and pain to succeed. He'd lost anything in him worth loving when his parents had died.

But in the first moment of hearing those words, when his body had still been so deeply embedded in hers, he'd not reacted with rejection—he'd felt a blooming sense of warmth, as if he were melting from the inside out.

Her saying she loved him had been a shock, that was all. She'd caught him off guard.

It was as if his brain had just taken a second to catch up, to realise what she'd said. And then he'd felt Flora's legs and arms around him, holding him, and he'd felt two very different impulses vying for supremacy—*Stay, sink deeper, never let her go* and *Go, leave now, run.*

So he'd run. He felt the tension thrumming through his body now. The urge to go. Put distance between them. Put distance between him and those words that even now felt as if they were living breathing things, whispering around him, making him remember what it had been like to bask in the unconditional love of his father and his mother. The feeling of security—that nothing would ever harm them, or their world.

But they had been harmed. And their world had exploded. And everything had been lost. So Vito would never trust that feeling again and he certainly wouldn't succumb to it.

The next morning Flora felt gritty-eyed. She'd showered and changed into her own clothes, faded jeans and a shirt. Hair pulled back into a loose plait to try and tame it.

She felt numb inside. She'd done this. She'd hastened the demise of her and Vito's relationship by revealing her feelings. But maybe it was for the best. She needed to get on with her life. Without Vito.

She went into the kitchen first and attended to Benji, giving him his food. She heard a sound and looked up but, heart thumping, discovered it was just Sofia, who told her that Vito was in the dining room having breakfast.

Then Flora blushed when she remembered the previous evening. 'I'm sorry, I made dinner and left everything—'

The woman smiled and shook her head. 'No problem, it's nice to see the kitchen get some use.' She winked at Flora, who smiled back weakly. The thought of seeing Vito was making her guts churn, but she steeled herself and went into the dining room.

He was taking a sip of coffee and reading something on

his tablet. He looked up and Flora instantly felt as wan and tired as he looked fresh and rested. Clearly not remotely heartbroken. But she was determined not to expose herself any more than she already had. Forcing a bright smile, she sat down. 'Good morning.'

'Morning. Coffee?' He held up the pot and Flora held out her cup, hoping her hand would stay steady. It did, as he poured her some of the fragrant drink. Small mercies. She took a fortifying sip.

Sofia came in with fresh fruit and pastries. Flora smiled at her. When she'd left Vito cleared his throat. Flora pretended putting together her granola, fruit and yoghurt was suddenly the most important thing she'd ever done in her life.

'Flora.'

Damn. She looked up. Vito had put down the tablet. He looked...

Oh, no, the worst.

She saw pity on his face.

He said, 'Look, last night—'

She put up a hand. 'I don't really want to discuss it. We said all that was needed. I'll move out today and we can move on.'

'You don't have to move out.'

The thought of living here in some kind of torturous limbo with Vito made Flora shudder. 'I do, but thank you.'

'No, you really don't. I'm going to New York today, within the hour, and then to London. I won't be back for about ten days.'

Flora had just stuffed a mouthful of granola and fruit and yoghurt into her mouth. It might as well have been cardboard for all she tasted of it. She managed to swallow without choking.

Vito said, 'I'm not just going to kick you out. You'll have time to get settled again.'

She knew from past experience not to be too proud. 'Thank you. I'll be sorted by the time you get back.'

'Will you contact the solicitor?'

Flora looked at him, the hurt at what he'd said last night still fresh. 'You mean, instead of trying to lure you into a more serious commitment?'

Vito's face flushed. 'I'm sorry. You didn't deserve that.'

The apology didn't mollify her all that much. 'But you're still not entirely sure, are you?'

'The only person I trust entirely is myself. I'm a loner, Flora. I never claimed to be anything different.'

Even now, Flora's treacherous heart squeezed. This man had so much to give. And maybe he would one day, but not to her.

'You are what you convince yourself you are, Vito. I'm surprised that you would limit yourself like that when you've had no problem breaking any other limits holding you back.'

Flora waited for his response—he was looking at her with such intensity—but then his phone rang and he glanced at the screen. She saw it too—the name *Massimo Black*— and her insides lurched. The dinner date. They were meant to be together.

Vito answered the phone and just said tersely, 'Can I call you back in a few minutes?'

Black must have answered in the affirmative because Vito terminated the call and put his phone back down on the table. Flora blurted out, 'I overheard you.'

Vito frowned at her. 'Overheard what?'

'Your conversation with Black in London. The night of the event in the art gallery. I heard him say to you that if we weren't together he probably wouldn't have agreed to do business with you. And I heard how you...didn't tell him that it was only a temporary affair.'

Vito's face flushed again. 'You think I misled him.'

'Not exactly...after all, we were together. I'm sure you saw no reason to assume we wouldn't still be together until such time as a deal was done. And you never hid that you were intending on using us being seen together as a way to restore your reputation.'

Vito stood up and went to stand at the window with his hands in his pockets. His back to her. She let her eyes rove over his tall powerful form, very aware that this could be the last time. She said, 'I don't think you set out to deceive him, Vito.'

He turned around. 'Still, I didn't make it clear that we weren't in a committed relationship.'

'If you want me to, I'll still come to London with you so he can see us together.'

But Vito shook his head. 'No, I wouldn't ask that of you. If Black won't do business with me for myself then it's better that the partnership ends now. It's not as if we would have been together for much longer, anyway.'

Flora absorbed that little dagger to her heart. Now she knew for sure that this would be the last time she saw Vito. She stood up. 'What I said last night, Vito—'

'You don't have to explain—'

'I know,' Flora said firmly, determined that he wouldn't stop her from saying this. She knew it was just going to add to the hurt, but she needed him to know. 'What I said last night I meant, Vito. I love you. I love the bones of you and the man you are, inside and out. You're a good man. You deserve more than to be a loner and maybe you'll find that some day with someone, because, for what it's worth,

I think you'd be an amazing father. I didn't say I love you wanting anything in return. It comes with no conditions or strings. It's just…love.' Flora stopped. She'd already said too much. Vito was staring at her.

There was a long moment of silence and then he said, 'You pay me a huge compliment, Flora. Especially after what I put you through. But I don't…' He shook his head. 'I can't say the same.'

Flora lifted her chin even though she wanted to crumple. 'You don't have to, Vito. You never led me on or promised anything. I just don't want you to think that I said that to extract something from you. I would never do that.'

She bit her lip and then said, 'I believed that you really saw me, in a way that no one has since my family died, but maybe it's good to know that that was just an illusion. Because I know I won't rest until I find someone who can really see me, all of me, and trust who I am. Goodbye, Vito.'

Flora left the room, quickly, before she lost her nerve. She went back to her room and stayed there until she was fairly certain he would have left, and then she emerged to an empty apartment, apart from Sofia and Benji, and set about getting through the rest of that day, and the next, and even though the future stretched out before her like a grey and lacklustre landscape she refused to let it bring her down. She would get through this. She'd been through worse, even if it didn't feel like it right then.

CHAPTER THIRTEEN

A week later, London

'YOU LOOK AS if you're thinking of doing serious harm to someone. Anyone I know?'

Vito looked around at Massimo Black, who was handing him a crystal tumbler holding dark golden liquid. Immediately it made him think of the way Flora's eyes darkened when their bodies joined, glowing dark golden. His fingers tightened on the glass. She'd been haunting him ever since he'd left Rome. Her words reverberating in his head like taunts.

'I love the bones of you...you'd be an amazing father... I won't rest until I find someone who can really see me... and trust who I am.'

Vito forced it all out of his mind. He'd been invited here to Black's office in London ahead of their dinner. They hadn't signed anything yet but his conscience rose up like bile in his throat.

He faced the man and said, 'There's something you need to know.'

Black raised a brow. 'Like the fact that you're no longer in a relationship?'

Vito couldn't have been more stunned if the man had just landed a blow to his gut. He felt winded. 'How do you know?' Had it got to the papers? He hadn't released a statement yet, telling himself he'd wanted to tell Black in person first, but also because another part of him had resisted it.

Black took a sip of his drink. 'Carrie got a phone call from Flora, who wanted to pass on a message to me.'

Black came to stand beside Vito at the window. Vito asked as politely as he could, 'What did she say?'

What he really wanted to ask was, *Was she all right? Where did she say she was?*

He knew she'd left the apartment in Rome because Sofia had told him she'd moved out, with no forwarding address. Was she homeless again? Was she—?

'She said that even though you were no longer in a relationship she hoped it wouldn't affect my judgement of your reputation, and that I'd be a fool to not go into business with you.'

Vito felt a rush of warmth around his chest at the thought of Flora advocating for him.

'I love the bones of you...'

He said, more tersely than he'd intended, 'And?'

Black gave him a look. 'I won't lie—if headlines in the paper feature your love affairs over your business affairs, I won't be inclined to continue investment. I favour discretion above all things.'

The bile stayed stuck in Vito's throat. The thought of even looking at another woman or taking another woman to his bed was almost repugnant to him. He muttered, 'I don't think you'll need to worry about that.'

'So why...? If you don't mind me asking.'

Vito chased the bile down his throat with a gulp of whiskey, and then, knowing he could very well be losing the best prospect of investment he could ever get, he said, 'I do mind you asking, actually.' Because he had no answers any more. He'd been so sure when he'd stood in front of Flora after she'd told him she loved him, but now that certainty was far less...certain.

Black said, 'Fair enough.'

'Do you still want to do business with me?' Vito would prefer to know now.

Black looked at him for a long moment and then said, 'Yes, I do, and this might sound crazy but, even though I only met her a couple of times, I trust Flora's judgement of you as a person. But I won't tolerate bad press going forward, Vitale, understood?'

'Understood,' Vito said, feeling grim, when he should be feeling ecstatic. But all he could think about was the fact that this man, who was little more than a stranger really, trusted Flora more than Vito had.

When Vito returned to the apartment in Rome a couple of days later, he expected that being back in the city would make him feel more settled. After all, he'd just spent time in the two places where he'd so recently had Flora on his arm and in his bed—he'd been bound to miss her presence.

Her scent, her smile, her infectious enthusiasm, her joy in everything, even the damned dog.

Vito scowled as he removed his tie and jacket. The apartment felt empty. Like a void. *Lonely.* In all his years since losing his parents he'd never felt lonely. He'd been too preoccupied. *And then obsessed, with Flora.* But now he felt it and it wasn't welcome.

He saw a box on the main table in the reception room and went over. A small black box. And a note. He picked it up.

Vito, I couldn't seem to take these back. Please accept them now as my thank-you. I hope you find happiness in your life, Flora. And Benji.

Vito opened the box but he already knew what it was. The cufflinks Flora had tried to gift him in New York. The eagles. Soaring high above it all, with that eagle-eyed vision. And suddenly Vito realised that the landscape below had become very barren and desolate.

I hope you find happiness...

It might never have occurred to him that it was a state he wanted to achieve, if he hadn't met Flora. It might never have been something he wanted to aspire to more than professional success. Because it hit him now that, for the last weeks...he'd been happy. For the first time in a long time. Since the tragedy of losing his parents. It had sneaked under his skin and into his head and heart without him even noticing. Teasing him with the possibility that he might have that again, in his life.

It was ironic. The Gavias had got the final word. The final revenge. Because Flora had cursed him, without even knowing it. Because now he knew what he wanted and needed and that the only way he'd ever find it was with her. But she deserved nothing less than his full surrender and the question Vito had to face was this: was he brave enough to admit that, in the end, after all he'd done and achieved, that he was still defeated? Because he hadn't realised until now where true success and fulfilment lay.

'I love it, Flora, you're a genius.'

'Thanks, Maria, but honestly, I'm not even qualified to be doing this. You should find someone who knows—' Flora stopped mid-sentence because someone had appeared in the doorway of the new offices of the women's aid centre.

Vito. Her heart palpitated. She was imagining him. So many times in the last couple of weeks, she'd seen a tall, dark-haired figure only to realise that it was a very poor facsimile of the real man. Maria saw her face and turned around. But Maria knew who he was, of course, because he was funding the charity's new home. Vito was a hero.

Maria went over and Flora could hear the emotion in her voice. 'Signor Vitale, thank you so much. You have no idea how far your money is going to go to help women and children who need a safe place.'

Vito looked at Maria and shook her hand and murmured something Flora couldn't hear. Then he looked at Flora and said, 'It's down to Flora. You can thank her.'

Maria made a half-chuckle. 'No matter what I say or do, she insists on coming here to work for us for free.'

Flora's conscience pricked. Maria didn't know about her inheritance yet and even though Flora had met the solicitor, she'd only taken enough money to find a small place of her own to rent. Maria had offered her board again, but Flora didn't want to take a space that could be given to someone who really needed it. She did have every intention, of course, of donating a significant amount to the aid centre, as soon as she'd got her head around the vast amount of money in her solicitor's bank account with her name on it. 'Don't be silly. It's a pleasure to help. You helped me.'

Maria said, 'What can we do for you, Signor Vitale?'

So far, Flora had somehow avoided making direct eye contact with Vito, but it was as if he was telepathically communicating with her to look at him. She did, and her insides somersaulted. He looked…different. Somehow undone. She only realised then that he was wearing faded jeans and boots. A T-shirt under a light bomber jacket. And that he was holding a motorcycle helmet in one hand. Pink.

He said, 'Flora, can I borrow you for a little while?'

Totally bemused and thrown by the dressed-down Vito and the pink helmet, she said, 'Okay.'

Maria said, 'You've done enough today, go on.'

Flora grabbed her light jacket and pulled it on, following Vito out and down the stairs to the street where a motorcycle was parked, leaning to one side. Some kids were looking at it and scattered. 'Vito…what's going on? Is this yours?' She pointed to the bike.

'Yes, it is, and do you know something? I've never even taken it out for a ride until today. It was a status purchase.'

Flora looked at him. 'But you do know how to ride it?'

'Of course.' He handed her the pink helmet. 'Here, put this on.' Flora took the helmet. Was this really happening? Or was she hallucinating? She put the helmet on her head and Vito—who was now sitting on the bike—said, 'Come here.'

Flora took a step towards him and he fastened the strap under her chin. The feel of his fingers on her skin shot through her like electricity. *Real, not a hallucination.* She put a hand on his and said, 'Vito, what are you doing here?'

He looked at her. 'I just want to talk. Is that okay?'

Flora couldn't speak. She was afraid to ask what about in case it was just to apologise or…ask her if she wanted to prolong the affair even though she was in love with him and he wasn't with her— She shut her whirling thoughts down and took a deep breath and then Vito said, 'Where's Benji?'

Flora found it ridiculously moving that he'd spared a thought for the dog. 'Upstairs in his bed. He had a big walk earlier so he was asleep. Maria will keep an eye on him.'

'Okay, hop on.' Vito held out a hand and Flora put hers into it, letting him help her to swing onto the seat behind him. She couldn't stop herself from falling into the groove of the seat, snug behind Vito. He put on his own helmet and said over his shoulder, 'Put your arms around my waist.'

Flora did so, and found herself slipping even closer to his broad back. The powerful bike throttled to life under them, and then they were off, weaving through the hectic Roman traffic.

It was late afternoon and the city was bathed in golden sunshine. Flora gave up trying to think about what Vito wanted to say or where they were going. She was enjoying the feel of his body against hers and kept her hands tied tight around his torso. She could feel his muscles bunching and relaxing as he drove with sexy confidence.

She realised where they were headed when he started climbing up out of the city onto Janiculum Hill, one of Rome's famous vantage points with amazing views of the city. There was a large car park and a wall where people stood to take pictures or just take in the view.

Feeling very bemused as Vito stopped the bike and got off, Flora let him help her off. She removed the helmet and he took it and put it with his in a carrier at the back.

Flora looked around at the people and the tourist stalls selling hats, water, pictures… 'Vito…what are we doing here?'

He took her hand and led her over to the wall, a quiet spot. He let her hand go. She looked at him and realised that he seemed nervous. He looked out over the city and said, 'I used to come here after my folks died, and after everything was gone but the name of the business. We'd even lost our home and were living in a cheap hotel…did I mention that?'

Flora shook her head. But Vito wasn't looking at her. He said, 'I know how terrifying it must have been for you to leave my office that day with nothing but the clothes on your back because after my mother died, that's pretty much all I had too.'

'Were you homeless?' Flora's guts clenched.

'For a little while, but I learnt to hustle and managed to scrape together enough to get by and find a hostel and then build up from there.'

Flora's mind boggled at the amount of work he would have had to put in, to start all over again from nothing. Just his name.

He continued, 'I used to come up here and look out over the city. And I used to imagine your uncle down there somewhere, wining and dining. Living in his palazzo, living off my father's ruined reputation and business.'

He glanced at Flora. 'Living off your inheritance, although I didn't know that then.'

He looked out at the view again. 'But now, it's someone else who consumes me when I look at this view.'

Flora's heart rate was erratic. 'Who's that?'

He looked at her. '*You*, of course. I'll be wondering where you are, who you're with. Wondering if you're happy. What are you doing? Are you using that money for yourself or giving it all away to the first person who comes along? Because I do know you, Flora, and I do see you. You're pure, and good and true, and kind. In spite of everything that's happened to you.'

Flora shook her head, embarrassed. 'I'm not. You're making me sound like a saint.'

He touched her cheek with a finger, so fleetingly she almost wondered if she'd imagined it. 'You are, compared to me. I let anger and grief dominate my life, crushing all the goodness out of everything. Crushing any hopes and dreams beyond achieving success and revenge.'

Flora couldn't speak. Vito continued, 'But then you came along and showed me how lacking my life really was and how empty my future was. I want a real future, Flora, full of happiness and fulfilment beyond material gains or success.'

Flora felt light-headed. She repeated his words. 'You want a real future.'

'Yes, but it can only exist with one other person. You,

Flora. I can't have that future unless you're in it, with me, by my side. I pushed you away because you exposed me for being a coward.'

She shook her head, not sure how she was still standing. 'You're not a coward. You're one of the bravest people I've ever met.'

Vito put a hand on her cheek, stopping her words. 'You're brave, Flora, you're braver than me. When you told me you loved me I pushed you away because I knew that to admit to loving you would mean surrendering everything I've identified with for years—grief, pain, loss, revenge.'

'What are you saying, Vito?'

He smiled but she could see the nerves behind it and the emotion in his eyes. 'I'm saying that I love you, Flora. Adore you. I lasted two miserable weeks before realising there was only one option. To surrender. But it's a happy surrender. I hand myself over to you, body, heart and soul, if you'll still have me?'

Flora looked up at Vito. He was stripped as bare as she'd ever seen him, and she'd never seen him like this. But she was taking too long. Doubt crept into his eyes, his expression started to grow tight. He said, 'You deserve the best, Flora. Maybe you've already realised that and you know that I'm not—'

Before he could self-doubt a second longer, Flora launched herself at him, wrapping her legs around his waist, almost toppling him, but he stayed standing, and wrapped his arms around her. 'Flora?'

'I love you, Vito. No one else would be good enough for me. You're the best. I told you before I love the bones of you and I always will and I want to live my whole life with you.'

She could feel the emotion moving in his chest as he sucked in breaths. 'Thank God. For a moment I thought it might be too late.'

She shook her head and said, 'Never too late.' She bent her head and covered his mouth with hers and a cheer went up from the tourists around them. Flora smiled against Vito's mouth and buried her flaming face in his neck.

Later, in Vito's apartment, after they'd moved Flora's and Benji's belongings back from where she'd been renting near to the new women's aid offices, they lay in bed, bodies cooling in the aftermath of spent passion.

Their fingers were entwined and Flora's leg was draped over Vito's thigh. They were pressed together, and her hair, wild and untamed, flowed over the pillow behind her head. She'd never looked more beautiful and Vito had never felt more content. He'd forgotten what it could feel like. True happiness. It still terrified him slightly but he wouldn't give it up again for the world.

Flora pressed a kiss to his chest and he tipped up her chin with his free hand. He came up on one elbow and looked down at her. She looked at him and smiled. His heart turned over. He said, 'By the way, there was one other thing I wanted to discuss with you.'

She smiled even wider. 'Yes, to whatever it is.'

Vito lay back and smirked. 'That was easy.'

Flora leaned up and hit him playfully. 'What was it?'

Vito grinned. He felt younger. Carefree. He let go of her hand and turned away to the bedside table and took the small black box out of the drawer. He sat up, suddenly nervous again.

Flora sat up too, pulling the sheet up. She looked from Vito to the box and back. 'Vito?'

He opened it and she looked down and he saw how she paled. She put a hand to her mouth and then looked at him again. 'Are you…is this…?'

He nodded. 'I don't want there to be any doubt... I want to spend the rest of my life with you, Flora. Will you marry me?'

He took the art deco yellow diamond ring out of the box and took her hand. It was trembling. 'Flora?'

She looked at him and tears were brimming in her eyes. She nodded, smiled, and said chokily, 'Yes, Vito...yes, I'll marry you.'

He slid the ring onto her finger and said, 'More tasteful than the first one?'

She half laughed and hiccuped. She threw her arms around his neck and he fell onto his back, happily under her lush body.

'Yes,' she said, 'infinitely.' She kissed him. When she pulled back, Vito tucked some hair behind her ear and said, 'One more thing.'

'Anything.'

'Some day, when you're ready and after you've done your graphic design course—'

'I'm doing a course?'

'Yes, you are.'

She grinned. Vito almost lost his train of thought, especially because a certain part of his anatomy was already coming back to life, but he forced himself to focus.

'You said that you'd like a family...'

Flora went still. 'You said you didn't.'

Vito pushed some of her hair over her shoulder. 'Well, that was before I knew you. I think now that a little girl, with her mother's golden-brown eyes and long wild hair, wouldn't be such a bad thing.'

Vito felt Flora's heart pounding against his chest. She said, 'Or a little boy with his father's dark hair and dark eyes and his fierce spirit.'

Vito kissed her. 'Or maybe, a little boy with his mother's curly hair and golden eyes and a little girl with her father's dark hair and eyes…'

Flora kissed him and Vito tasted the saltiness of her tears. She drew back. 'Yes, Vito, yes to all of it. I want it all, with you. For ever.'

He flipped them so that he was on top and between Flora's legs. She opened to him and as he joined their bodies he echoed her vow, 'For ever.'

A month later, Rome

Vito stood at the top of the church, waiting. He fiddled nervously with the cufflinks that Flora had given him. The eagles. Flora was late. The crowd were whispering and he knew what they were saying.

Was she was going to do to him what he did to her?

The tie around Vito's neck felt tight. He resisted the urge to loosen it. In truth, he'd never felt so exposed, laid bare, as he did in this moment, but he didn't even care. Because all he cared about was that Flora would come to him as promised, even though he deserved every ounce of humiliation she could dish out and more.

She's not like you…she's a good person.

He smiled tightly. And then, the crowd hushed and a ripple of expectancy went around the church.

Tension eased inside Vito. She was here. She'd come. She did love him. Music started up. He couldn't help it, he had to turn around. His heart stopped.

Flora stood framed in the doorway, a vision. In a simple white dress, off the shoulder, with little cap sleeves on her upper arms. A structured lace bodice with flowers embroidered into the lace, little pearls in the middle of each flower. It fell in soft tulle folds to the floor. It was simple, whimsical, romantic and very Flora.

Her hair was down, adorned by just a garland of white flowers on the top of her head. The only jewellery she wore, apart from her engagement ring, was the gold necklace Vito had given her. She held a simple posy of white wild flowers in one hand and by the other she held a lead. Benji danced around her feet wearing a white dicky-bow collar.

Vito could see that Flora was nervous, and wanted to scoop her up. She might be nervous, but she was brave. Braver than anyone he knew. And he watched with pride as she moved forward and started walking down the aisle, alone.

When she got halfway, Vito thought, *The hell with this*, and strode forward to meet her. He got to her and couldn't help grinning, his vision blurring a little.

She looked up, grinning too. She said softly, 'Did I have you scared for a second?'

Vito let out a short sharp laugh. He cupped her face in his hands and pressed a kiss to her mouth, ignoring the gasps and fevered whispers and the pointed coughing of the priest. He drew back and said, 'Every day, woman, you terrify me with your goodness and how much I love you.'

She winked at him, but he could see the emotion in her eyes too. She said, 'That's good, because someone has to keep you on your toes.'

Hand in hand, Vito and Flora walked the rest of the way to the altar, with their dog, and committed to a lifetime of love and joy.

* * * * *

ITALIAN BABY SHOCK

JACKIE ASHENDEN

MILLS & BOON

For my King of Cups

CHAPTER ONE

HER PHONE VIBRATED yet again but Lark Edwards tried not to look at it. It was nothing. Maya had a little cold, that was all. It wasn't life-threatening. It didn't require hospitalisation. The nanny who was looking after her for the night held qualifications in child health and was more than capable of looking after a fifteen-month-old with the sniffles.

If anything was gravely wrong, she'd contact Lark immediately, she'd promised.

Lark's fingers closed tightly around the phone.

She always tried to look on the bright side of things and stay positive, but perhaps there *was* something gravely wrong. Perhaps that's why her phone was vibrating. Perhaps Maya had suddenly become very ill and the nanny was trying to contact her to tell her.

Lark took a breath, calmed her racing heartbeat and gave herself a mental slap.

No. It was fine. She was only wound up because this was the first time she'd been away from Maya longer than a day. Mr Ravenswood, her boss, who owned Ravenswood Antiques, one of London's most exclusive antique businesses, had taken ill with the flu and hadn't been able to travel, so he'd asked Lark to go to Italy in his stead.

It was a very important assignment, he'd said, and it was vital someone from Ravenswood go. And since she was the only one who was free, it had to be her. She didn't have his knowledge of antiques since she was only his personal assistant, not to mention only being in the job a year, but he'd been giving her some basic training in the business for the past six months, and she was at least a little familiar with Italy, having been there once before. Also, all she'd have do, he'd assured her, was to view the pieces that the Donati family were wanting to sell to ascertain they were genuine—he'd told her what to look for—and to take as many pictures as she could.

It would have been easier for someone on the Donati end to send the pictures without the need to travel, but Mr Ravenswood had been adamant that someone had to view the items personally. Also, they were to speak to Signor Donati himself, since Ravenswood Antiques prided themselves on the personal touch. Mr Ravenswood had been very upset about the illness that had prevented him from flying to Rome. Then again, he couldn't ask such an important and busy man such as Signor Donati to rearrange his schedule purely for the sake of an old antiques dealer.

Also, the Donati pieces were special and could earn the business a lot of money, and Mr Ravenswood didn't want to do anything that might jeopardise the sale.

Lark had felt sorry for him. Jasper Ravenswood had given her a job just after Maya had been born and she'd been despairing of ever finding someone who'd employ a new mother. But he'd given her a position, and hadn't complained when she'd had to bring Maya into the office. So it was only the right thing to do to agree to go to Rome, see the pieces and talk to Mr Donati herself.

Jasper had been so effusively thankful, he'd paid for the very expensive nanny to look after Maya, Lark's daughter, for the night.

Lark took another calming breath.

Yes, it was only a night and Maya wasn't a little baby any more. The nanny, Emily, had been lovely too. She just had to stay positive.

As if determined to ruffle her calm, her phone vibrated once again and this time Lark couldn't resist having a quick look. But it was only a text from Mr Ravenswood wishing her good luck.

She smiled, typed in a quick thank you, then put the phone down on the overly gilded table in front of her, and forced herself to relax.

It could be just being in Italy again that was messing with her usually positive outlook, or maybe it was sitting on this beautiful velvet-covered couch—no doubt another antique worth thousands of euros—in this beautiful room, in the beautiful, centuries-old Donati palazzo just outside of Rome that was getting to her.

It wasn't all that conducive to relaxation.

It definitely *wasn't* being in Italy again. That night had been two years ago now, so if not the *distant* past, then very much *not* the recent past. It had no bearing on the future and she certainly never thought of that night in particular, not if she could help it.

She always tried to stay positive.

Leaning against the stiff back of the sofa, Lark looked around the salon—or so the member of the Donatis' house staff had called it, definitely not anything as common as a 'lounge'—and it was huge. The rust-red silk-panelled walls looked as if they had been hand painted and were hung with huge paintings of battle scenes in gilt frames. There seemed to be a lot of gilt on the ornate plaster cornices too, as well as on the intricately painted ceiling.

The parquet on the floor was ancient and worn and covered with hand-knotted silk rugs, while the armchairs and couch she sat on were velvet covered and as gilded as the old and huge fireplace that Lark sat in front of. Chandeliers hung from the ceiling and above the fireplace hung a massive portrait of two people in modern dress, which looked out of place with the rest of the room's stately opulence. A handsome man with cold blue eyes stood beside a seated woman with beautiful red-gold curls. Neither of them looked particularly happy and it somehow made the room seem dark and vaguely oppressive. Though that could have been due to the heavy dark blue silk curtains partially concealing the windows.

Not a place to slump on the sofa with a tub of ice cream and a glass of wine while watching movies on one's laptop, that was for sure. Which was exactly what she was going to do back at her hotel once she'd finished looking at the pieces Mr Ravenswood had wanted her to look at, taken the photos she'd been instructed to take and talked nice to whichever Donati family representative she was supposed to talk to.

Tomorrow she'd fly back to London and her daughter.

It was only a night, not a big deal.

She smoothed the fuchsia-pink skirt she wore and double-checked she hadn't spilled anything on her blouse. It was new and patterned with roses that matched the fuchsia of her skirt, and she loved it—wearing bright and cheerful colours always made her feel good. Luckily, there were no incriminating stains, which surprised her since being the mother of a young child meant clothing got stained on a regular basis and usually in mysterious circumstances.

It wouldn't do to appear untidy though, not today, not when she was here on behalf of Ravenswood Antiques. Mr Ravenswood had a certain reputation to uphold and she was determined to uphold it. He'd also been very clear that the Donatis weren't just any old Italian family. They owned Donati Bank, a private banking company that had been founded around six hundred years earlier, while the family's legacy went back even further. They were one of the oldest and most important families in Italy, their history and wealth equalling and even surpassing some of Europe's royal families.

It wasn't exactly a bright history, however.

Lark had done some research on the plane to Rome and the Donati family had been notorious in the Renaissance for all kinds of poisonings and stabbings. They'd had a thing for assassinations apparently, targeting anyone they viewed as a threat to their family. There wasn't any of that nowadays, of course, but their reputation in the business world was still as ruthless as it had been back in the day. Mostly courtesy of Cesare Donati, the last Donati heir, who drove the business like a racing car driver on the track. Fast and hard and with an aim to win.

He was an imposing, almost mythical figure, with a head for money and a reach in the finance world that spanned the globe, Donati Bank having offices in all the major financial hubs. He advised governments, held the accounts of many global corporations, as well as the personal accounts of some of the wealthiest people in the world, and had a reputation for being as ruthless as the Donatis of old.

She hoped the assistant she'd dealt with had passed on to him that he'd be meeting her instead of Mr Ravenswood. She hoped he wouldn't mind too much. He might even be too busy to meet with her, which would be fine since she didn't relish the thought of having to deal with a man like him. Her own father had been wealthy and powerful, and she and her mother had spent years running from him, so she knew what that type of man could be like.

Then again, she was good with people, and anyway, maybe speaking to Signor Donati would only take a few minutes. Maybe this whole thing would only take an hour or so, and then she might even be able to change her flight and leave Rome tonight. The flights had been full when she'd last checked, but being waitlisted was a possibility. Then she would get back to London and be there for when Maya woke up the next morning.

That was a bolstering thought and she felt much better, until her phone vibrated on the table again. She reached out to grab it, just as the salon's ornate double doors opened and a man stepped in the room. He closed them with a brisk click then turned to her.

And Lark's breath caught in her throat.

He was exceedingly tall—almost a foot taller than her modest five foot four—and powerfully muscled, the width and breadth of his shoulders and chest emphasised by the perfectly tailored dark suit he wore.

He was also beautiful, his face a work of art in the sculpted planes and angles of cheekbones, nose and forehead. His hair was black and short, the same colour as his winged eyebrows and sooty lashes, all of which made the deep, piercing blue of his eyes even more astonishing.

The same piercing blue of the man in the painting above the fireplace. Though unlike the painting, this man brought a crackling energy and force into the room, as if a fierce storm had come through the doors after him.

For a second Lark sat there, her phone forgotten, utterly transfixed.

She'd seen his face in many media articles, both online and in print. It was instantly recognisable. But that crackling energy he'd brought with him, the magnetism of his physical presence, made him completely unforgettable. And utterly mesmerising.

It was Cesare Donati, head of Donati Bank.

Her mouth dry, her heart pounding, Lark pushed herself to her feet, trying to resist the urge to wipe her sweaty palms down her skirt. She felt self-conscious all of a sudden, deeply aware that she was here as Mr Ravenswood's representative and yet not knowing a great deal about antiques. She'd learned a lot in the past six months, but that wasn't the same as someone who had a lot of experience in the field. And no doubt Signor Donati would expect her to have a lot of experience.

Well, there was nothing to be done about that now. She'd just have to be her normal bright, cheerful self, and hopefully that would be enough. He was a human being like any other and most human beings liked her.

Apparently, according to her mother, her smile could heal the world.

Signor Donati's attention was on his phone as he stopped near the couch, typing a message out to someone before slipping the phone back into the pocket of his impeccably tailored suit trousers. Then he looked at her and those piercing blue eyes of his widened, a look of shock rippling over his handsome face. He stared at her as if he'd seen a ghost.

Her heart was already beating far too fast and she had no idea why he was looking at her that way—perhaps he hadn't been informed that Mr Ravenswood wouldn't be here? Regardless, being friendly always put people at their ease, so she took a step towards him and held out a hand.

'*Buongiorno*, Signor Donati,' she said in her hastily practised and atrocious Italian. Then, switching to English, she went on, 'I hope my message was passed on? I know you were expecting Mr Ravenswood, but unfortunately he was unable to come due to illness, and he sent me in his stead. My name is Lark Edwards and it's a great pleasure to meet you.'

Cesare Donati made no move to take her hand. In fact, he didn't move at all. He only stared at her, his gaze twin spears of sapphire pinning her in place. 'You,' he murmured, his voice deep, rich and full of shock. 'What the hell are *you* doing here?'

Lark blinked. He'd said it as if he knew her, which was strange, because she'd never met him. She'd remember if she had, very definitely.

'Uh…me?' she asked uncertainly. 'Well, as I said, Mr Ravenswood was sick so I—'

'I told you there would be no contact between us,' he interrupted and then took an abrupt step towards her, his gaze sweeping over her as if he was meticulously recording every aspect of her appearance. 'I told you not to go looking.'

Lark blinked again, her surprise deepening into confusion. 'I'm sorry,' she said carefully, not wanting to offend him. 'Have we…met before? Or perhaps you've mistaken me for someone else?'

He said nothing. His fallen angel features were drawn tight to the perfect bone structure of his face, his beautifully carved mouth hard. A muscle leapt in his impressive jaw, his astonishing blue eyes studying her so intently she felt almost consumed by them.

A disturbing heat bloomed inside her, making her skin prickle and her breath catch yet again. It was physical attraction, she knew that, but a worse man to be attracted to she couldn't imagine, and not only because he'd never be interested in someone like her. He was also the very epitome of all she disliked about the male species: rich, arrogant and entitled, and even if he had been interested in her, she would have avoided him like the plague.

You did like one man, remember?

Yes. Maya's father. Except the problem was that she *didn't* remember.

Oh, she remembered her mother's death from cancer and then the dreary London winter that had felt as if it would never end. Then that fateful trip to Italy she'd taken to cheer herself up. And she remembered her handbag getting stolen in Rome but…the next thing she knew she'd woken up in hospital. Apparently she'd been hit by a car crossing the street and had banged her head hard, though she had no memory of it. No memory of the night she'd had either.

But she must have spent it with a man, because nine months later, Maya was born.

At first, she'd dismissed that night, because she hadn't had any long-term injuries and she seemed to be fine. But then, when the fact of her pregnancy had become apparent, she'd been terrified, and no amount of looking on the bright side and being positive had helped.

That her baby was healthy according to the midwife made no difference. She'd always wanted children, but hadn't expected to have them so soon let alone not have the slightest idea who'd fathered her child. In the end she'd visited a psychologist to talk through her fears, because no matter how her baby had been conceived, there was no doubting Lark would be a mother and she wanted to be the best mother she could be. She wanted to keep her baby and love it when it was born. The psychologist had helped, and after a few sessions, Lark had decided that her pregnancy wasn't something to fear. It was a last mystical gift from her mother, a blessing even. Because a blessing was exactly what a child was.

But there was no possibility though, that the man she'd spent the night with was this man. None whatsoever. She'd remember if she had, she was positive. He was so memorable in every conceivable way; it was impossible *not* to remember him.

Lark dropped her outstretched hand and gave him her brightest smile instead. 'Well,' she said. 'If I could just have a look at these pieces your representatives talked to us about and perhaps take a few photos, then I'll get out of your hair.'

It was *her*. There was no doubt. No doubt at all.

Cesare stood in the middle of his family's centuries-old salon, very conscious of the blood pumping hard in his veins and the shock that rippled like an earthquake through him.

It had been nearly two years ago, but he still remembered that night as if it had been yesterday.

The aunt who'd brought him up after his parents had died had just passed away after a heart attack, which meant he was now the last of the Donati line, and even though he'd been determined not to let that bother him in any way, it had. He'd gone out walking the streets, sending his bodyguards away because he'd craved solitude. They hadn't been happy about it, but since he was the boss and they valued their jobs, they did what they were told.

He'd walked for hours, telling himself he felt nothing, that the toxic combination of grief and fury in his gut didn't exist, and he'd been on the point of finding a bar to make sure the embers of it were well and truly drowned, when he'd come across a tourist who'd just had her handbag stolen. She hadn't spoken any Italian and she'd been upset. She hadn't recognised him, either, and though he didn't normally go out of his way to help people—he'd inherited his parents' selfish natures and he knew it—when she'd burst out that she'd just lost her mother, he knew he couldn't leave her on her own.

So he'd mobilised his staff to help her and while they'd dealt with the police, the banks, and the British embassy for a replacement passport, he'd taken her out to dinner. She'd had no money and was hungry, and he needed the distraction.

And what a distraction she'd proven to be, with her wealth of honey gold hair and beautiful sea-green eyes. He'd always had his pick of beautiful women, and while she wasn't who he'd normally choose for a partner, he'd found himself drawn to her all the same. She'd been so expressive and open, and even in the midst of her grief, she'd smiled. It had been the most astonishing smile he'd ever seen in his entire life, warm and generous and utterly sincere. No one had ever smiled at him that way and it felt like the most precious gift he'd ever been given.

Lark, she'd said her name was. Like the bird.

She hadn't had anywhere to go that night, and so he'd offered her a guest room in his villa. They'd sat up till midnight talking in the library and then the chemistry he'd felt all night and yet tried to ignore had sparked and ignited. And she'd been just as warm and expressive and sincere in bed as she had been during their dinner. Passionate too. Giving herself to him with an abandon that had spoken of deep trust. Another precious gift.

She hadn't known him, yet she'd trusted him with her body implicitly.

He'd never had a night with a woman with whom he'd felt such a connection.

It couldn't go anywhere, of course. Because by then he'd already decided that the toxicity of the Donati line would end with him. Selfish, his parents would have called it, and yes, it was. Petty and selfish, revenge for a childhood where he hadn't been a child so much as a possession to be fought over and used. A weapon his parents had aimed at each other.

They'd done their best to leave their scars on him, but he'd refused to be marked. And as for the legacy they'd thought had been so important, well… He could be as petty and selfish as they once had been.

He'd break up the precious Donati legacy, sell it off bit by bit, even Donati bank would go. He'd never marry, never have children. There would be no one else to take the name, no one else to shoulder the weight of that toxic history, no one else to ensure the whole bitter bloodline carried on.

Once he was dead, so were the Donatis.

Anyway, he'd made sure she knew that it would be one night and only one, and the next day, he'd left her sleeping in his bed. By the time he'd got home that evening, she was gone. He'd never heard from her again.

Until today.

Now, here she was, standing in the middle of the salon, dressed in a tight-fitting pink skirt and a blouse with roses on it, outrageously pretty and colourful in his over-wrought, overdecorated palazzo. Giving him that beautiful smile he remembered and yet looking at him as if she had no idea who he was. As if she hadn't spent an entire night, writhing in pleasure in his arms. He didn't understand. How could she have forgotten?

'Don't you know who I am?' he demanded before he could stop himself. Something he'd never had to ask because people always knew who he was.

Her big green eyes widened and a small crease appeared between her brows. 'Of course I do. You're Signor Donati, head of Donati Bank.'

He waited for her to add something more, something along the lines of 'yes, of course I remember the night we spent together, how could I forget that?' But she didn't.

Perhaps she didn't recognise him as the man she'd spent the night with, though again, surely that was impossible. They'd spent hours in each other's company, just talking. Then yet more hours not talking at all, only touching, kissing, tasting. Giving pleasure and receiving it. Did she not remember that?

Apart from anything else, he was head of the largest and oldest private bank in Europe, if not the entire world, and everything he did was the stuff of rumour and gossip. He couldn't go anywhere without being photographed by the paparazzi. Entire governments asked for his financial advice.

He was recognised everywhere and more than one woman who'd spent the night with him had sold their story to different news organisations around the globe.

All those stories were, without exception, glowing.

It was impossible that this particular woman didn't remember him. Unless, of course, she wasn't the woman he'd spent the night with... But no, he was certain she was the one. She'd said her name was Lark and it wasn't that common a name.

Yet, she was looking at him as if he was a total stranger.

Annoyance wound through him and it wasn't wounded pride, absolutely not. Merely irritation. He'd been expecting Ravenswood, not her, and that she just happened to be a woman he'd slept with a long time ago wasn't something he'd expected to have to deal with. It wasn't of note, though. And if she didn't remember him, he certainly wasn't going to tell her.

He'd been very clear, after all, that they'd only have a night and that there would be no further contact and she'd been in agreement. And up until this moment she'd been as good as her word.

Perhaps she was here because she'd wanted to see him? And pretending not to recognise him? Then again, why would she bother? And what had she said about Ravenswood?

Annoyed that his shock at her arrival had meant that he hadn't taken in anything she'd said, Cesare pulled himself together. Emotional control was vital and he couldn't let her unexpected appearance get to him. He was the head of Donati Bank, for God's sake, not a teenage boy with his first crush.

He gave her a cool look. 'Yes,' he said. 'That's exactly who I am. And as head of Donati Bank, I expected to see Mr Ravenswood himself not you.'

Her smile didn't falter. 'I know, but Mr Ravenswood has had a terrible bout of flu and he wasn't in any condition to travel. He also didn't want anyone to rearrange their schedule because of him, so he asked me if I'd be willing to look at your items on his behalf.'

She was still smiling warmly and shock was still bouncing around inside him, and he was aware that a very male part of him was noting how low the neckline of her blouse was, and how it showed off her pretty creamy skin as well as the dips and hollows of her collarbone. Skin he'd spent a long time tasting. Dips and hollows he'd spent a long time tracing with his tongue. In fact, he'd spent a long time following every line of that delectable, curvy body of hers with his hands and his mouth, and he'd relished every cry he'd brought from her. She'd smelled of vanilla, he remembered, like a sweet confection, making his mouth water…

He shoved the erotic memories aside, ignored the sudden increase in his blood pressure. No, he should *not* be thinking about that night. It was over and done with, and no matter how pretty this woman was, and no matter that she didn't recognise him, he wasn't going to let either of those things affect him.

It had only been physical attraction, nothing more, and he'd never let something as banal as lust rule him. He was in complete control of himself as he was in complete control of everything else he did, and while he'd enjoyed that one night, he wasn't going to pursue another. He'd never needed to chase a woman and he wasn't about to start.

'And who exactly are you?' he asked tightly.

She gave him that bright, sunny smile again. 'Oh, I'm Mr Ravenswood's personal assistant.'

'And do you know anything about antiques?'

'Not as much as he does, it's true.' This time her smile was self-deprecating. 'But I've been training with him for the past six months and he's told me what to look for. I'll also be taking some photos if that's okay.'

His annoyance, already simmering, deepened. He'd given up some of his precious time to oversee this particular matter himself. The pieces were valuable, dating from the Renaissance, and were worth a lot of money.

He was going to sell them—he was going to sell *every-thing* in the palazzo—and donate the money to charity, so he wanted to get the best price he could and that meant having them appraised accurately. He'd already had the list of charities he was going to donate to drawn up and all of them his father would have disapproved of. That satisfied him unreasonably.

What did not satisfy him was having his one-night stand turn up at his palazzo and apparently not remember that she slept with him. It shouldn't matter to him and yet for some reason it did.

'If all that was required were some pictures, I could have taken them myself,' he snapped.

Generally, when he took that tone, people leapt to either do his bidding or apologise for whatever transgression they'd made, but Lark merely gave him another of those pretty, sunny smiles, as though she hadn't heard the annoyance in his voice.

'Oh, no, that's not necessary,' she said soothingly. 'Mr Ravenswood was very insistent that I view them personally. Again, I'm so sorry you were inconvenienced. All you have to do is show me where the pieces are and I can do the rest.'

She really was very pretty, with a delicate nose and chin, and a perfect little rosebud of a mouth. And her expression radiated warmth and openness, her sea-green eyes sparkling.

It was as if a shaft of summer sunlight had suddenly illuminated the room, making everything feel lighter and brighter. Not so cold and oppressive and...dark.

She made him remember that night, the warmth he'd felt radiating from her, the way she'd opened her arms to him, welcoming him with such passion. And how no matter what he told himself, he had never forgotten her...

He didn't like it. He didn't want it.

Just then something vibrated on the small seventeenth-century table in front of the sofa. It was a phone, the screen lighting up.

The smile on Lark's face faltered, her expression tightening.

So, it was her phone. And clearly she was distracted by it.

His decision, already half made, solidified into certainty. He didn't want her here; she was distracting and he couldn't afford to be distracted now, not when he had so much to organise.

'I've changed my mind,' he said. 'There are plenty of other companies I can sell these pieces to. Companies who take this more seriously than—'

The phone vibrated again, interrupting him in midflight, and this time Lark made a sound. Her gaze darted to the phone on the table.

'Are you listening?' He knew he sounded demanding and graceless, but he'd come to the end of his patience and once that occurred, he was done. 'Because if you're not—'

'I'm so sorry,' Lark said quickly as the phone vibrated again. 'But I really need to get this. It's my daughter's nanny. This is the first time I've left Maya for longer than a day since she was born and well…' She broke off as the phone vibrated yet again, her attention on the screen. 'Sorry, I just have to…' Before he could protest, she bent to pick the phone up off the table, turning as she looked down at it, presumably to hide whatever text she'd received.

She wasn't very tall, though, so he could see the screen over her shoulder. On it was a photo of a very young child, a little girl dressed in a pink nightgown and smiling at the camera. She had a cloud of soft rose-gold curls and blue, blue eyes.

It was a singular colour that rose gold, as was the intense blue of her eyes. He'd never met anyone else who'd had hair that hue apart from his mother. And as for that blue...

That was Donati blue. Two hundred years ago the Donatis had been patrons of a painter who'd created a paint colour in their honour. And that's what he'd called it.

It was famous.

Cesare went very still as everything in him slowed down and stopped. Everything except his brain, which was now working overtime. Going back over dates. Going back over that night. Going over everything.

Because if there was one thing he knew, it was that the little girl in that photo was his daughter.

CHAPTER TWO

LARK IMMEDIATELY RELAXED at the sight of Maya's smile
on her screen. It was fine; of course it was fine. Emily had
only sent her a happy photo, making it clear that Maya
was feeling better.

Lark's central nervous system could stand down. Everything was okay.

Completely forgetting that she'd just broken off in mid-
conversation, she began to type a reply, only for a large
male hand to reach over her shoulder and pluck the phone
from her grasp.

She gasped and turned round sharply to find Signor
Donati staring down at her phone's screen, the expression
on his handsome face almost frightening in its intensity.

Lark's stomach tightened. Why had he grabbed her
phone? And why was he looking at the picture of Maya
as if he was…angry? She should have been paying attention, she knew that, and answering texts in the middle of
a professional conversation was very rude. But it was her
daughter. Surely he'd understand?

She plastered a smile on her face. 'I'm so sorry about
that text, but—'

'This is your daughter?' He looked up from the phone,
the blue of his eyes piercing her right through, the expression in them stealing her breath.

She didn't want to answer, an inexplicable unease sitting deep in her gut. Yet she couldn't think of a good reason not to. 'Yes,' she said slowly. 'That's Maya.'

He glanced back at the photo. 'Maya,' he repeated, his accent making her name sound like music.

Lark swallowed, her unease deepening. 'Can I have my phone back, please?'

He ignored her. 'When was she born?'

The uneasiness turned over inside her. Why was he asking her questions about her child? She didn't like it. She didn't like it at all.

'She just turned one a few months ago,' she said. 'I'm sorry, but why are you asking so many questions about—'

'And her father?'

Anger, heavy and unfamiliar, stirred to life in her gut. She tried never to get angry, it was such a depressing, useless emotion, but strange men asking her questions—deeply personal questions—about her and her daughter was a subject that she had no humour about.

'What about her father?' She kept her tone polite, because he was still a potential client, no matter his strange behaviour. 'I'm sorry, but I don't see how that is any of your—'

'Her father.' He looked up from the phone, his gaze all sharp blue edges. 'Who is he?'

He expected her to answer instantly, she could see that, and her usual reaction would be to soothe whatever was bothering him, because something clearly was. You caught more flies with honey than you did with vinegar, and Lark was an expert with honey.

But his line of questioning was deeply disquieting, not to mention that something about him had worked its way under her skin. His male beauty, the force of his presence, the air of authority that cloaked him, the way her heart suddenly seemed to beat out of rhythm when she looked at him... She wasn't sure which it was. Maybe all three. Whatever the reason, she didn't want to soothe him. Didn't want to give him her smile, smooth over all those sharp edges. So she didn't.

She gave him a cool look instead and said, still polite, 'I'm very sorry, but as I said, that's none of your business. I'm here to talk about the antiques you want to sell, not my daughter.'

His perfect features had hardened and the knuckles of his long-fingered hands were white where they held her phone. His gaze glittered and she was sure it was fury she saw there. He looked...dangerous and she was conscious that they were in the room together, alone. And he was a stranger, tall and powerful and so much bigger than she was. It wasn't that she was afraid of him exactly—or at least it wasn't *only* fear that wound through her. There was something else, something hotter...

'You don't remember me, do you?' he said.

Lark took a breath, her disquiet turning into a kernel of ice sitting in her gut.

No. It couldn't be. It couldn't...

'Should I remember you?' she asked carefully. 'I think I'd remember if we met.'

'We did meet,' he said. 'One night in Rome. You had your handbag stolen.'

The ice inside her froze her all the way through.

That night in Rome, the night she'd lost all memory of. The night she'd chosen to view through rose-coloured glasses because it had given her Maya. She'd thought she'd worked through all her fears about it, how her pregnancy could have been the result of rape or some kind of coercion, because she'd never had much to do with men and that was by choice. And after she'd seen the psychologist, she'd made a conscious decision not to keep revisiting that night, because how she'd got pregnant wasn't as important as its eventual outcome: Maya.

Her daughter was the most important person in Lark's life and she was all that mattered. Lark had told herself that it was even a good thing she didn't remember, because then it meant she didn't have to track down Maya's father and inform him of what had happened. She didn't have to deal with him or any demands he might make, and having witnessed that with her mother, it wasn't an experience she'd ever wanted for herself or for any children she might have.

It did mean that Maya wouldn't ever have a father figure in her life, but that wasn't a problem. Lark had never had one herself and her life had been all the better for it.

Except now Signor Donati was staring at her with sharp blue eyes, the force of his attention, the fury in it, almost a physical weight crushing her, and she was basically made of icy shock.

'No,' she said, her voice a tiny bit hoarse. 'I…don't remember.'

He didn't move and he didn't look away. 'I organised a new passport for you and then I took you out for dinner. We talked until the restaurant closed and then I invited you back to my villa. You said yes.'

Her mouth dried, the beat of her heart even louder in her ears. 'I… I…'

'We had some very good cognac in my library,' he went on relentlessly. 'And around midnight, we decided to move our conversation to my bedroom.'

No, it couldn't have been him. It *couldn't*. She would have remembered *him*.

'I told you that one night was all we could have and you agreed. I left you sleeping the next morning, and when I returned home, you'd gone.'

Lark shook her head, the cold shock making her extremities feel numb. She *did* remember her handbag being stolen and she'd been very upset about it. In fact, her last memory of that night was standing in a Roman street, wondering what on earth she was going to do, and then... nothing. Nothing until she'd opened her eyes and found herself in hospital.

Surely—*surely*—she would have remembered spending the night with him.

'I don't think that's what happened,' she said, her voice sounding thin. 'I'm sure I—'

'That's exactly what happened.' His gaze bored into hers. 'Why are you pretending you don't remember? Did you not want me to find out that I had a child?'

She blinked, the shock intensifying. 'No, of course not. And I'm not—'

'She has rose-gold hair.' He took a step towards her, still holding on to her phone, his gaze like a knife. 'My mother had hair like that, it's not a common colour. And no one but Donatis have eyes that blue.'

Lark couldn't help darting a glance at the portrait above the fire, at the woman sitting in the chair. Was that his mother? Because her hair was that colour and yes, if you looked at it in a certain light, it *was* the same colour as Maya's. And the man standing beside her with the blue eyes... The same blue as the eyes of the man standing in front of her.

Maya's eyes.

'Do you want money?' His voice was hard and cold and furious. 'Is that why you're here? Do you want to blackmail me?' He took a step closer and she found herself backing away. 'Did you do it on purpose? Are you planning to use your child to extort money out of me?'

The couch pressed against the backs of her legs, stopping her from going any further, and he was very close, towering over her, all six foot three of masculine fury. She could feel his heat, smell his aftershave, something warm and woody, like a cedar forest. And again she felt that tug inside her, her skin tightening. Not fear, and yet not unlike it. Anticipation, maybe or excitement, as if she relished that fury of his and wanted to see more of it. Which was crazy, because who wanted to see more masculine anger?

Also, how dare he shout at her? How dare he fling these questions at her, giving her no time to answer or think about what he was saying? And more than anything else, how dare he physically intimidate her in this way?

Lark never got angry and she never shouted. She tried to keep a positive outlook on everything she did. Years on the run from Lark's father had made her mother fragile and easily prone to depression, and God knew her mother didn't need Lark being difficult. She'd wanted her mother to be happy and her mother was only happy when Lark was. So she made sure to always be happy. Always be cheerful and optimistic, with never a bad word for anyone, and it hadn't been hard. Her mother had loved her for it.

So she had no idea where the hot anger that flooded her veins now had come from, or why. Because anger would only make this situation worse. She should be smiling at Signor Donati, soothing him somehow, or charming him out of his rage instead.

Yet she didn't do any of those things. She'd been worried about Maya and nervous about what Mr Ravenswood had expected of her, and then this horrible man had started throwing questions like daggers at her about a particularly sensitive time in her life, so now she had no interest in soothing him. And apart from anything else, anger was infinitely preferable to the cold fear that was now working its way through her.

So she lifted her chin and glared at him. 'Get out of my space,' she said angrily, and without waiting for him to move, she lifted her hands to his chest to push him away.

And froze.

He was very warm, the muscles beneath the wool of his suit jacket hard. That scent of his kept tugging at her, making her breathless. Making her skin prickle and tighten, as if her body knew something or remembered something she didn't.

He was looking down at her and there was something hot in his eyes now, a steady, hungry, blue flame and it mesmerised her. Her breath caught.

Men had never been a priority, not even as a teenager. Her mother had made her all too aware of how men could use you, trap you, hurt you if you weren't careful, so she'd always been careful. Which was why her pregnancy had come as such a shock and why she'd been glad that the accident had taken her memory.

So, she hadn't been expecting her own physical response to Cesare Donati, not the moment he'd walked into the room, and definitely not now. When she'd wanted to push him away and instead found her hands lingering on his chest, unable to tear her gaze from the hungry glitter in his eyes.

And when he said softly, 'Perhaps you'll remember this then,' and put a finger underneath her chin, tipping her head back, she didn't protest. And when he lowered his head and brushed his mouth over hers, she didn't avoid it.

Time seemed to stop, her world narrowing to this moment.

His kiss was unexpectedly light, unexpectedly gentle, his lips much softer than she'd thought they'd be. The touch of them on hers was electric, a bolt of white-hot sensation arrowing straight through her. Her nipples hardened against the lace of her bra, a pressure gathering between her thighs.

Sometimes at night she'd wake up aching, her skin sensitised, her head full of dreams of being touched and caressed. Of warm fingers stroking her, of a mouth on hers, of deep physical pleasure. She'd never understood where those dreams had come from and had never connected them with that night she'd forgotten.

But now…it was almost as if the memory was there. As if she could reach out and grab it. As if she even wanted to…

If he's Maya's father, he'll take her away from you and you know it.

The wave of cold fear swamped her, drowning the effects of the kiss and she pushed at him, hard.

He didn't resist, going back a couple of steps, his broad chest rising and falling rapidly. His eyes glittered. 'You do remember,' he said, his accent much thicker. 'You do.'

'No.' She tried to still the shaking in her hands. 'I don't. I don't remember anything about you. Yes, I was in Rome and yes, I remember my handbag being stolen. But that's all.' She took an uneven breath. 'I was in an accident. I was knocked over by a car in the street and the next thing I remember is waking up in hospital. My memory of that night is gone.'

His gaze narrowed. 'An accident?'

'I was concussed. They told me that my memory of that night would return, but it never did.' She swallowed. 'I'm telling you the truth, Mr Donati. I have no memory of that night. But one thing I do know is that Maya is not yours.'

She couldn't be. She absolutely couldn't. Maya was no one's but hers.

He took no notice, the focused look in his eyes unchanging. 'I'm afraid I must insist on a paternity test.'

'No,' she said before she could stop herself. 'I won't allow it.'

His jaw tightened. 'If you know for certain that your daughter isn't mine, then a paternity test wouldn't matter would it?'

Lark felt her face get hot, her anger mounting. 'She's *not* yours. And I won't have my daughter's privacy invaded.'

'I see.' He drew himself up to his full height, authority radiating from him. 'If that's how you want to play it then fine. But if you won't allow a paternity test then I'm afraid I'll be taking my priceless Renaissance antiques elsewhere.'

Her anger became outrage and she knew it was a mistake to give in to it. That she should be smiling and giving him what he wanted instead, because everything was always easier that way. There was never any point in being difficult.

But he'd casually upended her nice, safe little world, first with his claims of being Maya's father and then with that kiss. Now there was a part of her that was afraid. Afraid that he was right, that she had in fact slept with him, and her daughter was his. And that he'd take Maya from her the way her father had tried to take her from her mother.

Men did that, didn't they? They took what they viewed as theirs, including people. And if they didn't take, then they threatened, which was exactly what he was doing now.

Mr Ravenswood would be very upset with her at losing the Donatis as clients, but her daughter was far more important than any antique. Her daughter was priceless and Lark would fight anyone who dared to take Maya from her. She'd fight them to the death if need be.

'Fine,' she snapped before she could think better of it. 'Take them elsewhere. Because you will not be testing my daughter. Not today, not tomorrow, not ever.'

Cesare was utterly furious, yet he found himself almost admiring the way Lark Edwards stood there, with her pointed chin lifted, determination in every line of her small, curvy figure.

No one had stood up to him like this in a very long time and he had to respect the courage it must have taken her to do so. He was, after all, one of the richest and most important men in Europe and everyone did what he told them to. They certainly didn't argue with him the way she was doing right now, and most especially not when he was angry.

And he *was* angry. That little girl on her phone *was* his, he knew it in his bones, though he'd had no idea how it had happened. He'd always been meticulous when it came to protection and that night had been no different. She'd told him she was on the pill too. Nothing had been left to chance.

So there shouldn't have been a pregnancy at all and yet there was no denying the colour of the little one's hair or the blue of her eyes. No denying the instinct that had gripped him, the knowledge that had settled inside him as hard and sure as the earth beneath his feet.

Maya was his daughter. And that meant he had some decisions to make.

It would be easy to agree with Lark, to accept that indeed he wasn't her father, that he couldn't be. To let Lark look at these antiques, take her pictures, and then leave Italy. He'd never have to see her again, never have to think about her again, and certainly never have to accept that he even had a daughter.

Yet he'd seen that photo now and he knew he was no longer the only Donati left, that there was another. Nothing could erase that knowledge, nothing could change it. The Donati line *would* continue, whether he wanted it to or not, and so he had to alter his course of action.

He could never forget what his parents had done to him, how their petty jealousies and pointless grudges, their burning, relentless hatred of each other, had killed them both and nearly ended him. And he'd never wanted to repeat that cycle. Never wanted a family where that might happen.

But now Maya existed, and because she existed, the cycle could repeat itself. And he was almost certain it would. The Donatis were hot-headed grudge holders, not to mention rigid and dictatorial, and compromise had never been in their vocabulary. Their selfishness was innate, he was positive, and Maya had the potential to be the same.

He couldn't let her. He had to take charge, teach her how to manage the Donati flaws, help her grow up to be a better person, a better person than he was. A better person than either of his parents.

He also had the opportunity to create something new out of the ashes of the old, something different. Something new. A legacy without all the emotional manipulation his parents used, lashing out at each other and using their child as a go-between. A legacy without hatred or rage. Where a child was safe.

In fact, the more he thought about it, the more certain he became. Under his guidance, Maya could be part of a new generation, the start of a healthier legacy that would erase the toxic history of his family.

There was, of course, one small catch. Lark.

She was standing in front of him, that gorgeous smile of hers gone. Her face was pink with anger, her sea-green eyes fierce and determined.

Kissing her had been a mistake and he knew it. He'd hoped it would remind her of their physical chemistry that night, jolt her into admitting she'd been pretending all along. Yet it had backfired on him, reminding him of how good it had been to have her beneath him, and he didn't need any more memories of that. Especially considering she'd said that she had none.

An accident that had erased her memory...

He wasn't sure he believed her. It seemed far-fetched and a little too convenient, and made him wonder if she was lying in order to keep her child. He couldn't blame her for that. He might even do the same thing himself, though it wouldn't make any difference.

Maya was his and now he knew about her, now he'd made the decision to claim her, he was going to do so immediately and nothing and no one was going to stand in his way. He hadn't let anyone do so before and he wouldn't let anyone do so now.

Only your parents.

Ah, but that was different. He'd only been a boy back then, thinking that if he was obedient enough, good enough, they wouldn't argue about him any more. That they wouldn't argue, full stop. It had all been in vain, though. Nothing had made them stop hurting each other and him, and after they'd died, after his mother had nearly killed him, the only thing he could think was that if you couldn't beat them, you joined them.

So he had. People did what he said, jumped through his hoops, or simply jumped when he told them to because that's what he wanted and what he wanted he got.

He was a Donati through and through, and Donatis were selfish, and he didn't care.

'If you don't want a paternity test, then you don't want one,' he said. 'But I'm claiming my daughter regardless.'

A hot green spark lit in her eyes and perhaps it was perverse of him to enjoy that spark even more than her bright, placating smile. Nevertheless, he did. He liked the angry flush in her cheeks too. That same flush had been there the night he'd lain between her thighs and pleasured her with his tongue, leaving her trembling and crying out his name.

'You will not,' she said hotly. 'She's not yours. She's no one's but mine.'

'Do you really think you can stop me, Miss Edwards? I have governments in my pocket and resources you can't possibly imagine. If I want her, I'll take her and there's nothing you can do about it.'

He expected her to give in. That she'd realise how little power she had in this scenario and that giving him exactly what he wanted was the best course of action.

Except she didn't.

Instead she took a step forward, getting into his personal space in much the same way as he'd got into hers. As if she wasn't afraid of him or the fact that he was nearly a full foot taller than she was.

She looked up into his face, her eyes full of fury, and a very male part of him growled in appreciation. She was *exceptionally* pretty when she was angry.

'That's really how you want to play this?' she demanded. 'You'd take my daughter away from her home? Rip her away from everything she's ever known, including her mother just because you feel some kind of strange territorial possessiveness?'

He stiffened at her tone. 'That's not what—'

'How dare you?' She took another step, her eyes blazing. 'How *dare* you think you can take my daughter from me? Men like you are all the same. Just because you're rich and powerful, you think that can take whatever you want.' She took yet another step closer, and this time, rather to his own surprise, he found he was the one taking an automatic step back. 'She's only a little over a year old,' Lark continued fiercely. 'She's a *baby*. Don't you care how that might affect her?' She stepped forward again and again he stepped back. 'But no, you don't care, do you? You don't care about how that might affect her or me. And God, you *kissed* me, damn you.' She continued forward, her hands clenched into fists at her side, her green eyes glittering with outrage. 'Did you ever think that perhaps that wouldn't be welcome? That I might not want it? No, of course you didn't. It never occurred to you because the only thing you care about is yourself, you stupid, selfish, *horrible* man!'

Cesare found himself backed halfway to the doorway, Lark standing furiously in front of him, her delicate features pink, her eyes full of fire. And he was glad she didn't actually have a weapon in her possession, because he was pretty sure she might have used it on him. He was surprised she hadn't lashed out with one of those small, tightly clenched fists.

And while some of him was incensed that she'd had the gall to speak to him like that, most of him was shocked. Because no one *did* speak to him like that, let alone a woman he barely knew.

Are you surprised? You told her you were going to take her child from her.

Fine. Maybe he'd been hasty with that threat. Maybe he'd let his anger at the situation run away with him, which was *always* a mistake. The hot Donati temper was a flaw he had to keep in check, and he'd always prided himself on his control over his emotions. Clearly, though, in this instance, his control wasn't as good as he'd thought. He didn't give other people's feelings much thought either, but he had to admit that the fury in Lark's eyes got to him.

In fact, now that he thought about it, taking his daughter the way he'd threatened to wasn't the change he'd been hoping to make. Giovanni had taken *him* away from Bianca, his mother, and he knew how that had ended. He couldn't do the same thing, especially when he was hoping to start a new legacy.

Yes, he was a selfish man and he owned that. He was exactly as his parents had made him. But he didn't want that for the next generation, which meant he needed to set a better example. Start as he meant to continue and all that.

Cesare was used to changing his mind quickly. Being adaptable was vital in business, because rigidity meant stagnation and that's all the Donatis had been doing for centuries. Doing the same thing, going over the same ground. Wasting time killing the competition because that was 'the Donati way' instead of changing how they dealt with that competition.

He had to change now. Because while all the accusations Lark had thrown at him were correct, there was one that wasn't. He might be selfish and horrible, but he wasn't stupid.

Gritting his teeth, he put a leash on his temper and looked down at her, standing so small and indomitable in front of him. A wisp of golden hair had come out of her ponytail and lay across one pink cheekbone.

She was as lovely as he remembered, all soft and sweet and smelling of vanilla. He could still feel the brush of her mouth against his from that ill-advised kiss...

'You're entitled to your opinion of me, little bird.' He injected as much cool into his tone as he could to drain the heat from the moment. 'Some of it may even be correct. However, I'm nothing if not an excellent businessman and so I'll offer you a deal. You allow me a paternity test and if your daughter isn't mine, you'll never hear from me again. And if she is, then we'll sit down like civilised human beings and decide what to do from there.'

CHAPTER THREE

LARK WAS PRACTICALLY vibrating with rage, even as a part of her was appalled at how completely she'd lost her head. Calling him a horrible, selfish man was way out of line, especially when he was not only a stranger to her, but also a potential and very important client for Ravenswood Antiques.

Except not only had he brought up what had been a terrifying time in her life, that she'd thought she'd put behind her, he'd also gone after the one thing she'd do anything to protect: Maya. He'd threatened to take her daughter and she wasn't going to stand for it.

When her father had threatened to take Lark away from her mother, Grace Edwards's answer had been to run, and that had been fair since her father had been powerful and had money, while her mother had nothing. She'd taken Lark out of France, where she'd been born, and escaped to Australia, Grace's home country, where she'd managed to keep Lark hidden away for years.

Lark didn't know anything about Cesare Donati himself, but his family's history made it clear that they were ruthless and let nothing stand in their way when it came to getting what they wanted. He would come after her, she was sure of it, and then she'd be forced into the same situation as her mother had been. Grace had done what she could for Lark, but being on the run continually hadn't made for a great childhood, and God knew, Lark didn't want that for Maya.

Signor Donati had folded his arms across his broad chest and was looking down at her from his great height, his blue eyes now as cool as the ice in his voice. He was so much taller and more powerful than she was, and not only physically. Yet he'd still let himself be backed halfway across the room by her. And yes, he'd definitely *let* her.

She didn't know how to feel about that, whether to be pleased that she'd managed to unsettle him, or to be even more furious at being placated. But while she couldn't deny that allowing herself to be angry with him had felt oddly freeing, she couldn't permit herself any more. That really *would* be a mistake. She'd already called him a stupid, selfish, horrible man and that would disappoint Mr Ravenswood.

'Well?' Signor Donati demanded, impatience in his deep voice.

She tried to get a handle on her anger, forcing herself to put it aside and think objectively about the deal he'd offered.

He could be lying about being Maya's father; that was the issue, though, why he'd lie about it she had no idea. Also, he wasn't wrong. A paternity test *would* clear up that side of things. Certainly if Maya ended up *not* being his then Lark wouldn't have to deal with him again.

And if she is his?

He'd promised they'd sit down like civilised adults and talk, so that was something. Still, she didn't want to even think about that possibility yet, and she wasn't going to allow any testing to happen until she had that promise in writing. She wouldn't allow Mr Ravenswood to be penalised either.

'Okay,' she said. 'But I want you to promise that you'll also sell your antiques to Ravenswood. If you take your business elsewhere, Mr Ravenswood would be very disappointed, and this situation has nothing to do with him. It's between us.'

His gaze narrowed to sharp splinters of blue and he was silent a long moment. Then he said, 'I will not be apologising for that kiss.'

A sparking, prickling electricity shivered over her skin as the memory of his lips on hers stole through her, making her face feel hot yet again, and a thread of anger escaped. 'Like hell you won't,' she said flatly. 'You took it without asking and I'll be having that apology, in addition to all those other promises, in writing.'

A muscle in his jaw ticked. 'You don't trust my word?'

'No. I wouldn't trust you as far as I could throw you.'

He tilted his head, heat flickering in his eyes again. 'You did that night. You trusted me enough to come to my bed.'

The prickle of electricity over Lark's skin became more intense, a throbbing ache she'd never felt before gripping her. 'Do you have to mention that?' she asked tightly.

His hard mouth curved. 'It seems relevant to the situation at hand.'

Don't you wish you could remember, though? What it must have been like to sleep with him?

No. No she didn't wish it. She was glad, very glad, that she didn't remember. In fact, she'd come to a place of peace with it, and she would have been quite happy for those memories never to return, except...

There was a rising heat inside her, and she couldn't

help but notice how his suit jacket seemed to highlight the impressive width of his shoulders, while his trousers did wonderful things to his lean waist and powerful thighs. He wore a plain white business shirt and a silk tie that echoed the deep blue of his eyes, and he...

Her mouth dried. He was just beautiful.

'You were willing,' he went on, his voice softer, deeper. 'Very willing, in fact. Which also seems relevant.'

Unexpectedly, something tight and hard inside her that she'd thought she'd put behind her after Maya had been born, relaxed. The sessions she'd had with the psychologist had helped with her fears around that night, but there had always been a little splinter of uncertainty she'd never been able to get rid of.

You weren't raped or forced. That's something.

Perhaps. If she believed him.

'I only have your word for that,' she said, not wanting to admit anything to him just yet.

His imperious dark brows rose. 'You really think I'd take an unwilling woman to bed?'

'I don't know,' she said. 'Would you?'

'Absolutely not,' he replied, with no hesitation at all. 'Why would I? When I have an embarrassment of willing women to choose from?'

You're not making things better.

Lark took a deep, silent breath. No, she wasn't. And throwing around accusations of sexual assault wouldn't help the situation.

Yet even though her shock was wearing off a little, that kernel of ice was still sitting in the pit of her stomach. Him telling her that she'd spent the night with him hadn't jogged anything loose. Not even that kiss had. She also found it difficult to believe that he'd wanted her. Because why? She was a nobody, and while she might be inoffensive to look at, she certainly wasn't in supermodel territory. She didn't have much idea about what kind of women men like him went for, but she was pretty certain it wasn't women like her.

'Why me, then?' she asked, since as he'd said, that 'seemed relevant'.

The look in his eyes gleamed. 'Why do you want to know? Do you want to remember?'

She felt herself flushing yet again. She *didn't* want to know. She *didn't* want to remember. She'd put her fears and doubts about that night into a box and shoved them into a corner of her mind, never to be opened again.

Yet now Signor Donati, damn him, had opened that box and all those fears and doubts were spilling out again. What if that night had been terrible, for example? What if the conception of her beautiful daughter had been hurried, awkward and unpleasant? What if the man she'd slept with had been a liar? What if he'd been drunk? What if he'd been married? What if he'd slipped something into her drink and she had no injuries because she'd been unconscious?

What if he is *telling the truth? What if you* did *sleep with him? And what if that night was good?*

Yet even admitting that possibility felt dangerous, since she didn't understand how she'd ever have agreed to go to dinner with him, let alone go back to his villa, no matter how helpful or attractive she'd found him. She simply didn't trust men enough for that, and especially not a powerful man like this one.

So no, she didn't know why she was asking him about that night. She wasn't curious and she didn't need to know, because there was going to be no interaction between them after this.

That paternity test would prove that he wasn't Maya's father.

Why are you so sure about that?

Because she wouldn't accept any other outcome.

'No,' she said shortly. 'I don't want to know. Forget I ever said anything.'

His blue gaze never left hers and he studied her for another long moment. Then he said unexpectedly, 'I did not hurt you. And you should know that you wanted me every bit as badly as I wanted you.'

Lark's heartbeat thumped. She couldn't imagine wanting any man badly, let alone this one, not when he was everything she should hate. How had it happened? How had she managed to get herself seduced—

No, she didn't want to know. She didn't want to fall into an endless doubt spiral about what had happened that night, where there were too many questions and not enough answers.

Cesare Donati might have the answers you're looking for.

He might. But he could also be lying and as she'd already told him, she didn't trust him. Not an inch. All those stories about him that she'd read on the plane had mentioned his many lovers, and while he was supposedly childless, for all she knew he not only had a woman in every port, but a couple of unacknowledged bastards too. He was also reputed to treat his lovers well—who really knew? He could be abusive and paying people to stay quiet.

'Sorry,' she said, steeling herself. 'But I don't believe you. And as to the rest of your promises, like I said, I'm going to need them and that apology, in writing.'

He eyed her. 'I would not lie to you. Not about that night.'

'I don't care. If I don't have your signature on a piece of paper agreeing to all those things you just said, then you're not going to see Maya.'

His expression tightened a moment, then it smoothed and he shrugged as if none of this was of any moment. 'Very well. I will have my legal team draw up something for you.'

Lark, expecting him to keep arguing, gave him a suspicious look. Had she missed something? Was there a catch somewhere perhaps?

You catch more flies with honey, don't forget.

Oh, she couldn't forget. She had to stay calm, stay polite. Bury her outrage. However, she wasn't going to let him get away with dictating everything. He might have all the money and all the power, but she was Maya's mother. And if he wanted access, then he'd have to go through Lark to get it.

'Thank you.' She kept her voice cool.

'So, how long are you here?'

'Just tonight. I'll be flying back to London tomorrow. I want to get back to Maya as soon as I can.'

'Of course, you do,' he said. 'Would you prefer to leave tonight?'

Her gaze narrowed. Why was he being so agreeable now? 'I would, yes,' she said. 'But there were no flights available tonight and I wasn't sure how long it would take being here.'

'It will take no time at all,' he said smoothly. 'What time would you like to fly home?'

She stared at him, taken aback. 'All the flights were full. At least they were when I last checked.'

'They are not full.' There was nothing but supreme confidence in his voice. 'My jet can accommodate you.'

Lark blinked. 'Your what?'

'My private jet. It can leave whenever we're ready.'

'Wait.' Her gut tightened. 'What do you mean 'we'?'

His eyes gleamed, hot and blue. 'I mean, I'll be coming with you.'

'No,' Lark said, anger once more leaping in her eyes. 'You absolutely will not.'

He'd been expecting her to say that, but unfortunately, he wasn't going to give her any choice. He'd be coming to London with or without her, because now that she'd agreed to his deal—and he was glad she had—he'd decided that he wanted to see his daughter ASAP.

'Fine,' he said easily. 'Then I'll take my jet and you can fly commercial. I hope you can find a flight tonight, but if not, we can meet tomorrow in London.'

Her chin jutted, her expression tightening with frustration. 'Why do you want to come to London at all?'

He shouldn't feel pleased that he was getting to her or satisfied, because really, who was she to him? A one-night stand two years ago, that was all. Yet, he couldn't deny that he was relishing the anger in her lovely eyes and the stain of pink in her pretty skin. And the primitive male part of him wanted to keep pushing her, find out exactly how much she remembered of the night they'd spent together. Because he was sure that even if the injury had wiped her memory, her body hadn't forgotten him.

Her mouth had been soft under his when he'd kissed her, her hands on his chest exerting no pressure. She hadn't avoided his kiss and the pulse at the base of her throat had been beating hard and fast. Her pupils had been dilated as he'd raised his head, and he was sure the flush in her cheeks hadn't been anger then.

Until she'd pushed him away, of course, which she'd had every right to do.

Still, her body remembered and he was tempted, so tempted, to test that. Then again, she'd had to push him away because he'd forgotten himself and if one kiss had the power to do that to him, then testing her might very well test him, and he couldn't afford that. Not again. That night had been a one-off and he hadn't changed his mind.

In fact, perhaps it was even a blessing that she didn't remember. That way he didn't need to fight his own urge to revisit it as well as hers, since obviously if she had remembered, she'd want another night. They all did.

So there would be no more kisses, and whatever chemistry was between them, he'd let it lie. He didn't need to revisit that particular memory and he wasn't going to.

'Obviously I need to speak with Mr Ravenswood personally,' he said. 'And the sooner the better. I would also like to visit my daughter.'

Lark looked as if she wanted to shout at him again, and it was probably wrong of him to hope that she might. She was like an angry kitten, all small and soft, turning her sharp claws on him, and part of him wanted to see what else she might do if he got her really wound up.

She hadn't been like that the night they'd had in Rome. She'd talked to him openly about her life and how much she'd loved her mother. There had been something about a custody battle with her French father, and how her mother had taken her away to bring her up in Australia. How they'd had to move around a lot in case anyone found them.

He'd been intrigued by the story and had empathised

with her, making oblique references to his own struggles with his parents, though he hadn't told her the whole truth.

About how his mother had ultimately tried to kill him and then his father had shot her and then himself. That had been too dark a story and he hadn't wanted to go into it.

Lark had been so sympathetic and concerned at what he had told her. They'd been sitting in the library of his villa and she'd been leaning forward, listening. Then once he'd told her all about it, she'd put one small hand over his and that had been all it had taken for their steadily building chemistry to ignite.

Her touch had burned and when he'd looked into her eyes, he'd seen all that sea-green catch alight too, and when he'd pulled her into his arms, she hadn't resisted. Her mouth had been soft and hot, opening beneath his as if they were lovers already, and her arms had twined around his neck. She'd clung to him as if she hadn't been able to bear letting him go.

But he couldn't think about that night. It was over and done with.

'You can't see Maya,' Lark snapped. 'I forbid it.'

'Very well,' he replied smoothly. 'Then I'll wait until after the paternity test results come through.'

'You'll be waiting a while, so you won't need to come to London now, will you?'

'On the contrary. I can get test results the same day, and of course I'll need to meet with Ravenswood.'

She was breathing very fast, anger glittering in her eyes.

You are being unfair. She's Maya's mother and she's likely to be in shock. Why are you letting your wounded pride get to you?

The thought sent a sharp jolt through him. His pride wasn't wounded, of course it wasn't. And one woman not remembering their one-night stand didn't affect him in the slightest. His child was important and worth fighting for, that was all. It was true that if she'd indeed had an accident, then it wasn't her fault that she hadn't let him know about Maya's existence. It was also fair to say that since he was a complete stranger to her, him threatening to take her daughter must be frightening. Especially considering what she'd told him about her own father and how he'd pursued her and her mother.

It was clear she thought Cesare would do the same and doing nothing to dispel her doubts wasn't helping either of them.

Cesare had always been sure of himself and of what he wanted, and anger had propelled him to take charge of Donati Bank and institute all the changes his father had always refused to make, hauling a centuries-old bank into the twenty-first century.

He'd got rid of the accounts of tax evaders and money launderers, of arms dealers and drug barons, of dictators and terrorists. He made transparent secretive bank practices and opened special accounts for charities with excellent interest rates, zero fees and competitive financial management services.

Burning the old rules of his ancestors made Donati Bank *better*.

But anger wasn't his fuel any longer. Like love, it was a toxic emotion and one he'd put away. He still didn't much care for the emotions of others, though, and yet he was contemplating Lark's feelings now and it concerned him that he felt almost…guilty for threatening her. She was only defending her child and in her place he would have done the same. In fact, he'd probably have done worse.

'I just want to see her, little bird,' he said, softening his tone slightly. 'I'm not going to take her away from you.'

Lark's expression remained suspicious and angry. 'Why do you call me that?'

Something inside him jolted. He hadn't realised he'd even said it and now he had the impression that he'd said it more than once. 'I called you that in our night together,' he admitted reluctantly. 'You liked it.'

'Well, I don't now.' She eyed him. 'Nothing I say to you will make you change your mind will it?'

He was adaptable, it was true, but once a course of action had been decided on, he never changed it. Especially if he felt strongly about that course of action, and he did now.

'No,' he said. 'It will not.' He held her gaze, let her see the truth. Let her see the ruthlessness that made him a Donati of old through and through. He'd been brought up to be as terrible as his ancestors and he was. He made no apology for that.

But he would be the last of them.

Maya would be the first of a better, brighter generation. A kinder generation.

He'd make sure of it.

Lark took a breath and glanced away. Her hands uncurled from their fists, fingers stretching out a couple of times as if she was trying to relax them.

'Fine,' she said after a moment, looking back at him. 'But she'll be asleep when we get home and I'm not waking her up just so you can see her. You'll have to wait until tomorrow morning.'

'I can live with that,' he said.

It would do him no harm to wait, and there was no point antagonising her more than he had already. She *was* Maya's mother after all, and while his own had been a ridiculous excuse for one, it was obvious that Lark was a different kettle of fish. She was fierce and protective, which his own mother, too involved in her own petty jealousies and intrigues over his father, had never been. He approved. In fact, he'd already decided that she would have to be a part of Maya's life.

Is that really your decision to make?

Well, no, it was hers too. But he'd meant what he said when he'd told her that he wouldn't take Maya away from her—a child needed a loving mother and it was obvious that Lark was indeed loving.

However, he wouldn't allow himself to be cut out of her life either. She was a Donati, heir to a vast fortune and the poisonous legacy that came with it, and she would need him to guide her around the pitfalls and traps that being a Donati entailed.

She would need him to set her on the right path, to ensure that the poison that infiltrated his entire family tree stopped with him. That she would never carry the same stain.

Lark was still looking deeply unhappy at the thought of him coming to London. Too bad. She would have to get used to the idea of him being in her life now, the two of them tied to a little girl neither of them had expected.

'I just don't understand why you want this,' Lark said unexpectedly. 'You never even knew of her existence until ten minutes ago and now suddenly you want to run a paternity test and come to London to see her. Threaten to take her away from me. Why? She's nothing to you.'

'She is not nothing to me,' he said. 'And we shared more than our bodies that night, Lark. You won't remember, but I did tell you that I never wanted children. Never wanted a family, not with a history as toxic as the Donatis' history is. But then I saw the photo of her on your phone and I knew she was mine.'

'What? Just like that?'

He saw no reason to deny it. 'Yes, just like that. Call it an instinct. But whatever it was, I know she's my daughter, which makes her my responsibility. And I'm not a man who walks away from his responsibilities.'

'You can walk away from this one, believe me. I won't mind if you do. In fact, I'd even prefer that you do.'

'No.' He put every ounce of authority into the word. 'I will not leave any child of mine without a father, especially not a Donati child. She'll be my heir and inherit a wealth and a legacy that are beyond your wildest dreams, little bird. And she'll need me to guide her in how to manage both.'

Lark's lovely mouth tightened. 'Do you know how unbelievably arrogant that sounds?'

He shrugged. He didn't much care how arrogant or otherwise people thought he was. Arrogance was part and parcel of the Donati way, and he was all that and more. Arrogant, and selfish, just as his parents had been. But what made him different was that he owned it. They never had.

'I don't care how it sounds,' Cesare said. 'As long as you know that I will be part of Maya's life whether you want me to be or not.'

'Only if you're really her father. I could have slept with other men that night, you don't know.'

He allowed himself a smile at that. 'You were in my bed all night, Lark. And we didn't sleep. So unless you have the ability to be in two places at once, I'm pretty sure that the only man you were with that night was me.'

'I could have had a boyfriend.'

'But you didn't. You told me so.'

'I might have lied.'

But he was tired of this conversation. Now that he'd

made the decision to fly to London, he was impatient to be there. Impatient to see Maya. And he had to get his lawyers to draw up an agreement, then let his staff know he'd be taking the jet.

'You didn't lie.' He walked over to the table and placed her phone down on it, then took his own out of his pocket and glanced down at the screen. 'You were a virgin.'

'What?'

He glanced up at her shocked gaze. 'You told me you were a virgin and indeed you were. Now, are you coming with me to London or are you going back to your hotel?'

CHAPTER FOUR

LARK BADLY WANTED to tell Cesare Donati where he could put his stupid agreement.

He'd handed it to her the moment they'd got on his luxurious private plane—how he'd managed to have it drawn up in the time it took for them to go from his palazzo to the private airport where he kept the Donati jet she didn't know, but she'd spent all the taxi and taking off time going over it.

She wasn't a lawyer, but she'd had to deal with various legal documents while being Mr Ravenswood personal assistant, so it wasn't a difficult read. In fact it was unfortunately very clear. She almost wished it wasn't, just so she could keep on arguing about it with him.

She badly wanted to keep on arguing with him full stop.

Deciding to fly with him instead of flying commercial had been a mistake, but there had been no seats available on any flights to London out of Rome that night, and since she wasn't going to let him get to London ahead of her—she didn't want him seeing Maya without her present and given the arrogance of the man, that was something he might insist on to spite her—she hadn't had much option but to take up his offer of a flight.

Which meant that now she had to spend the next couple of hours in the company of the man who'd casually informed her that she'd been a virgin when they'd spent the night together. The night she had no memory of.

She'd had no idea what to say to that, not that he'd given her any time to respond since by then he'd taken his phone out of his pocket and had started arranging seemingly the entire world, leaving her to be carried along in his wake.

The next couple of hours had been spent fuming about his arrogance since that was easier than contemplating the ice that sat in her gut as they'd dropped by her hotel to pick up her stuff before carrying on to the airport.

Now she was sitting in one of the plush white leather seats of his private jet, trying to find her usual good humour and failing miserably.

She was furious and afraid, and she didn't know what to do with either of those emotions, since she'd always tried very hard not to dwell on negative feelings.

Anger was better than fear though, so she gripped hard to it, thinking about how he'd casually pointed out her virginity to her, as if that was something she'd forgotten too. Because no, of course, she hadn't forgotten. In fact, that was another thing she'd lost in the aftermath of that night, her first sexual experience. The memory of that was gone, there was no going back, and she didn't need him pointing that out to her.

Damn Cesare Donati. Damn him to hell.

Anger doesn't help, remember?

Yet knowing that didn't ease the hot, bright stinging emotion that sat inside her. When she'd been a child, her mother's fragility would sometimes weigh on her. The feeling of having to always be the one who was happy and strong, of never being allowed to be angry or sad in case that would push her mother into another downward spiral. As if she was the mother and her mother was the daughter who had to be protected and kept safe.

It had been hard at times, so she used to take herself off and bury her head in a book, a distraction from all that sharp-edged, hot emotion, and most of the time that had worked. The emotion usually faded.

But there were no books here and the thing currently making her angry was right in her face, pacing up and down the plane's small aisle as he talked on his phone in rapid, musical Italian.

He didn't seem to be a man who knew what stillness was, his presence a relentless kinetic energy that had her tensing in her seat every time he strode past.

She wished he'd sit down, because it was starting to get to her.

You like it. You find it attractive.

Lark gritted her teeth, trying to drag her attention back to the stupid agreement she'd insisted he draw up, but she kept getting distracted by him walking up and down, brushing past her in a delicious cloud of cedar and heat. Making her achingly aware of his physicality, of the way he moved, purposefully and with an athletic, masculine grace that made her pulse race.

Her gaze drifted from the words in front of her up to his tall figure coming to the end of the aisle and then pacing back.

Had he been like that in bed, when they'd slept together? Had he been this purposeful and powerful? Had she let it overwhelm her? Had she let him seduce her?

You'll never know now, will you?

She didn't understand why that made her ache with a hollow kind of loss.

Her mother had warned her about men and all the ways

they could hurt a woman, about how they could take advantage and manipulate. Lark had to be careful, she said. They might seem nice on the outside, wine and dine you and make you feel like a princess. But only once they'd caught you would their true colours become apparent, and that's when it became dangerous.

Lark's father hadn't been abusive until about a year into their marriage and by then Grace had been living in a country where she didn't speak the language and had no friends. She'd been isolated, cut off from her support networks, and then Lark had been born, making it impossible for Grace to leave.

It was your fault, you know that right? If you hadn't been born—

Lark shoved that thought from her head. It was a negative, depressing one and she didn't want it there.

Regardless, she'd taken to heart her mother's lessons on men and she couldn't think how Cesare Donati, arrogance personified and red flags from here to Australia, had managed to get under her defences.

He'd told her that they'd talked and talked for a long time. About what though? She couldn't imagine talking to him about anything, let alone for hours and hours. Then letting him seduce her, take her virginity… What had she been thinking?

It was true that she'd gone to Rome because she'd been grieving her mother. She'd just moved to England and escaping into a book wasn't enough this time to keep the dark thoughts at bay. She'd needed to get out of the cold, wet grey London, and had settled on Rome. Bright and sunny, with lots of history. Perfect, she'd thought.

Men had been the very last thing on her mind.

The first few days had been great, wandering the ancient streets and sightseeing, but then she'd been in a tour group at the Colosseum and had seen a family talking excitedly together. The man had hoisted a little girl on his shoulders while his wife had smiled and said something that had made all three of them laugh.

For some reason that had made her ache. She'd never had that. Never been part of a family laughing and enjoying each other's company. It had only ever been her and her mother, and her mother's relentless anxiety. They'd never gone on holiday, never even had a fun day out, not when Grace was constantly worried about the risk of discovery. It had been a tough childhood in many ways, though even thinking about it in those terms made Lark feel disloyal.

Her mother wouldn't have even been in that position if she hadn't had Lark.

Lark had felt…lonely. Then she'd had her handbag stolen, which hadn't helped, and then…she remembered nothing after that until the hospital. But in that blank space between realising her handbag had gone and waking up in the hospital bed, she'd met him. And he'd helped her, taken her out for dinner, taken her back to his house, and they'd…slept together.

He strode past her once again, keeping up a stream of Italian, and she watched him despite herself. Tall, powerful, authoritative. In total command of himself and the rarefied world he inhabited. Who was he talking to now? The prime minister of some country? The CEO of a huge multinational? The ruler of a nation?

She knew nothing about him beyond what was in the media, but he knew something of her and perhaps more than something. What had they talked about together? What had she told him? How had they connected so strongly that she'd given him her body?

Lark shut her eyes and tried to force her thoughts away from him. Thinking about him would only bring back her own feelings of dread about what had happened that night. About all the questions she didn't have answers to. It would undo all the work she'd done with the psychologist and the peace she'd come to with her lack of memories, and she didn't want that.

She had to look forward not back; that's what she had to keep telling herself. No matter how attractive he was or the current of excitement that hummed just beneath her skin, the unfamiliar ache of craving a touch she didn't remember.

Finally, the stream of Italian ceased as he stopped in the middle of the aisle and put his phone away. Then he turned and paced back to where she sat, pausing beside her seat.

'You have finished reading?' he asked. 'Is it acceptable?'

She badly wished there had been something she could nitpick, but she hadn't been able to find a single thing. Everything he'd promised was in there, even the apology for the kiss.

'Yes,' she said with very bad grace.

Without a word, he produced a pen, made her sign it then signed it himself with a flourish. Then he picked up the paper and like magic a stewardess appeared, taking the document from his outstretched hand and disappearing up the front of the plane.

'Does that always happen?' Lark asked.

He'd taken his phone out again and was staring at the screen. 'Does what always happen?'

'Someone appears out of nowhere to do your bidding without you even asking?'

'Generally, yes.' He put his phone back in his pocket,

stared down at her for a moment. Then much to her discomfort, he deposited himself in the seat directly opposite hers, stretching his long legs out in front of him. 'Is that supposed to be another comment on my arrogance?'

She needed to find her smile again, find the good humour and optimism that had helped her mother through so many tough times, because she didn't like this anger that sat like a burning coal inside her. It was as if he'd ignited a fire inside her that now refused to go out and nothing she could do would get rid of it.

'No, of course not.' She forced herself to smile. 'Please forget I said it.'

He stared at her silently, his blue gaze laser-like in its focus. 'You have a pretty smile, little bird,' he said after a moment. 'But I think I prefer your anger. That at least isn't fake.'

The coal inside her glowed hot and no matter how hard she tried to resist, she couldn't stop herself from snapping, 'It's not fake.'

'Yes, it is. You're very angry with me so why bother smiling?'

'Because I'm trying to be polite,' she said tightly.

He tilted his head, frowning. 'Why?'

'Well, aside from the fact that you're a complete stranger, you're also a potential client of Mr Ravenswood.' She was aware she was clutching the armrests of her seat far too hard, her knuckles white. 'Not to mention that you're also a very powerful—'

'Yes, yes, a banker, a Donati heir, etcetera,' he interrupted impatiently. 'But you didn't seem to find all those such an issue the night we spent together, so why are they now?'

'Because first you threatened to take my child from me

and wouldn't take no for an answer,' she shot back. 'Then you told me casually that the night we slept together, the night I remember nothing about, I was a virgin.'

'Yes,' he said without a single shred of shame. 'What of it?'

Lark took her hands off the arms of her seat and leaned forward. 'You don't think that I might be angry about any of that? That my child means nothing to me? That I might be horrified at the thought of my first time being with a man I'm liking less and less with each passing second, and who doesn't seem to care that I have no memory of being with him? Of losing my virginity to him?'

He tilted his head, studying her, and she could hear the anger and the thread of fear in her voice ringing uncomfortably loud in the interior of the plane. It seemed to be even louder than the engines.

Shame gripped her. Giving in to her anger was a mistake, no matter how afraid she was. There had been that time when she'd been ten years old and they'd stayed a couple of months in some tiny town in South Australia. She'd made a friend, the first one she'd had for years, and she'd been starting to think that maybe this time they might stay. That her father had stopped looking and finally they were safe.

Then something had happened to make her mother scared and she'd come home from school to find everything packed and Grace trying to get her into the car because they were leaving. She'd screamed at her mother then, an eruption of rage bursting out of her, that no she wasn't going and how could her mother do this to her when Lark finally had a best friend? She didn't want to go. She wanted to stay there.

Grace hadn't got angry. She hadn't screamed back. No,

what she'd done then had been worse. She'd burst into tears, sobbing and sobbing, making Lark feel like the worst person in the world.

'Please, Lark. I'm just trying to protect you,' Grace had wept. 'I'm just trying to keep us both safe. Don't you want us to be safe?'

Of course she did. And things were already hard. She didn't need to make them worse by upsetting her mother even more than she already had. So she'd swallowed her anger, done what Grace had asked and got into the car, and they'd left that small town, her mother silently crying all the way.

Anger hurt people. Yet Cesare Donati didn't look hurt or upset, or even annoyed. He just sat there looking smug, as if her anger hadn't touched him, and she had to admit that saying all those things to him in a fury had definitely felt…freeing.

'If you're waiting for me to apologise for that,' she said stiffly. 'You'll be waiting a long time.'

Signor Donati's blue gaze had become smoky, glittering as he studied her. 'Apologise for what?' His voice was deep and dark. 'You can say anything you like to me.' He was looking at her now as if he was hungry, as if she was a meal set before him and he was starving. 'You're pretty when you smile, little bird, but I think you're beautiful when you're angry.'

The excitement humming just beneath her skin crackled, her heart squeezing in her chest. No one had ever called her beautiful before and definitely not after she'd shouted in a temper.

'Don't say that,' she said huskily.

'Why shouldn't I? It's true. And all those things you said were true too. You have every right to be upset about your child, and as for your virginity… Well.' His gaze roamed over her as if he couldn't get enough of the sight of her. 'Let's just say you gave me a precious gift and I treated it as such.'

Her mouth was dry, her pulse still racing. 'I already told you, I only have your word for that.'

'And I am a man of my word.' One dark brow rose. 'If you doubt me, perhaps you need another reminder.'

The hot coal inside her flared, a burning ember, and this time she didn't know whether it was anger or something else, something hotter, something that matched the hunger in his eyes. Making her feel restless, making her ache.

He was turning her inside out, damn him. Making her feel as if she was a different person, someone angry and snappy and shrill. And no matter how freeing that might feel, she didn't like it.

'No, thank you.' She tried very hard to ignore that hot coal. 'I'm certain once was enough.'

Signor Donati said nothing, but his mouth curved and she found herself staring at the perfectly carved, full shape of his lower lip, the only thing that was soft about him. Everywhere else he seemed…hard. Certainly his chest had been hard when she'd reached up to push him, the muscles beneath the wool of his jacket like iron.

And that smile… There was a sensuality to it, a heat. A knowledge that taunted her, tugged at her. A knowledge echoed in the wicked glint of his blue eyes.

Her breath caught.

He was so devastatingly attractive and at the same time so completely smug, it was enraging.

He knows and you don't, so why continue to let him have that power?

A very good question. She'd been telling herself for

two years she didn't want to know what had happened that night. She had Maya and she had to look to the future, not keep going over the past. But now Cesare Donati had come into her life and had casually upended it, and now she was questioning everything.

She didn't like his certainty or how he had this knowledge of her that she didn't herself. It made her feel vulnerable, and she didn't want to feel vulnerable, not around a man like him.

She was also tired of not knowing. Tired of questioning. Tired of having no answers.

Perhaps now was the time to get those answers, take a little power back for herself.

'What exactly did we talk about that night?' she asked, for the first time not caring how demanding she sounded.

One of his perfectly arched, soot-black brows rose, that glint in his eyes becoming more pronounced. 'Are you sure it's our conversation you want to know about?'

Lark took another silent breath, the ache inside her intensifying. If she was honest with herself, although she did want to know what they'd talked about it, it was the other stuff she kept thinking about.

Other stuff? Such as how exactly you ended up in his bed and what you did there?

A flush crept into her cheeks. She wished she could deny those thoughts too, yet she couldn't. Her brain couldn't stop thinking about them. No, she needed to know. He was here and he could tell her, and she would be a fool to let the opportunity pass.

'I want to know everything,' she said. 'Everything we did.'

'Everything hmmm?' He studied her in that unnerving way a moment more, then leaned forward, his hands clasped between his knees, his gaze on hers. 'Well, first we talked. About books and movies. About the media and world events. About politics and scientific advances.' He paused. 'We also talked about our lives.'

Oh, God. What on earth had she told him about herself? 'What about our lives?'

'You told me about your mother and your years on the run spent hiding from your father in Australia. About what a wonderful mother she'd been to you, yet how fragile, and how you had to take care of her because of her mental health.'

Oh, no. It was worse than she'd thought. She'd literally spilled her guts to him. What had he done to make her trust him that way? She didn't understand. She might have understood if she'd met him *after* the accident, because then she could explain her apparent openness with him as a side effect of the brain injury. But not *before*.

'Why on earth would I have told you any of that?' she asked.

'We'd had a cognac or two and you told me you were in Rome because you'd just lost your mother and had wanted a holiday to get away. So I told you that I too had just lost my aunt.'

That did not make her feel any better.

She'd shared everything of herself with him and he still remembered. Yet while he might have shared with her, she'd forgotten. She'd forgotten everything. Tension gripped her.

'I was drunk?' She didn't want to ask, but she made herself. 'Is that what you're saying?'

'No.' His gaze very direct. 'You weren't drunk. I wouldn't have taken you to bed if you had been, please believe that.'

She had no reason at all to believe that, yet there was no doubting the look in his eyes. He meant what he said.

A small thread of relief wound through her. 'Okay, so if I wasn't drunk, why would I have told you all of that?'

'Because you were lonely and wanted someone to talk to, and we had a common experience.'

Lark shifted uncomfortably in her seat, remembering the family she'd seen at the Colosseum and how lonely that had made her feel. How the realisation had settled down in her that now that her mother was gone, she was essentially alone in the world. She didn't have any siblings and since her mother's parents were dead, the only other family she had was her father. But she had no desire whatsoever to connect with him.

For some reason, though, the person she'd chosen to connect with was sitting across from her now, in the shape of this arrogant, maddening, devastatingly attractive man.

'Why on earth would I chose you?' she asked.

'Let me remind you.' That smoky glint in his eyes glittered and he reached to take her hand where it lay on the armrest, holding it in his and turning it palm up.

He moved so quickly she had no time to protest and then at the feel of his fingers on her skin, she found she couldn't speak anyway. It was as if the humming static of his touch had deprived her of speech.

'I had just told you that I lost the aunt who'd brought me up,' he murmured, holding her hand in his much bigger one, his fingers long and blunt and capable. 'And you leaned forward and took my hand just like this.'

His touch was warm and he cradled her hand gently in his, stopping her breath. And she knew she should pull away, but for some reason she could only sit there as he brushed his thumb over her palm. The contact sent a burst of sensual electricity crackling over her skin and every thought flew straight out of her head.

She swallowed, staring into the vivid blue of his eyes.

'We stared at each other,' he went. 'Just like this. With our hands touching.'

'And then what happened?' she heard herself ask.

'And then?' The hungry glitter in his eyes was the only warning she got. 'Then I did this.'

And before she could move, he pulled her out of her chair and into his lap.

Cesare was playing with fire and he knew it. Yet he hadn't been able to help himself. He'd been exquisitely aware of her presence since the moment they'd boarded the plane. She'd been sitting bolt upright in her seat, studying the agreement he'd drawn up with fierce attention, and he knew that sitting near her would be a mistake. That he might try something ill-advised, something that he shouldn't do such as reminding her again of their night together.

He shouldn't, not when it was easier all round if those memories stayed forgotten. Yet there was a part of him—and no prizes for guessing which part—that desperately wanted her to remember every single second of the night she'd spent in his bed.

So he'd paced up and down the aisle of the plane, talking to various people, including his closest friend, Aristophanes Katsaros, renowned mathematical genius and self-made billionaire owner of one of the biggest finance companies on the planet.

Aristophanes, who rarely paid much attention to anything that wasn't equations or financial algorithms and had long made it known that he wasn't interested in having a family of his own, had been congratulatory about Cesare's new fatherhood status. But also dismissive of Cesare's self-control when it came to Lark.

'What does it matter if you have her again?' he'd said in his usual bored way. 'It means nothing, not if you don't want it to. Sleep with her or don't, another woman will come along in a couple of days anyway.'

Aristophanes was famous for having his assistants choose and manage his lovers, including putting them into his schedule, since he was far too busy to manage them himself. Cesare had asked him on more than one occasion what he did if his assistants chose someone he wasn't attracted to and Aristophanes had merely shrugged and told him that was impossible, since his assistants rigorously followed the checklist Aristophanes had given them.

Cesare still didn't understand, but then he didn't expect Aristophanes to understand why he was reluctant to have another night with Lark.

He barely understood himself. That night had been special, yet his doubts about repeating it had only made it even more so and he couldn't allow that.

Aristophanes was right about one thing: a repeat performance meant nothing, only that he'd enjoyed the sex and wanted to do it again. So really, did it matter if he wanted to sit down close to her? If he wanted to talk to her about that night? If he wanted to touch her?

More wisps of honey-gold hair had come out of her ponytail and the pink roses on her blouse made her pale skin even pinker, highlighting the blush that stained her cheeks whenever he looked at her. Those sea-green eyes of hers had flashed with annoyance and it satisfied him unreasonably that her annoyance was because of him.

He'd liked that he affected her and he'd liked it even

more when she'd started asking him what they'd talked about that night and getting angry. He knew that anger was because she thought she didn't want to know and yet hadn't been able to stop herself from asking.

He'd also been conscious of the way she'd watched him as he'd paced up and down the jet's aisle while talking to Aristophanes. She hadn't wanted to do that either, yet her gaze kept being drawn to him all the same.

She wanted him.

He remembered that light in her eyes, how the flecks of blue in her green eyes had glittered bright and hot when he'd pulled her into his arms. The same way they'd glittered when he'd kissed her a couple of hours back in his palazzo, and when he'd put his hand over hers just before.

The same way they were glittering now.

She was breathing very fast, her body a soft warm weight in his lap, her vanilla scent winding around him, making him relive that night all over again.

'What are you doing?' she asked, eyes wide.

'You wanted to know what happened,' he said. 'I'm telling you.'

'I don't recall asking for a demonstration.'

Her cheeks were deeply flushed, the pulse at the base of her throat beating fast. Her golden ponytail was draped over his shoulder, golden strands catching in the dark blue wool, and he felt a sudden and deep possessiveness grip him, making him tighten his hold.

'You really don't want to remember this?' he asked. 'You came into my lap that night without a protest, just the way you did now. And then you wound your arms around my neck and kissed me as if you hadn't been able to think of anything else except the way I'd taste.'

Her throat moved, her gaze locked with his. She'd softened against him, making all the blood in his veins rush below his belt. The pressure of her lovely rear against his groin making him ache.

He wanted her, he couldn't deny it. That morning when he'd returned to his villa and found his bed empty, he'd told himself he was glad. He hadn't wanted another night. He'd been there, done that, and trying to track her down was a fool's game.

He didn't chase women, not ever, and he wasn't going to change his habits just for her.

So he'd pushed her out of his thoughts, made himself forget.

But he hadn't forgotten. That night had imprinted itself on his memory and for the past two years, he hadn't been able to stop measuring every other woman he'd slept with against her. And it didn't matter how lovely or passionate or sexually inventive those women had been, something about them always came up short.

He'd told himself it wasn't because they weren't her, of course not. That night had been different because of his complicated feelings around the death of his aunt, leaving him the last Donati, nothing else. They weren't because she was special or different.

Yet looking down into her eyes now, he had to accept that perhaps she *had* been different. That the night they'd spent together *had* been special. And that he did want to revisit it after all.

It wouldn't be the same. She had no memory of their connection and while he did, he couldn't forget that she was the mother of his child.

You really want to complicate that with sex? Especially when she's clearly angry with you?

She might be angry with him, but she still wanted him;

he could see the desire flickering in her eyes. And after all, what was complicated about sex? For the past couple of months, he hadn't found himself a lover, telling himself that he was too busy. But he knew deep down that he hadn't found himself a lover because he was still searching for the experience he'd had that night, of Lark in his arms and the pleasure he'd found with her.

Now it was all he could think about.

Here she was and what they'd had that night, they could have again. Or if not that, then something similar. Where would be the harm? It could even be a good thing. Once those test results came back and Maya was revealed as his daughter, they would end up having to deal with things like custody and living arrangements, and he already had a couple of ideas about how he'd like to manage that.

In fact, he'd been thinking about it almost exclusively since he'd arranged for this little agreement to be drawn up and for the jet to be prepared.

'I might have done then,' she said. 'But I don't care how you taste right now.'

'No?' He raised a brow. 'Then why are you staring at my mouth?'

She flushed an even deeper pink, her gaze instantly lifting, her chin getting very set. 'I wasn't looking—'

'Would it be the worst thing in the world to admit that you want me?' he interrupted, tired of her denials all of a sudden. 'You had no problem letting me know that night. In fact, you didn't want to leave my bed.'

'Will you stop talking about that night?'

'Why? Does it make you feel things you don't want to feel?'

'I don't—'

Cesare laid a finger over her soft mouth, silencing her.

Her eyes narrowed, but she made no move to get off him. Instead, she opened her mouth and bit the tip of his finger.

A knife of sensation slid through him, white-hot and intense. Pure animal desire. The softness of her lips and the sharp edge of her teeth against his skin. And before he knew what he was doing, he'd taken his finger away, bent and covered that soft mouth of hers with his own.

She made a low, angry sound, but her hands were on his shoulders, her fingers digging in, holding him to her and her mouth opened, letting him in, the heat and sweet taste of her filling him.

He was hard instantly, desire gripping him by the throat. A desire he hadn't felt since that night two years ago. And he knew in that moment that it didn't matter how many other women he'd tried to bury that memory with, he'd never be able to bury it. That the only real answer was to relive it. Perhaps if he did, he'd be able to let it go once and for all.

Her mouth was so hot and so sweet and she was kissing him back the way she'd kissed him two years ago in Rome, as if she was starving for him. And he couldn't hold back. He didn't want to. He slid his tongue into her mouth, exploring, tasting, devouring her like the sweet treat she was, and this time the sound that escaped her was a sigh, a whimper of need.

Dio, he remembered that sound. When he'd first kissed her and then when he'd slid his hand beneath her shirt, touching her satiny skin. She'd arched into his palm that night, desperate for his touch, just as she was arching against him now, pressing her breasts against his chest, clearly wanting him just as much as he wanted her.

Her arms slid around his neck, her mouth hungry as she began to kiss him back, hesitant at first and then getting more needy, her tongue touching his, tasting him, exploring him.

His world began to narrow, hunger taking over, and it didn't matter that they were on his private jet that would be landing very soon, or that he wanted to see the daughter he'd never known he'd had—after all, it wouldn't be the first time he'd had a woman on his jet.

It would be so easy. He could push up the little skirt she wore, slip her underwear aside, and then he could take her in his lap. They wouldn't even have to break this mind-blowing kiss.

And then what? She's already furious with you, do you really want to make it worse? Especially when it's likely you'll have to talk to her about custody once your paternity has been confirmed. Also, have you ever thought that she might be frightened? Having no memory of a sexual experience that made her pregnant mustn't be easy.

Dio, that was all true. Anger, he liked, but he didn't want her afraid.

He broke the kiss and pulled back, staring down at her.

Her head was on his shoulder, her cheeks deeply flushed, her mouth full and red. Her eyes were as dark as a winter sea.

'Do not be afraid of me, Lark,' he said roughly. 'I know you don't trust me, but please trust this if nothing else. I did not hurt you that night and I will not hurt you now. You are safe with me.'

There it was again, the flicker of her temper. 'I'm not afraid of you.'

'Good.' He took a breath that wasn't quite as steady as it should have been. 'Because I want you. Right here. Right now.'

CHAPTER FIVE

THE PIERCING BLUE of Cesare's gaze had gone dark with desire.

For her.

Lark's heart was thundering in her ears, her skin tight, an aching pressure between her thighs. Her mouth felt full and swollen, the stunning effect of his kiss ringing through her.

One minute she'd been sitting there, fighting her anger. The next she was in his lap, surrounded by all that hard muscle and the astonishing heat of his body, his hungry gaze on hers.

She'd thought of making some protest or pushing at him the way she'd done in his palazzo, but something about the way he'd looked at her, his heat and the scent of his aftershave had made all her muscles feel heavy and slow. Then his grip had tightened, as if he hadn't wanted to let her go, and the really terrible thing, the terrible truth that had settled down in her, was that she hadn't wanted him to.

She hadn't wanted to admit to the sense of familiarity and recognition as he'd touched her either. The part of her that remembered what it had felt like to be in his arms, to be held by him, to have him close, his mouth on hers. That had felt safe with him, that knew he wouldn't hurt her, and wasn't afraid.

The part of her that *wanted* to remember. That wanted more. That was angry that her first sexual experience had been taken from her by the car that had knocked her down.

And it must have been good experience too, judging from the way he kissed you.

It wasn't fair that had been taken from her, it just wasn't, and as she'd thought just before, she was tired of not knowing. Tired of fighting herself too, because shouldn't she know? She'd talked to him, fine, but what about afterwards? When he'd kissed her and she'd kissed him back, and then he'd taken her to bed?

What had it been like? She'd experienced his kiss and to feel his mouth on hers had been so…good. But what about his touch? His hands on her bare skin? She wanted more and it was time to admit that.

He knew all these things about her and she knew nothing, and that was wrong. Yes, that gave him power and she was tired of him having all of it. Because it wasn't only the memory of that night he had, but a family legacy that went back centuries, massive wealth, and looks good enough to tempt an angel into sin. He also had authority and arrogance, and all she had was…what?

She had her child and a decent job, it was true. The flat she lived in was okay, but it was slightly run-down and there was no garden. Certainly it couldn't compare to his palazzo.

It's not just getting answers to your questions that will give you power. He wants you and that gives you power too.

The thought wound through her like champagne fizzing in her blood.

Looking up at him, she could see the need in his eyes.

The hunger. Yes, he wanted her. Right now, right here, he'd said.

They'd had one night two years ago and this powerful man, this man who had everything, hadn't been able to forget her.

There *was* power in that. Power over him.

Power and knowledge and *him*.

She might not ever get the memories of that night back, but that didn't mean she couldn't create new ones. She could give herself that couldn't she? Especially if he could make her feel as good as she suspected he could. As good as she had the night she didn't remember.

The admission eased something tight inside her, as if she'd been holding herself contained since the moment she'd met him, and now she didn't have to.

Now she could take what she wanted too.

But she wouldn't let him have it all his own way. She'd exert some of that newfound power of hers, see how that would affect him. Chip away at his arrogance. Make him wait. Make him sweat. Make him desperate.

Why not? There was also a power in not remembering too, because while she might not know the details, her body remembered. And she didn't feel nervous or unsure, because she'd already done this once. She knew he wanted her, that he hadn't been able to forget the one night he'd had with her. Which meant it had been good. Very good.

He'd buried the fingers of one hand in her hair, closing them into a fist, holding her tight, and she could feel his desperation in the strength of his grip. For the first time since they'd met, a sense of satisfaction filled her.

'Now?' she asked huskily. 'This is hardly private.'

'I'll tell my staff to stay up the front of the plane. They won't bother us.'

She lifted a hand and touched his cheekbone experimentally, her heart racing, feeling the warm satin of his skin and the faint prickle of whiskers. It felt thrilling, almost illicit to touch him like this.

Nipping his finger when he'd touched her mouth had been an automatic reaction, and she hadn't known where the urge had come from. Perhaps that was another thing to come out of that night. Whatever, now that she'd had a taste of his skin, all salty and masculine, she wanted more.

She'd never been kissed—or at least not that she remembered—and after hearing her mother talk about how terrible men were, she'd decided she never wanted to go there herself. But now, here she was in the arms of a man who wanted her, and she didn't feel threatened.

No, she felt powerful.

She let her fingers trail down his cheekbone and along his strong jaw, loving the prickle of stubble against her fingertips. Loving, too, the way his gaze flared as she touched him, blue darkening into twilight shadows.

She touched his mouth, tracing the line of his lower lip, the curve of it. It felt soft even though nothing else about him was, and it had felt soft too when he'd kissed her. Yet also firm, masterful…

He'd gone very still, making no move as she touched him, her fingers trailing where they would, his gaze fixed to hers. She traced the proud line of his nose then up to those sooty black brows with their arrogant arch, and back down again to his other cheekbone.

'Little bird.' His hold in her hair tightened. 'I'm getting impatient. Yes or no. Give me an answer.'

She liked that he asked her. She liked that despite him pulling her into his lap and kissing her, he'd waited for her to respond before he did anything more. Her mother had always told her that men took what they wanted, took what they thought was theirs, yet despite his obvious power and wealth, he was waiting for her to give him permission.

Maybe this was a glimpse of the man she'd met that night two years ago. The man whom she'd wanted enough to give him her virginity in spite of all the warnings about men her mother had given her.

'I'm thinking,' she said, flexing that power a little, wanting to see how far she could push him. 'I'm also trying to remember.' She stroked her fingers down the side of his strong neck to the knot of his tie, then pulled at it, the silk loosening, baring his throat. His pulse beat there, strong and steady beneath her fingertips, his skin warm.

She heard his breath catch at her touch, saw his eyes darken even further.

'Shall I tell you what happened after you kissed me?' he asked softly. 'After you wound your arms around my neck?'

Her own breathing was getting faster, the ache between her thighs a growing pressure.

'Yes,' she said, her mouth dry.

Blue flames leapt in his eyes. 'I did this.' He dropped one hand to the buttons of her blouse. 'I opened the shirt you were wearing.' He flicked the top button open. 'One button at a time.' Another one. 'I went slowly, because I didn't want to scare you.' A third button. 'And also, because I wanted to tantalise you.' A fourth.

Her heart beat like thunder in her head, her skin sensitised. She couldn't stop looking at his face, at the hunger etched in stark lines there, and all for her.

Cool air whispered over her skin as the fabric parted, making her shiver.

'And then,' he went on, undoing the last button so her

blouse was entirely open. 'I spread out the fabric so I could see you.' He pushed the two halves of her blouse wide, baring the white lace of her bra. 'Your nipples were hard. Just like they are now, and I touched them. Like this.' His fingertips grazed over the peaks of her breasts, first one and then the other, and sensation crackled through her, a knife of pleasure that tore a gasp from her throat.

She felt half hypnotised by his touch and by the deep roughened sound of his voice. By the pressure between her thighs that made her want to shift restlessly beneath his touch.

'After that,' he murmured, 'since your bra had a front clasp just like this one, I did this...' With a twist of his fingers, he flicked open her bra and the material fell away, the air cool on her sensitised nipples.

Lark took a sharp breath as he gazed down at her, desire glittering in his eyes. 'You were so beautiful that night,' he continued. 'As beautiful as you are now, and so I touched you just like this...' He cupped one breast in his hot palm, squeezing her gently, teasing her nipple with his thumb and drawing a shudder from her. 'Then I had to taste you, because you looked so delicious.'

He bent, his tongue touching her aching nipple and making her gasp aloud. Then he drew it into his mouth, applying gentle pressure, and she groaned.

This wasn't going as she'd planned. She'd wanted to push him further, flex her power even more, but she'd become a victim of her own hunger and now she didn't want him to stop. Not when it felt so good. Familiar, too, though her memory of that night was still a black hole. Her body knew, though. Her body was greeting him as if it had been starved for his touch, aching for him. Desperate for him.

Her eyes fluttered closed, her world narrowing to the

heat of his mouth on her breast, his fingers in her hair holding her exactly where he wanted her, his hard thighs beneath her, surrounded by his powerful body.

God, she loved it.

Weren't you supposed to the one making him *desperate?*

Oh, but did that really matter now? She didn't care about power games, not in this moment. In this moment all she wanted was him.

She groaned and arched her back, pressing herself into his mouth. Her fingers slid into his hair, the strands feeling like raw silk, soft yet with a delicious roughness to it.

'Do you remember, little bird?' he whispered against her heated skin. 'Do you remember me doing this to you?'

'No,' she replied, breathless. 'But keep going. What else did we do?'

He raised his head, the shadows in his eyes darkening into midnight. 'You have to say yes, Lark. I'm not going to show you anything more until you do.'

You were supposed to make him beg...

The thought drifted through her pleasure-fogged brain, but she couldn't remember why she'd wanted that. And anyway, all she had to say was yes and she couldn't think of a single reason to refuse him.

'Yes,' she whispered.

'Yes, what?'

'Yes, Signor Donati. Right here. Right now.'

His beautiful mouth curved, amusement warring with the satisfaction glinting in his eyes. 'I like Signor Donati, believe me. But that night you called me Cesare.'

'Cesare,' she echoed, his name sounding like music. 'Yes, Cesare.'

The amusement vanished, heat flaring hot and bright in his eyes. 'One moment,' he said, then shifted, getting his phone from his pocket. He hit a couple of buttons then is-sued an order in clipped Italian before throwing the phone down in the seat next to them.

'I've instructed my staff to not to bother us,' he said. 'We have privacy.' His gaze took on an intent look. 'Now, little bird. Why don't you take the rest of your clothes off for me?'

Lark shivered all over, her mouth going dry. 'Is that what I did that night?' she asked in a hoarse voice. 'After you t-touched me?'

Slowly he shook his head. 'I undressed you that night. But I wished I'd had the patience to watch you undress for me.'

She wanted to. She wanted to see more of that hunger etched on his face, more of his desire for her as she took her clothes off, baring herself for him. She'd missed out that night and she didn't want to miss out again.

So she slid off his lap and stood in front of his seat, reaching for the zip on her skirt and pulling it down. She felt no hesitation, no embarrassment. He'd seen her naked before and he'd liked it—he'd already told her so and any-way, there was nothing but heat in his eyes now. It didn't take a genius to work out that he was already loving what he saw.

She slid her skirt down, taking her knickers with it, then stepped out of the fabric, kicking off her little heels. She eased her blouse off and her bra, until finally she stood naked before him.

He sat back in his seat and let out a long breath, star-ing at her as if he wanted to eat her alive. 'Come here,' he ordered, soft and rough.

But now she could feel it, that power. He might have

called the shots just before, but this—all of it—lived and died by her will and only hers.

Lark gave him a slow smile then stepped forward, easing herself into his lap, sitting astride him so she faced him. Making sure she took it slow and easy, watching as the fire in his eyes leapt, his hunger burning bright as she settled herself on him.

'Ah, *Dio*...' he breathed, his gaze dropping down her naked body then returning to her face. 'I remember this. So beautiful...' He lifted his hands, cupping her breasts and she sighed, arching into his palms, wanting more of his touch. 'Say my name,' he said, demanding. 'Tell me how much you want me.'

'Cesare...' She caressed every syllable, loving how it made the fire in his eyes burn bright. 'I want you...' There was power in this too, in admitting her hunger for him, because that fuelled his, she could see it in his beautiful face.

It made her want to goad him even more. She reached down between them, her hand sliding over the fly of his suit trousers, finding him hot and hard beneath her, and lord...he was impressive.

He groaned as she squeezed him experimentally and she loved the sound, loved that she could draw it out of him.

'Lark,' he said roughly. 'If you continue doing that, I won't be responsible for what happens next.'

'What does happen next?' The words were breathless as she squeezed him again. 'I can't quite remember.'

'Witch,' he growled and lifted both hands, burying his fingers in her hair and pulling her in for a kiss, devouring her like a man starved.

He tasted like heaven. Like brandy or some other wickedly alcoholic sweet drink and it went straight to her head. Her arms lifted and she was twining them around his neck and arching against him, pressing her exquisitely sensitive nipples against the wool of his jacket.

There was something unbearably erotic in being naked while he was still fully dressed. It didn't make her feel weak. It made her feel as if she was the powerful one, using her sexuality and his own desire against him, bringing him to his knees.

'Say my name,' she whispered against his mouth, consciously imitating him. 'Tell me how much you want me.'

'Lark,' he murmured, the word rough and bitten off. 'And how about I show you instead.' Then he pulled her hands away from his fly and freed himself from his trousers. From somewhere he produced a condom packet that he ripped open with practiced ease. Then he sheathed himself before sliding one hand between her thighs, stroking her hot wet flesh, making her cry out as a flood of pleasure nearly overwhelmed her.

Then without another word, he positioned himself and thrust inside her.

She gasped, her head falling back, pleasure flooding her at the delicious stretch and burn of him inside her. She heard the sound of his harshly indrawn breath and he went still. His hand in her hair tightened and he pulled her mouth to his, kissing her with a hunger and passion that drove the last shreds of thought from her head.

She kissed him back desperately as he began to move, deep and slow, a rhythm that had her shifting on him, trying to match it. He dropped a hand to her bare hip, his palm burning against her skin, showing her the way, and then she found it. A rise and fall that was gentle at first and slow, then gaining pace.

Lark moaned against his mouth, as the pleasure became more and more intense, his hand on her hip pressing hard, his fingertips digging into her bare flesh even as his fist in her hair tightened still further, holding her still.

She put her palms flat to his chest, her nails against his skin, kissing him back hungrily as the pleasure rose in an agonising wave inside her. They moved faster, his thrusts harder, and then he slipped a hand between her thighs, stroking the sensitive bundle of nerves there and she came apart, crying his name as the climax took her and swept her away.

It was the sound of his name, hoarse and full of breathless pleasure, that catapulted him over the edge. As Lark sagged against him, he drove himself harder and faster inside her, both hands now on her hips to keep her still and then, long before he was ready for it, the orgasm hit him with all the force of a freight train, and he pulled her mouth to his as it took him, muffling the sound of his own release with her lips.

Afterwards he couldn't move. He could hardly breathe. She was a warm weight on him, her small, curvy body leaning against his chest, her face pressed to his shoulder. His fingers were wound in her hair, the strands soft and silky against his skin and he could smell her vanilla scent tinged with sweet feminine musk and sex.

Dio. He hadn't expected that to happen so fast. But tasting her mouth and then her pretty breasts, and then watching her as she'd taken off her clothes for him before sitting naked in his lap, her sea-green eyes dark with desire…

It had been a long time without sex for him and every other woman he'd been with since that night had been somehow…unsatisfying. Not that the problem lay with them. He was the issue and he knew it. Or rather, the issue was *her*.

Her and what had happened between them that night. The lovers he'd had previously had all been skilled and he'd had pleasure from them. But sex had always been a selfish thing. He could give a woman pleasure, but nothing more, and that was the beginning and end of it.

Not with Lark, though. Lark had been unpractised, a virgin, and so what an experienced woman would understand without a word being said, she wouldn't know. And she wouldn't understand. He'd had to be clear with her what he could give her and what he couldn't, and so he'd expected her to give nothing of herself to him, the way his other lovers had.

Yet she hadn't. That night in his arms she'd given him everything. She'd been so generous, giving him her complete and utter trust. He'd never had that before from anyone. He'd never felt as if he held someone's soul in his hands and never wanted to.

He was as his parents had made him, as selfish and self-serving as they were. Unlike them though, he owned it. He didn't pretend. They'd used him in their private war against each other, telling him that they cared about him, that they were doing this for him, but they weren't. He was the weapon they aimed at each other and when that weapon no longer had the power to hurt, they'd discarded him.

Everything he did, his every action was on them. He'd been going to tear apart their precious Donati legacy and plough any leftover ashes into the ground, take his revenge for how his father had locked him away for months in order to punish his mother. How his mother had then tried to kill him in order to hurt his father. She'd failed at that luckily, but not before his father had shot her and then himself.

Really, the whole thing had been almost farcical in its drama, so was it any wonder he'd turned out the way he had?

Of course, now he had an heir, things were different and he'd changed his mind about his revenge, but that still didn't mean he could be trusted with anyone's soul. He didn't want to be trusted anyway, and he was glad that this time Lark hadn't been so emotionally honest. She'd been angry and guarded with him since the moment she'd got on the plane, and he suspected the passion she'd let out to play hadn't been so much about him as about herself.

He wasn't complaining, though. He was familiar with the heat that lay beneath the surface of her cheerful smiles, and when she'd slid her hand down over the front of his trousers, desire darkening the green of her eyes, he'd felt nothing but pure satisfaction that she was giving in to it. She hadn't hesitated in touching him, her boldness gripping him by the throat and not letting go.

She'd pushed him, demanding he repeat the same words he'd ordered from her, and he had, without protest. Perhaps he shouldn't have allowed her that power, yet her response had been so very gratifying....

She shifted in his lap, but he tightened his arms around her, keeping her where she was.

He wanted to hold her a bit longer, his brain already running through plans about how he could have this again, keep her naked like this and in his arms. Not for ever, naturally, but for enough time that he didn't feel this nagging need. That he could finally look at other women and feel desire for them the way he used to instead of being consumed by thoughts of Lark.

And why couldn't he have this again? What was stopping them from sleeping with each other when the need arose? They had significant chemistry and gave each other great pleasure. She could hardly say no to that.

Her fingers spread on his chest, pressing herself away

and this time he reluctantly released his hold. She lifted her head, her cheeks pink, her hair coming out of its ponytail, all mussed by the grip of his hands. She looked thoroughly and totally ravished, the mere sight of her making him hard.

'I think,' she began in a husky voice. 'That that was a mist—'

'No,' he interrupted abruptly. 'No, it was *not* a mistake.' He lifted his hands and cupped her face, her skin like silk against his palms. 'It was perfect, little bird. Just as the night we spent together was perfect.'

She flushed. 'It can't happen again.'

'Why not?'

A breath escaped her and she pulled away, sliding out of his lap and reaching for her discarded clothing. 'Because I don't want it to.' She turned and began to dress. 'What I wanted was to remember that night or at least what it felt like to have sex with you. I still don't remember, but at least now I've had sex with you. I don't need another demonstration and especially not when we still have the issue of this stupid paternity test to deal with.'

She kept her face turned resolutely away, a thread of emotion in her voice that made him want to reach for her, turn her so he could look into her eyes and see what it was.

But that wasn't keeping it just about sex. That was engaging and he didn't want to engage, especially not with anything resembling emotion.

If she didn't want to sleep with him again, that was fine. It didn't matter and why would it? When he could get pleasure from anyone? He only had to crook a finger and women came running, so this one's refusal shouldn't affect him at all.

Yet he couldn't deny that something like frustration coiled like a snake inside him. Frustration at being denied.

Frustration because he wanted more, wanted her and only her. No one else would do.

If she hadn't been so passionate with him then he'd have accepted that no and never thought of her again. But she *had* been passionate with him. She'd come apart so beautifully in his arms, crying his name, and she was fooling herself if she thought she didn't want him again. Still Maya was a legitimate reason for her not to want anything more from him, and even though it was to his detriment, he admired her for putting her daughter ahead of her own desires. Unlike his mother, who'd fed him poison purely to punish his father.

Perhaps Lark would think differently once she'd accepted that he was Maya's father. Whatever the case, he certainly wasn't going to chase her. No, he wanted her to come to him. Still, that didn't mean he couldn't weigh the dice in his favour.

'Once on a plane is not really enough to know what sex with me is like,' he said, watching her dress, unable to take his gaze off her. It felt like a loss when she covered up all that pretty bare skin.

She gave him a sidelong look as she put on her bra then began to do up the buttons of her blouse. 'Did I mention how arrogant you are?'

He ignored that, leisurely dealing with the condom and his own clothes, not missing how she kept glancing at the movement of his hands as if she too couldn't keep her eyes off him. 'I'd reserve judgement until we have a bed if I were you.'

'But you're not me and my judgement is just fine, thank you very much.'

Cesare studied her, noting her pink her cheeks and the slight tremble of her hands. Remembering the way she'd clutched at him and how she'd cried his name as she came.

She'd wanted him very much and he suspected she still did, but she didn't want to admit it.

'Why is it so hard to admit you still want me, little bird?' he asked idly. 'I still want you.'

Her flush deepened. 'Because I don't. I was curious to see what sex with you was like and now I know. Curiosity satisfied.'

'Really? We had a whole night before. This was a mere fifteen minutes. Barely enough time to even get started.'

'It was enough for me.' She smoothed down her skirt and then sat opposite him, lifting her hands to deal with her hair, her lashes veiling her gaze.

And Cesare's frustration pulled tight inside him. She was lying or at the very least hiding something and no matter what he'd told himself about not engaging, he wasn't having it. Pushing himself out of his seat, he took a step over to where she sat and put his hands on the arms of her seat. Then he leaned down, getting into her space, his face inches from hers.

Her eyes went wide before darkening, her gaze dipping helplessly to his mouth.

'Really?' he murmured, satisfaction clenching inside him. 'Tell me you aren't thinking about kissing me again, having me inside you again, and maybe this time when we're both naked.'

Fire leapt in her eyes, the pulse at the base of her throat beating hard and fast. 'I'm not.'

'Yes, you were. Do you really want me to prove it to you?'

She took a little breath. 'I…no.'

'Then tell me, Lark. Tell me you still want me. You had no problem with saying the words when I had you in my arms. Why is it so difficult now?'

'Because…' Her chest rose and fell as if she was fighting something. 'Being with you made me realise what I'd missed out on. My first sexual experience and I don't remember it. I don't remember you. And what we just had now was…amazing, but it was also angry and fraught, and I don't like being angry. I don't like how you manage to get under my skin.'

Her honesty hit him in a place he wasn't expecting. A place that remembered that night and how special it had been. There had been no tension between them except delicious sexual tension and neither of them had been guarded or angry with the other. There had been pleasure and an intimacy he hadn't known he'd wanted until it had happened.

An intimacy he could not and would not have again.

He regretted that she didn't remember, he realised all of a sudden. He regretted that she had no memories of their intimacy or closeness, or of the passion they'd shared. It was a loss for both of them.

'I'm sorry, little bird,' he said after a moment, and he meant it. 'I'm sorry you don't remember that night. But I don't mind your anger. In fact, be angry with me all you want. Scream at me, shout at me, show me your claws. I like it.'

She stared up at him, searching his face for what he didn't know. 'I know what you're trying to do,' she said, her voice husky. 'And it won't work. I'm still not going to sleep with you again.'

Except she wanted to, he knew. He could see the truth in her eyes.

Why she was insisting on refusing him, he didn't know, but clearly it had something to do with her feelings around her lost memories.

He couldn't argue with that.

You don't need to sleep with her again. Sex is not just sex for her and that makes it complicated. Disengage, remember?

'Well,' he murmured. 'Far be it from me to insist.' His hands tightened on the arms of her seat momentarily, then pushed himself away from her and straightened to his full height. 'If you change your mind, you only have to ask.'

Yet more colour crept through her cheeks. 'Don't worry, I won't be changing my mind.'

For a moment, he stayed where he was, staring down at her, seeing the passion that lay deep inside her, burning like banked embers in her eyes. All it would take would be another touch, another kiss, and she'd go up in flames...

But no. He wasn't going to touch her again.

He smiled. 'Fine. If you do, though, let me know. I think you'd look pretty on your knees.'

Then he turned around, took his phone from his pocket and began to make the last of his phone calls.

CHAPTER SIX

LARK'S PALMS WERE sweaty as she sat her at tiny kitchen
table, unable to concentrate on the crossword puzzle she
was trying to do to pass the time.

Cesare—no, *Signor Donati*—would be here any minute and all the things she'd told herself she was going to
do that morning hadn't got done, because she hadn't been
able to settle.

Maya was playing in her playpen in the little living area
just across the hall and Lark could hear the happy sounds
she was making as she smashed a couple of wooden blocks
together. She hadn't started walking yet, but she wasn't
far off and Lark knew her playpen days were numbered.
Which meant Lark's life was going to get a little bit more
difficult.

There was a thump then a cry, and instantly Lark leapt
to her feet, her crossword forgotten. She went into the living room to find Maya sitting on her bottom and crying
loudly, lifting her arms to Lark as she appeared.

Lark went over and picked her daughter up, murmur-
ing comfortingly as she cuddled her close. Maya was getting heavy now and of course as soon as she was picked
up, she wanted to go back down. She was a very strong-
willed little girl and stubborn to boot.

Like her father, perhaps?

Lark kissed the top of Maya's rose-gold head, trying to ignore the anger that lay like a stone in the pit of her stomach. She didn't want to think about Cesare Donati and she especially didn't want to think of him as Maya's father.

The night before, after the plane had landed, she'd been terribly afraid he'd insist on coming back to her flat with her and seeing Maya. Either that or convincing her to come back to whatever palatial London house he occupied for the night.

She'd been too honest with him on the plane, when he'd loomed over her, surrounding her with his heat and his scent. Her mouth had gone dry and all she'd been able to think about was kissing him again, having him again. She'd wanted to tell him that the sex had meant nothing, her curiosity had been satisfied, but he'd surprised the truth out of her.

Deep down she'd been hoping against hope that sex with him would return her memories, yet it hadn't. That night was still a black hole. And now she'd had a taste of what she'd missed out on that night with him. What it must have been like that first time, to kiss him, touch him. Have him inside her. Those moments in the plane had been like missing pieces of the jigsaw puzzle falling into place, and yet... The whole picture remained hidden.

Being with him again would only remind her of all those other moments she'd lost, that she'd never get back. Of seeing his first reaction to her body, then the joy of mutual discovery, the thrill of newness, of shared wonder...

That was all gone and it had hurt more than she'd expected it to.

She hadn't wanted to tell him any of that, but she had, and there had been recognition in his eyes. And genuine understanding. And pity.

'I'm sorry,' he'd said…

That had made her ache, which in turn had made her angry all over again. She hadn't wanted him to be sorry, she'd wanted him to leave her alone, take his intense, distracting presence elsewhere. She had to look forward, not backwards, and sleeping with him again would definitely be going backwards.

Anyway, as it turned out, he'd neither insisted on coming home with her nor tried to tempt her into coming home with him.

As soon as they'd disembarked the plane, he'd told her he'd see her the next day and a car would take her home. Then he'd walked off, his phone stuck to his ear, got in another car and had been driven away.

She'd told herself she was glad, that she didn't want him anywhere near her. Yet that night, after she'd got home and the nanny had left, and she'd checked on her little girl, she'd gone to sleep and her dreams had been full of him. His hands and his mouth on her. His bare skin against hers. Stroking her, teasing her, taunting her. And then he'd whisper, 'Beg me, little bird,' before vanishing.

She'd woken up aching and restless and in a terrible temper.

Getting tied up in knots over a man, no matter how attractive, was a mistake and one she had to avoid at all costs. She wouldn't be her mother, falling in love with an awful man, marrying him and having his baby only to find herself trapped. Knowing that the only way to protect her child was to run and then be hunted to the ends of the earth.

Okay, so maybe Cesare—*Signor Donati*—wasn't quite as awful as her father had been. But he was terrible all the same. He was forceful, opinionated, arrogant and selfish, and those were enough red flags for her.

What if he's Maya's father?

Then she'd cross that bridge when she came to it. She just didn't want to think about it now.

As if on cue, the doorbell rang. Lark settled Maya on her hip and went to the door to open it, trying to ignore the nerves that leapt and jumped around inside her.

Sure enough, it was him. Cesare Donati. Standing on the doorstep wearing an immaculate handmade suit of dark grey wool. His shirt was black this time, his tie the same deep blue as Maya's eyes.

Behind him, a limo waited at the kerb, looking extremely out of place in her small suburban street, a couple of bodyguards standing nearby.

Not that she was really taking in the limo, not when he was bare inches away.

She'd thought that maybe she'd dreamed his effect on her, that after a night away from him, the force of his presence wouldn't be so intense, but she was wrong.

The impact of him was almost physical.

Her heartbeat sped up, nervousness coiling and tangling inside her. Then his blue gaze locked with hers and a flood of heat washed through her.

All she could remember were those moments on the plane, sitting naked in his lap. His mouth on hers, his fingers clenched tight in her hair. Of him inside her, moving deep and slow, and the intense pleasure uncurling inside her…

'*Buongiorno*, little bird,' he said in his deep, rich voice, his eyes glittering as if he was remembering the same thing. Then his attention shifted, the pressure of it releasing almost making her gasp aloud, and he stared at Maya instead.

He went very still, utterly transfixed by the sight of her,

and Lark was overcome with an urge to shield her daughter from the intensity of his gaze. And she might have if Maya hadn't been gazing back, studying him with the same intentness.

There was a moment's silence.

'May I hold her?' Cesare asked unexpectedly, his voice hoarse, still not taking his eyes off Maya.

Lark's first instinct was to refuse. Then again, he'd asked her politely enough and she knew he wouldn't hurt Maya. He'd promised he wouldn't take her away either, and while she didn't trust him, she was starting to think he might actually be a man of his word. He'd had that agreement drawn up, after all, and given his power, he didn't have to do that.

She glanced down at Maya. She wasn't a clingy child, though she had a certain reserve, and usually it took a little while for her to warm to someone. 'If she wants to go,' Lark said.

But it seemed that Maya didn't mind, going to him without a protest, seemingly as fascinated by Cesare as he was by her. In fact, she stared up at him as if she'd never seen anything so incredible in her life.

Then Lark saw the look on Cesare's face as he stared down at the child in his arms. Undisguised awe. Wonder. Amazement. He murmured something in Italian, not making a single protest as the little girl clutched at his suit with a hand covered in mashed banana.

And Lark's heart ached in response. Because she knew how he felt. She'd felt all those emotions too, the moment she'd first cradled her daughter in her arms.

Cesare settled Maya on his hip as if he'd been carrying babies all his life and glanced at Lark. 'Shall we go?'

Lark's stomach clenched. 'Go? Go where?'

'I thought it would better if we conducted this at my residence here in London. I want to spend a little more time with her and there is more privacy from the press there.'

A thread of panic wound through her and she took a half step towards him. 'No, what? Wait, I didn't agree to you taking her anywhere.'

He frowned, his blue gaze searching hers. 'I told you I would never take her from you and I meant it,' he said quietly. 'You will be coming with me. We'll go to my residence where some of Maya's genetic material will be taken and there we'll wait for the results. If the result is negative then you'll take her home. If the result is positive, we'll talk.'

He sounded so reasonable and yet the panic inside her refused to ease. All she could think about was how difficult would it be to run with her daughter, to go somewhere he couldn't find them, to hide Maya from him.

Do you really want your daughter to have the same upbringing you did?

Lark swallowed. Her childhood hadn't been the best, but Grace had done what she could. Yet Lark didn't want Maya growing up with the same fear. Growing up without friends or a safe space. Of never being able to put down roots because you never knew when you'd have to move on.

Maya reached up to Cesare's tie with one grubby hand and pulled on it. He paid absolutely zero notice, letting her ruin the silk as if it didn't matter. 'Come with me, Lark,' he said. 'Please. It'll be all right, I promise.'

Please...

He meant it, she heard the promise in his voice. And there it was again, the understanding in his eyes. The understanding she'd seen on the plane when she'd told him why she couldn't sleep with him again and how he affected her.

He knew her history, because she'd told him, and he knew why she was afraid. And for some reason he was trying to ease her fears.

'Okay,' she said, her jangling nerves settling, soothed by the quiet honesty in his voice, and then before she knew what was happening, she found herself walking down the path after him, to the limo that waited in the street.

His driver had already opened the door and Lark could see a child's car seat already in place. The driver said something to Cesare but Cesare shook his head, placing Maya in the car seat himself. Then he glanced back at Lark. 'Will you check she's secure, please? I think it was installed correctly, but I'd like to have you look at it just in case.'

She wasn't sure how he did that. He said he was a selfish man and yet here he was, finding those little threads of panic inside her and easing them with a please and some genuine reassurance, and by asking her opinion on the safety of her child, something that mattered a great deal to her.

A selfish man wouldn't have cared about her feelings. A selfish man wouldn't have even known she was afraid.

'You mean you don't automatically know everything?' she muttered as she leaned in, checking that Maya was belted in properly.

Cesare was standing beside her, his delicious cedar scent and the heat of his body winding around her, clouding her senses. Making her pulse race and her heart beat loud in her ears.

'...if you change your mind, you only have to ask...'

His words from the plane the night before drifted through her head, taunting her, her body's response to him making a mockery of her insistence that she wasn't going to sleep with him again.

But she couldn't give in to her desire, not when there were so many good reasons why she shouldn't, Maya and her future being the most important ones.

Annoyingly, Maya's seat was all good and he'd buckled her in correctly too. Though, being annoyed by that was stupid. She should be pleased, especially where her daughter's safety was concerned.

With an effort, she shoved her anger away and straightened, glancing at him. 'She's secure,' she forced out. 'Thank you for remembering the seat.'

He lifted one powerful shoulder. 'I consulted the nanny from the night before about what Maya might need. She's going to come here to collect some of Maya's important things if you'll allow it. That way we can get to my residence and take the test as soon as possible.'

It seemed ridiculous to be pleased that he'd asked her if she minded the nanny coming to get Maya's things, when he'd swept in and organised it all already. Nevertheless, she was pleased.

'That's fine,' she said. 'But do you ever get tired of upending people's lives to suit yourself?'

There was unexpected humour in his eyes and it suited him. It suited him far too well. 'Honestly? No.'

She snorted. 'Thought so.'

A soft, deep laugh escaped him, the sound moving over her like a caress. 'Did you really expect me to give you a different answer, little bird?'

But she didn't want to stand there watching the blue glints of amusement dance in his eyes or listen to that unbelievably sexy laugh again, so she only gave him a disdainful look and got into the limo without a word.

Sometime later, the limo pulled up outside a stately house in Kensington. Clearly old and eye-wateringly expensive, it was white, with a black wrought iron paling fence in front and ivy covering the walls.

As Cesare showed her and Maya inside, she caught a glimpse down the wide hallway of a lovely garden out the back, with trees and green lawns. But there was no time to look properly because then he settled her and Maya in one of the huge front rooms. New baby toys were scattered on the pale carpet and Maya squealed delightedly at the sight of them.

Cesare seemed to have vanished, so Lark wiped her daughter's banana-covered hands clean, then set her down, watching as she toddled happily over to a large plastic truck—she loved trucks—and banged it enthusiastically on the floor. She was still banging it when a woman in a white lab coat came in and asked Lark if she could take a swab from Maya's mouth.

Lark nodded and it was over painlessly, Maya going back to her truck as the woman left.

Lark watched her, trying to ignore the slow creep of dread.

You already know he's her father and continuing to deny it is only going to make things worse.

It was true. In which case she needed a plan, because she was sure Cesare already had one.

Upstairs, Cesare paced around in his study, gripped by a strange restlessness he couldn't quite describe. He didn't want to be here. He wanted to be with Maya, watching her play with the toys he'd bought her. Watching her play full stop.

She was amazing. Perfect in every way.

His daughter.

You don't know that for certain.

Oh, he was certain. He'd been certain since the moment he'd seen her photo on Lark's phone, and meeting her in person had only solidified that certainty.

She was a Donati from her curling rose-gold hair to the tips of her tiny toes.

He'd never held a child before and never wanted to, yet as soon as he'd seen her in Lark's arms, he knew his life wouldn't be complete unless she was in his too. And when Lark had given her to him and he'd held her, so small and fragile, he'd looked down into her blue eyes and known in an instant that he'd give his life for hers. Without hesitation. In a heartbeat.

Then he'd had the strangest thought. Had his parents ever felt that way about him? Had they ever experienced this moment of instant connection? He didn't want to call it love because love was a terrible, toxic thing and there was nothing toxic about Maya.

Perhaps it was protectiveness then, this feeling. A fierce, burning need to keep her from harm even to his own detriment.

No. Your parents never felt that way about you.

They couldn't have, could they? Otherwise they wouldn't have done what they had to him. His mother wouldn't have accused him of loving his father more than her, and his father wouldn't have punished him for being good for his mother.

He didn't care. They were gone now and good riddance to them.

What was important was her. She was the clean slate, the little innocent. Untouched by his family's toxicity, nothing but pure joy. She'd ruined his suit and his tie by grabbing at them with her little banana-covered hands, but he didn't care about that either. He'd wanted to keep holding her, his suit be damned.

Cesare paced around a bit more then reached into his pocket, pulled out his phone and called Aristophanes. His friend answered immediately, as he always did whenever Cesare called him since neither of them liked waiting for the other.

'I gather from this call that you're waiting for the paternity test results?' Aristophanes asked. His Italian was perfect, though there was the faintest hint of his native Athens in his voice.

'Yes,' Cesare said.

'Is that nervousness I hear?'

'Absolutely not.' Cesare reached the door of his study, turned and paced back to his desk. 'I know the outcome already.'

'I see,' Aristophanes said. 'So what is this call in aid of?'

Cesare let out a breath. 'I want to bring her back to Italy. She's a Donati and she needs to be with me. However...' He paused. 'Her mother will have something to say about it.'

And Lark *would* have something to say about it. And it probably wouldn't be good.

Still, he'd decided what he wanted and what he wanted he got. Also, he hadn't seen the inside of Lark's little flat, but he'd seen the outside and while it seemed decent enough, if small, it wasn't a suitable place for his child to grow up in. There was no garden for a start, nowhere for a little girl to run around in and play.

And you know all about how a child should grow up?

He knew enough. A child shouldn't grow up in the shadow of his parents' brutal war of a marriage. A pawn to be used to punish and undermine each other. A weapon to be used in a war caused by love turned into toxic obsession.

It was his father Giovanni's cheating that had started it. Cesare had been about five then, and his mother, Bianca, had then demanded a divorce after she'd found out. But Giovanni had refused. He wouldn't be the first Donati in history to divorce and anyway, Bianca had to stay and care for her child. Cesare needed a mother.

Bianca had been furious, but she'd stayed and things had been all right for a little while. Back then Cesare had loved his mother and had tried to be good for her in case his behaviour set off one of her rapid mood swings. She'd told him he was her good boy, her most loving son. That they needed to leave, to escape his father, who didn't love him the way she loved him. He'd believed her and so when she'd packed him a bag and held out a hand, he'd taken it and together they'd escaped.

It had seemed an exciting adventure, a chance to be with his lovely mother who'd sworn she'd protect him from his terrible father.

Then Giovanni had caught up with them, and he'd been furious. He'd dragged Cesare away by force, while his mother had screamed in rage, and taken him back to the palazzo. The next day Giovanni had told his son that he'd been worried for him, afraid for his safety, because his mother was sick. That she'd lied to him, that she didn't care about him. But Giovanni did. He loved Cesare. He was his heir after all. Oh, and he wasn't allowed to see Bianca again.

If Bianca had known what was good for her, she should have left then, but she couldn't stand that Giovanni had won this particular battle. Forgiveness had never been part of her makeup and so she'd stayed at the palazzo, living in a separate wing like a ghost, haunting her husband every chance she got.

She would leave little notes around the palazzo for Cesare, telling him that she was staying there for him, that she could never leave him, that Giovanni was intent on punishing her by keeping Cesare from her. But they couldn't let him win, she'd said. Cesare should be ready, because one day she would come for him and they'd finally leave for good.

Giovanni found one of the notes and told Cesare furiously that he was to burn them. That his mother was only telling him these things to hurt him, that the only thing she cared about was punishing Giovanni.

His father had been a proud man, arrogant and stiff-necked, and rigid. And he'd expected his son to be the same, and Cesare had tried. He'd hated the fight between his parents and he'd thought that if he was good enough for both of them, then somehow this terrible war would finally end.

But it didn't. It only escalated.

Giovanni tried to get Bianca removed from the house, but she refused to go. One day she turned up after one of Cesare's riding lessons at the stables, and he'd been so pleased to see her. When she said she'd brought them a little picnic, he'd gone with her without hesitation.

She'd taken him to one of his favourite spots on the grassy bank beside the river that ran through the palazzo's ground, and poured him a cup of some special drink she had in a thermos. 'Drink it all, my darling,' she'd told him, drinking some herself. 'Drink it all and you can be with Mama for ever and ever.'

There had been a feverish light in her eyes and she'd

seemed jumpy and tense, but he'd wanted to be a good boy for her, so he'd swallowed the whole cup. Then the world seemed to spin and he'd started feeling horribly sick.

His last memories of that day were of lying on the blanket Bianca had laid out and hearing his father's voice shouting angrily and his mother screaming back.

Then he'd blacked out and woken in hospital, where doctors stood around his bed, looking grim. He'd had no idea what happened, other than that he'd been very sick, and still was.

A day later, a stern-looking woman had appeared at his bedside. She was his aunt and she was there to look after him, because his parents had died.

Later, he'd found out that his mother had tried to poison him and herself that day beside the river, because she'd wanted to punish his father once and for all. The only reason he was alive was due to his father discovering that Bianca had taken him from his riding lesson and so he'd gone to find her. No one knew exactly what had happened then, but the facts were that his mother had died from a gunshot wound and his father the same.

The theory was, he'd killed her before shooting himself.

He certainly hadn't cared that his son had been poisoned and only saved by one of the stable hands who'd come to investigate the gunshots.

They'd told him they cared about him, that they loved him, but he knew then that his only importance was as a way to hurt each other. That no matter how good a son he'd been to both of them, hoping it would help them, it hadn't. Nothing he'd done had mattered at all. And if that was the case, then what was the point of being good? Of caring about other people, when no one had cared about him?

No, he had only himself to answer to and why not? Why

not accept the legacy his parents had left him? They were dead and gone, leaving him alone, and so why shouldn't he rip his father's precious legacy apart? Erase the memory of his mother?

That the best thing he could do with a family like his was to raze it then salt the earth, so that nothing ever grew from its poisoned soil again.

Except now there was Maya, who wasn't poisonous or toxic. Who'd been brought up by a mother who'd loved her and that was all she'd ever known. It had to stay that way.

'Cesare?' Aristophanes asked in bored tones. 'You've been quiet for an awfully long time. What were you saying about the mother?'

A jolt went through him. Why was he thinking about his parents? They had nothing to do with this.

'Maya's mother will not be pleased,' he said, trying to get his thoughts back in order. 'But I'm sure we can work something out.'

'Take her to bed,' Aristophanes said. 'I'm sure that will make her more conducive. Either that or offer to marry her.'

Cesare scowled. 'I assume you know why marriage is the last thing I would offer?'

Aristophanes, who knew Cesare's past, only sighed as if the topic was of the most utter disinterest to him. 'It would give her some legal protection and also money, which I'm sure she'd like. Also, I'm sure you'd like Maya to have your name.'

Cesare came to halt in the middle of his study, thinking.

He hadn't thought about marriage. Why would he? Marriage had never been something he wanted, not after the battleground it had become for his parents. Marriage seemed like a glass case, a trap where two people who couldn't get out turned on each other and destroyed each other, not caring if they took other people down with them.

'I didn't know you cared about my name,' Cesare growled.

'I don't, but you do. You being a Donati and all.' Aristophanes was a self-made man and had a healthy disdain for such things as family history and legacy. He'd long told Cesare that it was his considerable financial acumen that Aristophanes respected, not his name, and certainly not his history.

Cesare couldn't blame him. He didn't respect his own history either.

Still, now that Aristophanes had mentioned marriage, he couldn't let go of the idea. Marriage to Lark... There would be benefits to it, he had to admit. She'd obviously live with him and that would be useful. Maya should have her mother close and if Lark lived at the palazzo with him then they wouldn't need any messy custody arrangements. Also, yes, then Maya would take his name and legally be a Donati.

If he really thought about it, it wasn't marriage that was the trap, it was love. Love that could turn to hate in the blink of an eye, love that could make people do the most terrible things. He wanted nothing whatsoever to do with love. The good thing about his relationship with Lark was that he didn't love her. She certainly didn't love him, which meant they'd be spared that hideousness. Of course there was the issue of sex and how that would work between them since she'd told him she wasn't going to sleep with him again. Perhaps marriage might change her mind?

Then again, if it didn't, it was no problem. They could each have discreet lovers.

Really? You're saying you wouldn't mind Lark having a lover?

Something hot tightened in his gut at the thought, but he shoved it away before he could name it. Lark could have a lover. It wouldn't be an issue.

'Perhaps,' he said. 'It is important that Maya be a Donati.'

'I thought as much.' Aristophanes was clearly not interested in further discussion. 'Well, it's your funeral, my friend. Let me know when the happy occasion is and I'll make sure I have time in my schedule.'

Aristophanes lived or died by his schedule, Cesare knew. If it wasn't in the schedule it didn't happen. 'Of course,' he said. 'I'll let you know as soon as I have a date.'

He disconnected the call and then paced around a bit more, going over a myriad of plans.

Then the door opened and one of his assistants came in with the results of the test.

It was as he'd thought. Maya was his child.

He stared down at the piece of paper and the satisfaction that had settled down inside him became solid rock. There would be no more argument. No more discussion. Maya was a Donati and she would be raised one. She would be his hope for the future, a new generation rising out of the ashes of the old, and he had the opportunity to provide a better legacy for her than what his parents had left for him.

Are you sure she's not better off without you? Your parents certainly would have been.

The voice in his head was snide, taunting, but he shoved it away before the doubt had time to take root. No, she wasn't better off. She was heir to a difficult history and someone needed to help her come to terms with it. Someone would also need to teach her how to deal with her considerable inheritance, and he was the best person to do that.

He was her father, and although he didn't know how to be a good one, he'd certainly had experience of a bad one. He'd never be like his own father, never ever.

Cesare left his study and went down the stairs to the front room, pausing in the doorway.

Lark was on her knees next to Maya, both of them playing with the large plastic truck he'd bought. Lark was pretending to drive it around while Maya squealed with delight as she tried to grab it. And a peculiar sensation caught at him as he watched them.

His daughter playing with her mother, full of laughter and joy. Lark smiling at her child, her face shining. They were both enjoying themselves, clearly happy.

He'd never had that, he realised. Not in his own life. His childhood had been nothing but tension and hatred, a cold war with him in the middle. His childhood had been stolen from him by his parents and he wouldn't do the same to Maya.

His child would have a different childhood. He would give her joy and laughter and happiness, and he knew that the best way to do that was to make sure Lark was at his side.

That wasn't just important. That was vital.

Sensing his presence, Lark looked up, her pretty green eyes locking with his. She went still. Maya, taking no notice of her parents, grabbed at the truck, babbling happily.

'Oh,' Lark breathed, searching his face. 'So…it's true then?'

He didn't move. 'Yes. Do you want to see the results for yourself?'

A complicated expression passed over her features.

All the happiness disappeared, leaving disappointment, he thought, and fear, and also despair. She looked away sharply, hiding it from him. 'No,' she said in a curiously blank voice. 'I believe you.'

Cesare did not bother himself with other people's emotions or opinions. He didn't care about them, not a single iota. But he didn't like that expression on Lark's face. Not the disappointment or despair, and definitely *not* the fear. That wasn't what he wanted for her and he didn't want that for Maya either.

Lark's happiness was vital to his daughter's, he could see that now, which meant it was now going to be vital to him.

'We need to talk, little bird,' Cesare said quietly.

CHAPTER SEVEN

LARK TOOK A deep breath. She'd known this moment was coming, that she had to stop denying what she already knew. And she did know, even before she'd seen the look on his face as he'd stood in that doorway watching her and Maya.

Cesare *was* Maya's father and she had to accept it. She had to accept, too, that he wanted to be in Maya's life. He'd never made any secret of that.

She couldn't change it, just as she couldn't change that he was the father of her child, but that didn't mean she didn't have any choices or any power. In fact, she knew exactly what kind of power she had and while she'd waited for the results of that test, her brain running through various scenarios, she knew what choice she was going to make too.

She didn't have the resources to fight a man like him, and she wasn't going to run like her mother. Cesare was a man who knew what he wanted and she suspected that even if she did run, she wouldn't get far.

But she didn't want to run. She wanted her daughter to be happy. To grow up without fear, to have a home where she could put down roots and be safe. To be loved.

Cesare would no doubt insist on Maya living with him and Lark couldn't protest. He had a beautiful house with beautiful gardens, plenty of room for Maya to run around and play in. She'd grow up there, have a life there. She'd have everything she ever needed and Lark couldn't deny her that.

But she wasn't going to let Cesare take Maya without her. Where Maya went, so would Lark, and if he was going to take her to Italy, then he'd have to put up with Lark coming too.

He might protest, but there were ways she could make it attractive to him. Her body for example, could be a powerful inducement.

For Maya's sake.

Not for your own?

She caught her breath, a wave of heat washing over her.

Cesare had hitched a shoulder against the doorframe, his blue gaze fixed on her. He'd taken his jacket off and got rid of his banana-stained tie, so he was in his shirtsleeves. He'd rolled up the cuffs, strong forearms exposed, hands in the pockets of his suit trousers and there was something so incredibly sexy about them, about him leaning there casually, watching her...

She couldn't keep lying to herself. She couldn't keep pretending that she didn't want him. Couldn't keep telling herself that once had been enough and that all her curiosity had been satisfied, because it wasn't. How could she keep going forward when he was here? Reminding her of that night and of everything she'd forgotten?

Something had happened between them that night in Rome, something special and not only the conception of her daughter. Something else. Something that had kept him wanting her even though two years had passed. And she'd missed out on it.

It hadn't been just sex either, she felt it in her bones. It had been something else, something more, something that made her ache with a loss she didn't understand. Didn't she owe it to herself to find out what it had been? Who *he* had been to her and she to him?

She wouldn't find that out by continuing to deny herself, that was for certain.

'Okay,' she said, getting to her feet. 'Let's talk.'

Cesare pushed himself away from the doorframe. 'Not here. Up in my study.' He turned and made a gesture and Emily, the nanny who'd been looking after Maya while Lark had been in Rome, stepped through the doorway and into the room.

Of course, Lark thought with a hint of wry amusement. He'd thought of everything. Even making sure that Maya had someone familiar looking after her.

As Emily settled in, Lark gave Maya a kiss then followed Cesare out of the room and up the stairs. He went down a hallway, opened a dark oak door, and showed her into the large room beyond. Then he came in after her, shutting the door behind him.

'Please, sit.' He gestured to the chair that stood in front of his desk.

It wasn't an order. It was a request, so Lark did, settling herself in the chair. She expected him to go around the desk and sit in the chair behind it, but he didn't.

Instead, he came over to the desk and leaned back against it, folding his arms and looking down at her. He was very close, the warmth of his body and his scent making her mouth go dry.

She really had to get it together. He was going to start making proclamations and demands, she was sure, and she couldn't let him. Because once he started doing that, she'd be left carrying along in his wake, and she couldn't afford that. Not when she had demands of her own.

'I know what you want,' she said determinedly, before he could speak. 'You want to take Maya to live with you in Italy. At your palazzo presumably. And you want to bring her up as a Donati.'

Cesare opened his mouth, but she held up a hand. 'Let me finish please.'

He shut it.

'I can't fight you on this,' she went on. 'I don't have the resources, the connections or the power, and to be honest, it's better for Maya if I don't fight you. I know what it's like when parents are fighting each other and it's always the children that get caught in the middle.'

A strange expression crossed his face at that, but he didn't speak.

'I also know that Maya will have much better opportunities if she lives with you. She'll have room to run and play, she'll be safe. She'll have a home of her own rather than a rented flat and a mother struggling to make ends meet.'

Cesare opened his mouth again, but Lark shook a finger at him. 'I haven't finished.'

He shut it, but this time there was a glint of amusement in his eyes. She didn't trust it, but there wasn't anything else to do but go on. 'So, I'll agree that you should take her back to Italy to live, on one condition.' She stared at him fiercely. 'There will be no negotiation on this and I won't accept anything less. And if you want to honour the promise you made to me that you wouldn't take her away from me, you'll agree to this.'

He still looked amused, damn him, but all he did was make a *go on* gesture.

Lark took a breath. 'I will be coming too. Now, I don't care what you think of that or of how you'll find accommodation for me, but that'll be your problem. I will be coming with Maya because I'm her mother and she needs me. I won't accept separate accommodation from her and I will absolutely not be paying you any money for rent or board or—'

'Lark,' Cesare interrupted finally, his mouth curving. 'Will you allow me a word?'

'If you're going to tell me that you're not—'

'Lark,' he repeated, more gently this time. 'I agree.'

All the justifications and reasons she'd prepared about why he had to accept her offer flew abruptly out of her head. She gaped at him. 'You what?'

'I agree,' he said again. 'You're right. I do want to take her to Italy and bring her up as a Donati at the palazzo. And you're also right that she needs you at her side. A fight is the last thing I want between us, and I've already been planning to bring you with me to Rome. You will live at the Donati palazzo too and of course I won't demand any money from you.'

She'd been expecting to fight, to have to dig in her heels, and for a moment Lark couldn't think of a word to say.

'You...you won't?' she said at last.

'No.' He shifted against the desk and this time the glitter in his eyes wasn't only amusement, but something else. Something hotter. 'However, I do have a demand of my own.'

A thread of what felt suspiciously like anticipation coiled inside her, as if she was excited by the thought of whatever he was going to demand of her.

You like fighting him as much as he likes fighting you.

Of course, she did. The freedom she had with him to be angry was something she'd never had before, and yes, she liked it. Very much.

She caught her breath, trying to ignore the delicious shiver that crept over her skin. 'Oh? And what's that?'

Cesare smiled. 'I want you to marry me.'

Shock wound through her. That was…not what she'd expected him to ask. 'You want me to marry you?' she repeated stupidly.

'*Sì.*' More amusement glittered in Cesare's blue gaze, yet there was also the steel in it. This was something he would not be moved on. 'You're Maya's mother and I'm her father, and I think the whole thing would work best if we were married.'

'But…you can't *want* to marry me.'

'Not in the traditional sense, no,' he agreed, and why that should catch at her like a thorn, she had no idea. 'But in a legal sense I think it's absolutely necessary. Maya would have my name and so would you, which would give you resources and protection in case anything should happen to me.'

Lark felt her mouth go dry. Marriage had never been something she'd wanted for herself, not after witnessing the aftermath of her mother's experience. Her father had been abusive, Grace had told her, and yet there were some days when her mother refused to get out of bed and no amount of Lark's smiles would help. Where Grace would sit there slowly turning the wedding ring she still wore around and around on her finger, and staring at it. Grace had always told her she'd been glad to leave, that she'd had to in order to protect Lark and herself, but those days Lark would wonder if Grace was really as glad as she made out. If there was a part of her mother who still loved her father and missed him, no matter what he'd done to her.

That thought had horrified Lark, and she'd decided then

and there that she'd never get married. Never allow herself to be trapped by a man. Never fall in love.

Yet now, here she was, looking down the barrel of a marriage proposal and… Well. She wasn't in love with Cesare Donati—a small mercy—but she was actually contemplating marrying him. He was by his own admission a selfish man, arrogant and proud, and there was no way she should even be thinking about tying herself to him, and yet….

He'd kept his word about not taking Maya from her when he easily could have and he clearly believed that his daughter needed her mother. He was also serious about protecting her and putting her needs before his own, despite confessing how he hadn't wanted children.

The addition of a daughter wasn't going to make his life simpler and if he truly hadn't wanted her, he'd had plenty of opportunity to walk away. In fact, Lark had encouraged him to do so. But he hadn't. And now not only had he not protested at the idea of having another person come to live with him, he was also offering her his name. For Maya's sake.

'I…' she began, her voice husky. 'I…will need some assurances.'

One inky brow rose. 'Another agreement perhaps?'

'Um…yes.' She folded her hands in her lap to stop them shaking.

'You would have complete freedom,' Cesare said, watching her in that intense way he had. 'I understand what you'll be giving up to come to Italy, so I can use my connections to help you find another job or assist you into study if that's what you prefer. Or if you'd rather be a full-time mother to Maya then I will support you. You'll want for nothing.'

Lark's head spun. She'd never thought seriously about what she'd wanted for herself. Before Maya had come along, she'd had thoughts of going to university and had been looking into bridging courses since her constant moving around with her mother had meant patchy schooling. She'd never got university entrance. Then once she'd moved to London, and after a year or so of bouncing between temping jobs, she'd found out she was pregnant and all thoughts of university had been put on the back burner.

Taking up Cesare's offer meant that she'd finally have the time to think about university and what she wanted for herself, because Maya would be taken care of.

Don't get ahead of yourself. He's a businessman through and through, and he'll want something in return.

That was true. He *would* want something in return and she could well imagine what that might be.

Lark was conscious that her palms were damp and her heart was racing, but she forced herself to meet his gaze head-on. 'But presumably *you'll* want something,' she said.

'I will?'

'Yes, in return for agreeing to marry you.'

The hot gleam in his eyes became even hotter. 'Why? Is there something you want to give me?'

'Don't play games with me, Cesare,' she said, nerves getting the better of her. 'Not about this. You know what I'm talking about.'

He gave her a slow burning smile. 'If it's sex you mean, then no, I will not require sex from you. In fact, I won't require anything of you.'

Something tightened in her gut and she couldn't tell if it was relief or disappointment.

'Unless you want to exercise your conjugal rights of course,' Cesare went on. 'In which case I'll be happy to assist you. But failing that, since I have no intention of being celibate, I will be taking lovers. Discreetly of course, and I expect that you'll want to do the same.'

She swallowed. It was definitely relief, wasn't it? 'You mean be discreet if I want a lover myself?'

'Yes. You needn't stay celibate on my account.'

Except the thought of having lovers herself left her cold. *You only want him.*

She ignored that thought too. 'And if it doesn't work out? There'll be an option for divorce?'

A shadow flickered through Cesare's eyes. 'You want an escape clause?'

'Yes.' There was no point pretending. 'Don't you? You might meet someone else, for example, and fall in love and want to marry them instead.'

'Oh, that will never happen.' There was an unexpected edge in his voice. 'Love is for other people, little bird. Not for me.'

He said the word *love* with a certain distaste, as if it was poison and it caught at her, waking a curiosity she hadn't known she'd felt until now. He'd sounded so very emphatic and she found herself wondering why. What was love to him? Had he been disappointed by it? Hurt by it?

Again, she was reminded that he knew things about her yet she didn't know about him. Personal things. She'd told him about her mother, about her past, but had he told her about his? Had he mentioned anything about himself that night?

You'll have time to find out now, won't you?

Deep inside her, the anticipation that had gathered before turned slowly into a hot, tense excitement. Marrying Cesare Donati could prove to be interesting, very interesting, and she couldn't deny that it affected her in a way she hadn't expected.

'Well, little bird?' The look on his face was intense, as if her answer mattered to him. 'What do you say? Will you accept my proposal?'

The inexplicable, mysterious excitement pulled tight, making her breathless. Perhaps it wouldn't be a bad idea to say yes, to marry him. Perhaps it didn't need to be just for Maya's sake either. After all, how long had it been since she'd done anything for herself? How long since she'd had a place to call her own? A place to stay and put down roots. A home. She had her flat, it was true, and her job, but the flat wasn't hers and while she'd liked working for Mr Ravenswood and he'd been training her, it wasn't exactly a career.

She'd never have the money to buy her own place, not on her own, and having to provide for Maya meant study was out of the question too.

But all that would change if she married Cesare.

Was it even a choice?

'Is that really how you're going to propose to me?' she said, unable to resist the urge to poke at him just a little, to get revenge for him surprising her like this. 'Standing up like that with your arms folded?'

Blue flames leapt in his eyes, the heat intensifying. 'How else would you like me to propose to you?'

His voice was deep with a sensual edge she found unbelievably sexy.

Lark held his gaze. 'Surely on one knee.'

Cesare's beautiful mouth curved and for a second she wasn't sure if he'd do it. Then abruptly he pushed himself away from the desk, standing in front of her. Then he leaned down and put both hands on the arms of her chair.

He didn't let go as he lowered himself fluidly to the floor, on one knee as she'd instructed.

'Lark Edwards,' he said formally. 'Will you do me the honour of becoming my wife?'

Lark's pretty face was flushed, her green eyes glowing with a mixture of challenge and heat, and although he'd never taken kindly to being told what to do, he'd found himself going down on one knee all the same.

He could never resist a challenge and he could resist one from her even less.

Especially when he had an ulterior motive.

She'd surprised him, he couldn't deny it. He'd been all ready to launch into a detailed explanation about how she needed to marry him and why, expecting her to argue with him. Vociferously. However, then she'd taken the wind out of his sails by telling him she was coming to Italy with Maya whether he liked it or not.

It hadn't been what he'd anticipated at all, which had delighted him.

In fact, as she'd sat there primly in the chair, her hands folded, resplendent in a pretty green dress and telling him in no uncertain terms what she wanted now she knew he was Maya's father, he'd been delighted with her full stop.

She was beautiful for a start, and then she'd been very clear she didn't want to argue with him because of Maya, which had earned his fierce agreement. She wouldn't put her issues before those of her child's and he agreed fiercely with that too.

It wasn't a small thing she was giving up for Maya's sake. Her job and her life here in London, and any plans she'd made for the future. But she hadn't argued and she hadn't protested. She'd agreed it was in Maya's best interests and was prepared to back that up with action.

Really, his child couldn't have had a better mother.

But it hadn't been until he'd actually asked her to be his wife that he'd realised how much he wanted her to say yes. And badly. In fact, it had been quite disturbing how much he wanted it. Disturbing too to realise that though he could force her to say yes, he didn't want to. He wanted it to be her choice, the way it had been her choice that night two years ago.

Yet the real issue with wanting it to be her choice was that he had no control over her answer. As a man used to having control in all things, he did not like that at all, not one bit. However, he was also a man who knew how to turn things to his advantage so he was definitely going to do what he could to weight her choice in his favour.

She looked at him where he knelt on the floor in front her, and he was pleased to see surprise in her sea-green eyes. Clearly she hadn't expected him to kneel. But surprise wasn't the only thing in her gaze. He could see the flickers of sensual awareness there too, the embers of desire starting to glow.

He was still holding on to the arms of her chair, his body leaning lightly against her knees, making it impossible for her to ignore him physically. She was so small they were at eye level.

Pretty, pretty woman. She smelled so good. It was an aphrodisiac all on its own, and he could feel himself getting hard. He'd told her she'd look pretty on her knees, yet he was the one kneeling. Begging too, and not even for sex but for her name on a piece of paper.

He wanted her to say yes and not just for Maya's sake, but for his too.

His gaze held hers, the tension between them deepening the longer she stayed silent, the air around them becoming charged and crackling with static.

Cesare didn't look away as he let go the arms of the chair, putting his hands gently on either side of her thighs, just above her knees, and clasping her gently.

She gave a delicious little shiver but didn't pull away. 'I thought you weren't going to touch me again unless I asked?'

'I wasn't,' he admitted. 'But you haven't given me an answer yet and I thought I might offer some incentive.'

Lark's gaze drifted to his mouth, her gaze gone smoky. 'What incentive?'

'This.' He began to slowly ease up the hem of her dress, up the front of her calves and slowly over her knees, baring her pretty thighs. 'Our marriage doesn't have to be only about Maya. You could have something for yourself too. After all, don't you think you deserve it?'

'Do I?' She made no move to stop him, only staring at him, her breathing getting faster and faster as he pushed her dress even higher.

She hadn't asked for reassurance, and yet he found himself wanting to give it. Wanting her to understand too, that he was grateful for what she'd done for Maya. Because there were many choices she could have made when she'd found herself pregnant with a baby she had no memory of conceiving, and she'd chosen to keep her.

A difficult choice for a woman on her own, and he regretted that he hadn't been there to support her, to be with her when Maya was born. There was so much he'd missed. But one thing he knew was that this strong, beautiful woman had kept their daughter safe, had kept her happy and healthy and, yes, for that he was grateful.

'Yes,' he murmured. 'Of course you do.' He eased the hem of her dress up to her waist so he could see the knickers she wore, white cotton with a bit of lace. Very practical. Incredibly sexy. 'You kept her when you could have chosen differently, and that must have been very hard.' He slid his hands up her thighs, stroking her silky skin and she took a soft breath. 'Especially having to do this all on your own.'

Lark's gaze became liquid, her full lower lip trembling slightly. 'I wanted so badly to be a good mother to her,' she whispered. 'But sometimes...'

'It's okay.' He stroked her slowly, hoping she saw his sincerity, because he'd never been so sincere in all his life. 'I'm sorry I wasn't there to help you. But I am now, understand? You've done a fantastic job with her, but you're not alone in this any more.'

Her throat moved, and she stared at him as if she was drowning and his gaze was a lifeline. He could smell her vanilla scent, tinged now with the delicate musk of her arousal, and something primitive and powerful turned over inside him.

She needed him, he could see that now, it was there in her eyes, and he liked it. He'd never been needed before, not like this, and it made him want to be there for her, protect her the way she'd protected their daughter.

He would get that yes from her. She would be his wife. She and Maya were his now and it was his responsibility to keep them both safe and happy.

And touching her now wasn't only about weighting the dice in his favour. It was also a token of his gratitude for what she'd done for their daughter, and his appreciation for her strength and courage. Pleasure, just for her and her alone.

Cesare looked into her eyes, seeing the flickers of her

passion beginning to ignite, and he bent his head, brushing his mouth over the top of one thigh and then the other.

Her breath hitched, yet she made no move to stop him. So he reached up and hooked his fingers in the waistband of her knickers and slowly drew them down. She sighed, lifting up to help him, then leaning back in the chair as he pulled them all the way off and dropped them on the floor.

Then he leaned in again and gently eased her thighs apart.

'Cesare...' she whispered, shivering.

'Little bird.' His thumbs stroked over her skin as he glanced hungrily at the soft golden curls between her thighs. *Dio*, she was gorgeous. Then he met her gaze once again. 'You are so beautiful. So strong and brave. Our little girl is healthy and happy, and that is all down to you. I want to show you how much that means to me, give you the pleasure you deserve. And I won't lie... I also want to show you what you could have as my wife, what a good husband can give you.'

Her eyes had gone dark with arousal, her face flushed. 'Yes. Yes, please...'

His own hunger was becoming demanding and he was hard, but for once in his life Cesare wasn't interested in his own pleasure. The only thing that mattered was hers.

He bent, nuzzling gently at her inner thighs, pressing kisses there as he went, hearing her breathing get faster and faster. He remembered how she'd tasted that night, remembered her cries of delight as he'd brought her to the edge of orgasm and held her there. That memory had lived in his head for so long and he'd never thought he'd ever get the chance to taste her again.

Yet here she was, between his hands and he couldn't wait.

He was so damn hungry.

He gripped her thighs and leaned in, nuzzling against the soft curls and kissing her there. Then he tightened his grip and using his tongue, began to explore the soft, damp folds of her sex.

Lark cried out, moving restlessly in his hands, but he didn't let go. He leaned in further, exploring her deeper, wanting to drive her to the edge of sanity and hold her there for as long as possible.

She was delicious. He wanted to do this all day, have her shaking and trembling and crying out as he gave her all the pleasure she deserved and then some.

His groin ached, his own need becoming demanding, but he shoved it aside. It wasn't important, not right now, not compared to her.

He knew how to pleasure a woman, knew how to bring her to the brink and hold her there. Knew how to use his hands and his mouth to give her the greatest ecstasy, and he did so now. Kissing her, licking, feasting on her. Devouring her as if she was the most delicious treat he'd ever tasted and she was.

She twisted in the chair and he felt her fingers in his hair, clutching at him as he continued to tease and to lick and to nip, using his fingers and then his tongue, circling and stroking that most sensitive part of her.

And he finally got what he wanted, her begging at the end, her fingers knotted in his hair, twisting in his grip as she tried to get that final friction that would send her over the edge.

But he denied her and denied her, wringing as much pleasure from her as he could until finally, with a light flick of his tongue, he gave her what she needed most.

Lark screamed, her body convulsing as the orgasm swept her, and he tasted it, salty and sweet and addictive.

Then he held her in his hands as she sobbed and trembled through the aftershocks, and only once she'd quietened did he ease back, looking at her.

Her head had lolled against the back of the chair, her eyes shut and her mouth slightly open, the gleam of perspiration at her throat.

He waited a moment then dealt with her clothes, calmly pulling her dress back down and covering her, while she watched him from beneath long, golden lashes.

'What about you?' she asked eventually, her voice hoarse. 'Don't you want—?'

'No,' he interrupted gently. 'That was for you. I don't need anything in return.'

She stared at him a long moment. 'You want me to say yes, don't you?'

He could tell her it didn't matter, not let her know how much he wanted it, but he couldn't lie, not to her. Not now.

So all he said was, 'I do. Very much.'

She was silent a long time, just looking at him. Then she said unexpectedly, 'I don't want another lover, Cesare. I want you. I want this.'

There was triumph inside him and a wave of satisfaction so intense it should have been a warning sign. But if so, it was a warning he paid no attention to, because he wanted more of this too.

'Then what is your answer, little bird?'

'Yes,' she said softly. 'My answer is yes.'

CHAPTER EIGHT

Things moved very quickly after Lark had agreed to be his wife. Cesare Donati was a man who apparently didn't let any grass grow under his feet.

He gave her some time to collect her and Maya's most important items from her flat, and to hand in her notice to Mr Ravenswood, then a week or so later, Lark found herself on a jet back to Italy.

Mr Ravenswood hadn't been too happy to lose her, though he'd been even more unhappy at losing the antiques since Cesare was now not going to sell them. However, he was mollified by Cesare promising to use his connections when it came to sourcing other items, and soon gave Lark a glowing reference.

Cesare had also organised for his staff to pack up her flat and clean it, which was a relief since she didn't relish having to do it herself.

As far as the whole marriage thing went, Cesare had asked her what she preferred in terms of a ceremony since he didn't much care, though he did warn her that since he was quite a public figure, media interest would be high. But she didn't want to make a big deal of it since it wasn't as if theirs was a love match and told him so.

He didn't waste any time with that either and as soon as they'd landed, Emily was sent to the palazzo with Maya, while Lark found herself having an impromptu wedding ceremony in a tiny chapel near the airport.

Afterwards, she sat in the limo staring at the rose-gold ring on her finger as she and Cesare drove to the palazzo. Somehow he'd found the time to get her the most beautiful ring. It was inset with tiny emeralds and was actually very beautiful.

She could hardly believe it. She was Signora Donati now and Maya had a little family. Perhaps she should have felt afraid or even had a hint of foreboding, but she didn't.

This had been the right thing to do, she knew it.

Of course, what life would be like now she was Cesare's wife was another story, as was what kind of marriage they'd have once they were settled.

He'd been true to his word and had had another agreement drawn up, and this time he'd had a third party look over it for her. There had been nothing in it to cause alarm. He hadn't even bothered with a prenup about his wealth in the event of a divorce. There had only been mention of custody arrangements for Maya and a certain amount of money for her upkeep too.

Lark had signed the agreement without protest, though she still felt a degree of uncertainty.

She couldn't stop thinking about the day he'd asked her to be his wife, and how he'd knelt before her chair, his hands stroking her, telling her that she was strong and beautiful, and that she'd been an excellent mother for Maya. And that she wasn't alone any more.

The sincerity with which he'd said it, so totally unexpected, had made her heart clench tight in her chest and unexpected tears rise. She had no idea how he'd known about the doubts she'd buried so far down she'd forgotten they were there. Doubts about the kind of mother she was, and whether she'd made the right choice in bringing Maya up by herself. They were always there, those doubts, and somehow Cesare had seen them, had brought them to the light, and then had looked into her eyes and told her that yes, she'd made the right choice. That he was glad she had, and that Maya was happy and healthy and that was the important thing. That she'd done a good job and he appreciated it.

He appreciated her.

Then he'd given her the most intense pleasure, taking her quickly and skilfully apart with the touch of his mouth and hands. He'd told her she was beautiful and brave and then he made her feel both of those things. He'd told her she wasn't alone and for the first time in her life, she actually felt it. Even as a child, loneliness had stalked her, because although she'd had her mother, it had never seemed as if Grace was really there. She was either in the depths of a depression, or staring off in the distance, turning that ring on her finger, gone somewhere in her thoughts that Lark couldn't follow. Her mother's attention had seemed a fleeting thing. There and then gone again in the blink of an eye, even though she was physically present.

But Cesare had knelt at her feet and looked at her, seeing her. Focusing all his intense attention on her, and she'd felt the weight of that attention settle on her. It wasn't heavy though, only deeply reassuring on a level she couldn't describe.

He meant it though, she'd seen it. Every word he'd said to her that day, he'd meant.

And now he was her husband; she didn't have any desire to go searching for a lover. She'd half thought, before he'd got down on his knees and made her feel so unbelievably good, that perhaps she wouldn't mind being celibate, since it had never bothered her before.

But he'd shown her the error of that particular piece of thinking, and in addition to reassuring her doubts, he'd somehow awakened the passion inside her, until she hadn't been able to think of anything else but him. Of what it would be like to be in a bed, naked, with him. Of how good it would be and how starved she'd been for physical touch.

As they pulled up to the palazzo, her new home, Lark made a decision. They hadn't discussed what kind of marriage they were going to have in the days leading up to it, such as whether they'd share a room and sleep together every night, or whether she'd have her own.

But she knew what she wanted. Sharing a room, sharing a bed.

He might not like that, but she was going to ask for it nonetheless.

Cesare got out of the limo, opened the door for her. 'Emily will be looking after Maya all afternoon,' he said as she stepped out onto the gravel, the blue of his eyes burning fiercely. 'I organised specially so you and I could have a wedding night.'

Emily had been looking after Maya on and off over the past few weeks, and Cesare had employed her to come to Italy with them since he wanted Maya to have someone familiar looking after her when her parents weren't able to.

Lark could feel her own desire start to rise in response to his, yet he must have picked up on some of her uncertainty, because he frowned all of a sudden. 'What is it?' he asked. 'Did you not want—'

'No,' she said quickly. 'No, it's not that. We just… haven't discussed anything about this marriage, Cesare. I mean, how it will work and what it will look like.'

'What is there to discuss? You'll be living here with me and Maya, and I'm hoping you feel the same way I do about sharing a bed.'

She swallowed and looked him in the eye. 'Every night? And it will be "our" bed, not just yours?'

'Yes.' He held her gaze. 'You will have your own space, but it will be "our" bed and "our" room.'

The last shred of tension left her and she let out a breath. 'Okay, so apart from the living arrangements and sex,' she said, as staff bustled around, taking luggage out of the car and into the house. 'I also don't know anything about you and I'd like to.'

He shut the limo door then paused. 'What do you want to know?'

'I told you all about my childhood and my past. About my mother and growing up on the run. You know about me, but I don't know anything about you. Unless you told me that night?' She looked up at him, part of her hoping that it hadn't only been her who'd opened her heart, that he too had reciprocated.

But slowly he shook his head. 'No. My past, my family history is…dark. And I didn't want to talk about it that night. You were so warm and open, and you needed someone to talk to. I didn't want to make it about me or drag you down into a discussion about my family's dramatics.'

The words sounded casual, but she heard it again, the slight edge. The edge that always carried in his voice whenever he spoke about his family.

It was something bad—she could see the shadows stealing through his gaze—and part of her wondered if now was a good time to talk about it, especially since they'd only just been married. Then again, maybe now was the perfect time, so she knew immediately what she and by extension Maya were getting into.

'Well, I'd like to know,' she said. 'I mean, shouldn't I know something about the man I married and the family I married into?'

'You are looking at the entirety of the family you married into.' His voice had gone curiously blank. 'I'm the last heir. Or at least I was until Maya appeared.'

She'd heard about that. It was what the media called him. Perhaps she should have done some internet research on her own about him, but she'd been too busy the past week with moving and getting things organised.

'Will you tell me about it?' she asked.

His blue gaze had gone dark. 'Are you sure you want to know? A quick internet search should tell you everything.'

'Maybe. But I'd rather not get Maya's family history from the internet. I'd prefer to hear it from her father.'

He was silent a moment. 'Well, don't say I didn't warn you.' He held out a hand. 'Come with me.'

She took it, his fingers threading through hers warm and strong, then followed him as he led her in through the palazzo's ornate entrance and into the huge salon where she'd first met him only a couple of weeks earlier. He let go of her hand, stopping before the fireplace and glancing up at the portrait hanging above it, of the stern-looking man and the pretty woman with rose-gold hair.

'Those are my parents,' he said. 'Giovanni and Bianca Donati. They married for love by all accounts, not that you'd know it in the end.' He put his hands in his pockets, still staring up at the portrait. 'I don't remember a time when they weren't fighting. My first memory was of them arguing about whether I should have a nanny or not. My father insisted that I should, while my mother insisted that I shouldn't, that I had her. Mama was intense about her opinions, hated to conform, harboured grudges and never admitted she was wrong, while my father was proud and rigid and fanatical about traditions. *Compromise* wasn't a word either of them understood. They spent an entire month arguing about it. Papa kept hiring nannies and Mama kept sending them away until she eventually got her way.'

Lark folded her arms, watching him.

'Then came my schooling. Papa wanted me to go to the boarding school he attended, Mama refused to let me go. She wanted to teach me herself. They argued about that on and off for six months, until eventually Papa hired tutors for me at home. That wasn't good enough for Mama and she continued to complain about it both to me and to Papa. She didn't like it when I was given riding lessons at six either. She thought I was too young and she and Papa had a shouting match about it. Papa won that round too.'

A sense of foreboding crept through Lark. This was not going to end well she could feel it.

'Papa had a business trip to London not long after that, and so my mother took me to America without telling him for a fun "holiday". He found out and was furious that she hadn't told him and that we went without security. She accused him of stifling me, he accused her of being lax and not putting my safety first, and so it continued. For some reason I became the thing they argued about almost constantly, and because they couldn't let anything go, it escalated.

I fell off my horse one day—it wasn't anything major— but Mama ordered my riding lessons to stop, and when Papa told her she was overreacting, it blew up into this huge screaming match. She demanded a divorce, but he refused, so she retaliated by waiting until he was on another business trip, then walking out and taking me with her.' Cesare's blue gaze came to hers and there was something in his blue eyes she didn't recognise. 'Donati staff found out and alerted Papa. He arrived at the airport in Rome just as we were about to go through security and he stopped us. Mama didn't care that we were in a public place, she screamed at him and he shouted back, while I was pulled between them.'

Lark's chest tightened. 'How old were you?'

'Eight.'

God. Eight and caught between shouting, screaming parents. She couldn't imagine how awful that must have been for him.

'Oh, Cesare,' she said softly.

'You think that's bad?' He smiled, but there was no amusement in it. 'Just wait. It gets worse. Papa took me home and refused to let her see me, telling her that he was happy for her to leave, but she wasn't taking me with her. Mama of course couldn't let that go. She always hated it when Papa won. So she told him the only way she was leaving was with me, and stayed. She camped out in one wing of the palazzo, arguing with him constantly, insisting that I be allowed to see her, that he was cruel to keep a mother from her child, etcetera, etcetera.' Cesare turned back to the portrait, his expression bitter. 'Eventually she wore him down and he allowed her supervised visits with me, but that only enraged her more. She didn't consider it a victory, telling me that he was a terrible father and didn't I want to be with her? That she loved me more than he ever would.'

Cesare paused a moment and she could see the tension in his tall figure, could feel it thread through her too, a crawling, aching dread.

'I was ten by then and one day she turned up for a scheduled visit after my riding class. We were going to have a picnic, she said, and somehow she managed to send the staff member who was supposed to be supervising us away. I hadn't seen her for about two weeks and I was… reluctant to go with her. She could never leave the subject of her grudge with Papa alone, and I always felt as if it was my fault somehow, especially since all they fought about was me. Anyway, that day she was…happy and seemed excited to see me, so I went on her picnic. We had it beside the river and there was delicious food. She poured me an orange juice from a thermos and gave it to me. Told me to drink the whole thing.'

His voice had become colder and Lark felt herself get colder too, the dread tightening.

'I started feeling dizzy and sick, and very sleepy, so I lay down, and she stroked my hair telling me that soon we'd be together and free of him. My last memory before I blacked out is of my father suddenly arriving and shouting, and her screaming back, and when I woke up, I was in hospital.'

Lark caught her breath in shock. 'What happened?'

Cesare glanced at her once again. 'Mama wanted to punish Papa once and for all and had poisoned the orange juice. Apparently she'd planned to poison me then herself. But the staff member she'd sent away went straight to Papa and he found us before she could drink the rest of the juice. He'd brought a gun and when he found out what she'd done, he shot her. Then he shot himself.'

Lark stared at him, horrified. She'd thought her childhood had been pretty bad, but that was nothing in comparison with his. That his own mother had tried to kill him and herself… Then his father shooting her…

'Cesare,' she began faintly yet again, only to stop, because she couldn't think of a word to say.

'Yes,' he said, the word full of bitterness. 'What kind of response can you to make to that? It's almost farcical in its dramatics, don't you think? But then that's the Donati family way. Our history is full people shooting, stabbing or poisoning people we don't like. It's a history of self-involvement. Of selfishness. Of putting our feelings ahead of anyone else's including our children's.' He gave a laugh that was utterly cold and cynical sounding. 'It wasn't exactly the world's most loving environment as you can imagine.'

Lark's mouth was dry, her chest tight. She felt almost crushed by the weight of a terrible sympathy for him, for a little boy caught between two self-involved individuals who'd cared more about their grudges than for their son.

At least her mother had cared. She'd escaped her marriage because she'd wanted to keep Lark safe.

Sure, but let her fear and paranoia make things difficult for you. You weren't allowed any bad feelings either, because it upset her.

Lark shoved the thought aside. That might be true, but if it hadn't been for Lark then her mother would never have had to run at all; she was not forgetting that.

Anyway, this wasn't about her. This was about Cesare.

She wanted to cross the room to where he stood and put her arms around him, give him some kind of comfort because it was the only thing she could think of to do.

It was a horrible story, a terrible one, and no child should ever have to experience their own parent trying to harm them the way he had. No child should ever have to think that it was their fault either, and from what he said, it was clear that part of him still blamed himself.

She took a step towards him, but he'd turned back to the painting, going over to the fireplace and putting his hands on the mantelpiece, staring up at the portrait. And there was something about his posture now, a subtle change in tension that kept her frozen where she was.

He didn't seem bitter now. He seemed furious.

'Anyway,' he went on. 'For years I ignored what they did to me. My aunt cared for me until I reached my majority, but she wasn't exactly a loving caregiver either. She died two years ago and it was then that I decided I was done with the Donati legacy. That I was going to burn it to the ground, break it up, sell everything and donate the proceeds to charity.'

Yet more shock echoed through her. 'What? All of it?'

'Yes.' He pushed himself away from the mantelpiece and turned to face her. 'Don't mistake me, little bird. I'm as selfish and self-serving as my parents. I tried to be good for them, to be the perfect son for them. I listened to my mother's complaints and I obeyed my father's every directive. I thought that if I was only good and obedient enough they'd finally stop arguing about me. But nothing I did made any difference, and for a long time I blamed myself for their deaths. They hadn't made a will, because they couldn't agree on the terms, at least that's what my aunt told me before she died, and that's when I realised the truth.

'Nothing I did made any difference to them, because they didn't care about me. Their arguments and grudges and petty slights were more important to them than providing for their child. So why should I care about them? Why should I blame myself for something that wasn't my fault? They were gone, but I still had their toxic legacy to look after and that's when I decided I was done looking after it.'

She didn't have an answer to that, mainly because she could understand why he felt that way. Who wouldn't? After they'd been treated the way he'd been treated?

'But you changed your mind about that, didn't you?' she asked.

'I did,' he agreed. 'I changed it the minute I saw Maya's picture on your phone and I knew she was mine.' His blue gaze gleamed suddenly. 'I decided she would be my new start. My new beginning. A chance to create a different Donati legacy, a better legacy. She's untouched by my history, by what my parents did to me, and I want her to stay untouched by it. I want her to grow up knowing what happiness is like, to put something better out in the world that isn't just selfishness.' He paused a moment. 'I want her to grow up to be a better person than I am, a better Donati.'

The tightness in Lark's chest wouldn't ease. He saw himself in such a negative light, didn't he? He called himself selfish, thought he wasn't a good person, though she didn't understand why. Then again, he'd grown up in the middle of a cold war, where the people who were supposed to protect him had been more interested in hurting each other. And they'd argued over him as if he was the problem, and he'd felt that way too. And she suspected that no matter what he'd told her about deciding he was done with blaming himself, a part of him still did. Why else would he keep seeing himself as selfish when everything he'd done so far was the opposite?

Well, however he felt, while she hated that he'd been forced into that position, she admired his resolution. Sometimes when she'd been younger, she'd often used to wonder what it would be like to just be allowed to be angry.

To shout if you wanted to, cry if you wanted to. Not be told that your smile was the best thing about you and how great it was that you were always happy. How your positivity made the world a better place.

Then how your one bad mood could cause a depression spiral that ended with your mother not leaving her bed for days.

What would have happened if she'd been a little bit selfish herself?

But there was no point in thinking that. Her mother was gone and those kinds of thoughts were disloyal. She'd been in a terrible situation and she'd done her best with Lark, so who was Lark to criticise?

'You're not a bad person, Cesare,' Lark said. 'Why demonise yourself? It was your parents who had the behavioural issues, not you.'

'I'm not demonising myself. I'm only accepting who I am. No one wins in a situation like that one and certainly not the child caught in the middle of it.'

'You're not selfish, though. Why would you think that?'

He lifted a shoulder. 'Because I want what I want when I want it. I wanted revenge for what my parents did to me, so I put it in motion. And then when I realised I had a child, I wanted to make sure she was the new legacy I put out in the world. It's not about her, Lark. It's about me and what I want. Don't ever forget that.'

But there was something in that statement that just didn't ring true, especially not after seeing him with Maya. And not after he'd knelt at her feet, the look on his face nothing but sincere as he told her she wasn't alone.

'You do care about her, though,' she said. 'You wanted me to come with her because she needed her mother and her happiness was important to you. And what you said to me—'

'It's the legacy, Lark,' he corrected her gently. 'That's all I care about. Creating a new and improved dynasty, that's all. Now.' The flame in his eyes leapt. 'I'm tired of talking about this. Why don't we get to our wedding night?'

There wasn't much distance between them and yet he felt suddenly as if any distance at all was far too much.

Nothing about his recitation of his terrible childhood should have been difficult, because it had been a very long time since he'd woken up in that hospital bed and his aunt had told him the truth about what happened.

Yet…he'd found himself tensing as he'd told Lark about it. Found that the fury he'd thought he'd buried, the fury that had consumed him as a teenager and that had no outlet because the people he was furious at were gone, was back. It simmered like a field of burning magma just under the earth's crust, scalding, melting anything in its path.

He'd hated that anger. It reminded him of his parents, of his mother's shrill rage and his father's outraged roaring. Of standing in that airport as the two of them had yanked him back and forth, fighting over him as if he was a bone between two dogs. Of the feverish brightness in his mother's bright eyes as she'd poured him that orange juice, and the satisfaction in his father's expression as he'd told Cesare that he was forbidding Bianca to see him.

No one could understand what had happened in their marriage to make the two of them hate each other like that. Cesare had read all about it in the media, the articles and the think pieces, the theories on why, but he knew, because he felt it himself.

The why was in the ferocity of his anger, an anger that had come from love.

Love was the issue. Love was the problem.

He'd loved his parents, yet they'd continually made him feel as if he was failing one or the other of them, and so that love had turned to rage. He hated them now and that hate was the same hate they'd turned on each other, which was why he had to be careful.

Anger could turn into toxicity so quickly, and he himself might have been consumed back when he was younger, if he hadn't funnelled it into determination. A determination to not let his parents ruin his life. To not be scarred by it or harmed by it. To come out of it unmarked and strong and successful.

So that's what he'd done. Yet his anger was still with him, still bubbling away under the surface. He'd thought he'd managed to get rid of it, but clearly he hadn't, which meant he'd made a mistake somewhere along the line.

He'd let himself care; that was the issue. He'd let himself care about Lark, about what she thought of him, and now he was angry that he cared. So he'd thrown his own self-ishness back in her face so she knew what kind of man he was. Yet she hadn't flinched from him. She'd only looked at him levelly and told him not to demonise himself, that he wasn't selfish and why would he think he was?

He didn't like that and he didn't like the way she was staring at him now, with an expression of sympathy and understanding. Looking at him as if he was still that hurt little boy all those years ago.

'Don't look at me like that,' he said abruptly. 'I don't need your pity. It was years ago. I am done with it now and I am done with them.'

'It's not pity.' Her voice was quiet. 'I'm sad and horrified for you, Cesare, and I'm sorry you had that happen to you. No child should be treated that way. To be fought over like a…a possession. And then to make you feel as if you were to blame—'

'I don't feel that way,' he interrupted harshly. 'Not any more.'

She didn't even blink. 'Don't you? You're certainly still angry with them.'

'Perhaps,' he forced out, not wanting to admit it, yet not being able to deny it either. 'But having you and Maya here will be a new beginning. A way to leave this particular piece of the past behind.'

Lark nodded slowly, studying him for a long moment, making discomfort twist inside him. He didn't like the way she looked at him, as if she could see right through him, through every lie he'd told himself since his parents' death, even the lie that he was done with both it and them.

Then she said, 'You have every right to be angry with them, Cesare. They were terrible parents and they should have done better.'

It was such a simple statement and trite in its way. Yet he felt something twist inside him, though he wasn't sure what it was. He didn't want to examine it, though. Neither did he want a conversation about his own motivations and thoughts with Lark.

'Yes,' he agreed, keeping his voice very neutral. 'They should. But now you know my history and Maya's.' He took a step towards her, taking his hands from his pockets. 'Come upstairs with me. I want you naked.'

She didn't move, her gaze level. Today she wore a plain blue linen dress that caught the blue hints in her green eyes and her golden hair was loose and curling over her shoulders. It wasn't a white wedding dress, but she didn't need a white dress to look feminine and delicate, like a princess. A princess he wanted to ravish completely.

His wife now.

If you'd really wanted to create a different legacy you should have had a different beginning. You should have married her properly. Given her a beautiful dress and a wonderful ceremony, then taken her on a honeymoon that she'd remember for ever.

Perhaps he should, but it was too late now. It was done. He'd been impatient to get his ring on her finger and now she was his wife.

The primal, possessive part of him, the part that he never let out from its cage, growled like a beast. He wanted her in his bed and now, and what he wanted he got.

He'd told her he was selfish and what he wanted was all that mattered.

He stalked towards her, closing the distance, loving the way she gave a little gasp as he reached out and gripped her by the hips, pulling her hard up against him. She was all soft and warm against the hard length of his sex, and he was starting to think that maybe he'd just have her here, on the sofa. Or perhaps he'd bend her over it. Either way would suit him nicely.

Lark lifted her hands and put them on his chest, not pushing him, but certainly holding him at bay.

'Wait,' she said breathlessly. 'I need us to discuss a few things first.'

'Things?' He slid his hands over her rear, fitting the soft heat between her thighs over his aching groin, impatience gripping him. 'What things?'

Lark's hands remained firm on his chest. Her face was delightfully flushed, but the expression in her eyes was all determination. 'I told you, Cesare. Our marriage.'

'You wanted my history so I gave it.' He flexed his hips against her, watching with satisfaction as her gaze darkened, arousal glowing hot beneath her determination. 'What else do you need?'

She took a sharp breath. 'It's not just that, and it's not just being in your bed and living together. It's about how we treat each other. That will have an effect on Maya—you can't deny that. We're both living examples of it after all.'

She's right. She has thought about this. Have you?

No, if he was honest with himself, he hadn't. All he'd thought about was making her and Maya his and then having Lark in his bed. That was the extent of it. And he was finding it difficult to think about it now, because her warmth and vanilla scent was driving him crazy.

Still, she had a point, they did need to talk about it. 'We can discuss later, surely?' he asked, his voice now slightly roughed with desire.

'I don't want us to start this marriage off in a way that might end badly for all of us.' There was doubt in her eyes beneath the determination and the arousal, and that doubt caught at him. He didn't like it. He didn't want her doubting this new life. He wanted her feeling safe and secure and happy.

So he forced his desire aside for a moment and met her gaze. 'I don't either,' he said, letting her see the conviction in his eyes. 'So know that I will always treat you with the utmost respect. Any issues or disagreements we have, we discuss privately and do everything we can to find a compromise if we can't agree. Aside from that, you and I will share a bed every night, but during the day we can go our own ways. We will come together as a family when it's required for Maya, and we will never, ever argue about her in front of her.'

Lark stared up at him silently for a long moment, searching his face. Then the doubt in her eyes began to fade. 'We both want what's best for her, don't we?'

'Yes,' he agreed and meant it. 'She comes first. Always.'

Lark's hands relaxed, desire glowing bright in her eyes. Then her fingers curled in the material of his shirt and she tugged him close. 'Good,' she murmured. 'I like the sound of that.'

Then she went up on her toes and pressed her mouth to his.

CHAPTER NINE

LARK FOUND THE next few weeks unexpectedly happy.

For all that Cesare had told her that they'd go their separate ways during the day, he ended up staying at the palazzo quite a lot. He told her he was 'working from home' but seemed to spend a good deal of his time with Maya. Helping her 'settle in', apparently.

Not that she was complaining.

Not when every night she was naked in his bed, in his arms.

There was so much pleasure to be had from him, and yet another reason why she didn't understand why he thought he was selfish, not when he was the opposite in bed.

He was inventive when it came to wringing orgasms from her, encouraging her to tell him what she wanted and how, then welcoming her passion whenever she gave it. He never refused her anything and seemed to get as much enjoyment from her pleasure as he did from his own.

There was nothing selfish about that, nothing at all.

Some mornings she'd come down to breakfast in the palazzo to find him lying on the ground with his daughter, letting her climb all over him and pull on his expensive silk tie with her dirty hands, or playing trucks, which really just consisted of banging them on the ground. Once, she'd come down to find Maya asleep in the crook of his arm and him singing softly to her in Italian.

That in particular had caught at her heart, her daughter's red-gold curls nestled against the dark wool of his suit, golden eyelashes fanned over her rosy cheeks. He'd been looking down at her as he sang and the expression on his face had stolen her breath. She'd had to look away, feeling as if she'd invaded his privacy somehow.

He'd told her the day they'd got married that it wasn't Maya who was important to him, but his legacy, and maybe he believed that. But it wasn't true and Lark knew it. Not when he'd also said, not five minutes later that Maya came first, always.

Whether he knew it or not, he loved his daughter. It was written all over his face.

He didn't just spend time with Maya, though. He was very insistent that they do things together 'as a family'. Again, not something she'd object to, since she enjoyed those things as much as she suspected he did.

Sometimes it was as simple as having dinner outside on one of the terraces, with Maya in a highchair and Cesare insisting on feeding her himself as he listened to Lark tell him about Maya's day. Afterwards, they'd lie on a blanket on the lawn, in the warm summer evening scented with the lavender that grew in the garden beds nearby, idly chatting about nothing as Maya played with her growing collection of trucks.

Sometimes it was more of an outing, such as the time Cesare took them to spend a few days in Venice in a luxurious palace beside the canals. They'd had gondola rides and Maya had squealed with delight at the pigeons in the Piazza San Marco.

He took them to other places around Italy too, Tuscany

and the Cinque Terre, to Florence and Naples, and Milan. He said he wanted to show Maya the country since she was part Italian, but Lark had a sneaking suspicion that he wasn't quite telling the truth about that. Because Maya was very little and probably wouldn't remember or appreciate the beautiful scenery, but Lark did. Lark did very much.

Then in Rome, after a day spent wandering the streets with Maya in a buggy and all three of them eating gelato, Cesare organised a private tour of the Colosseum, and even though Lark had told him she'd already seen it, he insisted she go. Because Maya hadn't seen it, he told her, and neither had she, not without all the crowds.

Privately Lark doubted Maya needed to see the Colosseum just yet, but she didn't really mind. Yet as they stood there in the ruins of a once mighty empire, Cesare bent and picked Maya up, putting her up on his shoulders, and as her squeals of delight rang off the ancient stones, Lark remembered standing in this same place nearly two years earlier. And she'd watched a family standing together like this, a child on their father's shoulders, the mother standing by. And she'd been hit by such a feeling of such isolation and loneliness, or wishing she'd had a family just like that one.

Now she had, yet it wasn't the same. Not quite.

She had a daughter and a husband, but their marriage was lacking one thing. They were only married for Maya's sake not their own, and while she and Cesare loved Maya, they didn't love each other.

They respected each other—he'd kept his promise to her that he'd treat her with nothing but respect—but love wasn't a part of that.

Why do you need love? You didn't want it, remember?

She hadn't, no. But now the lack of it made her worry for the future of their little family. Cesare had promised that Maya always came first and she agreed, but would that be enough to hold them together?

If she'd learned anything from her unsettled childhood it was that a broken relationship between a child's parents could hurt their child, and Cesare too had been a prime example of that.

She didn't want that kind of tragedy for her daughter. Not that she thought she and Cesare would suddenly turn on each other like their respective parents' had, nevertheless... He'd promised he'd be faithful, but what if he got tired of sleeping with her? What if he wanted someone else? What would happen and what would she do?

The very thought of it sent a hot, bright bolt of unexpected jealousy straight through her, and because Cesare had chosen that moment to glance at her, she'd had to turn away quickly in order to hide it.

How ridiculous to be jealous. He'd been very clear that love was something he didn't want, and that they'd be sleeping together only as long as this desire lasted and then they'd be done.

She'd agreed to it. She'd let him put that ring on her finger. She'd known exactly what a marriage to him had meant. Being jealous hadn't never been part of this scenario.

You never thought you'd feel something for him, though.

Lark's stomach dropped away.

The tour guide's voice rose and fell, but she'd stopped listening.

She *did* feel something for him, it was nestled there close to her heart, and what it was, she didn't know and didn't want to. But whatever it was, it made the thought of him finding some other woman to hold at night...difficult.

A selfish man wouldn't have noticed her sudden quiet. A selfish man wouldn't have paid any attention to her at all. Yet after the tour was over and as they got in the car to return to the palazzo, Cesare glanced at her. 'You're very quiet, little bird. Is anything wrong?'

She couldn't tell him about that jealousy, about that feeling in her heart, not when she didn't have the words for it herself, so instead she pasted on her sunniest, most cheerful smile. 'No, of course not. Why would there be? I've had the loveliest day.'

He looked as if he was going to say something more, but right then Maya dropped her soft rabbit on the floor of the car and started shouting with annoyance, which distracted Cesare nicely.

She should have known better than to think he'd forgotten, though.

When they'd got home and a very tired Maya had been settled in bed, Cesare slid an arm around her waist and pulled her in close in the hallway outside Maya's door.

'Now that I finally have you alone,' he murmured. 'You can tell me what's wrong.'

Lark swallowed, the familiar warmth of his body against hers working its magic.

Damn him. She couldn't tell him and it certainly wasn't worth upsetting the balance they'd found in their marriage to even try articulating her strange doubts.

And it would upset it. She had no idea what he'd think about her feelings for him, but he certainly wouldn't like it.

'Nothing.' She took a breath and then forced herself to look up at him, giving him the same bright smile that she always gave her mother. 'Honestly. I was just a bit tired earlier.'

His gaze narrowed into glowing blue sapphire splinters. 'You can smile at me like that till kingdom come, little bird, and I still won't believe you.'

Annoyance gripped her. That smile had always worked for her mother. Why wouldn't it work for him?

'There's nothing—'

'Lark.' His hands tightened on her hips. 'You went very quiet at the Colosseum today and wouldn't look me in the eye after the tour. Why? Something's bothering you and I want to know what.'

She couldn't help herself, she had to glance away. He'd see straight through her, because he always seemed to. He'd see her jealousy and the feeling that was growing inside her, the fear that she didn't want to examine or even articulate.

That she was falling for him.

Instead she stared at the buttons of his casual black shirt and put her hands on his chest, feeling the steady beat of his heart, trying to think of something to say that wasn't the truth and coming up with nothing. 'It doesn't matter, Cesare,' she said at last. 'Leave it.'

But then her chin was being gripped in long fingers as he forced her gaze up to meet his. 'Why do you do that?' he demanded abruptly. 'Why do you smile and pretend nothing's wrong?'

Her annoyance deepened. 'I'm not pretending.'

'Yes, you are. I can see it in your eyes and your smile is fake as hell.'

The annoyance became anger and for a minute it was all she could do not to snap and rip herself from his arms. And she didn't want to snap. She didn't want to ruin what had been a perfectly nice day with a foul temper.

'Little bird,' Cesare said, quieter this time, the look in his eyes softening unexpectedly. 'You don't have to pretend with me, you know that, don't you?'

She wasn't sure why her anger faltered right then. Why it simply flickered and went out like a candle flame. Perhaps it was because of his gentle reminder when she'd been expecting him to argue, or the concern in his eyes when she'd been expecting irritation.

And that was the thing, wasn't it? She'd never pretended with him. She'd never been able to, not even right from the very beginning.

So she let herself relax against him, lean into his warmth and his strength. 'I know,' she said. 'It's just... Mum was so fragile emotionally and getting angry or being in a bad mood always made her worse. Even just being sad was an issue. And I...didn't want to make things harder for her than they already were. So... I made sure I was always in a good mood, that I was always smiling, because it was easier for both of us if I was.'

Cesare's thumb stroked over her chin in a gentle movement. 'Well, I'm not your mother, Lark Donati. I'm your husband and I'm not afraid of your temper, and you know that. We wouldn't be standing right here if I was.'

Lark felt something inside her ease, a tightness that she hadn't realised was there. 'That's true,' she admitted. 'You never have been.'

He was frowning, though. 'I don't like that she made you feel responsible for her moods.'

'She wasn't well,' Lark said. 'I didn't want to add to it. And sometimes—' She broke off all of a sudden, not wanting to say the doubt out loud, because part of her didn't want her to acknowledge it even to herself,

'Sometimes?' Cesare let go of her hips, only to thread his fingers through her hair, holding her gently as he looked down into her eyes. 'What about sometimes?'

She sighed. 'Sometimes I used to wonder if she wouldn't have been happier if I hadn't been born at all. Then she wouldn't have had to go on the run and maybe she wouldn't have—'

'She might,' Cesare interrupted gently. 'But also, she might not have. Also, as a parent, I know that even though Maya completely upended my life and yours, I'd much rather she was born than not.'

Lark let out a breath and the words she'd been keeping inside for far too long came spilling out along with it. 'There was nothing I could do to fix her,' she said huskily. 'I tried to be happy, tried to keep smiling. Tried to stay optimistic. But nothing worked. Or it would work for a bit, but then she'd spiral again. Sometimes, she'd stay in her room with the door locked for days and days.' Her throat tightened, the old fear flooding back. 'And I used to be so afraid that one day she wouldn't come out.'

Cesare's blue gaze somehow became no less fierce, no less sharp, and yet there was something protective in it that wrapped around her heart and pulled tight. 'I know your mother was in a difficult situation and that she was afraid. And that she might have been sick, as well, but why did she not get help?'

'It was difficult, because she didn't want anyone to know our names in case my father found us.'

'So what provision did she make for you?' His fingers tightened in her hair. 'What if one day she actually hadn't come out of that room? What would have happened to you then?'

Unexpectedly, Lark felt her tears fill her eyes. She'd been so afraid back then, and sometimes she wondered if perhaps her mother had infected her with her own fear and paranoia, that it was a vicious circle, each of them feeding off the other's fear.

'I don't know,' she said huskily. 'She didn't have any friends and wouldn't allow me to have any either. She thought the less people who knew about us the better.'

Cesare's mouth hardened and she saw the blue glow of anger in his eyes. But not at her she knew.

'You can't get angry at her,' she said, feeling protective. 'She did the best she could.'

'No, she didn't.' His voice was flat. 'The best she could would have been not to make you responsible for her well-being. That was her job, not yours.'

It was her most secret doubt, the anger that she kept locked tight away inside her. Anger at Grace for doing exactly that, for ensuring her childhood was one town after another, a cheap flat, a grotty motel room, a stranger's basement…

No friends. No steady school. Only fear and the sense that she was always walking on eggshells around her mother, never sure what would send her into another depressive incident. The knowledge that she was the one who had to look after Grace, not the other way around.

Lark felt hot tears fill her eyes, though she wasn't sure why. Maybe just the fact that he'd said it aloud and it was such a relief to have someone else acknowledge it. 'I was… angry at her,' she said. 'I know it wasn't her fault and that she wanted to protect me, and I loved her. But I'm angry with her all the same.'

'You can love someone and be angry with them at the same time,' he said. 'And I know it doesn't change things, but you should have had better, Lark.'

He believed it, she could see. There was a fierceness to his stare that for some reason felt like cold water on a burn, easing her. Soothing her.

'Thanks,' she said huskily. 'That helps. And you know what? I don't even feel angry any more.'

'Good.' The fierceness in his stare somehow intensified. 'Then you won't mind telling me what was bothering you earlier, will you?'

* * *

Cesare saw reluctance flicker through Lark's wide sea-green eyes. She didn't want to tell him, that was clear, though he couldn't imagine why, not when over the course of the past few weeks they'd grown closer.

Having her here at the palazzo, in his bed at night and waking up to her in the morning, then sharing coffee on the terrace as Maya played at their feet…it had been so unexpectedly fulfilling. And while he still saw flashes of her delightful temper, she'd started to relax with him, the truth of her becoming apparent, so warm and open and genuine. Intelligent, funny and honest too.

She was a delight. The way she'd been that night two years ago.

Their daughter too was a delight.

He also hadn't realised how completely fascinating having a child was. How a deep part of him kept getting drawn to this little girl with the big blue eyes the same colour as his own. Maya, too, had a temper that he admired and she was also very stubborn, which he also admired. She was very loud sometimes and he admired that less, but he respected her commitment to it.

She'd started smiling for him now and lifting her arms to him whenever she saw him, and he was sure she'd babbled *Papa* at him on more than one occasion.

He had no words to describe the strength of feeling inside him on those occasions.

The only thing he knew was that going places with his little family or even just staying at home with them had made him for the first time in his life…happy.

This was what he'd wanted to give his child that he'd never had himself. This happiness. He'd once thought that all families were like his, that most parents screamed and hated each other like his did, but it wasn't until after they'd gone that he'd understood that no, most families weren't like that.

Perhaps it had been then that all the anger he'd suppressed while he'd been a child trying to make two irrational people happy had started spilling out like poison. Anger at them and what they'd put him through, the childhood he'd been denied. Happiness. Security. Love.

All his parents had given him was their own rage, which they'd nurtured with their dysfunctional relationship and so now he was cursed with it too. There was no escape for him. There was always the doubt that if he gave in to it, he'd turn into them, violent and irrational and toxic.

But he'd been good these past few weeks. The simmering rage that had burned just beneath the surface of his skin had receded back down to where he'd buried it deep inside, and hopefully now it was gone for good. It hadn't touched Maya or Lark, and he was glad.

He'd been feeling very glad at the Colosseum today, too, enjoying the feeling of Maya's warm little body on his shoulders and hearing her laugh. He'd turned to glance at Lark to see if she was enjoying herself as much as he was, only to catch a glimpse of some troubled expression on her eyes, something painful. Then she'd looked away, avoiding his gaze.

A strange feeling had stolen through him then, an urge to find out what it was that was hurting her and take it away, soothe her. It was unfamiliar this feeling, yet he hadn't questioned it after they'd got into the car. He'd asked her straight out what was wrong, but she'd only smiled, told him it was nothing and turned away.

Maya losing her toy had distracted him, yet he hadn't forgotten. The smile Lark had given him had been fake. And he knew the difference. He'd been seeing Lark's genu-

ine smiles for the past few weeks, after all. When she held
Maya in her arms and looked down at her. When he kept
the light on at night, so he could watch her face as he made
love to her, and after he'd given her as much pleasure as
they both could handle, and after they'd both recovered,
she'd smile slowly, like the sun coming up, lighting her
face, lighting her green eyes.

That was a real smile. But the one she'd given him in
the car was not.

Perhaps he should have let it go, but he couldn't. The
knowledge that something was bothering her nagged at
him like a shard of glass caught in a place he couldn't
reach, and he knew that he couldn't ignore it. He had to
find out what was wrong.

Her happiness was vital to his new legacy plan, which
meant he had to fix it.

He'd got sidetracked by talk of her mother and he could
see now why she'd been pretending today. It had made him
inexplicably angry the way she'd been treated as a child,
the burden of responsibility that had been put on her shoulders by her mother, and he'd found himself wishing he
could change it. Go back in time and tell Grace Edwards
to get out of her head and look at what she was doing to
her daughter. An irrational wish. Nevertheless he wished
it. But all he could do was tell Lark that she shouldn't
have had to deal with that, that it had been wrong of her
mother, and hope Lark believed him. Also, that he wasn't
her mother and she didn't need to do that with him.

Lark's lashes lowered, veiling her gaze as she toyed
with one of the buttons on his shirt. 'It's nothing,' she said
slowly. 'Only…that night we met two years ago, I'd also
just been to the Colosseum and I saw a family there. Parents and a child, and they were having so much fun. I re-

member wishing I could have had that as a kid.' She let out a long breath and looked up at him. 'Then we were there today and I realised I did have it. With you and Maya.'

He frowned, dropping his hands to her hips and then lower, sliding over the curve of her rear to bring her closer, where he preferred her. 'You didn't look happy, though,' he said. 'You looked as if someone had stabbed you.'

She stared up at him for a long moment. Then abruptly she pushed herself away and out of his arms. His first instinct was to grab her and pull her back, but he crushed the urge. If she wanted space then he had to let her have it. Her needs were important to his plan and he couldn't let himself forget it.

'What's going to happen, Cesare?' she asked. 'When you find someone you want more than me? When you get tired of me? What will we do?'

His frown deepened. He didn't understand why she was asking him this. 'What has that got to do with you realising you have a family?'

'That family I saw, they loved each other.' Lark's voice was flat. 'All of them loved each other.'

'So?' He still didn't quite see what she was getting at.

'Our marriage isn't a real marriage,' she said. 'We're only together for Maya's sake. So what happens if it breaks down between us? What happens if you decide you want someone else?'

'Our marriage is very real,' he insisted, slightly irritated because they'd already had this discussion right before she agreed to marry him. 'You've taken my name. You wear my ring. You sleep in my bed. We live together. How is that not real?'

'Because we don't…care about other, do we?' There was an odd pain glittering in her eyes that he didn't quite understand. 'And it's the children that suffer when two people don't care about each other, Cesare. You know that and so do I.'

A flicker of shock went through him, because he hadn't been expecting this. It felt as if she'd taken a hammer to the most perfect mirror and now there was a crack running straight through it.

How could she think he didn't care about her? When he'd done nothing but make sure she was happy for the past three weeks?

'That's not true,' he said, itching to grab her and drag her back into his arms and show her just how wrong she was. 'I do care about you. Haven't I been proving it to you since we got married? Haven't you been happy these past few weeks?'

She let out a breath, the expression on her face difficult to read. 'Yes,' she said, almost reluctantly. 'I have. I just...want Maya to know what a good relationship looks like. What respect means. I want her to know what a good man looks like.'

That hit him hard, in a place where he knew he was vulnerable. Because he wanted that for Maya too, but he wasn't a good man. He never had been.

You'll just have to try harder then, won't you?

Yes. He would.

'I agree,' he said. 'And she will know, Lark. I promise on her life that she will know.'

Lark said nothing, her gaze was unreadable and he didn't like it.

'What more do you want?' He was impatient now to get whatever this was out of the way so they could get on with being happy. 'Tell me and I'll give it to you.'

She remained silent a moment more, then said, 'I don't

want you to sleep with anyone else while Maya is still a child. You'll be faithful to me and I'll be faithful to you.'

He hadn't even thought about another woman since being with Lark and couldn't imagine being with one either. So he answered without hesitation. 'I don't want another woman, Lark. I want you.'

'Promise me, Cesare.'

He couldn't ignore his instinct any longer. Reaching out, he pulled her back into his arms, settling her where she belonged, against him. 'I am not going to get tired of you,' he said. 'In fact, I can't see myself wanting anyone else for a long, long time. So yes, while Maya is growing up, the only woman in my bed will be you. I promise.'

Lark's gaze was searching as she looked up into his face, so he let her see the truth, the force of his conviction to his promise.

Is this really just for the sake of your legacy now? Or is this for her?

But he didn't understand that thought, because the two were the same, so he ignored it.

'You mean that?' Lark asked, the tension slowly bleeding out of her.

He raised a brow. 'Do you want me to write out another agreement?'

'God no.' She flushed. 'I think I've had my fill of legal documents from you.'

He laughed, pulling her closer as satisfaction stretched out inside him. 'Does that mean you trust me, little bird? Trust me to keep my promise?'

'Yes,' she said on a long breath. 'I do.'

'Good. Now let's seal the deal.'

And he bent his head and covered her mouth with his own.

CHAPTER TEN

LARK STOOD IN the doorway to the terrace, watching her husband as he sat at the big stone outside table with Maya in his lap. She'd just turned two and Cesare had wanted to do something special to mark the occasion, so they'd had a small afternoon party with a few of her friends from the little play group she attended with Emily.

All their guests had gone now except one: Aristophanes Katsaros, who owned one of the biggest finance companies on the planet and was apparently Cesare's closest friend.

Lark had been slightly startled that Cesare even had a close friend, let alone that he'd invited him to Maya's birthday. Especially since Aristophanes had seemed absolutely mystified by the little girl.

He and Cesare were talking now in fast and fluid Italian, and as Lark watched, Maya slid off her father's lap and toddled over to where Aristophanes was sitting. She tugged on his trouser leg and lifted her arms to him, apparently unafraid of this stern stranger. Cesare laughed as his friend, with obvious reluctance, lifted the child up and gazed at her in apparent bewilderment.

Amusement stole through Lark. Aristophanes was an inch or so taller than Cesare, which put him at nearly six-five, with black hair and the kind of steel grey eyes that looked like storm clouds. He was definitely a…presence.

He tended towards unsmiling silence, his grey gaze watchful, but there was something very compelling about him.

Clearly Maya thought so too, because she babbled happily at him, while he stared back in stunned silence.

The afternoon had been a wonderful one, with the little ones running around on the lawn with lots of games and sweet treats. Maya had loved it. She'd especially loved being carried around by her father all day as he showed her off to all the guests like the little princess she was. Lark had felt her heart clench tight in her chest every time.

These past nine months had been so wonderful. Since the night he'd promised her that he wouldn't be with anyone else, easing her doubts, she'd felt so much more secure. Safe, almost, and she hadn't been able to say that for a very long time.

Cesare had been a caring, attentive husband, not only keeping her happy at night, but also helping her enrol in university, and supporting her as she worked her way towards an art history degree. She wasn't sure what she was going to do with it yet, but after her training with Mr Ravenswood, she'd become interested in antiquities and the preservation of them. She was now thinking she might like to do some museum studies, but she wasn't quite sure yet.

There was no pressure, though. She was creating a life for herself and a home here in Italy with Cesare and she loved it.

She leaned her head against the doorframe, watching him as he finally took pity on Aristophanes and took Maya from him, tossing her into the air a couple of times and making her squeal with excitement. The look on his face was so full of joy it made her chest hurt.

It had been hurting like that for the last few months, whenever she saw him with their daughter. He'd had such a terrible upbringing, with parents who hadn't cared about him, with one even trying to kill him, yet he hadn't let that stop him from being the best father to his child. He was so wonderful with her, never letting his own terrible history touch her.

She didn't understand why he'd ever thought of himself as selfish. She didn't understand anything when it came to him.

You do. You understand too much.

Her mouth dried, her eyes prickling. Perhaps she did understand. Perhaps she'd been lying to herself all this time, telling herself that she didn't know what the feeling that gripped her whenever she looked at him with their daughter, whenever he took her in his arms, was.

The feeling that had wound itself around her heart and made itself part of her.

He'd made good on every single promise he'd given her and since that night where they'd talked outside Maya's room, he'd never given her a single moment's doubt either.

He made her so happy.

He was beautiful inside and out.

Lark's vision swam and her throat tightened as she felt that feeling grow bigger, taking up every part of her, making it hard to breathe.

It was love. She knew it with every cell of her being.

Somehow, at some point in the past few months, she'd committed a cardinal sin and fallen in love with her husband.

She turned away, her heart beating far too hard, furiously blinking away her tears.

Love had never been what she wanted—had never been what either of them wanted—and yet it had happened all the same.

He accepted all the passionate feelings that lived inside her that she'd had to keep under control for her mother's sake, and had never turned away from them, not once. He even liked her anger as he'd told her on more than one occasion.

And all through these difficult months of starting a new life in a new country, he'd been there supporting her. Caring for her and her daughter, damn him.

Now she understood why she'd trusted him the night she had no memory of. Why she'd told him everything, why she'd given herself to him. Perhaps she'd even fallen in love with him that night and now, here she was doing it all over again.

Now, it was all so clear.

He'd made himself so much a part of her life, she couldn't imagine being without him.

He'd told her that all of this would be his new legacy, a new start for the Donati family, and that was what was important to him. Not Maya and not her. He kept insisting that he was selfish, that he wasn't a good man, and yet everything he did proved the opposite.

She wanted to show him that. Show him what an incredible man he was and what a fantastic father he'd been, and make him believe it.

She wanted to make him as happy as he'd made her.

She wanted to love him. Yet that was the one thing he didn't want.

So? What difference does it make? You have a life with him that's already perfect, so why not keep things as they are?

Lark pushed herself away from the doorframe and stepped into the cool of the salon, trying to get a breath.

She desperately wanted to keep things as they were,

but there had been rare occasions where he'd shut himself away in his study or left on a business trip and not asked her to join him. Moments where there were shadows in his blue eyes and a tension in his powerful shoulders. And it was in those moments that she wanted to ask him what was wrong, to help him the way he'd helped her. Soothe him. Love him. But whenever she asked about it, he'd brush it aside, change the subject or simply kiss her and distract her with pleasure.

He wouldn't let her in and he never would. Because he'd told her right at the start of this marriage, and nothing had changed, not for him.

Yet everything had changed for her. Everything.

Your love wasn't enough to make your mother happy. Why would it be enough for him?

Tears slid down her cheeks.

It would never be enough. His past was too dark, his wounds too deep. Some hurts couldn't be healed with a smile and a good mood, and she knew that all too well.

She didn't know what to do. Leaving him wasn't an option. Cesare loved his daughter so much, and Maya loved him too, she saw it every day in her daughter's eyes. Lark would never tear them apart by taking Maya from him, never.

Leaving without Maya also wasn't an option. She couldn't bear to leave her child. Her falling in love wasn't Maya's fault after all.

But she had to do something, protect herself somehow. Loving someone who didn't want it was a terrible thing and she didn't want the relationship she had with Cesare to break down because of her own hurt feelings.

Which left her with only one option. She had to tell Cesare that she couldn't sleep with him any more, that she couldn't be his wife, not in that way. Friendship was all she could do, and at the moment she wasn't even sure she could do that.

It would hurt him. He'd probably be furious, but there wasn't any other way. Not if she wanted to keep this little life she'd made for herself and Maya.

'Little bird?'

Cesare's deep voice, full of warmth and tenderness, came from behind her and she caught her breath, wiping frantically at her eyes.

Then she turned, forcing a smile on her face. 'What is it?'

He stood in the doorway, casual today in a black T-shirt and worn faded jeans, and she loved him as much in casual clothes as she did when he was in a suit, perhaps even more so.

He looked relaxed, his beautiful mouth curving in a smile he kept just for her. He was so beautiful. Everything about him, from the exquisite planes and angles of his perfect face to his eyes, a deeper blue than even a summer sky.

But even more than his physical beauty, she knew the beauty of his soul. He thought he kept it hidden from her, but she saw it all the same. She saw it in his eyes every time he looked at Maya, even now with wonder, as if he couldn't believe she existed.

He was a good man. He didn't believe it, she knew, but he was.

'I've invited Aristophanes to stay for dinner,' he said. 'You don't mind?'

'No,' she said, her voice husky. 'Of course I don't mind. He's most welcome to stay.'

A faint frown crossed his brow. 'Are you all right?'

No, she wasn't all right. She was desperately in love

with him and she didn't know what to do. Or rather, she did know what to do, she just didn't want to do it.

Sooner rather than later. You'll only make it worse for yourself by waiting.

She would, but she couldn't do it now, not with his friend here.

But even later, after Maya was in bed and Aristophanes had left, she could hardly bring herself to say the words she needed to say. And what made it worse was after they'd both sorted through Maya's birthday cards, and organised all the new toys she'd got for her birthday, Cesare pulled Lark close in the hallway and ran his hands over her, making it clear what he wanted.

There was no perfect time to tell him of her decision, but…she could have one last time with him, couldn't she? She could never resist him and one last night to touch him, kiss his beautiful mouth, have him inside her wasn't so much to ask, was it? He'd been talking about having another child and she couldn't think of anything she wanted more than to have another of his babies.

Except how could she bring another child into the world whose parents' relationship was so fraught?

Especially when you already have one who might be hurt by your decision.

No, and there were no good solutions either. Everywhere she turned someone was going to be hurt, no matter how hard she tried to limit the damage.

'I want you,' Cesare murmured in her ear, as he kissed his way down her neck, his hands stroking down her sides. 'Let me take you to bed, little bird.'

And abruptly Lark was tired of thinking about it, tired of the pain shredding her heart. She wanted him, wanted this, and if it was the last time, so be it. She'd take it.

'Yes,' she whispered and let herself relax against his chest as he picked her up and took her upstairs to their bedroom.

As he set her down next to the bed, his hands already at the zip of her dress, she abruptly pulled away. Her heart was beating far too fast and she was desperate for him in a way she hadn't felt before, but she wanted to do this her way.

'No,' she said huskily, turning to face him. 'Let me undress you first. I want to touch you.'

He smiled, the beauty of it making her ache. 'Be my guest.'

He never denied her anything when it came to sex, yet part of her wished he'd deny her now, because this was only going to make it harder for her.

Still, she stepped up close to him, taking the hem of his T-shirt in her hands and drawing it up slowly, exposing his flat, chiselled stomach and smooth olive skin. Then she lifted it higher and he raised his arms, helping her get the fabric off the rest of the way.

Dropping the T-shirt on the floor, she then let her hands wander over his bare chest, feeling the hard muscle beneath his warm satiny skin and the crisp prickle of hair.

He felt so amazing. He always did.

Leaning forward she kissed her way along his pecs, her fingers trailing down to his narrow hips, then toying with the buttons of his jeans. He made a delicious sound of male satisfaction, one of his large warm hands cradling the back of her head as she continued to kiss her way down his rock-hard torso, undoing his jeans then sliding her hands inside.

He growled, his fingers clenching tight in her hair as

she took the long, thick, hard length of him in her hand, stroking him, teasing him.

She loved him. She loved his body and the sounds he made. The way he touched her when he was aroused. And he should know that he was loved, know that he was cared for. No one had ever cared for him; no one had loved him. She couldn't bear it.

She didn't want to ruin this moment by telling him, but she would show him. She would worship him the way he deserved to be worshipped.

Kneeling at his feet, she slid his jeans down over his hips, taking his underwear with them, and he stepped out of the fabric, finally, gloriously naked.

Lark ran her hands up his powerful thighs to the hard length of his sex. He was beautiful there too and he should know it. She leaned forward and took him in her mouth, tasting his delicious flavour, all salt and musk and heat.

He made another deep growling sound, his fingers a fist in her hair as she drew him in deep. 'My beautiful wife.' His voice was low and rough. 'You make me so hungry.'

He made her hungry too. He made her want more. He made her want everything. But she couldn't ask that of him, not when he'd been so clear what love meant to him.

It wasn't his fault she wanted something more.

Eventually he got impatient and pulled her up from where she knelt, tossing her on the bed and following her down, pinning her beneath him. 'Now,' he murmured. 'Where were we?' Then he pulled her clothing off and she helped, desperate to have nothing between them but skin.

So when he reached for a condom in the bedside table drawer, she stopped him. 'No,' she said when he looked down at her in surprise. 'You wanted another child. Let's try for one.' She could give him this gift, couldn't she?

But what about your decision?

Maybe she didn't have to leave him now. Maybe she'd wait to see if she was pregnant and then make a decision. She just hadn't realised how much it would hurt.

Cesare smiled at her and it was as if the sun had come up on a bitter winter landscape, the promise of summer and warmth and life.

It made her want to cry, but instead she reached up and pulled his mouth down on hers, kissing him desperately, gasping in pleasure as he slid inside her.

He felt so right. So perfect. She wanted to keep him there for ever.

She wound her legs around his waist, holding him where he was, and when he put his hands on either side of her head and looked down into her eyes, she stared back. She couldn't help herself.

He began to move, deep and slow, and she could see the pleasure glow bright in his gaze, and the hunger too.

His eyes were so blue.

She loved him so much.

She wanted to tell him so, but she couldn't do that now. He'd stop and she didn't want him to stop. Instead, she raised her hand and touched his beautiful face the way she had on the plane that day, so long ago now. Tracing his features as he moved inside her, the pleasure growing deeper and deeper.

'Lark,' he said softly, turning to brush his mouth over her fingertips. 'My little bird.'

Yes, she was his. She'd be his for ever; she knew it deep in her soul.

The orgasm hit her without warning, hard and fast and when it did, she had to bury her face in his neck to stop the tears that came along with it.

* * *

Cesare felt the orgasm hit, pleasure pouring through him, and he couldn't move for long moments. Not that he wanted to. He was quite happy with Lark lying beneath him, all soft and hot, her legs wrapped around his waist, her face turned against his neck.

Every part of him was relaxed and heavy with physical satiation, pleasure echoing through him, yet something was bothering him and he couldn't figure out what.

Then he realised that Lark was weeping.

Shock cut through the pleasure like a knife, and he moved off her, lying on his side and looking down at her. Tears were rolling down her cheeks. She turned away, flinging an arm across her eyes as if she was trying to hide from him.

His chest tightened and he grabbed her arm, pulling it away so he could see her face. It was flushed and wet with tears.

'Lark?' he demanded, rougher than he'd intended. 'Did I hurt you?' Fear gripped him. Had he done something terrible? He must have to make her weep like this. 'Lark,' he said again, trying to pull her close. But she wriggled out of his grip, turning away.

He stared at her, bewildered by her sudden change in mood. She'd been so passionate and hungry for him just before, her eyes full of some unearthly light that had gripped him by the throat and hadn't let go. She had never seemed more lovely to him.

Yet something had changed and he wanted to know what.

'Lark,' he repeated, sharper this time. 'What's going on?'

She was still a moment, then he heard her take a deep

breath and turn back to him. Her cheeks were wet, her lovely green eyes red. 'I'm sorry, Cesare,' she said thickly. 'But I can't do this any more.'

He stared at her, not understanding. 'What do you mean? You can't do what?'

'I can't be your wife, not like this.'

A feeling of foreboding began to gather inside him. She'd touched him reverently. Kissed him as though he were precious, and no one had ever done that to him before. No one had ever held him as if he mattered, as if he was important.

But even so, there had seemed something deliberate about the time she'd spent doing it. As if she was savouring it, savouring him. Then that light in her eyes as he'd slid inside her that he didn't understand. It had looked like grief.

It was a goodbye.

He went cold all over. 'Tell me what you're actually saying,' he demanded. '*Exactly* what you're saying.'

'I can't keep sleeping with you.' She sat up abruptly and turned, slipping off the bed. 'I can't keep being…intimate with you. That has to end.'

'What?' He stared at her in bewilderment. 'Why?' And then, in a hot flare of jealousy, he scowled. 'Have you found someone else?'

'No, no, nothing like that.' She was dressing and he found it unbearable all of a sudden. He reached out over the mattress, catching her hands and pulling her back down on the bed again.

'Tell me,' he growled, turning her over and pinning her beneath him. 'Why can't you sleep with me any more? And why are you crying?'

She swallowed, her jaw tight. 'Let me go, Cesare.'

'No. Did I do something to hurt you? What?'

'Yes,' she burst out suddenly, passionately. 'You did do something. You made me fall in love with you.'

The words echoed around the room, a slow horror dawning inside him.

'Love?' he echoed stupidly.

Her eyes glittered and this time she didn't look away. 'I know you don't want it and I know you said love would never be any part of this marriage and I thought I was fine with that, but… I'm not. I love you, Cesare. I love you so much.'

This time, he was the one who pushed himself away from her as if she'd burned him, horror deepening, the anger that he'd thought he'd vanquished rising along with it.

'No, Lark,' he said in a rough voice. 'No. I told you—'

'I know what you told me.' She sat up, pain stark in her eyes. 'And don't worry, I'm not asking for you to love me in return. I know how you feel about that. And I'm not going to leave—I would never take her away from you and I'm not leaving her—but I can't keep pretending we have a real marriage when we don't.'

'Why not?' he demanded, fury abruptly running through his veins. At her for changing everything when he'd thought things were perfect, and at himself for not realising that making her happy might have had this effect on her. For not seeing her growing feelings.

Another way you're selfish. You didn't even think about how she *might feel. All you wanted was your damn new legacy.*

Yes, and why shouldn't he? He was a selfish bastard and he'd never made any secret of the fact. Yet something like self-loathing wound through him all the same.

'Because I can't.' More tears were rolling down her

cheeks and for some reason the sight of them hurt, like small slivers of glass pushed beneath his skin. 'I spent my childhood loving my mother, hoping it would help her, fix her somehow, but it didn't. I don't want to do it again.'

The fury felt as if it was choking him. 'I'm not broken, Lark. Why the hell would you think I need fixing?'

'You don't,' she said passionately, wiping futilely at her tears. 'It's not that. It's just… I want to love you so much. I want to make you as happy as you made me, but sometimes I feel as if there's a part of you that you keep shut away, a part that you don't want me to see. And it's like that night again, Cesare. Where you have all of me, but I have nothing of you.'

He knew what she was talking about. The days when the pressure of trying to keep both her and Maya happy, to not give them any reason to doubt and mistrust him, got to him. Sometimes he found himself furious for no reason and always when he should have been happy. It felt as if he was missing something, lacking something, and he couldn't pinpoint what, which angered him. He didn't want her to see that, didn't want his anger to become something toxic, the way his parents' had, and so he'd shut himself away and dealt with it, only coming out again when it had gone.

She didn't need to see that. No one did.

'You do have all of me,' he insisted, fighting his anger. 'But there are some things that you don't need to see.'

'What things, Cesare? What is so very bad about you that I shouldn't have to see it?'

He gritted his teeth. He kept on telling her what kind of man he was, but she didn't seem to believe him. Perhaps he needed to drive the point home. 'You know what my parents did to me,' he said flatly. 'You know how sick they were, how they let their anger consume them. Well, I'm no different. I was furious with them after they died, for the hell they made of my childhood, and for a long time I let that fury take charge. And I nearly let it consume me the way it consumed them. But then I decided I'd had enough of letting them control the course of my life, and so I decided to break up their legacy and finally move on. Then you came along, Lark. You and Maya. And you both gave me hope that I could do something different.' He found his hands had curled into fists and he tried to relax them. 'But that doesn't change who I am. I'm what my parents made me, Lark. Angry, and bitter, and selfish. That's the part of me that you don't need to see.'

'No.' Lark's eyes suddenly burned, her voice fierce. 'No, you stupid man. You might be angry and bitter, and God, if anyone's got a right to that, it's you. But you're not selfish. You're the opposite. You put your daughter first, every time, and you're caring and kind and supportive. Why do you think I fell in love with you, you idiot?'

'It's not for her,' he insisted, an odd pain starting up inside him. 'It's for the new—'

'Legacy, yes, so you keep saying,' Lark interrupted furiously. 'But I don't believe that and I don't think you do, not for a second. You're doing all that for her, because you love her. Because *she* matters to you, not your stupid legacy.'

His heart was beating far too fast and he felt like a man drowning and trying to grab onto a life vest as it floated past. And missing.

She's not wrong.

She was, she had to be. Love was toxic. Love had killed his parents and it had nearly killed him. And he didn't want any part of it. Ever.

This time it was he who pushed himself off the bed

and reached for his clothes. 'I'm not having this conversation,' he said in a hard voice. 'In fact, we will never speak of it again.'

Lark didn't move as he dressed, sitting on the bed naked and so achingly beautiful she stopped his heart.

'That's too bad, Cesare,' she said, still fierce. 'Because I can't have half-measures. I've given you all of me, but if I can't have all of you, then I have to do something. I don't know if I can do friendship, but that's all I've got to offer you right now.' Tears gleamed on her cheeks even as anger glittered in her eyes. 'I'd like to tell you I'm sorry, but I'm not.'

He had no answer to that. It was a futile argument anyway, and he knew how those kinds of arguments ended. Very, very badly.

So he said nothing and strode from the room instead.

CHAPTER ELEVEN

LARK DIDN'T KNOW what to do after that. She didn't know where that left them, she only knew that while he still believed those terrible things about himself, there was no hope for them. No hope for their marriage at least.

Eventually, her heart tearing itself apart in her chest, she slept, but he didn't join her.

And she didn't see him the next day at breakfast either. Apparently, according to one of the palazzo staff, he'd gone in to the office and didn't know when he'd be back.

Three days later, he still hadn't returned, and Lark began to wonder if he ever would.

It wasn't fair. She didn't care about herself, but denying Maya his presence was a terrible thing to do. She tried calling him to tell him so, but he wouldn't answer. He didn't respond to her texts either.

Eventually, after much thinking and then some hunting around, she found Aristophanes's private number and called him instead.

'Lark?' Aristophanes's deep, cold voice was full of surprise. 'To what do I owe the pleasure?'

Lark took a breath. 'I need you to talk to Cesare. He won't answer any of my calls and I'm getting desperate.'

'Oh?' This time Aristophanes sounded wary. 'Why?'

She swallowed. 'I…um…told him I loved him and I

couldn't be his wife any more, not in the way he wanted, and we argued. Then he left.'

'Oh, dear,' Aristophanes said, his voice very neutral. 'That does sound…difficult.'

'He seems to believe he's some terrible person,' Lark said, fighting tears and quite unable to stop herself. 'But he's not. He's the most wonderful man I know and I just want him to believe—'

'Yes, yes,' Aristophanes interrupted, sounding distinctly uncomfortable now. 'I see your point. Well, we can't have that. I'll give him a call.'

After he'd disconnected, Lark sat with her phone in her lap, staring at it, only for Maya to come running into the salon the next moment, closely followed by Emily.

'Sorry to interrupt,' Emily said, looking apologetic. 'Maya was trying to find Signor Donati.'

Lark swallowed. Maya had been finding Cesare's absence difficult and that had upset Lark too.

'It's okay,' Lark murmured, reaching for her daughter and cuddling her on her lap. 'Why don't you take the rest of the day off, Emily? I'll look after her.'

Lark held her daughter's warm little body after Emily had gone, rocking her gently while Maya curled up against her.

Every part of Lark hurt. Every part of her ached. She couldn't let it break her, though. She couldn't afford to be broken, not for Maya's sake. And if Cesare didn't return? Well, she'd fill in the gap he'd left in her daughter's life. Maya had started out without a father and luckily she was young enough that she'd forget him if he never returned.

If this was what life was like from now on, then so be it. She would endure for her daughter.

But she wasn't going to love again, that was for certain. Cesare was the only man for her and always would be.

* * *

Cesare sat in his office in the Donati Bank building in central Rome, a nearly empty bottle of whisky sitting open on his desk, the couch he'd been sleeping on for the past few days still covered with the blanket he'd found from somewhere.

He hadn't been back to the palazzo. He missed his daughter and his wife so badly it felt as if he'd lost part of his soul.

But he couldn't go back, not now. He'd thought he could keep Maya and Lark safe from him, from his anger and his selfishness, but it was clear that he couldn't.

He'd hurt Lark, he knew. He'd made her cry. And he wished he could go back and soothe her, comfort her, tell her he'd never hurt her again, but he couldn't promise her that.

Because he would. She loved him and he couldn't bear that, not when love always ended in destruction. Far better he steer clear of both her and Maya for the foreseeable future. That seemed to him to be the only way forward.

He poured the rest of the whisky into his glass and sipped at the fiery liquid.

Why couldn't she have kept it to herself? Why couldn't she *not* have fallen in love with him? He couldn't give it back to her and eventually that lack would fester, and then who knew what would happen? She had a fiery temper and love could turn that toxic.

You know it wouldn't. She's nothing like your mother.

Maybe, maybe not. There were no guarantees.

Love ruined everything.

His phone was sitting on his desk, the screen full of missed call notifications from Lark. He hadn't contacted her since he'd walked, mainly because he had no idea what to say to her, not when the only things he could think of would hurt her and badly.

Just then his phone buzzed, but it wasn't Lark this time. It was Aristophanes.

Reluctantly, Cesare answered it. 'What?' he demanded gracelessly.

'I see,' Aristophanes said, as if something had been confirmed for him. 'You're sulking.'

Cesare glowered at his office windows, at the sun sinking over his ancient city. 'I am not. Why are you calling me anyway?'

'Because your lovely wife asked me to.'

Cesare's heart contracted. 'Why did she do that? I didn't ask her to.'

'I know you didn't.' There was the faintest hint of censure in his friend's tone. 'She's desperately worried about you. Apparently she told you she loved you and you left.'

His jaw felt tight, all his muscles tense. 'I had to. You know my past. You know that I can't—'

'I know that you're lying to yourself,' Aristophanes interrupted mildly. 'And I know you're being a coward.'

Cesare growled. 'I had to leave her. She seems to think that I'm this paragon and I'm not. I never have been.'

'No,' Aristophanes agreed. 'You're not a paragon. But you're not as bad as you seem to think you are. And anyway, it doesn't matter what you think. She's the one that really matters to you and I think you know that.'

Deep inside, something shifted painfully in his chest. 'It's my legacy that matters,' he said, but even to himself his voice sounded uncertain. 'Not her.'

'What did I say about lying to yourself?' Aristophanes said. 'You think I didn't see the way you looked at her at Maya's birthday party? Your heart was in your eyes every time. You're in love her, you fool. And I think you're telling yourself any lie you can get your hands on so you don't have to admit it.'

'No,' Cesare said hoarsely, even as the truth settled down inside him and wrapped around his heart, filling him with an icy terror. 'No, that's not true.'

'It is,' Aristophanes said, relentless. 'You're in love with her and you're afraid. And I know why.' He paused. 'You're not like your parents, Cesare. You do know that, don't you?'

'Do I?' His voice sounded strange. 'I am angry for what they did to me. I thought I was past that, but I'm not. And I can't trust myself around Lark or Maya when I'm angry because—'

'Because what? You think you'll harm her? Harm Maya?'

He stayed silent, frozen all the way through, the terror of that thought robbing him of speech.

'No,' Aristophanes went on calmly. 'You wouldn't. You're not that kind of man and you never have been.'

'You don't know that.' His voice had gone hoarse.

'I do,' his friend said. 'And if you won't take my word for it, take Lark's. She's a smart woman and she's in love with you, and I don't think that would have happened if you'd been anything like your parents.'

Cesare took a breath, and then another, fighting his fear.

He'd always told himself he was a selfish man, but part of him had always known that was a defence. A defence against caring. Yet all the lies in the world hadn't stopped him from caring for Maya. And he knew, in a sudden flash of insight, that they hadn't stopped him caring about Lark either.

He'd told himself that making Lark and Maya happy was for his legacy, but that was a lie too.

He was making them happy because he loved them. He loved his daughter, and he loved his wife. He loved them so much it hurt. And he was terrified of it. Terrified that he was just like his parents…that love would turn him into someone he wasn't. Someone toxic and violent, who would hurt those he cared out.

There was a silence down the other end of the phone.

'What if you're wrong?' he said hoarsely. 'What if I really am just like my father? Or my mother?'

'Don't be ridiculous,' Aristophanes said briskly, because he'd always been uncomfortable with emotion. 'You haven't killed anyone yet that I know of.'

'Ari, don't—'

'Cesare, stop. Your parents ruined your childhood, it's true. But you don't have to let them ruin your future. You have a beautiful daughter and a lovely wife. Be a shame to throw all that away because you're not brave enough to man up.'

Cesare shut his eyes.

His friend was right. He was giving in to his fear, letting them ruin his life the way they'd always done.

His beautiful, courageous wife had set him an example. She'd had a child on her own, had loved her and cared for her despite her own doubts. She'd created a wonderful childhood for her—she hadn't let her own run her life—and then she'd moved with him to Italy, sacrificing the life she'd made in England for Maya and for him.

She'd shown him what love was. That it didn't have to be toxic or destructive, or full of rage and pain. She and Maya had shown him that love was happiness. Was laughter and joy and wonder and awe. It allowed for anger and hurt, gave space for those emotions, yet didn't allow them to linger or fester. Love allowed for honesty. Love allowed for fear.

How could they give him all of that and he give them nothing in return?

His love for Maya had been instant and irrevocaable and he'd had no control over it. But Lark had been different. She'd slipped under his guards and wrapped herself around his heart and now he couldn't get rid of her. She was there for life.

And he didn't want to get rid of her. He wanted her to stay there for ever. Doing anything else would *really* make him like his parents.

'Sorry,' he muttered to his friend. 'I have to go.'

'I thought you might,' Aristophanes said.

And laughed.

Lark was sitting in the salon, her books on the table in front of her, trying to study when Cesare suddenly burst through the door.

His hair was standing on end, his shirt half undone. He had no jacket and no tie, and he looked as if he hadn't slept for a week.

He was also the most beautiful sight she'd ever seen.

She pushed herself to her feet, her heart beating suddenly very fast. 'What are you doing—' she began, but didn't get any further, because Cesare had crossed the distance between them without a word, pulling her into his arms before she could finish.

'I need to tell you something,' he said roughly. 'I've been a coward and a fool, and you will never know how sorry I am for running out on you the way I did.'

Lark put her hands on his chest, aching at the feel of him, at the familiar warmth of his body surrounding her. 'Cesare, what are you doing?'

'I'm coming home.' The look in his eyes burned. 'I'm

coming home to you, because I love you, Lark Donati. I've loved you since that night we spent together, I think, but I told myself it was only physical. Because I was afraid. Afraid of my anger. Afraid of love. Afraid that I would become like them. I didn't want to fall into the same traps of emotion, to love someone so much it became an obsession and then hatred.' He took a shuddering breath. 'I didn't want to end up hurting you or Maya.'

Lark's eyes filled with tears, her heart full and painful in her chest. 'You wouldn't. You *never* would, Cesare. I told you that you're nothing like them, *nothing*. Because what they did to you and to each other wasn't love.'

'Yes,' he breathed. 'Yes, I think I'm beginning to see that.' His arms tightened around her. 'And I'm beginning to see what love actually is, and you taught me that. Love isn't an ending. It's a beginning. It's creation. It's joy and happiness, and my life here at the palazzo. My life ever since I married you. Love is you, Lark. You and Maya.'

Her throat hurt and she could feel tears start to slide down her face, but they were happy tears. Joyful tears. She touched his face. 'So what does that mean?'

'It means, little bird, that I want you to be my wife for real. I want to be faithful to you, to love, honour and cherish you, in sickness and health, until the day I die.'

Lark smiled, aching with love for him. 'In that case, I do.'

And that's what they did.

Lark never remembered that night they spent together, but it didn't matter.

She lived it every night, in Cesare's arms, for the rest of their lives.

EPILOGUE

'IT'S TWINS,' ARISTOPHANES SAID. He sounded…angry.

Cesare bit back a smile. 'Congratulations?'

His friend had called him in a fury, because apparently he'd found out that a woman he'd spent a night with three months earlier was now carrying his child. Two children, to be exact.

'I don't need your congratulations,' Aristophanes snapped.

'I fail to see what you're so angry about,' Cesare said patiently. 'Weren't you supposed to be trying to get her pregnant?'

That had been the case, according to Aristophanes, but he had refused to give Cesare any details. Annoying. Especially because Aristophanes had always made it clear he didn't want children.

'Don't you understand?' Aristophanes growled. 'I can't *not* have them in my life. They're mine.'

'I don't think you really want me to say I told you so, do you?'

Aristophanes said something filthy in Greek then disconnected the call.

Cesare put his phone back on his desk and smiled.

Just then, the doors of his office opened and his wife came in. She was wearing the most beautiful sea-green gown, the exact shade of her eyes. It wrapped around her figure deliciously and he wondered if perhaps they could change the time of their dinner date. Maya was with Emily; she was taken care of. They could make it later. Give him some time to—

'Cesare,' Lark said, looking stern. 'No, we don't have time, and anyway...' The stern look faded to be replaced by the smile she gave for him and him alone, the one that lit her face, that made him ache to hold her. 'I have something to tell you.'

It couldn't be bad, not judging from her smile, yet his heart started beating faster all the same. 'Oh?' He pushed his chair back and got to his feet, coming around his desk to where she stood and taking her gently into his arms. 'Something good, I hope?'

Her face shone. 'I'm pregnant.'

It *was* something good. It was the best news he'd ever had.

And a little under eight months later, when Lark delivered their twins, a boy and a girl, it got even better.

He realised then what he'd subconsciously known the day he'd chosen Lark and his child over his own fear.

That the true Donati legacy was love and always had been.

* * * * *

COMING SOON!

We really hope you enjoyed reading this book.
If you're looking for more romance
be sure to head to the shops when
new books are available on

Thursday 24th October

MILLS & BOON

MILLS & BOON®

Coming next month

HUSBAND FOR THE HOLIDAYS
Dani Collins

In so many ways, this was her dream come true. Could she really complain if it wasn't exactly perfect? "Yes. I will marry you, Konstantin."

"Good." He slid the cool ring onto her finger, then looped his arms behind her.

Eloise's hands were on his lapels, quivering with pleasure at having this right to touch him.

She looked up at him, expecting him to kiss her, but he only caressed the edge of her jaw with his bent finger.

He dipped his head into her throat and nuzzled his lips against her skin.

She gasped and shivered. Her nipples stung and her knees grew weak.

His breath pooled near her ear, fanning the arousal taking hold in her. This was surreal. Too perfect. Like a Christmas miracle. Not that she believed in such things, but maybe it was?

Continue reading
HUSBAND FOR THE HOLIDAYS
Dani Collins

Available next month
millsandboon.co.uk

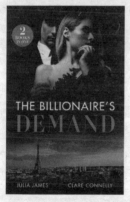
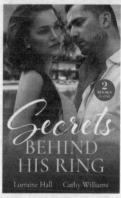

LET'S TALK

Romance

For exclusive extracts, competitions and special offers, find us online:

MillsandBoon

@MillsandBoon

@MillsandBoonUK

@MillsandBoonUK

Get in touch on 01413 063 232

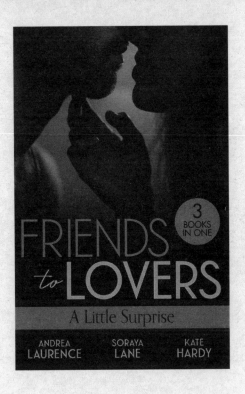